Shattered dreams

I just want to stop thinking about forever in the dark and my endless, claustrophobic tunnel of a future. Because I'll never drive or get a job, or get married or lose my virginity. Maybe I'll never even kiss anyone.

Because how will Zach Haze—or anyone—fall in love with me now? I'm definitely not invisible anymore. Everyone has noticed me now that I'm "famous," as Logan says. But having everyone know who you are isn't fabulous if it's because you're the star of a gruesome tragedy. Or because you're disfigured. The way people stare and fuss makes me feel like I'm trapped under a magnifying glass, gasping and sweating, in danger of catching fire. Again.

OTHER BOOKS YOU MAY ENJOY

BLIND

RACHEL DEWOSKIN

speak

SPEAK
An imprint of Penguin Random House LLC
375 Hudson Street
New York, New York 10014

First published in the United States of America by Viking,
an imprint of Penguin Group (USA) LLC, 2014
Published by Speak, an imprint of Penguin Random House LLC, 2016

THE LIBRARY OF CONGRESS HAS CATALOGED THE VIKING EDITION AS FOLLOWS:
DeWoskin, Rachel.
Blind / Rachel DeWoskin.
pages cm
Summary: After a horrific accident leaves her blind, fifteen-year-old Emma, one
of seven children, eagerly starts high school as a sophomore, and finds that nearly
everything has changed—sometimes for the better.
ISBN 978-0-670-78522-3 (hardback)
[1. Blind—Fiction. 2. People with disabilities—Fiction. 3. Family life—Fiction.
4. Interpersonal relations—Fiction. 5. High schools—Fiction. 6. Schools—Fiction.]
I. Title
PZ7.D537Bli 2014 [Fic]—dc23 2013041189

Speak ISBN 978-0-14-242455-1

Printed in the United States of America   Designed by Jim Hoover

10   9   8   7   6   5   4   3   2   1

For brave girls everywhere, keeping
each other inspired, un-lonely, beloved.

Including the dazzling ones who
compose my world:
Christine, Donna, Erika, Heidi, Jill, Julia,
Kirun, Lara, Melissa, Olati, Shanying,
Tamar, and Willow.

Thank you for seeing me for real,
in the most important ways.
I see you, too.

Bring me the flower that leads us out
where blond transparencies rise
and life evaporates as essence.
Bring me the sunflower crazed with light.

EUGENIO MONTALE, 1948
TRANSLATION, W. ARROWSMITH, 1994

-1-

Going blind is a little bit like growing up. Maybe because the older you get, the more you have to close your eyes partway. From the time I was tiny, if I thought the words, *When I die, I'll be dead forever*, I could actually understand, in my bone marrow, what *forever* meant. It was like falling into something textureless, silent, unscented, absolutely blank. And never stopping the fall. I grasped that terror early, and had just started forgetting it when my accident happened. Now I remember again. So I might not be "sighted" anymore, but maybe I'm not that much blinder than anyone else, just a different kind of blind.

If you're me, then you see that we're all only a half-second disaster, mistake, or choice away from being changed forever. Or finished. If you're not me—like my sisters and brother and parents—then maybe you don't see that. At least not in the same way. Maybe you don't think about forever in the dark. Or what it means to feel colors, to relearn

Sarah, Leah, Naomi, Jenna, Benj, and Baby Lily by the shapes of their voices and the textures of their breathing. I know my sisters and brother by the baby powder, cheerio, and blue toddler toothpaste feeling of the little ones; the pickle, bubble bath, tousled pillow hair of my middle sisters; and the lemon and licorice of the two oldest. Maybe you don't think about what it means to see or not see; you squeeze those thoughts shut, because who can stand to stare straight at what's happening? No one. We have to learn to look away so we can say—the way my parents still try to tell the seven of us—*you'll be okay; everything will be fine*. In other words, we lie. I don't do that anymore.

I don't say much at all, because I have to keep track of what's going on around me. And I was quiet anyway, even when I was still sighted. I learned that word from my doctors; I'd never heard of *sighted* until I wasn't it anymore, never considered *blind* until it locked onto me like a parasite. I hadn't noticed what an odd and colorless word it is, how it can suck the meaning out of whatever it attaches to: Blind love? Blind rage? Blind faith? Why are those the unthinking kinds? And who's more lost or hopeless than the blind leading the blind? The most amazing love happens at first what? Right, sight. Seriously?

This July was the one-year anniversary of my accident, and I was shocked to find it hot again. Time was keeping its same pace, even though for me, the world had flipped onto a flat axis where days were dark and nights lit up my mind.

Hot didn't make sense, and neither did the idea that a year had passed. I had missed half of ninth grade and spent the second half at a place called the Briarly School for the Blind. Until the accident, I never skipped thirty seconds of Lake Main, the school I went to my entire life. And then all of a sudden I dropped out and found myself at Briarly, where they teach history and braille and cooking and laundry. My life was like a horror movie about someone else's life. One I couldn't watch. Briarly was for The Blind, and I was *the blind*. The truth is, I keep getting surprised by that, even though everyone else seems to have accepted it.

This summer, while my best friend, Logan, and all our friends from Lake Main were at the lake, shading their eyes, dipping in blue, falling in love, I was in summer school at Briarly, pressing the six long, flat keys of an old Perkins Brailler, listening, practicing, sliding and tapping my white cane, finding shorelines where the grass meets the curb, where the wall meets the floor, where each stair starts or stops. I was listening for traffic to the right, to the left, thinking, if I heard a chorus of engines rev, *Stop!* But if they idled, I thought, *Okay Emma, okay me, okay, now you have the whole light, strike out, walk, okay, now, go.* With chopped-up words in my mind and a million sounds and my ears and brain exhausted, I stuck my white cane out ahead of me, waiting to see—was anyone turning? Had I made a mistake? And if my cane remained uncrushed, then I struck out into the walk, tried to stay straight, to keep my body safely within the white lines. Hug the right, stay straight. I was working, focusing, trying not to panic, panting with the hope of being what the Briarly School for the Blind referred to as "mainstreamed," my dad called "back on track," and Logan and I knew was just me going back to real school. Back to Lake Main, to my actual life.

And then it happened; in August, we got the yes, the "paraprofessional," the promise of "special-needs dispensations," and even though it was humiliating and I still couldn't see, I was going back to Lake Main, and a rainbow blew up around me. Logan was at my house, as always, and she grabbed me and we danced through the living room, until I banged into my older sister Sarah. She screamed at me, but I didn't care. I had learned to walk, read, and survive life in my house and at Briarly, so everyone was assuming I could manage tenth grade at Lake Main.

I would get my assignments early, either braille or audio versions, and have my paraprofessional read the chalkboards out loud to me. I would eat in the lunchroom with Logan and have my life back. I was flying with pride, and so was my dad. My mom was terrified, but faking that she wasn't. Sarah was furious that everyone was paying so much attention to me "again," because I had used up my quota after the accident. And my crazy, lovely, oldest sister, Leah, was talking about how we'd walk every day and pick up the little kids from Lake Main primary, and how great it would be for all of us to be together again.

It seems insane now, but my family and I were actually— after one small, terrible year—backing into the warm groove of things-might-be-okay again. That's how easy that mistake is. Even I had started thinking *it*, whatever *it* is, couldn't happen to us; had started feeling stupidly safe again, the way people do, even though we should know better by now.

Because right as I finished summer school and Logan and I were planning what I'd wear my first day back, a girl from Lake Main, Claire Montgomery, disappeared. At first we all thought her ultraconservative parents were exaggerating— she was probably just in the city again, since one time she'd gone for a day with her best friend, Blythe Keene, or maybe she had run away. But then the days multiplied, and it seemed like something might be really wrong, so people started freaking out and searching frantically. News teams came and circled like turkey vultures. Then the last Sunday night in August, when it had already started to cool down and smell like fall and school and burning leaves, Sarah screamed in front of the TV.

We all ran. I came last, sliding my cane along the hallway wall, with my dog, Spark, barking in front of me. Spark and I hate screaming. I listened while everyone else watched.

Even my dad was home, because it was Sunday and he wasn't on call for once. We were scattered all over each other and our huge gold couch, red chairs, tan rug. I was at my mom's feet, on a pillow, one of my hands holding the ankle of her jeans. I felt the scratch of paint on the hem, wondered what color it was, what she had been making and when. Because she doesn't paint anymore. Leah was on the floor next to me.

"They're showing Lake Brainch," Leah whispered, her voice quiet and steady in my ear, competing with the newswoman's vicious report. The worst words tore up to the top: *body of . . . washed . . . drowned . . . local teen . . . don't know . . . foul play . . . haven't said.* I smelled lemons. Leah had leaned in toward me, set her head on my shoulder. "I'm Emma-izing," she said, pulling my hand up to her face so I could feel her closed eyes, lashes against her cheek. "I'm just listening, too."

Words have vivid edges and colors now, and listening to Leah is like being inside a book with glistening pages, or seeing the sun from the roof of our house. When I was little, Leah used to take me out there some mornings before anyone else was awake, including our parents or Sarah, Leah's cranky, inferior, one-minute-younger twin. Leah liked to see the sun as it woke, and to show me, too. Now, when she speaks, I can feel each tile's smooth curve and the way my body tilted into the rise of the roof. Mostly I remember what the sun looked like, hot over the sliver of lake we could see from up there, hot over our small bodies. Like "our own burning gold balloon," Leah once called it. She said since we were the only ones up, the sun belonged to us, even if just for a moment. And it was true. That sun is one of the things I can still see, in my mind. That and my mom's face. I remember exactly what my mom looks like. Maybe because her voice and face are everywhere in our house, or because she keeps us all in a loose orbit around her, I still see her in a different way than I see anyone else. Now Leah and I will never climb out onto our roof again—Leah is seventeen and a senior and busy with college applications and I'm, well, it's obvious.

I steadied myself on the floor in front of the TV, tucked my head, and rocked as Sarah said, "They found her body. Oh my god. How can they be showing this?"

I felt like I was falling. Sarah smells like pepper, and her words sound like stilts, hooves, or heels. She and Leah are each other's opposite, maybe like most twins. Sarah's hair is so dark it's hard to believe her eyes could be darker, but they are. Flat, black, and glinty. Leah's are almost black, too, but they shine like stones you'd hold in your pocket for comfort. When Leah tells me what's on TV, it's because she doesn't want me to feel left out. When Sarah does, it's so I'll have to suffer, too.

My mom, slapped back to consciousness suddenly, took a sharp breath and stood.

"Benj, Jenna, time for bed!" she sang out in the cracked plastic voice she puts on to hide fear. She leaned over me to hand Baby Lily to my dad, and then herded the little kids out of the zone of dangerous news. My dad stood, too. "Come on, Benji," he said. "Let's take Lily to her crib."

But they were too late. The scary part was over, and we had all heard or seen it. Naomi, who's ten and not really a little kid anymore, but also not one of the big kids, asked, "Um, should I go to bed, too?" I felt bad for her. No one answered—maybe my parents didn't hear—so I said, "Come sit on my lap," and she did. The words had turned to cooking sugar over whatever the shot was: . . . *beloved by her family and friends,* the television was chanting. *Friends say fifteen-year-old Claire loved animals and sports; she was a star on Lake Main Middle School's Sweet Pea Synchronized Swim Team. According to authorities, foul play does not appear to have been a factor. What a shock to the tiny town of Sauberg, where residents are stunned by the occurrence of such a tragedy in their own backyards.*

I buried my face in Naomi's hair as a new reporter joined in, her words at first squeezed white and flat and then pumped up with the breathy thrill of someone dying. Someone young. Someone she didn't know but we did. At least I didn't have to see those anchorpeople with their mannequin faces, pretending to be heartbroken while they practically sang about misery and death. Since my accident, I've noticed that the gorier and more horrible the story, the lower the reporters' voices go; there's a drumbeat under their words, a music that blooms and swells like it's leading to a love scene. But it isn't, at least not in Sauberg, where before Claire, the biggest story was my eyes, my "horrific tragedy," as they put it, so everyone would look. Everyone except me.

And now Sauberg is in the news again because Claire's dead—streaky-haired, allergic, freckled, daring, athletic Claire. Claire of the clear lip gloss and chipped front teeth, of the skin so thin you could see through it, of the lopsided smile and shockingly strong legs. Soccering, swimming, smoking, partying Claire. Claire of the usual contradictions times a thousand. The one who could do everything, including get in deadly trouble, better than the rest of us.

I'm probably the only one in Sauberg—including the toddlers—who hasn't seen the footage of her body being removed from the lake. Which may be why I can't believe she's gone. Kind of like I still can't fully believe I'm blind. If there's any truth to that stupid expression "see it to believe it," then what can I believe? I still wake up thinking, *Okay, Emma, now open your eyes*, and then—well, then nothing. I can practice the facts of my accident, just like I can repeat what I know about Claire: she drowned and washed up. But in neither case do the "facts" really help, maybe because facts aren't exactly facts. They're just names someone puts on what happened, and then we all repeat them straight into the encyclopedia. What actually happened to Claire? And maybe more importantly, *why?*

Maybe we can't make sense of things like my accident or Claire because there is no sense. Maybe we're all stunned numb because we thought my eyes were enough karmic tragedy for our whole town. We believed nothing else so terrible could happen again. Lightning twice? Not here. Not to us.

But actually, getting struck once doesn't change your odds for getting struck again, and I spent my first day of mainstream tenth grade feeling like a lightning rod. In the Lake Main High School building, where I've been waiting to go my whole life, I was lost in a maze of friends I once knew but couldn't see or understand, waiting to see what might electrocute us next. Most of them were too traumatized about Claire to care about anything else; some were angry that I had ignored them for the entire year since my accident, and others were vicariously curious in the way people get when something awful happens to someone else. It wasn't exactly the homecoming Logan and I had dreamed of.

Logan tried hard to help. She kept a running commentary as she walked me down halls rushing with gossip I couldn't quite get. There was so much movement and noise. I was in a barrel, spinning and falling down some huge flood. I tried to push the thoughts of Claire and last year at Briarly back down into my bones, to focus hard on Logan's voice. "Not a germ on it!" she said, and laughed until she snorted. Adrian Woyzniak must have walked by. I shared a desk with him in second grade, and one time he said, "Hey, Emma, look at this!" And when I looked over, he had unzipped his pants, and there it was, resting on the outside of his corduroy bell-bottoms like a forlorn class pet. I said, "Oh my god, Adrian!" and he responded, "Not a germ on it!" It's Logan's favorite thing anyone has ever said. Whenever she hands me anything, usually something to eat, she says, "Not a germ on it."

Now she was whispering names in my ear. But even though I remembered all the people Lo could still see, it felt like none of us knew each other anymore, least of all me. And Logan didn't seem to get that now I was one of the actual weirdos, someone who would probably never be normal or okay. Before my accident, we both thought that with enough of her influence, I might eventually be less of a silent shadow girl, but what hope is there now? If I was too shy to be any fun before my eyes, how will I ever be more like Logan after them?

"Oh my god, Elizabeth has gained another fifty pounds," Logan said, and then, "Blythe got her nose pierced, and has on four-hundred-dollar boots I bet she stole from Claire M.'s closet—" Here she paused, and then decided to go the worse of two routes I could hear her consider: "Or her body."

"God, Logan," I said.

I reached down to feel my outfit: the usual striped hoodie, long-sleeve V-neck T-shirt, and jean skirt. I had on blue Converse with tennis socks, and pink, cat-shaped sunglasses with jewels in their corners, from Logan. She likes to accessorize, which means she's always hanging scarves and necklaces and glittering things off us so we sound like wind chimes. I love this about her; she's festive and likes to decorate things, including me. Even though she has no money, she has bought me eleven pairs of sunglasses since my accident, including the athletic ones with a band to hold them on. At first, she was big into encouraging me to take my glasses off whenever I was ready, but I don't want to, and I'll never want to, and I can't even stand to talk about it. And she's figured that out. So we haven't mentioned it in months. Kind of like how we've stopped saying the words *driver's ed, license,* and *car.*

As we walked, I tried to lead Spark, who Lake Main let me bring, maybe because they don't know he's not a real guide dog, or they don't care, or probably they just figured it wasn't worth arguing, since my parents fight so endlessly over everything that everyone else has to give in, just to avoid dying of exhaustion. Lake Main already knows that, because my parents love the separation of church and state, and famously made Lake Main take down all the Christmas decorations and remove "Away in a Manger" from the roster at the annual holiday concert.

All day I kept checking the parts of my body, making sure they hadn't disappeared just because I couldn't see them. I counted my fingers, felt my knees, ankles, and elbows. I had to work not to rock back and forth or tuck my head down, habits I started when I first got out of the hospital. Last year at the Briarly School for the Blind, the king of my ninth-grade universe, a boy named Sebastian, used to come up and hold my shoulders whenever I rocked. His hands were so confident they felt kind of rough, and he smelled like leather jackets and tangerines.

"Okay to rock out with me, Emma Sasha Silver," Sebastian told me, "but you can't do it with sighted people or they'll think you're a freak."

"Please don't call me Emma Sasha Silver," I said. "Just Emma." And I kept rocking. But every time I wanted to rock at Lake Main, I remembered Sebastian telling me it would make me look like a monster, and stopped myself. Because unlike Briarly, Lake Main was throbbing with people who could see me; everyone I'd been to nursery school with, in school plays with, eaten cookies and Jell-O and macaroni with my entire life. I didn't want them to think I was a freak. And knowing them wasn't the relief I'd thought it would be. Not just because

I stayed blind, but because they had all changed, too.

Logan held my hand and pulled me along, whispering about where classrooms were, the newly lime library ("someone barfed green paint on the walls; you're lucky you can't see it"), electronic doors to the gym. "Don't trip on that backpack, Em."

We were on our way to the office to "check in with" Principal Cates, which meant reassuring her that Spark and I had gotten to school without dying, and that Logan would get Spark and me to my locker, English, art, and the lunchroom without us getting trampled, lost, or devoured by rubberneckers. At the end of the day, Logan was to deliver me to Leah, who would take me home. Leah. Leah was my walk home, my finish line; she was like an icy lemon drink at the edge of a desert I still had to cross.

Leah was hours away. The office smelled like the core of school-earth, an even more intense version of the hallway's sloppy joe meat and hot Xeroxed copies, Bactine, Windex, sneakers, molding books. There was no laundry smell; there were no kitchens. I guess kids at Lake Main don't have to learn "life skills," or they get to learn them privately at home. The office, unbelievably, was noisier than the hall had been, and I couldn't make any sense of the sounds until Principal Cates's voice came both over the PA system and into my ears directly, because we were standing next to her. Her words doubled in my head.

"Welcome back back to Lake Main middle middle and high high school school." I inched away from the door, thinking I might be able to avoid the echo if I could hear only the PA and not also Principal Cates's live voice. I thought, *Focus in, Emma, focus in.* Logan followed me. "Where are you going?"

I didn't answer; tried instead to tune into individual words: *We . . . are . . . thrilled . . . to . . . have . . . you . . . herethisyear. PleaseriseforthePledgeofAllegiance.* I felt the thunder of chairs being pushed back, bodies standing, hands clasping, and then more words, a chorus, vibrating under my bones and above me, the whole school shaking in unison with *liberty and justice for all.* At the end, I thought, as I often do, *Okay, now I'll just open my eyes.* I can't tell anyone that this still happens, because how stupid is it to keep getting re-surprised by what should be obvious now? After more than a year? I haven't even told my therapist, Dr. Sassoman. She would just say it hasn't been long at all and I've made amazing progress and blah blah yadda yadda. I don't have to tell her anything anymore, because I already know what she'll say. It's almost like she lives inside of me. I shuffled back toward Principal Cates, disoriented, trying to feel Spark ahead of me and Logan to my left.

"Emma Silver, glad to see you," Principal Cates boomed. She shook my hand so vigorously I thought she might rip it out at the shoulder. Principal Cates is weirdly competitive. She was a runner when she was young, and then a running coach, and now she's a principal who loves slogans. Her favorite is "Champions are made in the morning," because she gets to school before dawn and roams the grounds, congratulating any other human being also running in circles before the sun comes up. Champions, in other words. She also likes to say, "Now is the time to do more than the minimum." Until I lost my eyesight, she had no idea who I was. Which I preferred. I liked being invisible in my family, too, recording what I saw without being seen myself. I used to be the secret keeper of words, but in some very unfair way, being blind is the opposite of being invisible.

"Logan, we're all counting on you," Principal Cates was saying. "Be a team player, please, and make sure Emma gets to her locker and her classes."

"Will do, Principal Cates."

"Good-bye, young ladies." No matter what comes out of her mouth, it's a cheer.

And we were free. As if she were programmed to do it, Logan resumed her commentary instantly: "Oooooh. There's Trey, more beautiful than ever. Be a team player, Emma, and go ask him if he wants to check out my Monday undies." She laughed until she snorted again.

"You're still wearing day-of-the-week underwear?" I asked. "Are you in third grade?"

"They're thongs."

A crowd of people surrounded us suddenly, most of them to pet and play with Spark, and the first bell hadn't even rung. I apologized to Logan for the nightmare of having to be my tour guide/bodyguard, but she slapped me and said, "Don't be stupid. You're famous. I'm living vicariously."

I *am* famous in the gross sense that my showing up means that everyone has returned from the new horror of Claire's death to the passé buzz about my eyes. But only for a moment. Claire's "accident" is a distraction from mine— and even though this makes me mean, I'm grateful for the weird demotion from worst-luck-girl-of-all-time in our town. What happened to Claire is so much worse than what happened to me that it makes getting blinded seem sneezy and manageable. Of course, Claire doesn't have to come back and face whatever her story is. Or the crowds of people telling it to each other. I couldn't help wondering—if this was what my dad called "back on track," then what was a track? And why be on one at all, let alone *back* on one? Maybe if there was anything worthwhile about being blinded, it was that it knocked me off the unthinking, lemming track I was on. For a moment, anyway.

Someone came up and said, "Hey, Emma, nice to have you back," and I realized it was Coltrane Winslow, and I tried not to rock, managed to squeeze "Thank you," out right from the top of my throat like a bird, just as an adult voice, maybe belonging to a teacher, came from above me: "Excuse me!"

I was still hoping to say something normal to Coltrane, who is a calm, really smart guy we all figure will be on the Supreme Court someday because his parents are both lawyers and he's super ambitious and fair and nice to everyone. But I was dizzy and unsure if Coltrane was even still standing there when the big voice interrupted. Whoever it belonged to had cleared a pathway, because she was standing right in front of me. And judging from how high up her voice was, she was apparently the Jolly Green Giant.

"You must be Emma Sasha Silver," she boomed, so loud it sounded like she was standing on a building shouting down into a megaphone. I knew then that she was my "paraprofessional," Ms. Mabel, because who else would be in the hallway armed with all three of my names? My parents had met her over the summer, but I'd refused to come.

Logan sang, under her breath but not quietly enough for my taste, "Wonder Woman, Diana, Princess of the Amazon!" I tried to slap her quietly, but missed, and ended up waving my arm around like some kind of useless flapper. Spark perked up, anxious to see why I was moving and whether we were headed somewhere. I bent and petted the top of his head. It was hard to stand back up, honestly. As soon as I touched Spark I wanted to fold up on the floor next to him. But I didn't. I stood back up, straight, like I was proving to myself that I could.

"Are you Ms. Mabel?" I asked.

"Yes, dear. I certainly am. May I walk you over to English class, Emma Sasha, and help get you situated? And who is this?"

"Um, my friend, Logan."

"Hi, Logan. And your dog's name?"

"Oh," I said, realizing that she had meant Spark the first time and I had introduced Logan. I flushed. "He's Spark."

"Hello there, Spark," she said. "Come, Emma Sasha, we'll go meet Ms. Spencer."

I wanted to tell her that Sasha is my middle name and I prefer to be called just Emma, like a normal person, but I couldn't think of a way to do so politely, and anyway, as soon as Ms. Mabel took my hand, Logan said, "See you after class, Emma Sasha! Good-bye, young lady! Be a team player!" and took off, laughing and snorting down the hall. It was the first time all day that I'd been away from her, and my knees wobbled as I took my first solo steps. I wondered if anyone was watching. Or everyone.

Logan had promised both my mom and me that she wouldn't leave my side for a single second except during English, because I'm in accelerated and she's in regular, what she calls Lobotominglish. Logan doesn't care about school and she hardly tried last year in ninth grade, because her dad moved away to California and I got blinded and went to Briarly and she skipped a bunch of school and didn't turn in her papers, so she got put in the lower-level class. It's not because she's slow. She's amazing at the things she cares about. But in my family, if you don't turn in an English paper, you might get executed or, worse, disappoint Dr. Dad, so none of us would ever skip a single class or turn in anything thirty seconds late, let alone miss an entire paper. Well, except Sarah, who didn't start her college applications on time and apparently also got a snake tattoo around her ankle, according to Leah. But our parents either think the snake itself is punishment enough or they pretended not to care that Sarah had defiled her skin, because Leah said they just shrugged and Sarah's been wearing kneesocks lately. Sarah once joked in front of me that it was a good thing I got blinded in the summer, or I might have missed a day of school, God forbid. Of course that was before I had no choice but to miss half of ninth grade. And who knows how I might be this year, who I am now?

Spark nosed my leg, which gave me enough confidence to keep walking. And Ms. Mabel lowered her giant hand onto my shoulder and guided me, pointing out the girls' bathroom, the teachers' lounge, rooms 214, 216, 218, and then, maybe sensing how overwhelmed I was, she tried small talk and told me her family had lived in Sauberg for three generations, her father was the chief of police for forty years, and she lived with him until he died, and yadda yadda. Maybe she hoped she'd be the Anne Sullivan to my Helen Keller. Then she asked about my family. I said there were seven kids, and she whistled low under her breath, and thought about my parents having sex while I thought about her thinking about my parents having sex. Whenever anyone finds out that there are seven kids in my family, they imagine my mom and dad having sex. I mean, be honest. You hear "seven kids," and you're immediately like, "Wow, those people love having sex. It's all they do. Constantly."

When we finally arrived at English, I was exhausted and ready to go home and hide under the cushions of our gold couch. I heard frantic scratching and clicking, and smelled so much white dust I felt like I'd swallowed a hopscotch. Spark sneezed.

Ms. Spencer either didn't notice Spark and me, or she chose not to say anything as we settled ourselves in the first row. I was grateful to be left alone. "I'll read what she's writing on the board as soon as she's done," Miss Mabel told me.

Ms. Spencer was scribbling so fast and wildly I wondered if we were starting the year with *The Odyssey* (which Leah read to me when I was frozen on the couch, missing ninth grade, and trick or treating, and homecoming, and everything else). Maybe Ms. Spencer had decided to transcribe the entire text in chalk. A piece snapped and I heard it hit the floor.

People were shuffling in, some pausing to gasp over the

sight of me, others stopping to say hi, maul Spark, or marvel over my HumanWare brailler, the one Sarah made sure I was aware cost almost six thousand dollars. Ms. Mabel read the board into my tired right ear: "Assignments, reading, writing, journal, two analytical papers. Books: *A Raisin in the Sun*, *Macbeth*, *To Kill a Mockingbird*, *The Stranger*, *The Inferno*, *Antigone*." I jotted the titles down in my brailler, and Ms. Mabel stayed the entire time, telling me whenever Ms. Spencer wrote anything on the board, which was approximately seven hundred times a minute. Had teachers always written on the board this much? How had I not noticed, and how would I ever manage without help? Before my accident, I would have celebrated extra hours to write my in-class exams or finish assignments. But now that I need extra time and someone else to read the board to me, I feel furious and proud and want to show everyone that I don't need anything "special," even though I clearly do. I hate the word *special*.

I was considering this when someone started crying uncontrollably. I didn't know who it was, except that it wasn't me, thank god. No one was surprised; since Claire, crying is like clearing your throat in Sauberg. People walk the streets weeping. Ms. Spencer just clucked her mouth and said there were grief counselors downstairs to help us "deal with our feelings." When class ended, Ms. Mabel stayed to talk to Ms. Spencer about getting me my assignments in advance so she and I could translate them into braille, and I tuned them out until they were done, when Spark and I felt our way toward the door and stood there groping around for Logan. But she wasn't back yet.

"Hey, Emma," someone else said, and I recognized Blythe Keene's musical, twinkling voice.

I thought maybe I could feel her gloaty, working eyes bore a hole into my face, like she was trying to melt my sunglasses and get a glimpse of the damage. But then she put her hand on my arm and said, "Welcome back."

I said, "Thanks," and she left her hand on my arm, like she wanted me to know she was still there, or was going to lead me away or something. People are weirdly casual about touching me now. It's like I have to see by feeling, so everyone gets to feel me. Or maybe they just don't want to shock me; it's like the animal way of warning some other animal that you're nearby and aren't going to pounce. The truth is, I was surprised Blythe had come up to me at all. She's like a dream girl, beautiful and funny and, I don't know, herself, I guess. She doesn't try as hard as everyone else, and she never has. I don't know why. She didn't ask how I was, and I was glad.

But then I couldn't think of anything to say and we were standing with her hand on my arm, so I asked how she was.

She said, "I'm managing," which was very Blythe— honest, not insane or melodramatic or anything, just okay

and true. Because Blythe and Claire were best friends like
Logan and I are. Inseparable. So even though Blythe's life is
perfect in every way, it's also ruined. Then she offered, super casually, to walk with me to art. She wasn't like, "Can I
medevac your basket-case ass to art class because you're blind
flying the halls"; she just said, "Wanna walk to Fister's together?" like we were old friends. Which I guess we are, in a way.
I mean, I've known Blythe my whole life, but it's not like she's
ever really paid attention to me.

I tried to say, "Sure, thanks," in a normal human voice,
without crying or throwing myself into Blythe's arms. I didn't
wait for Logan, just followed Blythe like a pitiful puppy.

When Blythe said, "Hey, Zach," my heart catapulted up
into my throat. Zach Haze. I tried not to rock, not to turn my
head too wildly toward the sound of his voice when he said,
"Hey, Blythe. Hey, Emma, nice dog," as if nothing had happened, a year and a half hadn't passed, I hadn't been blinded,
and I hadn't brought my K9 buddy dog to Lake Main after
missing ninth grade. As if I weren't an invalid. I knew if I
opened my mouth I would barf my heart straight into the
hallway, so I stayed mute, as usual. I've never been able to
talk to Zach Haze. Once, in sixth grade, right after Benj was
born, Zach asked me if my family was Catholic, even though
he must have known we're not, since my family is famously
the only Jewish one ever to live in Sauberg. I'll never know

why Zach asked, because I tried so desperately to think of a fascinating answer that would engage him forever that I stood there for ten minutes like an absolute salt statue. And then he assumed there was something profoundly wrong with me, and never spoke to me again. Which is a tragedy, because I love him desperately. I always have. And he's one of the few people who has only been made better by my new ability to listen closely: his voice is amazing, deep and smooth and patient—not like he's slow or searching for the right word, but like he has all the time in the world to talk to you, and wants to mean what he says, so he gets his words right. They always sound sweetly musical, and you can feel the vibration of his voice coming up from the floor, so it shakes you up a little, makes your bones rattle and chatter.

As soon as Blythe and I got to the art room, Mrs. Fincter, alternately called by everyone Fister, Sphincter, or Spinster, pulled me aside to say, "I heard you were going to be in this section. Do you think you can handle a regular art class?"

As opposed to what? Not handling it? Dying? Taking an irregular art class? I waited as long as I could. Mrs. Fincter knows my family because my mom is an artist, and even if she weren't, she'd still be famous, just for rocking her Old Mother Hubbard vibe so hard. But I didn't know if Mrs. Fincter liked my mom or not, or how she thought of us.

"Um, yeah," I finally said. "I hope so. I have—"

I was going to tell her that Ms. Mabel could help me, but she interrupted. "I guess we'll have to come up with an individual plan of study for you."

Blythe was probably still nearby. I wondered if she was listening to me and Mrs. Fincter, hoped not.

"Okay," I said, wanting the conversation over. I wasn't able to tell whether my individual plan of study was a happy challenge for her as an artist, teacher, and person, or a horrible inconvenience. But since I had actual problems to deal with, I put Mrs. Fincter's feelings about me where they belonged: under *who has time to give a shit about this?* I just let Ms. Mabel help me get my supplies ready so I could participate absently in our first free-drawing session. I felt the waxy ridges of the crayon create raised lines on my paper. I ran my fingers over the page, felt my drawing take shape while Fincter talked about how we heal through art and blah blah we could work out our grief through projects blah. I was thinking it would be nice to heal through someone actually telling the truth once in a while, when a girl's voice asked, "Is that your dog?" and I jumped.

I didn't know who had said it, or whether she meant Spark or my picture, because I was drawing a dog. Or even for sure if she was talking to me, although the voice was so close to my right ear that I assumed she must be. I nodded silently. *Don't rock.*

"It's pretty good," the voice said, so she must have meant the crayon work. "That's amazing that you can do that."

"Thanks," I said, but I couldn't bring myself to ask who I was speaking to. Ms. Mabel didn't say anything. Maybe she thinks I have to get my social life together on my own. Or maybe they only pay her to help me with my academic struggles.

Last year at Briarly, a blind girl named Dee said I should just ask who had come up to me, or who was talking, or whatever I couldn't figure out myself. She said no one would mind, not even sighted people. We had just had this nauseating conversation because I asked where she'd gotten these delicious Korean pastries she was sharing with me and Sebastian, and she said, "My mom brought them back from Korea." I asked what she'd been doing in Korea, even though I didn't really care. And she was like, "Well, she was visiting my grandma, who lives there, because she's Korean."

My mind reeled backward and forward at the same time. I asked, "So your mom is Korean, too?"

Dee laughed. "That's generally how it works, Emma," she said.

"Are you Korean?"

"I'm half," she said. "My dad is black."

"Wow. I guess I've never seen you," I said, and she laughed again, like we were bonding, but my throat started to burn, because I hadn't meant it as a joke. In fact, it set alight a new dread in me, one that was hard to name. I knew nothing. How would I ever find out anything about anyone again? Without having to ask questions no one is supposed to ask?

Dee was someone I wouldn't have been friends with at Lake Main, and I can't even explain why this is, or what point there is in it, but since my accident, I can't stop dividing the world up into things I do "because of it," and things I "would have done anyway," like there's some ethical reason for me to do only things the "other Emma" would have done. But everything I've done since was something the new blind me had to do. So I can't win.

Asking people who they are is obviously something I would *never* have done. And I don't want to start now. So I said nothing to the mystery girl in art. I just ran my fingers along the lines I'd drawn again and again, unsure what color my sad crayon dog was, wanting to ask Ms. Mabel but not asking, dying to rock but not rocking. Maybe people make too much of having to know everything all the time. Maybe I can do fine without knowing who's talking to me or crying in what class, who's here and who's gone.

One thing I know, maybe the only thing, is that I'm here. Claire is actually *gone*, in the permanent dark. Which is not the same as my dark. My dark is complicated and sometimes lovely. I have to keep reminding myself. I can hear and smell and feel the people I love, which is the opposite of absolute nothingness. I'm still alive. I'm still me—just this other me. It's going to be fine. Right?

I said nothing in any of my classes, or the hallways, or the lunchroom, where I ate my clammy sandwich in a whirl of activity that felt dangerous. Logan translated the entire time, even told me who was eating what, but eventually I had to tune her voice out. All day I felt twisty and dready and alternately so hot I thought I might be feverish and so cold I was immobilized. I listened and tried not to listen, waited and tried not to be waiting, since what was I waiting for?

The final horrific event of the afternoon was a mind- and butt-numbing mandatory assembly. Logan and I sat together, and in a miracle coincidence, Zach Haze sat with us. As I parked Spark and my white cane at my feet, I couldn't help thinking, *If only*. If only I was the old me, Emma of the working green eyes, sitting with Zach and Logan, I could endure anything, even this performance about how shocked we all were, how a loss like this, how a scholar athlete, how as a community, how healing. How grief counselors. How "available to us." How the hows made Principal Cates's voice into the lowing of cattle in a field I was driving by. How none of it told us anything real about Claire, about who she had been or what had actually happened. We knew that our parents and teachers were calling Claire's death an accident, but Principal

Cates didn't come near any words with actual information in them. What kind of accident? Had Claire killed herself? Slipped into the lake alone? What could she have been doing there by herself?

I sat as still as I could, focusing in and, for some reason, imagining reds: Twizzlers, lipstick, traffic lights, blood. Logan passed me a sticky, already unwrapped Jolly Rancher, whispered, "Not a germ on it!" and I tasted the joke and the pink bloom of fake watermelon in my mouth at the same time. Logan and Zach whisper-bantered about the bullshit assembly, school, the bright world they were still part of. While I listened. While I felt terrified, like Claire's and my tragedies—even though they're not related and hers is worse—melted together into one dark.

Then it was three fifteen. Leah swept me up from Logan at my locker, and carried me home on a wave of my sisters. Leah asked me a million questions about my day, her voice full of awe and joy. I complained about the assembly and Mrs. Fincter. Leah grabbed me into such a violent hug that I thought Spark might attack her. "You made it through your first day, though! I knew you could do it! What did people say? Did they stare? How was Logan? How was Ms. Mabel? Did you see *him?*" She dropped her voice to a whisper, even though she didn't even say Zach's name out loud.

"I didn't see anything," I said, and she laughed her howling belly laugh, which made me laugh until I almost felt like it had been kind of funny, even though nothing had seemed at all funny while I was still at school. Leah always puts me somewhere other than where I've been. On the roof of my life. I wish I could do that for Naomi, but I don't know how. Especially now.

Leah darted into Jenna's kindergarten room and came out with Jenna, both of them singing "Down by the Bay," Leah terribly, ear-wreckingly out of tune, and Jenna with her shocking, little-kid glass voice, her own verse, all the notes lining up just right: "Have you ever seen a fish stick wearing ketchup lipstick?" She and I are the musical ones; she has perfect pitch and I can hear it. I used to love piano, singing, any music, really. And now Jenna does.

Naomi came out of her fourth-grade homeroom with a drawing she'd been working on all day. She kept holding the open notebook, coloring as she walked out of the school and down the eleven front steps. Leah said she should wait until we got home to keep working on her picture. Naomi said, "Emma gets to walk without looking. And it's a comic."

"My bad," Leah said, "but please stop working on your comic while we're walking." I don't know if Naomi obeyed or not. At the bus stop, Benji bounced off the preschool bus like a Super Ball, terrifying Spark. I could feel us rolling home like a force, a five-star Silver parade, missing only Sarah and Baby Lily. Naomi was now busy directing Benj and Jenna to stomp on all the cracks, and to guess how many steps we were from home, while she counted to see who was closest. I wasn't allowed to participate, because I had the advantage of having figured out how many steps there are between most places in our house, so I was "too good at it." Naomi is a busy person, always making crafts, rules, or games; she never slows down. She's the leader of the little kids, but lately she'd rather be one of the big kids. I get that, since there are so many things I can't do that I sometimes don't know if I count as an actual big kid anymore.

Our walks home are how the slow hours of that first day morphed into a week and then that week into two and three and a month, and even I settled surprisingly into the dim lull of school. Everyone wanted something: good grades; a starring part in the Lake Main Players' production of *Annie Get Your Gun*; someone to go to the first football game with; someone for the second game; an escape from parents, from church, from whatever was eating away at your particular insides; to get a driver's license; to get a car, a boy, a girl, someone else's lips or body pressed against theirs. Meanwhile, I just wanted to make it from room to room, not to get hit by a car or pitied too much by anyone but myself. To keep doing well in school, which used to be easy for me, but maybe won't be anymore, with Ms. Mabel and my brailler and my ears. I just want to stop thinking about forever in the dark and my endless, claustrophobic tunnel of a future. Because I'll never drive or get a job, or get married or lose my virginity. Maybe I'll never even kiss anyone.

Because how will Zach Haze—or anyone—fall in love with me now? I'm definitely not invisible anymore. Everyone has noticed me now that I'm "famous," as Logan says. But having everyone know who you are isn't fabulous if it's because you're the star of a gruesome tragedy. Or because you're disfigured. The way people stare and fuss makes me feel like I'm trapped under a magnifying glass, gasping and sweating, in danger of catching fire. Again.

Because that's what happened. The summer before I should have started ninth grade at Lake Main, I went to a Fourth of July party with my parents and my sisters and Benj. It wasn't quite dark out yet, and we were standing on a stretch of green lawn, clutching paper plates imprinted with stars. My mom spread out a blanket, but my dad and Leah and I stood waiting for the first fireworks. It must have smelled like barbecue, wet grass, summer, dogs. I didn't notice, because I didn't have to care about smells then. There were people everywhere, our neighbors and friends, carrying flags and balloons, laughing and chattering. In my memory, it's like the "before" picture of my life and our town. And then the sky darkened and the show started and maybe Leah went to throw our plates away or something, but my dad and I were still there, holding the rope they'd strung up like a boundary, watching.

I loved the way the giant booms sent out wheels of spinning pink, red, yellow, and orange. I loved standing there dizzily, everywhere hot rocket smoke, colors shooting up and exploding into art that disappeared almost instantly. Even then, I got what's so thrilling about beauty we see briefly or only once, the kind we can't hold on to. Maybe I jinxed myself by thinking that? Because I tilted my head back to watch, like I was drinking the magic of each explosion of color, waiting for the next and the next. My dad had his hands on my shoulders, and he pulled me toward him a little. I took a step backward as he said, "Maybe we should—" and then I felt the spray of heat and pain across my face and my hands flew up to catch it, stop it, protect my eyes from whatever the sharp, shocking hot, melting, screaming blaze was, but then there was nothing.

My dad never finished his sentence. Maybe we should . . . what? Back up? Duck? Cover? Run? Not have come to this place that will ruin our daughter's life in 3, 2, 1. Well, there wouldn't have been time to count, or he'd have gotten at least the next two words out. Lie down? Move back? Who knows what he would have said if a rocket hadn't blown backward and shot into the crowd. Right where I was standing. I've tried to stop wondering why the tiny band of my eyes—that one spot in the universe—was the place it hit, because, as my therapist Dr. Sassoman likes to say, that kind of wondering is "unproductive." I used to ask obsessively, what were the chances? Chances are funny, though, because now that it happened, they're 100 percent.

Sometimes the accident seems like the beginning of my entire life, because I can't fully remember who I was before. Even though—or maybe because—I work so hard to keep what I used to be able to see: colors, light, shapes, my mom's and Leah's and Benj's faces, even the way those fireworks looked.

I found myself in a cold, blank, metal-smelling hospital. That's where I woke up, where I first heard my mom crying and my dad talking in his doctor voice about sockets, scarring, loss, regaining. Where were my sisters? Benj? Where was I? Was I awake?

I remember thinking, *I can't be waking up*, because waking up and opening your eyes are the same thing and I couldn't open my eyes. But then, all of a sudden, I knew I was awake. And that my eyes wouldn't open. That they were sewn shut, or something; something was wrong. It was after that realization that I felt shrieking, amazing pain. How had I not felt it first? Nothing happened in order. I reached up, but my hands found only band after band of cotton pads, fabric, tape. I couldn't see. I couldn't think. I used to believe that seeing and thinking were the same thing.

"Emma," my mom said. "You're awake." I don't know how she could tell. Her cool hand arrived somewhere near my forehead; it must have been on a patch of skin uncovered by the bandages, but I couldn't tell exactly where. Was it near my eyes? Where were my eyes?

"Where am I?" I screamed. "What is—Take this off!" I tried to peel the bandages, to tear them off, to see where I was, but someone held my arms down—I don't know who. One of my parents? A nurse? I'll never know, because then I was out, and then I was me again, thinking, screaming.

Whoever came up with the words "out like a light" knew something terrible. Because even when I was on, I felt out, off, gone. I could not calm down, could not stop shrieking about the pain and where my eyes were and where I was. My parents were a desperate loop, trying to answer, trying: "You had an accident; you're in the hospital; you're awake; you're okay, you're Emma. Emma. Emma."

Then everything—the words, the rustle and scrape of the hospital, the robotic reports of machinery I couldn't see, even the air—would go gauzy and soft. Like curtains, fluttering in the sort of light that's about to turn into nighttime. There were needles in my arms. Someone pushed buttons. I heard beeps, and the room drowned out until I was awake again, screaming. That's how it was then, when I was a prisoner in the hospital, in that metal dark. I couldn't have said if ten minutes or ten months had passed until the day someone peeled the tape and then lifted off the cotton and cloth from my eyes. I asked if I could open them now, but they were already open; I knew because I reached up and felt my right eye. It was open. And I saw nothing.

"What do you see, Emma?" someone asked me.

"Who is that?" I asked, trying not to yell, not to panic.

"I'm Dr. Walker," he said, and put his hand over mine. It felt to me like a cooked steak, a heavy piece of warm meat on my cold hand. I shuddered.

"It's Dr. Walker," my dad said. As if we all knew each other, or that might mean something to me.

I screamed, "Why can't I see?"

For a few days, they held out hope for my right eye, but then Dr. Walker wasted no time in declaring that neither eye's sight was going to "be restored." So I lived those weeks in the hospital learning to be alive without my eyes. That's when Dr. Sassoman showed up, talking about "therapy," smelling like vanilla lotion, holding my hands, and putting whispered questions into my ears, where they stopped and stayed. I did not answer "how are you feeling?" or "what do you remember?" My parents talked noisily, far away from my ears, but in a buzz somehow around my head, about how great Dr. Sassoman was, how she was "the best in the business." She was going to help us "get through this," and I saw a tunnel. If I could just gasp and squeeze through a tunnel, I thought, maybe I'd be able to see. Light at the end. I said nothing. And

Dr. Sassoman, as lovely smelling and whispery and practical as she was, wasn't a magician. She still isn't. She just guided me around the hospital and objected—like my parents—whenever I said I was going to die "without my eyes." Like it mattered what the hell I said.

"You are decidedly not going to die, and you still have your eyes," Dr. Sassoman told me on countless mornings, as I wept and wound my way around the room, crashing into things, unable to move properly, to believe that this had happened, was happening, would continue. "They don't work the way they did, but you are not without eyes."

"They're ruined!" I told her, as if she didn't know. She considered this progress—any time I spoke, it was "progress"—and several weeks later, when I tried to run from the room but hit the door? Progress. Once, I hurled a useless braille block at her; some well-meaning friend of my father's had sent a box of "tools" for me, but I never figured that one out. Dr. Sassoman was there when I opened the box, all cheerful and encouraging, so I punished her. She dodged the block, I guess, although I couldn't see and hadn't yet learned how to calm down enough to pay attention to what was happening around me. She never lost her patience or raised her voice. My parents tried to be that patient, but couldn't be, because they were so traumatized that my mom was screaming and throwing things at night when they thought we couldn't hear, wouldn't know. But even I knew, as dark and floaty as I was then. She wrecked her studio, sliced open canvases with an X-Acto, poured her paints out, shattered and sawed apart her beloved easels. She hasn't painted since. My dad became her doctor, which, if everything else hadn't been so disastrous, might have been the worst part of all.

My parents met in a hospital in the city when he was a resident. The maternity wing bought a bunch of my mom's paintings, and my dad apparently saw her in the lobby, carrying canvasses. She must have looked like no one he'd ever seen, because my mom has long, curly red hair and has dressed the same way since she was my age, in painty jeans and hoodies and glittery Converse sneakers. And figure everyone else was either a sick person or a puffy-eyed doctor in those terrible, sagging, light-blue scrub pajamas. I bet my mom lit the lobby on fire. My dad says he knew as soon as he saw her, and in spite of his debilitating social awkwardness, he apparently walked right over and asked, could he help her with whatever she was carrying? And then—alert the fairy tale police—it was her spectacular paintings! And I'm not kidding; her paintings used to be beautiful, full of the feeling of light on water, the way Leah's words are.

It's no surprise my dad practically fainted with love the first time he saw my mom. The part about why she fell for him is less clear; it's almost as if, because he was a doctor, she naturally loved him, too. He's very stiff and difficult and she's floppy and easy to be with. But people adore doctors, because they save you. Although it turns out they can't save you from everything, not even when they're your parents. Maybe my mom just liked the way he's handsome—the strong, square-jawed, clean-shaven, sleek-haired way. It's the opposite of how she's beautiful—her wild-haired, rule-hating prettiness. My mom smells like pasta and lavender, and sounds like traffic and music and the beach. My dad smells like mint and rubbing alcohol; he's a smooth motor, gears, keys clicking, machinery that works. In fact, my parents are so different from each other that it sometimes seems like the two of them combine to make one whole person. But after my accident, they couldn't keep the parts in sync anymore; the world was spinning on a faster, looser axis suddenly, dark, brutal, everything out of control. And I knew everything, the way kids always do and parents either don't realize or can't face that we do. In my family, whatever the little ones don't understand, the older ones translate. If you're a grown-up and you have a pink vibrating toy in the drawer by your bed, for example, you might as well keep it on the mantel in the living room, because your eleven-year-old daughter, who is me, will find it while she's looking for a flashlight and she'll think it's a perfect rocket for her American Girl doll until her older sister, Sarah, who's mean about knowing everything, will tell her what it actually is.

Obviously our parents' fake daytime optimism didn't trick any of us, least of all me. I knew my life was wrecked, and every time I thought about it, my hands and face would go numb and then I would black out and wake up later, with my parents' and Dr. Sassoman's voices standing over me.

"You can calm down," Dr. Sassoman said finally. "You can tell yourself to calm down."

And I said, "You can tell yourself to fuck off." I had a momentary pang of power, before my shame and helplessness overwhelmed me again. I had never said anything like that to anyone, not even Sarah. I had no idea who I was, and couldn't find a way to apologize.

But Dr. Sassoman said nothing, just let it go, just let me scream for weeks, until my throat was raw and her point was made. She was still there, waiting for me. Just like my parents and sisters and brother. And Logan. And my own body, which I could feel but no longer see. My arms, there. My fingers, one through ten, there. My neck, throat, cheeks, collarbone, my small breasts, which Logan and I had joked about since we had both started getting them the year before. We had a contest about whose would get bigger, even though it was obvious that it would be hers, because she's a breasty, bouncy, dimply person and I'm a stick figure, just like my parents and my sisters and probably Benj, although he's still baby-chubby so it's hard to say. I was even more knees, bones, and elbows then; it seemed a miracle that I had any breasts at all, but I did, and they were still there. Everything was there; I just couldn't see it. Nothing had been altered by my shrieking about everything being altered forever. By my not being able to see it. If a tree falls in the forest and I can't see it, it still falls. That's what it feels like to have the world tell you to fuck off.

Logan came to the hospital six times a week. Her parents were breaking up and saying incredibly terrible things to each other and about each other to her, and her mom was suing her dad, and he was moving out. On Saturday mornings Lo's mom tagged along to my room. She brought perfume samples, Pixy Stix, stickers, chocolate kisses. The stickers were always textured. I traced the shapes: hearts, stars, puffy animals with googly eyes that clicked around inside their clear plastic half-globes. I often let my fingers linger on the eyes of those lucky bunnies and ducks. Logan stayed all day every Saturday, reading out loud to me, playing me songs. She climbed into my bed with me, talked about her parents, cried over them and my eyes, laughed until she snorted, spelled out boys' names on my back with her long fingernails, and brought stuff I could feel: coins, sandpaper, beach glass, feathers. Once, a giant conch she definitely got at one of the souvenir shops on Lake Street, Sauberg's pathetic "downtown." Lake Street has a strip of stores, partially because if you live here you occasionally need things, and partially because of Lake Brainch, the big freshwater lake that gets called "Branch" by the tourists who come to swim and boat and water-ski and bring home beach souvenirs. Because of them, all the shops on Lake Street are vacation colors: pale yellows, sky blues. They sell taffy and temporary tattoos, straw hats and swim toys, seashells and flamingo wind chimes, even though no flamingo has ever set a bony pink foot anywhere near this place. But I loved the shell Logan brought, and was certain it held the ocean in it. I could hear the water rushing through, and smell the salt.

Logan asked about everything she handed me: "What does it look like to you, Em?" And I worked on what words I'd use to describe the world—maybe for the rest of my life. While she listened. In late August, I stopped screaming. Just before Logan started ninth grade, I got out of the hospital. The nurses hugged and kissed me and gave me cards, and Dr. Sassoman made a chart about what I'd do and when and how. I would apparently come to her office every week for eternity, and other people, including her, would come to my house and teach me, and I pretended to listen and then staggered home after my mom and dad. And sat down, numb, on our gold couch. And tried to open my eyes, rocked, counted my legs and arms and fingers. I didn't cry. Or talk.

Then the world moved forward *anyway* in the relentless

anyway way it does. Dozens of mothers came to our house with frozen blocks of pasta and breads and cakes they'd baked and their daughters, my friends from another life. I wasn't hungry. I hid, refused to see anyone, and hung the green curtain over my bed in the guest room on the first floor, which was suddenly Naomi's and my bedroom. My mom thanked everyone in what Sarah dubbed her "suburb-drug" voice. Sarah also later pointed out that our mom got pregnant with my littlest sister, Baby Lily, that August, so, well, whatever. That was what it was, but she was taking drugs? When our mom was pregnant with Benj, she wouldn't even drink a soda or touch a piece of fruit that wasn't organic and grown in front of her, but now her unhappiness and guilt were so profound that she was poisoning our new baby just to keep from dying of misery or maybe killing herself. Because of me. Knowing the depth of her fear doubled mine.

I met Dr. Sassoman every other week at her office, which smelled like vanilla beans and the color beige. It was so quiet the thoughts in my head pounded, bounced, and echoed: "It's fall, fall, the world is racing by without me. Without me. Where am I? Where am I? Open your eyes, Emma, open your eyes." On the in-between weeks, Dr. Sassoman came to our house, and talked with my parents, too. It was September and I was on our gold couch, in Dr. Sassoman's office, back on the couch. Everyone else started school and I became part of the dark, scratchy couch fabric. I was clutching the braille cube I never learned to use, not moving, cold-sweating. When Logan said her dad was moving to California, the words sounded like they came from outer space and floated down. I couldn't hold on to them or respond. I wasn't there for her or anyone. It felt like I literally wasn't there; everyone else was still human, living on the same earth I'd once been on. They were doing human things like starting ninth grade at Lake Main, but I had dropped out of the world. I lived in this weird, dark, spinning void. I lay back on the couch. *Open your eyes, Emma.* I thought of myself as "Emma" then, or "you," or "she," anyone but me.

Logan came over every day after school, and asked all the time when our other friends could come and see me. When I could manage to respond at all, I said, "Never."

"But it might cheer you up, Em," she said. "Everyone misses you."

I said nothing. She brought and read me notes from girls I'd known since preschool: Deirdre Sharp, Claire Montgomery, Monica Dancat, Elizabeth Tallentine—their names were dimly familiar, like words from a language I'd once spoken but no longer knew. Logan said Lake Main was hell without me, that she was going to die if I didn't come back. But I could never go back. If I'd never see anyone again, why should they see me?

My mom made me walk outside occasionally, made me

feel the grass, the sunlight, fresh air, the world. She begged me to shower, but I couldn't stand water on my face. No matter what she asked me to do, I said no, burrowed deeper. Then, a million no's later, it was October. And even though July, August, and September had been the longest, worst months of my life, October's arrival felt sudden. I was furious. How dare it be October? I was lying on the couch in sunglasses, fingering a braille alphabet page, trying to use it to line dots up in some meaningful way, but failing: A: 1; B: 1 and 2; C: 1 and 4; D: 1, 4, and 5; E: 1 and 5; and so on. I had just figured out that turning letters into numbers just took a 3, 4, 5, 6 in front and A became 1, B 2, C 3, D 4, E 5, and F 6, when my awkward dad I could no longer see came into the living room.

"Hi, Emma," he said. Was he looking at me? I felt his weight at the foot of the couch, and smelled something funny and alive. I heard scratching. Fear rose in my throat, indistinguishable from the fury I couldn't temper. "What are you doing?" my dad asked, waiting for a second, as if something was caught in his throat, before adding, "Sweetie," my mom's word.

"I'm learning my fucking ABC's. What are *you* doing?" I responded. He swallowed a gulp of sorrow so hard I heard it. I had been so quiet my whole life; maybe my parents thought the vile things I now said were representative of who I'd been all along. I hoped not, even though I couldn't stop being cruel to them. I wished I hadn't been so quiet before, when my life had been easy. Why didn't I say cheerful and clever things when I was still intact and happy? Now there's no chance of it. My dad and I both tried to think what to say next; it's hard to know who felt more lost or miserable. My dad is like me; he doesn't like to talk, either. But the scratching sound saved us both, and a bark sat me up like I'd been yanked by a string. I dropped my cube and groped around.

"We brought you something, sweetie," my mom said. So she had come in the room, too. My dad handed me Spark. I put my face right up to Spark's, felt his warm, silky face with my cheek, his wet nose with my nose, his furry ears with my hands. He licked my face wildly, not even avoiding my sunglasses. It was love at first whatever isn't sight.

My dad was talking: "He's a K9 buddy, Emma, blah blah, so he's not really allowed in restaurants or blah blah real seeing-eye dog, blah blah." This turned out not to be true, except at the Briarly School for the Blind, where they were strict about distinctions between "real guide dogs" and "pets." Other than at Briarly, I've yet to meet the shop owner who throws the blind kid's dog out the door, pet or not. But there is a rule that you have to be sixteen to get a guide dog and my dad loves a good rule. "As soon as you're sixteen, you can go to training school and choose a genuine mobility assistance dog, blah."

I had tuned him out at "He's," was burying my face in

Spark's fur, crying. My mom and I were both crying and my dad was not. I was furious at my mom for crying and at my dad for not crying. And the more I hated them and myself, the more I loved Spark. I don't know if that makes sense, but I loved him completely, the way I couldn't love anyone or anything else anymore. Everything else was ruined and he was perfect.

"Spark can help by keeping you company as you get up and about more," my dad continued.

I couldn't stop crying. But I stopped kissing Spark long enough to say, "I'm not going anywhere."

"Yes, you are," my dad said, but in the pause that followed my mom either shot him a withering look or grabbed him quietly, because he added, "When you're ready."

Then my mom came and put her arms around me, but I kept mine around Spark, who was wildly licking my face. Spark! Who understands me without any effort, who doesn't care what I look like, who asks for nothing but love and to go on walks, and who is the only one who actually *always* helps. He has never once made being blind worse for me. I spent the rest of that day off the couch, roaming the house with Spark, laughing as he sniffed everything in the house and tackled and licked me. It was the first time since the accident that I'd heard my own laugh. July, August, September, October is a long time to go without laughing.

• • •

My father's entire life has been a study in how patients who walk soon after their surgeries recover, whereas those who "mope about" stay bedridden disappointments to their parents forever. Which is why he was all over me to work my way back into the land of people who move and live. He got me Spark, my white cane, and, to my fury and embarrassment, a mobility coach named Mr. Otis who came and pried me off the couch so I could learn to walk, find my own room, pour and drink a glass of water without spilling it everywhere, and get to and from the bathroom without tripping and cracking my spine.

I could hardly breathe when Mr. Otis first started coming. While I tried to keep my hands and face from going numb, he showed my mom and me how to organize drawers, make braille labels, and sew them into my shirts and skirts and tights so I could choose my own outfits. We labeled the individual items with premade tinfoil labels Mr. Otis suggested at first and then, later, with pieces of plastic milk gallon cartons my mom cut up and used, her sculptor's inspiration. But mostly, I tuned his bright red voice out and streamlined my clothes. I wore only jeans, V-necks (T-shirts when it was hot, long-sleeve T-shirts for in between, and striped hoodies when it got cold), and blue Converse all the time. I have three pairs. And four red nightgowns. I still dress that (and only that) way, because why change? All of my bras are nude, so they'll never show through, no matter what shirt I choose.

Mr. Otis spent countless hours helping me click and slide the white cane in front of me, in step, back step. I thought of the ballroom dance class Logan and I had taken on weekends when we were eleven, trading off who had to be the boy: triple step, rock step, triple step, rock step. In step, back step, spark step, rock step. She was so loud and extroverted and crazy in those classes, and I was so quiet. I loved her, loved listening to her joke and be confident and laugh and stomp all over the place. It's hard to believe how shy I already was. How will I ever dance again with anyone other than my white cane or Spark? Mr. Otis once told me, "The cane is an extension of your pointer finger, Emma. You are feeling your way. Touch, touch, find a shoreline, find a landmark. Indoor, outdoor, find a shoreline, where's your shoreline?"

This was what music would be for me: Mr. Otis's voice; this was my sad dancing: my "feeling my way" with a long, bony, witchedy digit scraping the sidewalk. My graphite finger tapping, searching for a shoreline. I can't remember how many times Mr. Otis showed me a new one, or asked me to name a landmark: here's where the grass becomes a curb, where the curb rolls into the street, where the carpet meets the wall. Here are the planks of the porch, down one stair, two stairs, three stairs, grass. Maybe ten million times, maybe twenty. My mind gets melty when I think of his voice, of those gasping weeks or months or whatever they were. Listen to the traffic. Hear it stop on your left, and when the rush of it starts on your right, stick your cane straight out into the crosswalk in case. Everything was "in case" with Mr. Otis: in case someone is turning, in case you've made a mistake and it's not actually a red light, your light. Listen. A landmark can be the smell of the Mantroses' rosebushes, or the sound of cars at the end of Oak Street, the grind of engines stopping or starting up at an intersection. Once you've stuck your cane out and no one has hit it with a car, then okay, strike out into the crosswalk, try to stay straight. If the engines have just begun to idle, then you have the whole light, Emma. Remember, the band of that walk inside the white lines should be approximately the same width as the sidewalk. It's Mr. Otis who told me that, and when I have that thought, even now, I have it in his urgent red voice. Hug the side away from the cars that are moving, try to stay straight, in case.

In case. In case. In case. Even though we were too late, because the worst thing ever had happened, in spite of whatever "in cases" I had tried my entire life leading up to it. Mr. Otis and I walked down the five porch steps, our minds humming a stupid chorus of "in case." We moved, slid, tapped, stumbled onto the band of sidewalk over and over and over, and when Mr. Otis wasn't there, my mom used Spark as an excuse to get me out of the house and make me practice. She told me what was going to happen before it happened, every second, like some kind of psychotic robot: "Now I'm going to turn the coffee grinder on." *Wherrrreww, grrrrrrrr.* "Now I'm going to start the car." *Griiiind.* "Now I'm going to light the burner." *Foooshmp.* Now I'm turning on the water now I'm closing the door now I'm walking behind you now I'm opening a drawer now blah blah now now now now, Emma, Emma, Emma? I was so sick of her voice, but so terrified each time a sound ignited without any warning that the terror made me furious, too.

Mr. Otis programmed my phone to speak to me, but I couldn't find the right spots to enter my password, couldn't stand the speed of the voice-over voice, maniacally shouting, "Insert passcode, four digits required, one a b c, two d e f." Mr. Otis's voice was the opposite; his was human and patient: "Tap the number twice," he said, "and then tap elsewhere on the screen twice." I hate the word *elsewhere*; it's where I used to be, where everything I used to be able to see still is. One, tap, tap, six, tap, tap, nine, tap, tap, three, tap, tap: Leah's age last year, followed by Naomi's and Benj's. Every year I change my passwords for everything and learn a new finger tap dance.

My life with Mr. Otis was another life, another surreal tutorial in how to relearn everything I'd known as a toddler. My dad, who believed rehearsing moves would make me feel happier and more confident, demanded progress reports. He reminded me between five and twenty times a morning to practice, and on the rare nights when I could be forced to sit and rock miserably at the dinner table, he asked what progress I'd made, even though for me practice and progress felt like opposites. The work was a choking, incessant reminder that I was back at a zero flatter than any baby starts at, learning to guess which sister was which. To use a fork and knife. To know where I was standing, whether I might get run over, what I might be eating. To survive. It was all a matter of survival, even though it was literally stuff like learning to walk down the sidewalk or across the street.

My mom fed me grilled cheese sandwiches cut into tiny triangles, baby carrots, pizza, and fake-chicken tofu nuggets, all of which I could pick up and eat with my fingers. She stopped short of mashing my food up or cutting grapes in half, but just barely. And only because my dad, who made me eat tomato soup on Sundays, just because I couldn't use my hands, told her I would never recover unless I "gained my independence." Late at night, when they shouted and fought, she screamed about how and what chances and danger, and he said I had to learn braille, had to learn to walk around by myself, eventually to "take the bus." My dad's big goal for me was to take a bus, even though I had never taken the bus anywhere before my accident, so I didn't really see why that would be such a major breakthrough. My mom argued that I should practice at own pace, figure the world out slowly if I wanted to, and see people only when I was ready, talk about school when I felt up to it. He said no; they had to help me, had to push me, or I might something—fall into something. Depression? Death? I can't remember, because it was too terrible and because it was the same night that I heard my dad cry, the only time I ever have, and it was so sad that I shut the sound out of my mind so fast I can't hear it now, even if I try to.

I was pretty sure I did want to die, but as furious as I was, I didn't want to tell my parents that. I tried to make progress, tried to be better. On his last day, I even tried to thank Mr. Otis, mainly so my dad would be happy. I said, so quietly I wasn't sure Mr. Otis had even heard me, "Um, so, thanks. For everything." He didn't respond, so I worked up enough words to ask how he knew so much, whether he was blind. I meant to be nice, but he said, in an apologetic voice with broken glass in it, "No, I'm not blind. But I . . . well, you're welcome, Emma."

And then he left, and I imagined him pirouetting into his light, sighted life, weightless with relief that he would never have to deal with me or my darkness again.

School week afternoons, Leah and Naomi and Jenna— and sometimes even Sarah—got home from school and sat with me. I could smell the world on their coats, the town outside, the music they had played and listened to, the friends they had seen, hugged, and gossiped with, kids who no longer tagged home to our house to eat or play, because I didn't want them to. And until this fall, for a year basically, my family accommodated this wish. Naomi made clay figures and handed them to me silently. Once, I told Leah that I missed Mr. Otis and Sarah said, "Yeah, he was hot," even though I hadn't realized she was in the room and I wouldn't have said it in front of her, and then we all sat stunned. I had the new brailler my parents were so excited about on my lap, and was feeling the ports on the side, the long, sleek display of braille dots I couldn't yet read. But when Sarah spoke, I reached up to touch my sunglasses; thought, *Hot? Mr. Otis?* What did that even mean? Would I ever find anyone hot again? My sunglasses were in place. I reached for Spark. I was always reaching for Spark.

"Can I see that thing for a minute?" Sarah asked. Maybe she was mad that I ignored her stupid, hideous comment about Mr. Otis. How dare she find him hot? I hated her, but I couldn't have said why.

"This?" I extended out the brailler, and she clucked her tongue and said, "It's hard to believe that's worth six laptops."

"Come on, Sarah, leave her alone," Leah said. And I

thought, *Six laptops?* What did that mean? How much had the brailler cost? And why was it so expensive? How did Sarah always know everything? And would we run out of money because of all my doctor bills and machines? Had Spark cost money, too? I thought about money, which I never had before. My parents had enough money; we weren't rich, but they didn't seem to worry about food or even raising a huge brood of kids. But now, would I both cost them everything and never be able to repay them? I would never get a job, never make enough money to support myself, never be okay. I would stay here, on the couch, for the rest of time, until my parents were gone and there was nobody to buy top-of-the-line braillers or tomato soup. What else could I do? School was an utter impossibility, as was walking or running or biking or eating complicated food that required a spoon or reading for real again or taking the bus. Who would fall in love with me? Was I unlovable? Would I always be unlovable?

"Mom!" Sarah was shouting now. "Can I borrow the car to meet Chris or no?"

I heard my mom saying blah, blah, she had to take someone somewhere and something and some o'clock and some errand, and then I heard Sarah slamming the front door and walking out into the bright light of her perfect life. Jenna was singing and Naomi was in the kitchen hammering something that turned out to be a bunk bed for her and Jenna's dolls, and Benj was on the couch with me, watching a cartoon that sounded inflatable, rubber. I couldn't hear Leah anywhere. Why had my parents bought such a fancy brailler? Couldn't they have gotten the eighteen braille display? Or even gotten an old-school one? Did I actually need the one that's really a computer, or was it another desperate gesture of guilt? Were they trying to make better something that couldn't be made better? And if so, at what cost?

Nights, I lay back and tried to block out all the noise, to sleep, to stop thinking, to vanish. Sometimes Naomi would whisper down to me in my bunk, "Emma, are you asleep?" I never was, so I'd say, "No," and then she'd say, "Are you okay?" And I felt sad and swirly and sick, because I knew she was worried about me, even though she was littler than I was and I should be the one asking her if she was okay and now I'd never be her Leah. But I couldn't take care of anyone else, so I just said, "Yeah, I'm fine. Goodnight, Nomi," which was her nickname, because Benj couldn't pronounce *Naomi*.

My memories of that time are the opposite of a photo album. I can't see the holidays, whether my sisters went trick-or-treating or to Halloween parties, whether we had turkey for Thanksgiving or lit candles at Hanukkah. I remember instead the tiny, unimportant parts of every day, maybe because they were so monumentally difficult. Or maybe because remembering what holds the days together is more truthful than remembering a few big-ticket, smile-for-the-camera events. Or maybe just because I can't see.

Benj was everywhere, every day, un-ruined by my tragedy. He spent the days tearing through the house like a tropical storm, often jumping onto the couch with me. By November our traumatized mom was barfing every twenty-five seconds, even though her first trimester was done. Sometimes, she'd be taking care of me and Benj, making cheese sandwiches or talking to one of us, and she'd say, "Excuse me," go to the bathroom and throw up, and then come back and start the conversation right where she'd left off. When she wasn't throwing up, she and Benj cut out egg cartons and sewed sock puppets and did laundry while I listened to the dark and snuggled Spark.

By December my mom had lost the battle over asking me to shower and so began pouring baths for me. It was one of the many ways in which I went back to being a baby. I brought Spark into the bathroom, and he sat next to the tub while I climbed in. Sometimes Spark leaned into the tub and drank the water or gobbled whatever bath bubbles my mom had added. The soap felt foamy and smelled like different colors to me, depending on the time of day and my mind's mood. One ice-blue night in mid-December, Jenna, who had just turned five, got into the bath with me. She left her squeezy, noise-making, water-squirting toys in their plastic bucket, and sat quietly for my sake, a feat for her. I was tracing my fingers along the surface of the water, listening to Spark breathe, thinking, *Come on, Emma. Dark is safe, dark is water, dark is safe, dark is water, water is safe,* until I could almost believe it.

Then Jenna asked in a tiny voice, "Emma? What are you thinking about if you're so quiet?"

I answered her honestly, maybe because I was failing with Naomi, or maybe because I've always had trouble determining how much truth is too much.

"I'm thinking about the dark, J," I said. I don't think I meant to be mean.

But her breathing stopped. She waited a little bit before she asked, "Is it really scary, Emma?" with so much fear that the words turned an internal organ mix of blue and purple. I backed away and made up a half-truth I now tell all the time, maybe because I'm still hoping to convince myself.

"Being blind is okay—it, um, it makes the dark not scary, J. I'm used to it. It's calm. Like water."

Jenna said, "Oh! Like the bath. With bubbles." And her raspy, choppy, little-kid breathing started up again cheerfully. Knowing she felt better made me feel better, too, almost as if what I had said was true. Sometimes words matter, even when they're not true. And other times, repeating lies can be the worst possible human crutch. It's something I can't work out. That night in the bath, I kissed Jenna's wet face. She felt like a little soapy seal, my five-year-old sister, and all I knew was how glad I was that she was less scared for me. Or of me, if there's any difference.

Then Jenna said, "Um, Emma? Is it okay if I tell Nomi that being blind is okay, like a bath? Because, well, maybe she thinks it's scary, too."

I tried not to cry.

Last winter made me realize that even if I stayed on the gold couch without moving for fifty years, we would all still get old and die. In case getting blinded hadn't made it clear, recovering taught me that my small life didn't matter to the world overall, which I don't think is something you're supposed to understand until you're old. But I had to learn it early for some reason. My mom would say it made me smart, but actually it just made me desperate. When it snowed in December, I knew in this weird, sudden way that after winter it would be spring, which meant summer would come again. I'd have been blind for an entire year, the year itself another utter loss. I told Dr. Sassoman that I was scaring my little sisters and myself and losing my mind. It was snowing outside of her office window, and I was trying to feel the cold sound of it.

"I can't stop thinking really fast, so fast it's scary. And I can't sleep. And I can't stop making up weird refrains—like 'dark is cool, light is heat'—and repeating them to myself," I admitted, scared, and suddenly embarrassed, too. But to my surprise, she clapped her hands together. The pop made me jump, and she touched my wrist with her cool, papery fingers. I thought of snowflakes cut from coffee filters, wanted to use scissors again.

"I'm glad to hear about the sayings, Emma," she said, squeezing my wrist a bit. "Those are coping strategies you're creating for yourself."

She waited. Dr. Sassoman has a big appetite for awkward pauses.

"No!" I said, my voice too loud and hard for the soft white room, the snow, the moment. "I'm not coping! I'm crazy. I've missed an entire half a year of school, and I'll never catch up, and if I have to be in a different grade from Logan and all my friends for the rest of my life, I'm going to die. And I can never go back. How can I go back like this?"

"You are not going to die," she said, as usual. "And you *are* coping. That's what those 'sayings' you're making up are—that's you coping. Human beings are capable of curing our own miseries if we are courageous enough," she said.

"I'm not," I said. "I'm not courageous enough."

"I think you are," she said, and then she repeated it, like

I was deaf, too. "We have to figure out a way to help you sleep better, though."

That night, right before bed, I asked my mom if my brailler had cost six thousand dollars.

"I don't remember the exact price, sweetie," she said, "but we got a good one, so you'll have it for a long time and it can be both your laptop and your brailler. And we wanted to . . ."

"To what?" I asked.

"I don't know—make braille more fun?"

We both waited, me because I wanted to punish her—for trying to bribe or comfort me, for pretending there could be anything fun about this. She was quiet because she wanted to get this right, but couldn't. Finally she just said, "Please, don't worry about it, Emma, okay?"

I wanted to rat Sarah out, to tell my mom that she had made sure I knew how much that stupid thing cost. But I didn't, not because I'm kind—or even because I'd rather be nice than right—but because I knew my mom already knew. She bent to kiss me and left, and like so many nights that have followed it, I lay with my arms around Spark, thinking, *Okay, dark is safe, dark is water, light is terror, light is fire, focus in, focus in*, until I thought my mind would snap with the effort. Then I used, *Dark is cool, light is heat*, and then, *Relax and close your eyes, close your eyes, relax.* And, *Feel it, Emma, feel it, Emma, read it to feel it, feel it to read it.* Finally I fell asleep.

The next time Dr. Sassoman came for one of her home visits, she talked with my parents for a while and then asked me privately where I was "keeping my anger."

I didn't answer.

"Is it in your stomach?" she proposed. "Your heart?"

I shrugged.

She handed me something it took me a minute to recognize. Eggs. A carton of eggs.

"What is this?" I asked.

"A dozen eggs," she said. "Do you want to throw them?"

This suggestion made sense to me, and I nodded.

"Where? At the walls inside? Or outside? Anywhere you want."

We went outside first, even though it was brutally cold: step one, step two, step three, four, five, end of porch, here's the grass, the walkway, sidewalk, maple, crosswalk, traffic, oak tree. I listened hard for the engines, and then, instead of sticking my cane into the street, I threw some eggs, hard, at the sidewalk, at trees I couldn't see, into the crosswalk I hadn't realized I hated. Here's a shoreline where the shell meets the pavement, shatters, yolk, white, blood. Your light, my light, red light, egg light. I listened for the cars to come and smash what was left of the eggs into nothingness. Then I felt around in the carton. I still had four eggs.

"I want to throw these inside," I told Dr. Sassoman, and

she said that was fine; that she would clean them up afterward and I didn't have to worry about whatever mess we made.

Hearing the eggs crack into the walls—of our living room, Naomi's and my bedroom, the kitchen, and the upstairs bathroom, I thought, *This is a sound I never realized I'd hear, an experience I wouldn't be having if my accident hadn't happened.* But that was it. I didn't feel anything about it one way or another, and I didn't stay to listen to Dr. Sassoman or my mom—or whoever did it—clean the egg off the glass cabinets in the living room, the bathroom mirror, or the wall above my desk.

When Dr. Sassoman asked later whether it had helped, whether I was feeling any better, I said nothing. Because I had no idea. How can you know the truth about anything you're still inside of?

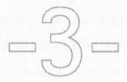

It's mid-October again—surprise. We all made it through September and two weeks of October, even me. Before they left for fresh death elsewhere, the carrion reporters wrote lists of the drugs in Claire's blood and stomach: Oxycontin, Percocet, Vicodin. Those are names I remember from after my eyes; they make me feel newly burned. Now we've all agreed—without even saying so out loud—to call Claire's death a tragic accident. No one really wants to talk about it, even at school, where people are pretending to talk about it by listing the same hows over and over. How tragic, how surprised, how, how. But what I want to know is, how did Claire gobble a giant fistful of drugs and fall in the water "by accident"? What the hell was she doing picnicking on painkillers alone at the lake? Did she throw herself in on purpose? And if so, what does "accident" even mean?

The drugs were apparently "recreational," like she took them as an after-school sport she could have put on her resumé if she hadn't accidentally died instead. Lake Main is blazing with warnings about the dangers of drug use and "teen suicide prevention." Of course, I haven't asked any real questions out loud, either, so I should hardly be flinging rocks at other people's glass walls. But I can't help wondering: if beautiful, talented Claire M. couldn't bear to stay alive, how will I?

The school put up a display case in the tenth-grade hallway "to honor Claire's memory." Ms. Mabel described the trophies and pictures to me: Claire as a six-year-old, in a tutu and slippers; Claire kicking a soccer ball; Claire in a swimsuit, her arms around a teammate; Claire in the sunlight, with her streaky hair everywhere. While Ms. Mabel was talking, I remembered Claire's long, pale neck, and a locket she wore every day when we were kids. It had in it some shards of teeth she'd lost when she fell off her bike. She showed them to me once and I said, "Gross." She just shrugged and said other people wore shark teeth around their necks, so why couldn't she wear her own? I remember thinking it was a good point. And even though I didn't touch the little chips of ivory then, only saw them, now I remember what they felt like.

Ms. Mabel started to tell me what was on the floor, but I stopped her; I could smell the sickeningly sweet lilies, and I reached down to feel the crinkly wrappers on candy and bouquets, the marble-eyed bears, swim goggles—maybe for Claire in heaven, which my parents don't believe in. I wonder if Claire's still do, if they think she's swimming in the afterlife even though she drowned in this one. They weren't the most religious family in our town—that would be Blythe's or Deirdre's—but maybe they think she's "gone to a better place."

Heaven or not, there's definitely a better place than Sauberg somewhere. But I don't see how that makes what happened to Claire any more palatable. Nothing does. Now words sound hollow, falling out of people's mouths to the ground like dead seedpods: *We're just so shocked! In this place, of all places! Such a nice community. Such a safe town. We still can't believe it happened here.* To hear us tell it, Sauberg is not the kind of place where *that kind of thing* happens—although I've never heard anyone be like, "Yeah, our town loves this kind of thing," when a girl's body washes up. Mostly, people are surprised by totally pointless and horrifying death, so maybe no town is that kind of town. Or maybe every town is.

Sarah calls Sauberg a "conservative, small-town lunatic asylum stuck in the nineteenth century." She's angry that we live here. Sarah and Leah and I were born in the city, and it was because of me that my parents decided they had to move here, which of course Sarah holds against me. As if I got a vote about whether to be born. Or when. Or being their third kid under three, which meant that they couldn't even hold all of our hands crossing the street. Not to mention they were about to have four more kids. Sauberg is close enough to the city that my dad can drive to the hospital where he works in under an hour, and far enough away that we can have wholesome childhoods and a four-bedroom house. We're two to a room, with Baby Lily in my parents' room, which is pretty civilized for a family with seven kids. If we were in the city, we'd all be sleeping on top of each other. By the time Baby Lily needs her own bed, Leah will be away at college, and so will Sarah, if she can manage to finish a single application and get in anywhere. It's funny that even though she's the one who can't wait to get out of this "vile dump," she hasn't even started her applications and they're due in December.

It's almost Halloween again, the biggest see-and-be-seen holiday of the year. I'm planning to read or sleep through it. The truth is, I've been mainstreamed for almost eight weeks, but I've only left the house to go to school and to doctor's appointments. I've only asked to leave twice with Lo, and both times my mom said she'd prefer that we hang out here. She wants me safe in the house, and I don't know if it's because of me, or because of Claire. All our parents are stricter and more annoying than ever. But that's been true for me since last year, and lately I can actually *feel* that year underneath this one, like something jagged and dangerous, slicing up and tripping me back in time. I'm trying to forget about last year, the gold couch, Mr. Otis, braille lessons, Briarly, the way Seb smelled like tangerines and leather jackets.

Benj helps most. Maybe because he lives in the present tense, which makes it easier for me to be there when he's around. Or because other than Spark, he's been the one least freaked out by my accident. Little kids have an easier time than the rest of us adjusting to "I see with my hands and ears and mind instead of my eyes." Once I promised Benj that I remembered just what he looks like, he was okay with the rest of whatever my accident meant.

All we'd been talking about all week was Halloween, which I didn't want to think about, when he tumbled down the steps of the preschool bus on Thursday afternoon, shrieking, "I winned! I winned! The rabbit will come!"

"I *won*," Naomi said. She was swinging her violin case against her legs.

"What rabbit?" I asked.

"Bigs," Benj said, grabbing one of Leah's hands and one of Naomi's and swinging and leaping between them. I could both hear and feel his legs kicking, his rain boots stomping and bouncing on the sidewalk. Then Naomi tripped and I heard her violin case go flying.

"Hey!" Leah shouted. "Are you okay?" She picked up Naomi, who was wounded but not crying, and poured some water on her knee, which she had apparently scraped badly enough to tear through her tights.

Jenna rescued Naomi's violin and there was a scramble of kids as we fell all over each other. I wondered if there was anyone else on the sidewalk, anyone who could see us. When there are other people looking at us, I don't know how to think of my family, don't know if we're clean or dirty, sane or crazy, tame or wild. Even when I could see, it was hard to imagine what my own clan looked like from the outside, maybe like it's difficult to gauge anything you're inside of. When we all started walking again, I was thinking how I hadn't been any help. If it weren't for my eyes, Benj would probably walk between Leah and me, instead of between Leah and Naomi. Naomi wouldn't have fallen over. Leah wouldn't even have to walk us all home every day. She'd be hanging out with her friends instead, like Sarah, who, when my mom asked if she could help with drop-off and pickup, just said, "No thank you." Maybe I'd be in charge. I wonder if I'd be happier if I were in charge. Probably I'd be resentful of having to help so much, and not even realize how little I had to complain about. It's not like I spent my whole sighted life being like, "This is so fabulous, to have my eyesight."

I wonder when I'll be done with the what-ifs and if-onlys. I hate them, and they play in my mind on a loop, like the voice-over lady in my phone, screaming for a password I can't type in fast enough. Will the questions ever stop?

I held my white cane with my right hand and Spark's

leash with my left, trying to calm Spark down. Naomi's walking was odd and jolty. She was probably either trying to avoid the cracks or to step on all of them. Benj was shouting: "Sometimes he, I mean she—you know, that rabbit—will come to my house when we have no school, because it will be my turn for Bigs!"

"Ow," Naomi said. "Stop pulling on my arm like that."

"It's my house, too, Benj," Jenna said. Scratch, click, scratch, click. I felt something—a stick, maybe—something in the way.

"Careful," Leah said, seeing me notice it. "There's part of a tree branch there."

When an actual rabbit arrived the next day, which was a Friday, Jenna was almost as delighted as Benj, because the kindergarten gecko died and they haven't replaced it yet. Naomi pretended for about six seconds to be above the excitement, but as soon as Bigs showed up, she immediately wrote a star vehicle play for the rabbit, mysteriously called "Buffalo Rabbit on the Jungle Shore."

I was in the living room, waiting for Logan, listening to cabinets opening, drawers sliding along their metal tracks, Jenna and Naomi fumbling and shuffling, drawers slamming shut. Then came the furious, thick snipping. Pop of the hole punch and Jenna's, "Mom? Where's the yarn? Nomi and I can't find any yarn," to the discovery that we were out of yarn and they'd have to use string or ribbon. To tie what they were making—construction paper ears—around Benj's and Jenna's heads, so they could be rabbits, too. The doorbell rang and I felt my way along the wall until I reached the foyer table. I opened the door.

"Hi, Lo," I said as she came in. She smelled like herself, candy with a faint chemical spritz. She took quick stock of the scene. "More animals joining the Silver circus?" She laughed. "Let's go to your room."

But we hadn't even sat down on my bed when Jenna screamed and we raced back into the living room with Spark, who didn't know what to make of the chaos. "Bigs had a pee accident," Jenna told us in her teacher voice, the one she uses when she's trying to sound like Naomi, who's trying to sound like her teacher. Jenna was calm now, but Benj was crying.

"Gross," Logan said.

"Don't cry," I told Benj. "Just go get Bigs, and Logan and I will clean up the pee. Where is it? On the rug or the wood?"

"The wood. Over here," Jenna said. I leaned down to pet Spark, who was frozen in his warning position. "It's just the rabbit," I told him. "Don't worry."

"If you have pee in your body, you have to go to the potty right then," Benj told me and Logan, sniffling. "Don't delay!"

"Right," Logan said. "I guess Bigs didn't get that memo."

She had already picked the rabbit up and now she handed

it to me, and I was surprised by how un-fluffy Bigs was. Maybe she was some hideous, short-haired, prickly rabbit breed. Logan saw my face and laughed until she snorted.

"Ew, right?" she said. "And you should see her creepy-ass red eyes. Like a picture no one fixed."

"*Ass* is not a nice word, Logan," Jenna said, drawing out the s's so the word lasted a full ten seconds. "You can't say *ass* at school. Only at home."

"Help me with this, will you, Jenna?" I asked. I felt for the edges of the cage and gently set the rabbit back down in it and went with Spark to get some paper towels from the kitchen. My mom now keeps everything in its perfect place on the counters or in the drawers, so I can find whatever I need. It's the thing we're most organized about. She tries to keep toys off the floor, but that's been a bigger challenge. So I'm careful. Naomi reappeared, wearing tap shoes and carrying a bin of blocks, which she immediately dropped. I couldn't tell whether by accident or not, but the noise was enormous.

While Jenna and Naomi collected the blocks, Logan helped me mop up the pee puddle. Logan hates animals, except for Spark, whom she loves because he's part of me. I could feel her thinking sarcastic thoughts. Logan and I know each other so well that most subjects require almost no discussion, including family and the fact that mine is better than hers, and she's always over at my house, so that's why it's okay for her to complain about how many kids there are, how there's always some kind of crisis or other and we're always cleaning something horrible or looking for lost toys or consoling someone who's hysterically crying or eating a dinner with so much shouting and interrupting and craziness it's a circus. Calling my family a circus is Logan's second favorite shtick. And coincidentally, since we were cleaning up after the rabbit, Logan got to say her first favorite thing about whatever drama is unfolding at the Silver house: "This is all because your parents are like rabbits."

Saturday morning, Bigs was not in her cage and no one knew where she'd gone. I heard my mom come down the stairs barefoot, carrying something she set down—a plastic basket, from the sound of it—and start looking right away. This meant she considered it a genuine emergency. Usually she "triages demands," as she and my dad like to call it, which means throwing the laundry in first and taking care of whatever crises there are with the epic pajama washing already underway. But she went straight to the couch and ripped off each of its eight velcroed cushions. No rabbit. There were creaks and scrapes as she pushed the couch across the floor, checking behind or under it. She sighed. Still no rabbit. She unlatched and opened up the iron and glass cabinets, although how a rabbit would have launched herself into them—or opened the doors—is anyone's guess. Maybe my mom thought Naomi or

Jenna had stuffed Bigs into one—with the sculpture of us my mom made recently, a tangle of cooked, painted clay I can't stand to feel for some reason. It's the first thing she's made (other than Baby Lily) since my accident, and she's very proud of it. Sometimes she goes into the old carriage house in our backyard, where she used to paint, when she's not hopping through the house with Baby Lily tied to her body or running the small country of our family.

My mom headed out of the living room, and I heard the basement door swing open and, at the same moment, heard Benj come wailing and stomping down the stairs in his rain boots (which he wears every day, with Batman pajamas and a cape), creating such a thunderous racket that Baby Lily started crying, too. Crying is contagious in our house. I felt my way into the kitchen and crouched down, touching the floor under the counters until I got to the part between the stove and the fridge. I don't know how else to explain it, except that my hands sensed her there, and sure enough, I reached into that small groove and felt fur. I grabbed Bigs, but as soon as I did, I knew something was wrong with the way she felt. She was too floppy, too limp, too . . . I don't know, she felt like a toy.

My mom was back in the doorway of the basement staircase, and she must have been watching, because she said, "Leah, take Lily," and then came rushing over and grabbed the rabbit. She stayed bent over me for an extra second; I felt her hair tumble down—long, curly, red—and she kissed the top of my head. Benj came running in then, his rain boots squeaking across the kitchen.

"Naomi and Jenna, come with me! We're taking Bigs to the doctor, Benji. We'll be right back."

Then my mom and Naomi darted outside, with Jenna behind them, still in just her socks, as far as I could hear, leaving the door open. When it didn't click shut, I felt my way over and closed it myself.

"Will Bigs have to get a shot at that damn doctor?" Benj asked.

"I don't know," I said. I made my way back to him and knelt down, reached out and touched his face, the cold little nose and scrunched eyebrows. Wet streaks on his cheeks. I pulled him toward me: toast with butter, bubblegum toothpaste, and tears. Baby Lily was still crying, too, and Logan was holding her now. Logan's heels tapped the floor. She was rocking, and her hands went *thump, thump, thump* against the romper on Baby Lily's hot little back. So Leah must have handed her Baby Lily and gone somewhere. I hadn't heard her leave, but she wasn't in the room. Sometimes I have to figure out what's happening now before I can guess what happened a minute ago.

When I stood up, Logan handed me Baby Lily, and I

rocked her while Benj kept clinging to my leg. If someone else is holding her, Lily feels to me like a puppety collection of little parts: chubby dumpling face, short arms, a leg here or there, and a *voice*—she screams like she's being dipped in boiling oil. But when I hold her myself, I can feel the weight of her being a whole human being. I kissed her doughy rolls of neck.

Leah reappeared from the basement in a cloud of laundry steam. "Here, baby, come to Leah," she said, taking Lily and tucking her into the wrap she must have tied to herself on the way up the basement stairs. As soon as she was in the cloth, Lily started snoring. Babies are like those cars that go from zero to a hundred in under one second. There's something surreal about their ability to go from screaming to sleeping instantaneously, but also something practical about it. I held Benj's hand again then, but I didn't say anything else, because I don't believe in lying to little kids, and I didn't think "I have no idea what's going to happen" or "I think the rabbit's going to be dead when mom comes back" would be especially comforting.

After a minute, I smelled fire, heard the flash and splatter of butter, reminded myself to breathe. Leah was shuffling through the third drawer over, the one that jams a bit and sticks when it opens, then sinking a knife through something soft to the surface of a plastic cutting board. Cheese. She was making grilled cheese sandwiches. I smelled bread land in the popping butter. The cupboard opened, and she took out a can; hooked and snapped it into the mounted opener, where it turned a slow, grinding circle until it came open with ragged edges and the opener stopped. The red smell arrived: tomato soup, my favorite. Leah unlatched the can and poured the soup into a pot that was already as hot as the butter, from the splatter of it. Logan was helping while I stood there, listening and working to follow, and when the food was ready, she put ours on a tray and took it to my bedroom, where we sat on my bed, pulling closed the green, filmy curtain and eating our soup in my tent. I left half of mine for Spark and put the bowl down next to the bed where he was resting; listened to him happily slurping and gobbling. I love him so much that when I hear him eating, it makes me feel full. Logan and I sat without talking for a long time. She was lying on her back, with her socked feet kicking the bottom of Naomi's bunk bed. Metal springs. Creak, kick, creak, kick.

"Are you okay?" she finally asked me.

"Not really," I said.

"The rabbit?"

"I don't know. That too, I guess."

"Yeah." She thought for a minute. "It's been kind of a rough year."

"Unlike last year?" I said, and she laughed. Last year, we

both almost died of misery. But then Claire actually died, and now here we were, still alive. Logan's laugh wasn't a happy one; she always snorts when she's actually laughing—right at the end of her laugh—and she sighs when she's not.

She sighed. "Yeah, that was crazy, too. Maybe we're due for some good luck."

"I don't want luck," I said. "I just want to know what's going to happen some of the time. Instead of getting shocked to death constantly."

"We should get a crystal ball," Logan said. "Or try out some of your magical rabbit-finding powers on the future." She pulled the curtain back and hopped off the bed, went to turn on some music. "How about 'Sweetness'?" she asked.

"Whatever you want," I said. Logan's always introducing me to music, but I prefer the terrible stuff my parents play, Simon & Garfunkel and Tom Petty. Maybe because embarrassing music played by old people reminds me of being a baby, makes me feel safe or something. No one knows about my horrible musical taste except Logan. And when I pretend to be cool in front of other people, she never rats me out. Lately, I do so much listening that I prefer not to have any music on, but how un-fun do I really want to be, even with Logan?

I lay back and put my feet up flat against the bottom of Naomi's bunk, stretched my legs. "I wonder what it would be like to be in charge."

Logan bounced back onto the bed and my legs bent. "Of what?" She sounded kind of surprised.

"I don't know," I said. "Anything. How we live? What we do? Whatever."

"I think there'd be major problems," Logan said. "Like, who'd go to school?"

"I would," I said. "And so would you. We'd all probably do the same things we do anyway; we just wouldn't feel like prisoners about it." I reached down and felt for Spark's head, rested my hand on his lovely skull, scratched behind his ears.

"No way," Logan said. "No one would follow rules if we didn't have to. Everyone would be having sex in the streets and eating Twizzlers three meals a day. Including me."

Logan loves red candy, which I find really weird and gross. She has a thing about fake cherry flavor, even though she hates actual fruit, including cherries.

"That's not true. You could already do that when your mom's not looking, and you don't."

"But if I got to make up the rules for everyone, we'd all be crazy, sugar-eating sluts. Maybe I'd say there's a rule we have to be."

Logan has been obsessed with sex since we were thirteen. Or with virginity, depending on how you look at it, since neither of us has had sex yet. Her third favorite shtick, after my parents being rabbits and my family "the Silver circus," is this thing she came up with in seventh grade about our virginity. We were talking in social studies about destiny and free will, and Logan decided that whom we're going to lose it to is preordained, so the universe already knows and we just haven't found out yet. She can't decide if what we do will or won't change the outcome. I doubt the question of whom we'll lose our virginity to was supposed to be the central focus of Ms. Paton's unit on free will, but it's very Logan to take something academic and make it sexual. Of course, destiny's plans have gone kind of badly for me, so maybe I just have less faith in the universe than Logan does. I'd rather make my own plans than rely on anyone or anything else, fate included.

"Forget it," I said. "Let's take Spark for a walk." He perked up, barked.

But Logan went to the window and opened it, and cold rain blew in sideways. I had heard it anyway, hitting the window and the bushes outside.

"You don't have to drench me. You could just say it's raining."

"Maybe we should do a story," Logan suggested.

"I don't feel like it."

Logan and I sometimes write stories where I come up with a few lines and then she writes a few, but her lines always make the stories into weird, sci-fi ones. We'll have a great character, fighting her way through the regular impossibilities of being a girl, or even a warrior or whatever, and then it's Logan's turn and the girl grows horns or wings or an alien lands on her head and wants to have sex with her in outer space, and I have to quit before the story is ruined forever. So we never finish any of them.

I felt incredibly restless. "I wish everyone weren't so full of shit all the time," I said. "Do you think Claire killed herself on purpose? Do you think they know what happened, or why, and just aren't telling us?"

"You know I have no idea. We've been over this. And anyway, who's *they*?"

"I don't know," I said. "Her parents? The cops? Why do we keep having to have these bullshit meetings at school? Why can't we have our own meeting, where we tell the truth?"

"You want to have another grief meeting?"

"No, not a grief meeting. Not hideously fake, with the weird other version of us that we all become in those meetings. I hate those conversations."

"Yes, I know."

I couldn't resist. "They make me feel crazy, like we're all robots. Or in a terrible play."

"I know."

"I guess I just feel like everyone's so apathetic and full of it. Claire was by herself, taking 'recreational' drugs for no reason? And now she's dead for no reason? And we're all just going to live with that and move on, with our parents and the school even more all over us than ever? It just seems—"

"Unfair," Lo said. "Yeah, it's unfair. But what's new?"

We heard Benj start crying again, followed by banging. Leah must have set up a pot-and-pan band to distract him from Bigs.

"The world is a very stupid place," I told Logan, picking up speed. I felt choppy and staccato, excited.

"Yeah? And how do you propose we make the world less stupid?" Logan asked.

"I don't know. What if we talked about Claire *for real*, for one thing? About what she did—and if it's what I think, why. I mean, how could she . . . we have no control over anything that happens. What if we—"

"But we do," Logan said. "Have control, I mean. If she killed herself, then that's the ultimate control, right? Or even if she fell into the lake drunk or high or whatever, she made the choices that got her to that point—some people are super fucking crazy. Maybe Claire was just way crazier than we realized."

I was fretting about what this might mean for me and my accident, what I considered my own secret insanity, when I heard the little clicking sound Lo makes when she chews her hair.

"Why are you nervous?"

"I'm not."

"Stop chewing your hair."

"I can't. I'm biting the split ends off."

"Why don't you just get a haircut?"

"I'll get one if you do."

I didn't respond to this. When my mom came home, she gathered us in the living room and said Bigs was "going back into the earth so that other things can grow and live." Jenna was crying, either because she was old enough to make sense of this tortured description or because the vet had been more straightforward.

But Benj asked, "Did Bigs die?" directly, so my mom was forced to say yes. He did not cry, just stood there, swallowing and holding his breath. I could feel him quivering with sorrow. Apparently Bigs had eaten something that poisoned her. Naomi asked what, and my mom paused before saying, "Maybe part of a lily plant in the living room?"

Her voice was candy pink and pitched up, maybe because she was lying and didn't want whoever's toy it had actually been to die of guilt. I imagined a rabbit-shaped X-ray with a matchbox car or Lego, a Polly Pocket doll head or foam block in the stomach. I knew instantly that my mom had picked the lily because it belonged to her and my dad and it was sitting on the floor, so the rabbit would have only herself to blame if she had snacked on it. My mom is a good and kind liar.

I told Benj what I hoped was the truth, that someday it would be okay. Naomi was comforting Jenna. Then I asked my mom if Logan and I could go out for a walk, and she said if I didn't mind, she'd rather we stayed in. I did mind, but I didn't argue. Logan and I went up to Leah and Sarah's room, since they were out, and talked about what the rabbit ate, whose fault it might have been, and why lie. Logan cares more than I do about blame; she blames her dad for leaving her mom, and whenever she mentions him, she uses her lime voice and I can hear her face squeeze tight and sour. She's an only child, and since he moved to California she only sees him on school vacations, in huge week- or month-long doses, which is just really awkward—like, for example, she got her period for the first time while she was visiting him last year. She was the last to get it by an entire year, and she would have been totally thrilled except she didn't want to tell him, so she had to come up with an excuse to go running to the drug store. And when she got home and told her mom, her mom cried because she hadn't been there for it, and Logan ended up comforting her mom instead of her mom comforting her. Logan's mom works all the time because they need money, and her dad doesn't have much, either. And he's never on time with anything, including sending checks. When her mom's not working she's out "making friends," so she won't die of loneliness, which I think is really selfish, because who cares if she has friends?

Once you have kids, it's your responsibility to take care of them until they're old enough to be alone.

Obviously my parents can't stop blaming themselves for what happened to me, especially my mom. Which is, I bet, how Claire M.'s parents feel. They were so strict; maybe she picnicked on drugs at the beach to punish or escape them. Or maybe they're the types who think—as you have to, if you want to survive—that there was nothing they could have done. There was nothing my parents could have done about my eyes, either, but they still blame themselves, in a general, feel-like-shit-forever way. I wish they would stop, but I'd probably be furious if they did, too.

Sunday morning, Naomi woke Logan and me, knocking on Sarah and Leah's door. When I answered it, she said, "I waited forever to wake you guys," even though it was only seven thirty.

"What's up, Nomi?" I asked.

"Why did you want to get away from me last night?"

"What?"

"How come you and Logan never want to sleep in our room when Logan is here? Can I play with you?"

I sighed. "We didn't want to keep you up, okay? And yes, you can play with us. Let's go have breakfast."

We headed to the kitchen, where Baby Lily was babbling and shouting and crying. Benj, apparently recovered from the loss of Bigs, was racing a plastic dump truck manned by Champon, a dirty stuffed toy turtle he definitely meant to name Champion but got wrong. Jenna was dancing and singing—kind of beautifully, actually—to a princess video called "Bella Bella Dancerella."

Naomi hustled over to the fridge and then from there to the electric mixer. Apparently she had lost interest in playing with Logan and me, but I couldn't tell what she was working on with the mixer; either one of her "science projects," which usually involve food coloring and cornstarch; or hopefully pancake batter. She used to make me help her with all her experiments and I found it annoying, but now I feel bad that she never asks me anymore.

The phone was ringing and Leah came in from the back door, home early from her sleepover. She kissed our mom hello and said hi to me while mom ran to the phone. The kitchen felt bubbling and orange, and I liked it. Because it's what I'm used to, because it's cheerful and tastes like cooking sugar, and because it doesn't change. Having six siblings has its drawbacks, obviously, but there are good things about it, too, like there being a high likelihood of at least some of us liking each other. If you're in a room with six other kids, you might be friends with one of them, whereas if you're in a room with just one other kid, there's more than a 50 percent chance that the kid will be a total asshole and you'll hate him—and what if that person is your only sibling?

I listened tightly to my mom's phone voice, organizing a funeral for Bigs. She was sniffling. The turtle dump truck Indy 500 had stopped, so Benj was listening, too.

"Right," my mom said. "In the back garden." She paused. "I can bring one."

Benj's boots shuffled over to where I was. "Emma? That rabbit will get bernied," he told me. He reached up and put his sticky left hand in mine. Spark barked and Logan shushed him. I could feel Benj lift his right hand and use it to wipe his nose—with something he was holding. Champon, probably.

"*Buried*," Naomi said, from the counter. She had turned the mixer off. "Not *bernied*, Benj. *Buried*."

"It's okay," I said. "I knew what you meant." I squeezed his little hand, and wondered if my being on his side had made Naomi feel bad. She was just trying to be a big kid, showing off her vocabulary. I moved closer to where she was, and smelled butter.

"Are you making pancakes, Nomi?" I asked.

"Yeah, do you want some?" she asked hopefully.

"I would love some, thank you."

"Buried," Benj said to himself, practicing, getting used to it. "Bigs will have to get buried." I felt him tense his body, trying to get the word right, trying not to cry again. The princess music stopped and Jenna came into the kitchen, her feet sweeping—ballet slippers.

"Can I help?" she asked Naomi in a whisper, upset that our mother was crying.

"I'm done with this part," Naomi said to Jenna. Then I heard Naomi step down carefully; heard the stool squeak, which meant she was probably carrying the giant mixing bowl full of batter over to the stove. "Can I help with the next part?" Jenna asked.

Naomi sighed impatiently.

"Be nice, Nomi," I said. "And wait until Mom gets off the phone to turn the burner on."

"I'll do it," Leah said, and she touched me on her way to join them. I tensed, waiting for the sound of the gas, the flame catching it, the smell. Logan started clacking plates around, setting the table, and then I heard the gas ignite, the fire turn colors, the batter sizzle on the griddle. I inhaled, exhaled, sat, with Spark at my feet and Benj pulling up a chair on my right, coming closer and closer until he was practically on top of me, then taking my hand again while we waited for our mom to hang up, calm down, come back to us. I could feel the flame under the pancakes, and my mom, dropping her voice to a whisper I'm pretty certain only I heard, said, "Uh, yes, in the freezer." *Focus in,* I told myself. *Focus in. Breathe.* I tucked my head and rocked a little at the table. Was the dead rabbit in the freezer? Had Claire been in a morgue, frozen? Had her parents come to identify her? How did blind people identify their loved ones? Did you have to feel the face of a corpse?

Weirdly, I felt a flutter of colorful hope. Maybe Lo and I could at least talk about something meaningful, like what Claire had done and why, whether there was any way to keep ourselves or each other safe, maybe take some control over our own lives or stories, anyway. Before it was too late and we were adults, with other people relying on us to pretend we could keep them safe.

Before my accident, I thought I knew a lot. I used to take endless notes in a little book I made, with a pencil holder and an eraser holder and a bunch of paper taped in. I spied on my family, and my parents and Leah and Sarah called me Mata Sasha Silver, after Mata Hari. I hid with my ratty notebook under the dining room table while everyone else was eating and talking and talking and talking. That's after I was done with my food, and had already asked quietly, "Can I be excused?" And my mom had said, "Sure, Emma, sweetie," and my dad had said, "May I. May I be excused." And I had nodded, repeated his words like the sweet, obedient parrot I was. And then slipped off my chair, and vanished. I loved that feeling, of being safely unseen. There are so many of us, and there was always such a storm of chaos; I got to organize a little bit, even if only by recording boring descriptions of my parents. I guess I was trying to understand something about us, even back then. Or maybe it was more than that. Maybe I was storing up information, even though I didn't realize I would need it. Because I do. The spying trained me to pay attention, and I still have, locked into myself, most of what I learned when I was other-Emma, Emma with my working eyes. I can still see the blur of all my sisters whirling up from dinner into dishes, bath times, pj's, last snacks, singing, shouting, toothpaste, stories. I'm still listening, even if I can't disappear beneath the table with its curving legs and toed feet that almost match the ones on our upstairs bathtub. I know those cold bath feet well, and now they're how I understand white. Our round, wooden table is what brown feels like; the scratch of the couch fabric, gold. There is nothing in our house I haven't touched, both when I was a spy and now that I'm blind—no surface, no pillow velcroed to the sofa, no part of any wall or windowsill. Now I have to focus in all the time, so my mind and I can stay sharp and alive without eyes. I have no choice.

The tablecloth I used to flutter up and peek out from has dark blue flowers that are an ink-soaked cartoon in my memory. Deep blues can be as scary as water where it drops off to too-deep, but sometimes those same blues are cooked and delicious. Sometimes they're the hot berries my mom pours over Naomi's pancakes, when the smell of the room goes indigo.

Some blues have ice-cube edges, and gray itself smells like smoke. Now the lake, which used to be sunny and layered, is all wrong, gray and dangerous. Now our town, which was fresh-cut green before Claire, has a cracked outside and a scarlet, pulsing center. It's volcanic, like my fear.

Logan said we should ask Zach Haze to meet us for coffee at the Bridge Café downtown, and ask what he thought about maybe getting some people together to talk. I agreed, of course, because he's the future love of my life and also reasonable and smart. So she pulled him aside after lunch at Lake Main, and we stood outside the cafeteria for a few minutes. My back was against the wall, which made me feel steadier, safer, slightly less nervous. Zach smelled light blue, clean like chlorine—maybe the pool that morning, or some sky he had carried in with him, or a bleachy T-shirt. There was also peppermint gum, and the forever-chemical-fruit scent of Logan's hair. People moved in a constant rush down the hall, and as soon as there was a pause, I spoke into it: "So, uh, Zach, we wondered if you wanted to meet us for coffee to talk about an idea we had—about maybe getting some people together for a, um, conversation about . . ." This was a sad imitation of what I'd practiced at home, even recorded and played back to myself twice. I hate speaking. I wanted to open my eyes, check what was happening. I pressed my right palm flat against the wall.

There was a long pause, and I pushed my own "on" button and started blabbering. "It's no big deal, I mean, it's just Logan and I were trying to figure stuff out, about what's going on in Sauberg, and we were wondering—"

"Hey, man!" Zach shouted, because someone had walked by and slapped the back of his head—Carl Muscan, I realized, after hearing him whoop and laugh. I paused, waiting for them to work it out in whatever bizarre way guys do, but Zach didn't chase him down the hall or tackle him or put him in a headlock or anything, because he's not that kind of person. Mainly I was just relieved that the weirdness I had sensed—correctly—had nothing to do with me. That's usually true, I guess; everyone's thinking about their own problems, not yours. Unless you're Claire and you drown yourself in Lake Brainch, in which case your drama infects the whole town and everyone has to think about it all the time.

"Okay, cool," Zach said. "So, you just want to meet at Bridge?"

"Yeah," Logan said. "And then maybe we can talk. We were hoping you'd help us, you know, get some people together or help lead or whatever."

She turned and started walking away, probably because

the word choice embarrassed her, especially, if I had to guess, the part about "help lead," which had sounded good when we thought of it but now was a little much. Logan often walks off in the middle of a conversation; it's a theatrical habit for her, and it works, in the sense that it makes you feel like you want more of her. She's always leaving before you're done, because she hates awkward pauses and is worried that if she stays too long people will think she's pathetic.

Zach called out after her, "So, how about Wednesday, Logan? For Bridge?"

I heard Logan call out, "Perfect," from ten feet away. And then she didn't come back; just left Zach and me to be like, "Uh, okay . . . so, see you Wednesday," which was not generous of her, especially since Spark and I had to run after her and catch up.

"That was good, right?" I said.

"What?"

"That, just now, with Zach."

"Yeah, of course," she said. "He was totally Zach about it."

I asked if she would come to the bathroom and help me sneak a text to Leah asking her to call my piano teacher, Mr. Bender, and pretend to be our mom saying I was sick and couldn't make my lesson. I can't go to my lessons anymore because all of a sudden the sound of piano music makes me feel like I can't breathe, almost like something is pressing the notes into my throat. I used to love piano—I was really good before. And I could read music easily, learn new songs without much effort. Even when I first lost my sight, piano was okay; it was the first thing that made any sense to me after my accident. I could still see the keys in my mind, their straight, dark edges, the little blank spaces between them, the off-white shine of their surfaces. It was a relief, kind of, the opposite of braille when I first started that—no raised cells, nothing to ponder or suffer over; just the smooth, easy feeling of something under my fingers that has always relied on my fingers to make meaning. But now I feel stupid playing; I haven't been able to learn anything difficult, since I can't see the music. And if I move at all, I look like I'm trying to imitate Stevie Wonder and am totally self-conscious. I don't want to think about where to put my fingers or listen for my own notes. My ears are tired.

So I'm adding piano to the growing list of things I can't do: see, sleep, get anywhere near water or fire, show my eyes to anyone, figure out the truth about things that really matter, listen to or play music. My mom will be devastated when she finds out. Maybe I'm about to start breaking my winning streak in school, skipping actual classes, too. I never skipped class at Briarly, because what else did I have to do there, other than go to class or let Sebastian guide me around and try to make me a better person than I'll ever have a chance of being?

Sebastian's name is like piano music. It sends me spinning back sickeningly fast to the feeling of last spring and the wet cut grass and laundry smells of Briarly. To his voice, always in my ear. When he had to write a paper on *King Lear*, Sebastian insisted on reading me practically the entire play out loud. Maybe he thought that since I'm one of a giant litter of children, I might have to compete for my parents' kingdom at some point and that listening to him mangle iambic pentameter would put me at an advantage. He said his English teacher had told them in class that the point of *Lear* is that "nothing can come of nothing." I didn't say anything, and Seb said someday I would appreciate the wisdom of that, even if I couldn't see it now.

I said, "I can't see anything."

And he said, "That's what I mean, Emma. Something only comes of something."

I walked away, aware that he meant something about my self-pity, and annoyed enough not to care exactly what it was. Seb disapproved of my negative attitude, because he belongs to happiness like it's a conversion religion. He's a year older than me, in eleventh grade now. I wonder how it's going for him. He told me last summer, before we never spoke again, that he was going to take the driver's ed test, no matter what his parents said. I wonder if he did.

Seb is a total now, like me. He has no vision left, not even the sliver he had as a kid. So maybe he faked his way through the driver's ed test. If anyone could do that, it would be Seb.

I wonder what he's doing now. Probably driving by clicking his tongue and listening to the sound bounce off stop signs. He's probably running a marathon, getting in a year early to Harvard, starting his own company, and curing cancer. I wonder if he has a new basket case to take care of now that I'm gone. I wonder if he misses me. And if I miss him. I can't think about it. I have too many other problems to wade through, without remembering Seb or what happened last year.

Once, only once, I was crying at Briarly—I never cried in front of people before my accident, and I hardly wanted to become a sobbing public wreck after it. But I couldn't find my brailler or my phone and I was groping wildly around my cubby (we had cubbies instead of lockers there, one of the few patronizing concessions they made to our being blind) and I just started crying, and Seb's hand was instantly on my shoulder and he sat me down in a chair I hadn't known was there and he found my brailler and my phone, both in the inside pocket of a newish backpack I had hung in the wrong cubby and he had found somehow.

All he said was, "Sit for a sec, Emma," and that was it. He handed me the things as soon as he found them, and then he walked away calmly as if nothing had happened, leaving me sitting there. Later that day, he introduced me to a bunch of kids as "my awesome friend, Em," and I rocked wildly and didn't speak and didn't listen to—let alone try to learn—any of their names. They were all going skiing that weekend with some teachers from Briarly on a school trip, and Seb begged me to come.

"Are you nuts?" I asked. "I can't speak for you, but I can't see anything, including trees or other people in my way, if I'm plummeting down the side of an icy cliff."

"I know," he said, laughing his deep tunnel of a laugh. "I'm familiar with that scenario. But they do have skiing for blind kids like us."

I took the "like us" part and put it away in the place in my mind reserved for festering and denial.

"Really? How do you avoid breaking your neck? Because I'm not available for any more maiming."

"You have a guide," Sebastian said. "How about my mom calls your mom and they talk it over, and then see if you want to come? Me and Dee do it every year—they're open through spring. A bunch of the teachers come, and they have ski instructors for beginners."

"It's really empowering," Dee said.

I didn't like the word *empowering*. And I didn't like Dee. I had the sense that she didn't want me to go skiing, but I wasn't sure why and I didn't care. Maybe because she was in love with Sebastian and preferred not to share him.

Or maybe because I was unbearable to be around. Both things were true. Lately, I can't stop thinking about Seb. But I also can't face him. Or Dee, for that matter. He called me last week and then again this week, both on days when I'd skipped piano, been miserable and scared all day, and couldn't do anything, least of all talk to him. When I heard my phone say his name, my pulse accelerated so much it was like I'd been running every second since I saw him last. Maybe picking up and hearing his voice might have been a break, breath, rest from the racing. I remembered the way his hands felt, what his laugh sounded like. But I wasn't brave enough to talk to him; I couldn't bring myself to, maybe because I don't deserve it. Or maybe I'm just too ashamed. I can't be that fragile Seb-Emma and also the new tough person I'm trying to be. So I can't talk to Seb until I am actually her, until I have something to tell him that isn't utterly pathetic.

Because Seb, more than anyone else, makes me remember something I've been pushing down into my bones, which is where I put things I can't think about now, things I don't have facts for, can't understand or face, can't say. Something about myself, some kind of truth. He didn't leave a message.

Yesterday at school, I decided to test myself. Maybe I'm bored of being so needy. Or maybe I just thought I had a better chance of being awesome at our coffee date with Zach Haze if I had done something, anything brave before it. Like going to the lunchroom without Logan.

Sometimes this happens—an idea or challenge or whatever you want to call it will come to me, and then I'll feel like I *have to* do it. Once, when I was ten, we had just started building the tree house in our backyard, but not yet put up walls, and I climbed up on the platform and sat there with my legs dangling over the edge. I looked down at the ground. It was only five feet up or so, but I had this terrible feeling that I had to jump, just because the idea of jumping had come into my head while I sat there. I told myself I couldn't get down unless I jumped, that I wasn't allowed to use the rope ladder I had climbed to get up in the first place. So I sat there for almost an hour, trying to get my brave on to do it. Finally, Sarah came outside and yelled at me, "What are you doing up there, Emma? Mom wants you to come inside," and I squeezed my eyes shut as tight as I could, and made sure I was remembering to bend my knees, and I jumped. It wasn't even that bad once I'd done it. My feet and knees hurt a little, but I was fine.

"Are you insane?" Sarah shouted. "Why didn't you climb down the ladder? You didn't have to kill yourself to get inside this instant—thirty seconds would have been fine!"

I walked over to her. "I didn't do it so I could hurry. I just wanted to see if I could." She sighed as if I were stupid, but later, when I told Leah, she was like, "I totally do that sometimes. But you should let yourself off the hook if the thing is really scary or dangerous. Come and tell me if you think of something and start to convince yourself you have to do it. I'll help you do it if it's a good idea, and I'll talk you out of it if it's a bad one."

But Leah was somewhere in class, and all I had to do was get to the first floor alone; it didn't seem like a bad enough idea to warrant looking for Leah or even talking myself out of it. So as soon as Ms. Mabel left, I pretended I was going to wait for Logan like I usually did, but then I quickly steered Spark and my white cane out the door and down the hall and into the first door, which led to a stairwell I didn't usually use. There was such a rush of people that I lost my focus and my way. My heart was banging around and coming loose inside me and I thought I might cry. I didn't want to ask anyone where I was, so I listened and held the banister and got out at the first platform, pushing through what I assumed were the second-floor doors. I walked a bit, holding the wall, until I heard flushing, and made my way to the door of a bathroom, which I determined from some high voices was the girls' room. I slipped in, locked myself and Spark into the big, handicapped stall, found my cell phone, called Logan. I listened to it ring, praying she would pick up, trying to block out the deafening smell of the air freshener, cheap perfume, contraband cigarettes, and Lysol, the rattle and bang of people coming in and out. Lo picked up.

"Em! I'm in the cafeteria. I can't be on the phone. Where were you? I went to Ms. Spencer's, but Amanda said you'd already—"

"I'm in the bathroom," I choked out.

"Which bathroom?"

"I don't know. Second floor?"

Three minutes later, she was there. Maybe she ran. Maybe she heard in my voice that I was sad or scared. I don't know, because I didn't say anything about it and neither did she. She just knocked on the stall door and I opened it and then she took my hand and led me quietly down to the cafeteria, where I bought a sandwich in the cold lunch line while she waited. Then we sat at a table together somewhere, and I didn't ask who was near us or next to us or even if there was anybody we knew or anything happening. Usually Logan tells me who's saying and doing and wearing what, but she stayed quiet, too. We were surrounded by a lunchtime so loud in my ears that the room might as well have been filled with indiscriminate screaming. I unwrapped my sandwich mechanically, took several dry bites, felt around for a small plastic package of mustard, tore it open, and squeezed it onto a piece of bread I had worked to place flat up in my hand. When I bit into the sandwich, it was covered with mayonnaise, which I

hate but thankfully Spark loves. Logan held my hand after, as
we walked down the hall together, and I knew she was trying
to make me feel better, because she spent an eternity telling
me what everyone was wearing, and I half listened, half detached and floated up above us.

What everyone is wearing is something I barely cared
about before the accident and obviously can't bother with
now. Logan claims not to care, either, because she thinks caring about that is fun and doesn't want me to feel left out, but
she can't keep herself from telling me that Amanda Boughman is still super gorgeous even though her dad left and her
mom has no money, so where does she get all her clothes?
And Monica Dancat, who Logan says must buy all her clothes
at the army supply store, because she looks like she's "going
to war in a lesbian costume." I don't know what "lesbian costume" means—maybe Monica wears camouflage? I never ask
any follow-up questions. Because I hate that kind of conversation. Whenever I say someone is pretty or cute at Lake Main,
people laugh, even Logan, like what can I mean by cute? But
there are ways to be pretty that don't involve the things Logan looks for.

She described Blythe Keene's leather jacket for ten minutes. Maybe she's obsessed with Blythe, just like everyone
else. Blythe moved to Sauberg in sixth grade, years after the
rest of us, so she's been the beat of Lake Main's gossipy heart

ever since she got here and moved in next door to Claire's giant castle of a house, which Claire's parents built themselves, making everyone else's parents angry.

By middle school everyone knew Blythe and Claire had danced naked on the roof of the school, on a dare. The roof is slanted and dangerous, and it was still light out, and apparently they took pictures, although I never saw them and neither did anyone else I know. They also went swimming at night, even when it wasn't summer, in other people's pools and in Lake Brainch, and they were the first ones to drink. Blythe once got sent home from school for wearing a skirt so short you could see her underwear. She was always older and more rebellious than anyone else, and Claire had a better shot at being like her than anyone else. Maybe because her family was different; they were a catalog family, 2-D, shiny and shellacked. Claire's hair was a mix of colors that didn't occur in nature—so streaky she looked like some artsy god had poured paint on her head and shoulders. Blythe's hair was straight white blonde, until Claire died, when, according to Logan, she dyed it a horrible, oily black. It still smells blonde to me, like a clear, square mint.

Logan says it's their parents' fault that Blythe is always in trouble and Claire's gone. Because they were fanatically strict, and apparently hated each other. I'm not sure that's right, but I get what she means: if you forbid your kids to live, they'll live anyway, probably harder than they would have. And lie to you. If you were over at Blythe's house and you said "God," even just like "Oh my god" or something, her mom sent you home for taking the lord's name in vain. They weren't allowed to say or do anything, which might be why they did so much of everything. Although Claire wasn't wild with boys the way Blythe is; we all know Blythe has slept with lots of guys, and that she doesn't care about the rumors or the boys themselves.

Even my older sisters know about Blythe having sex with seniors, and then afterward not caring whether they call her. And not picking up when they do call, or calling them, for that matter. I once heard Sarah say Blythe is "the guy about it," I guess meaning she cares more about whom she likes than who likes her. It kind of makes her the movie star of my mind. I don't even get to try to be like Blythe, because of what happened. But maybe I would have if I could have. Been wild, I mean. And proud. I wish I were wild and proud.

I interrupted Logan's Lake Main fashion monologue to ask if she wanted to come to dinner, but she said, "I can't," and then went quiet. Which she never used to do, but lately does a lot. Like she didn't want to tell me about the Halloween party she went to. Which is my fault, because I didn't want to go, but I kind of thought she'd describe it to me later.

Then I remembered she had driver's ed. The idea of everyone in the world getting their licenses in the next few months isn't something I want to chat about. My regular shrink appointments are Friday afternoons, interspersed with occasional Dr. Walker appointments to look at my scar, so when I'm on a table with hot lights and hands all over my blank face, or sitting on Dr. Sassoman's couch, talking about forever in my dark, Logan has her hands on the steering wheel of a car, with a teacher in the passenger seat and bright, laughing friends in the back, waiting for their turns, looking out the open windows at whatever is still there for everyone who can see: house, house, tree, tree, playground, runner, sunlight, flowers, 3-D life, the way that movement looks. On Fridays, I sit still. And try to remember to breathe.

So maybe Seb is right and this is the kind of self-pity that nothing will come of, but *never* being able to go anywhere myself or have the same freedom as Logan and everyone else gives me a dropping feeling, like the *forever* of being dead. It's just such a long time not to be able to drive. Not to grow up for real. I can't tell anyone. I mean, Seb still skis and plays soccer and "beep ball," which is baseball with blindfolds and a ball that beeps. Even after he gave up on getting me to ski, he invited me to come and at least "watch" one of his beep ball games, but I never did. Because I didn't want to watch what I couldn't see. And unlike him, I'll never take the driving test. But Logan will. And Naomi and Jenna and Benj and even Babiest Baby Lily.

• • •

After my accident, only Logan told me the truth. My parents asked both her and my sisters not to read me the stories about me, but Logan did it anyway. I was the "local girl" with the "horrific tragedy." I was Job and Oedipus. My tragedy was "biblical," my accident "freak," my loss "blinding." I was unlucky and tragic; every single article called me "disfigured."

Logan had to tell me. We have a rulebook called L&E, which we made when we were little and still try to live by. Leah always told me that the most important thing was to be nice to other girls, because people love to lie about how girls are competitive, jealous bitches caught in an endless cycle of catfighting and competing. ("And for what?" Leah always asks me. "Boys? Limited positions of glory in the world?") Leah says there are plenty of boys or girls or jobs or trophies or whatever you want in the world, so share. She says it's our job in a family of so many girls to help correct the stupid beliefs people hold about girls. I don't know how Leah figured this out, or why Sarah never did, but Logan and I wrote it down like a girl bible. We vowed to be one person, with indivisible hopes and happiness: If one of us did well, we both felt joyful. If one of our hearts was broken, we were both devastated. And Logan kept her part of that deal; she almost died when my accident happened. Sometimes I'm surprised she didn't actually gouge her eyes out.

We wrote that we would tell each other the straight truth all the time, although the L&E book has helped me get why an occasional white lie or omission isn't always a bad thing. Like the time in seventh grade when I overheard Blythe Keene and Amanda Boughman talking about how Logan twitched her butt so much when she walked that she looked like "an epileptic pony," and of course I told Lo right away because it was the loyal L&E imperative, and anyway I thought if Blythe and Amanda were talking about me that way, I'd want to know. But leaving the actual pony part out might have done the job just as well, without ruining everyone's friendships for an entire year.

I guess Logan could have left out some of the worst parts of those reports about me. Or maybe she did. Maybe they were even more horrible than I know. I just thanked her for not patronizing and lying to me like everyone else did. I said it would have been worse not to know what everyone was saying. I said that people could write whatever they wanted, but no one would ever get to see my disfigured eyes again.

"But you have to leave the house someday. And see people again," Lo said quietly.

I said, "I can't see."

She never made that mistake again; just stopped using the words *look*, *see*, or *burned*, and started buying me "Emma Silver Star Glasses." And once I put the first pair on, I never left my room without sunglasses on again.

Because my left eye is closed, and there's a scar along the lid that runs in a diagonal line from the top to just underneath my eye. I've only asked about it directly one time, and it was the last time anyone has said anything about it to me. No one is allowed to mention it ever again. Because on an odd and awful night almost exactly a year ago last fall, I woke up thrashing and stumbled into the kitchen to get some water. My mom had forgotten to leave a bottle on my nightstand, because we didn't have any systems yet. I went without sunglasses or Spark or my cane, feeling the wall, trying not to trip or cry. I thought it was the middle of the night because I had fallen out of space and time. I was so thirsty and so scared that the thirst and fear felt confusing, like they were the same feeling.

Then I heard breathing, and my mom's voice said, "Hi, sweetie," and my hands flew up to my eyes. I smelled something thick, muddy, chemical.

"What are you doing?" I asked, jittery and still covering my eyes, even from her.

"I'm having a glass of wine," she said. "Why are you up, Em?"

So that was the smell. Why was my mom having wine in the middle of the night? "I can't sleep," I told her. I was glad she'd mentioned the wine, because I wouldn't have liked it if she was hiding things from me just because I couldn't see them.

She asked, "Would you like a sip?"

"Of wine?"

"Yes, wine. Here." She stood up and I heard her getting a glass down. Then I heard the pouring, a thick, purple sound, and the smell came closer to me. She put her hands on my shoulders, pulled a chair out, and helped me into it.

"Try a little," she said. "It's better than that Manischewitz Passover crap, that's for sure." She laughed a deep, sad, throaty laugh that made me feel very scared.

"Are you drunk?" I asked.

She laughed again, but this time it was her real laugh. "No!" she said. "Certainly not. I've had about four sips of wine. I'm afraid even I have more tolerance than that."

"I thought you said Jews don't drink; that self-medicating is for anesthetized WASPs."

"You heard that?"

"Yes."

She sighed.

"Why are you drinking?"

"Having a glass of wine once in a blue moon isn't drinking," she said.

"But it's the middle of the night," I said. "And you're alone."

"It's ten o'clock, sweetie. I'm waiting for your dad to get home from the hospital and have a glass of wine with me.

And I'm not alone. You're here with me, and I'm glad."

I took this in. I had never considered the possibility that my parents sat at the table late at night, drinking wine, either alone or together. In spite of myself, I felt left out. And then stupid for that. I mean, this was last year. It wasn't like I was a baby. I drank a big gulp of my wine, and it tasted sour, made my tongue sweat.

"Yuck," I said. "I like the Manischewitz better. This tastes like coins. Or"—I pushed my lips together—"Band-Aids?"

My mom laughed her real laugh again then, and I felt less sad, less scared.

Then I sat right next to her at the table and asked, "What does it look like?"

And she didn't ask me what, because she knew I was talking about my left eye.

She just said, fast, "It's much better, Emma, sweetie. Not so livid as it was."

That word, livid, for something on my face, my eye, made my throat close with fear. Even though she was using it to make the point that the scar wasn't livid anymore. My mouth was thick with the choking taste of the wine, but I made the shape of livid again and again, silently, pressing my tongue up against the back of my teeth. I was trying to make livid lose its meaning, the way repeating a word can. My mom was still talking when I came back from the work of undoing her stupid adjective. The scar had "calmed down now," she was saying, and I looked like I had "as a baby, when I was asleep but about to wake up, with one eye closed and the other one open."

"You always looked a little suspicious when you were a baby, and that's how this looks now, too. You look beautiful, vulnerable, strong," she said. "You look just like yourself."

I wasn't going for it. "The scar is disgusting," I said, pushing my chair back and standing. "You're lying. It's thick and ropy and red and purple and horrible." Because that's how it felt to my fingers, crazy and jagged and maybe like a multi-colored, furious, mountainous ridge jutting off my face. "I'm a sickening, livid monster. Why can't you ever tell me the truth about anything?"

I leaned in then and put my hands on my mom's face, to see if she was crying. Wet, yes. Tears. I had put it meanly to make her cry, and it had worked, and now I felt the meanness bubbling, boiling inside me. But I said nothing to fix it; I couldn't. I just stood there. The skin on my mom's cheeks felt thin and fragile, the tears toxic, like they might eat away at her face. I let my hands fall back to my sides hopelessly, and thought about salt, how weird it is that tears contain it, that our eyes produce something they hate.

"Nothing about you could ever be disgusting," my mom said. But I knew she was wrong; I was ruined inside and out.

I went back to my bed, forgetting to get water. I lay there, dying of thirst.

Our Bridge date with Zach was on November 2. It was so rainy and windy that leaves swirled like cartoon tornadoes and the lake roared, wanting to swallow us all up. I knew I would never get near water again. It seemed impossible that summer had ever been to Sauberg, that any of us had ever swum in Lake Brainch, seen sunlight, watched actual clouds move across the sky like spun sugar. It should have been beautiful. Claire should have been alive. I should have been able to see the leaves. The leaves should have been red and gold and yellow, but they were nothing but a wet smell, dirty, decaying. What I could feel of them, under me, sinking into the ground, was a reminder of the wrong, worst things. When I picked up a handful of leaves, hoping to feel the red and gold of them, they disintegrated in my hands. What about leaves raked into crisp piles? Why were these so soaking, peeling from the ground in only the most furious gusts of wind, sticking to our jackets? On our way to Bridge, Logan screamed when a muddy leaf pasted itself to her face. It felt like the world was ending. And I'm aware that having no control over how to fix the world is a typical human predicament, but it felt desperately, uniquely urgent to me.

Zach and I both got hot apple cider and muffins and

Logan got coffee. We sat at a corner table in the back of the café. Spark was shivering. I took my jacket off and put it over him where he was lying at my feet. He did the funny thing with his paws where he pats them on the floor like he's dancing or running in place. This seems to warm him up. Maybe Zach was cold, too, because he left his jacket on and sat very still, and it wasn't until we had already started eating that I heard him unzip his coat and shrug it off. I was relieved, like this meant he would stay for a little while.

He finally said, "So, you guys wanted to talk? What's up?"

I leaned my leg into Spark's body on the floor next to my feet, while Logan said we just wanted to talk about what was going on at school and in Sauberg in general—you know, with Claire and our parents all being crazy and strict and the school acting like we were talking about it but not really talking about it, and what the fuck. She went on for a long time, and I knew she was nervous. I was grateful that she took over, but also felt left out. I wished, as I do more and more, that I could be Logan for a few minutes. But not that she would have to be me, because why would I wish that on her?

Zach was quiet again, for a long time, the way he is, which makes me nervous, even though I know he's just collecting his thoughts. I've noticed, since I have no choice but to listen, that people who think before they speak say better things than the ones who open their mouths and let the words go without choosing which ones will matter and which ones might as well be clutter, dust, or puddles. Go figure. It seems obvious, but you'd be surprised how many people either haven't realized it yet or just can't turn off the faucets of their mouths in time to save everyone from drowning in floods of stupidity.

"That sounds really good to me," Zach finally said, and I warmed up like a heater. "Do you guys just mean people from school?" Zach asked, slowly, his voice a golden color. "And where would we do it? Maybe here?" Zach asked.

"I was thinking somewhere more private," Logan said. "So people feel like they could say whatever they wanted. What about the Mayburg place?"

"That's a great idea," Zach said, quicker than usual. I was shocked that Logan hadn't run this terrible idea by me. The Mayburg place is an abandoned house at the mouth of I-92, between Lake Street and the outlet mall. It's set back from the road, close to Point Park Beach, which Leah says they've cordoned off. The path to the Mayburg place is so overgrown with plants and trees that you have to hack your way in there. I've only been in the house once, two years ago in the daytime with a bunch of girls after an afternoon school picnic. It was me and Logan, Amanda, Blythe, Claire, and this girl Melanie Glass, who moved away the summer of my accident. We did it on a dare, and the place was full of old, ruined things, including a calendar from twenty years ago, clinging to a rusted nail on the wall. We all took one look, touched the door to prove we'd done it, screamed, and tore out of there. Except Claire. She went all the way in and took an old bowl as a creepy souvenir. I remember she and Blythe showed it to all the boys and how they were impressed.

"The Mayburg place? Won't people be afraid to show up?" I asked. And right away, all the blood from my limbs went straight to my face. I became a piece of humiliated chalk. And Logan made it as bad as it could be by saying, "Of course we'll help you in, Em."

One of the main L&E rules is that Logan and I never fight in front of other people, so I just said, in a voice so fake not-angry that I sounded even more medical than my dad, more pastel than my mom, "I meant other kids, not me—just, you know, younger kids or whatever." I planned to shout at Logan later for betraying me and making Zach think I was a disabled basket case.

"Of course," Logan said, realizing her mistake. "Good point. Maybe we should meet up at Cock Dick or something, and then walk over in a group. If anyone's scared we can remind them they're totally safe as long as we're all together, looking out for each other. And without adults. In a way, it will be a chance to enact our goal of being there for each other or protecting ourselves or whatever we talked about at your place,

Em." Good, so at least Logan was embarrassing herself, too.

Cock Dick is the statue on Lake Street; it's of this guy named Thomas Johnson, who apparently founded this tiny strip of an uptight place and therefore got a stone version of his body and face made for everyone to look at (and touch) for the rest of time. The statue is wearing tight hunting pants, and has a shotgun slung over its shoulder, but mainly, the crotch is out of proportion and shiny from everyone touching it all the time, especially for a town where most people never talk about sex, and we have no sex ed at school, and no one is allowed to wear short skirts. Maybe that's why everyone wants to fondle Thomas Johnson. And apparently *John Thomas* is also a word for that, because most words mean both what they mean and also something else, usually something dirty that you can't guess in advance of some asshole being like, "Oooooooh! You said Peter—ha-ha!" And you're like, "But your name is Peter."

Zach was saying, "So what if we each choose five or so people to invite, make lists . . ." Then he waited again and I could feel Logan struggling to keep quiet, to resist filling the silence. "Let's say five people—that would be fifteen, eighteen with us. And we won't say much; just that we're meeting at the Mayburg place on Saturday night. Should we say ten?"

Ten o'clock. We were going to ask fifteen people to weed-wack their way out to the Mayburg place after dark so we could talk in private about our dead friend? It seemed certifiable. I wrapped my arms around myself and said, before Logan could respond, "Ten sounds great. It will help show who's actually interested enough to come." Spark whined for a minute at my feet, as if he knew I had betrayed us both and was about to get us into trouble. I wondered how much trouble, and threw him the rest of my muffin.

We made our lists based on who was most likely to be into the whole idea, and brave enough not to tattle or panic. We all agreed that Zach would ask future Supreme Court justice Coltrane Winslow, because he was perfect for this sort of thing, whatever it was, and I would ask Deirdre Sharp, for her huge math and science brain. Amanda Boughman would be helpful getting more people, because she was a popular butterfly. Elizabeth Tallentine was shy and weird, but I've liked her since third grade, when we were voting on which cause to support with money we made at a "restaurant" we had in our classroom, where we served bread and water to our parents for cash. Everyone was like, "Let's do animals," because they're cute and furry and we love them, but Elizabeth shocked us by disagreeing. So our teacher, strict, mean Mrs. Jackson, made Elizabeth stand up and give a speech about why she didn't think our cause should be animals. Elizabeth's face was a shiny balloon. She said, "I love animals, too. But some people have cancer—some kids, like my cousin Max.

He's four. And doctors need money to do science so they can save him." She gulped a bunch of air. "So, um, maybe if we can save kids like Max, then more animals will get saved, too, because kids love animals." I looked up at Mrs. Jackson and her eyes were sparkly and tears poured out of them, and we all had the stunned revelation that she was a human being, that teachers could cry. I think I'll remember that moment forever, and I'm glad I saw it. We voted to give our restaurant earnings to cancer research. And when Elizabeth was absent for three weeks in fifth grade, we all made cards to say how sorry we were that her cousin had died. Apparently the fifty-four dollars we collected at our "restaurant" wasn't enough to make the difference. When Max died, I cried, too, even though I hadn't known him, hardly even knew her. I knew then, like I know now, that we hadn't done enough.

I reached into my backpack and took out a slate and stylus Sebastian gave me last year, which I have to admit was a show-off move. I hoped Zach would find it cool, wanted him to notice something about me. I could have written the list on my fancy electronic brailler, but everyone's already gotten bored of that. And I think the slate is beautiful—it's metal and it fits over the paper neatly, and then I use a small stylus with a round bulb on one end and a point on the other to poke into the cells and write. I wrote the names quickly: 1. Deirdre Sharp, 2. Joshua Winterberg, 3. Elizabeth

Tallentine, 4. Amanda Boughman, and 5. Blythe Keene.

Then I flipped the page over and ran my index fingers over the names to see if I'd made any mistakes. I could tell Zach was watching by the sound of the silence. And I was right, because he asked, "You write them backward first?"

I felt a flush of excitement, followed by acute embarrassment, and smothered both by reaching down to pat Spark. "Yes," I said, blushing. "They're mirrored."

"That's amazing," he said. There was a long silence. "Can I see it?"

I handed the slate across the table, and heard Zach snap it open and inspect it. "You learned how to do this last year at your other school?" he asked, and then, "Hey, do you want to invite anyone from there?"

"Uh, I don't think so," I said. "I mean, not yet. It would be, you know, hard for them to get out and, well—" I stopped myself. I didn't want to say anything about other blind kids that might implicate me. "But, uh, thanks for thinking of it."

"No worries," he said. "Here." He handed me the slate back. "This thing's cool."

I could hardly get the words out, but I did, and they sounded sharp and clear, like the beautiful icicles we snap from our roof in the winter, no echo of the struggle I felt in speaking them: "Thanks, Zach."

I felt brave.

Ten months ago, last January, my parents sent me to Briarly like a prisoner off to labor camp. They didn't ask what I wanted, which was to fossilize on the gold couch. Maybe Dr. Sassoman told them they had to send me to a blind school or I was going to die. Or maybe my mom was just totally out of patience and ready to throttle me, because right after Hanukkah, at the end of December, she said, "We've found a school for you to attend, where you can keep practicing some of the skills Mr. Otis helped you with, where you can build confidence and—" Here she paused, the hope in her voice so bottomless it embarrassed us both. "And make some friends. You'll start in January."

It had been six months since my accident. And I had left the house only to walk Spark, sit with Dr. Sassoman, throw eggs at trees, and be poked by a blur of doctors chosen by my dad, every one of them "the best in the business." But the business of what? None of them could save my eyes. Or my mind.

And now my parents had found the Briarly School for the Blind, and I was going to start the following week. Halfway through ninth grade, blind, full stop. Now my dad called me "sweetie"; now my pregnant mom spoke orders to me like she was my dad. I didn't even bother to put up a fight about Briarly—I didn't have the energy, and anyway, what difference did it make? I obviously couldn't go to real school. It would be better to start somewhere fresh, where everyone was blind. Like me. *Blind like me*, I thought, and lay back down against the pillows, pulling Spark over me like a blanket.

Briarly was an hour from our house, in Silverton, a town I had never heard of until my mom took me there for my first day. She got up at five thirty, made breakfast, sent Leah and Sarah and Naomi to Lake Main and Jenna to preschool, then helped me dress in a new outfit she said was beautiful: a short black corduroy skirt, tights, a silver V-neck long-sleeve T-shirt, and a striped hoodie. I asked for every detail of every piece, feeling each to see if the truth of my fingers lined up with what my mom said. I wore the red metal sunglasses Logan had gotten me, and they were hard and cold against my face.

My mom put Benj in pull-ups and overalls, and packed him and his endless stuff: goldfish crackers, string cheese, a slobber-marinated copy of *Fox in Socks*, a plastic truck, mittens and clips to hold them to his coat, and Champon the dirty turtle. I could smell Champon: mildew and Elmer's glue, maybe, a pasty smell like papier-mâché, wet flour, melted crayons, kid paint. Benj still loves to flop Champon's head against his cheek while he sucks his thumb at night. The turtle has had its head sewn back on five times, but Benj will perish if it gets lost or washed. And frankly, if anyone washed it, I'd probably never be able to "see" it again.

I could also suddenly feel—hear? smell? how did I know?—a kind of smoky exhaustion emanating off my mom, and I had a moment of pleasure at my ability to tell what was happening, followed by a dropping fear that she might snap and leave us. Everything seemed possible then, every worst-case scenario.

I was sweating in the front seat. She had six kids, and now one of them was blind. And she was pregnant again; how could she stand it? Maybe she could hear me thinking, because she suddenly reached over and touched my cheek. Her hand smelled like coffee and white soap. Spark barked from the back, where he was trapped next to Benj.

"I was just showing him," Benj said, and I didn't even ask what. I was in the front, because putting me in the backseat with Benj would have meant admitting I had fully, formally lost my position in the family, something my mom denied. Last May, when Baby Lily was born, Benj was thrilled not to have to be the runt anymore, and he told everyone that Lily was "the babiest baby" and he was "the biggest big boy." That's how we all started calling Lily "Babiest Baby Lily." I still feel like I might as well be Babiest Teenager Emma.

Spark kept barking, maybe because Benj was annoying him, or maybe because he realized he wasn't going to be allowed to come into school with me. We had been over and over it with Briarly; Spark wasn't a registered assistance dog, and Briarly wouldn't budge. I hated them, wanted to turn around and go home, wanted to open my eyes. By the time we arrived, I was welded to my seat. I couldn't move, because I couldn't see anything, couldn't imagine what this day would mean, couldn't believe that this was my life, that this was the school I went to.

Now that I can stack that first day at Briarly underneath my first day back at Lake Main, I have to admit that things are getting better. If I had closed off the future part of my brain and focused on what was actually happening in the moment, I might have been able to manage better. But maybe it's precisely because I was forced to get through those months at Briarly that I now know how to shut parts of my brain down and forbid the fear from melting me.

My mom helped me out of the car, and then we walked up a rocky path and a staircase. I kicked my feet forward to feel where the stairs were, sliding my white cane until it hit the edge of each step so I could judge its depth. My mom was describing everything to me: "The building is brick, the lawn is green, there's a baseball diamond, oak trees, maple. Holly. Mums. It's late for mums. Purple, Emma, purple mums. It's a beautiful place, Em," my mom said, interrupting her own frantic monologue only to yell, "Benj, don't do that on the stairs, you'll fall!"

"Why bother making a school for the blind beautiful? It's lost on everyone anyway," I said, and my mom kept holding my hand.

"Stop, honey," she said, and I didn't know whether she was talking to me about being negative about the beautiful school I couldn't see, or talking to Benj about whatever he was doing, probably standing on his head on the cement staircase. But then she said, "Stop a sec," and held on to me, and I realized she meant that I should stop walking, so I jolted to a stop and put my hand out, in case I was too late and about to hit something. I felt suddenly like I might fall down the stairs, like all the walking and hearing and smelling and finding I'd been doing at home was being stripped away by this new place. I caught my breath, listened, and heard a door opening, a giant metal door. It sounded prison-heavy. It struck me as odd that they wouldn't have an automatic door at a school for the blind, or that they would have stairs, but Briarly's idea wasn't to build a separate world for blind kids but to teach us how to be blind in the regular world. We'd have to open doors and climb stairs, so why not start now?

We went in and everywhere was a different dark, the smell of school, but off somehow—not Lake Main. A different kind of Lysol, meatloaf, unfamiliar kids, dryer sheets? Why did it smell like laundry? There were blind kids everywhere, and I kept thinking, *I'm one of them. Am I one of them?* It's impossible to know yourself when you're not around the things and people who made you you. The Logans and Zach Hazes. I felt confused, upside down, dizzy. I could feel the heat of the other kids' bodies, hear snippets of their excited chatter: what they had done over Christmas, this party, that movie, what homework, Teacher X, Teacher Y, none of the names meaning anything to me. I was the new kid, new kid, new kid, the new blind kid, all the dimensions of my outsiderness and newness washing over me like waves, trying to suck me under while I struggled to float or swim toward some familiar land. Lake Main suddenly seemed like shore.

My mom held my hand down the hallway to the office of the principal, Mrs. Antoine. She welcomed me and said how sorry they were to hear of my accident but how glad they were to have me. How she hoped starting in January, midyear, wouldn't prove too difficult. The word *difficult* turned bruise colors in my mind, and I rocked back and forth. My mom put a hand on my shoulder, but I shook it off.

"We will do everything we can to make the Briarly

School a place for you to thrive and learn, Emma," Mrs. Antoine said, and her voice was an expensive, soothing alto. I realized suddenly that Briarly was a private school. My parents
had never spoken about it, neither to nor in front of me. But
sending me there must have been both costly and painful, because my mom is a big believer in public schools. She thinks
"parents like them" should stay with the public schools, because that ostensibly makes the schools better. Although how
my parents have made Lake Main better is anyone's guess.

"Your classes here will be regular academics," Mrs. Antoine was saying. I was thinking about Spark in the car, about
how unfair it was that I couldn't have him at school with me.

". . . blind-friendly ways. This way, if you choose to be
re-mainstreamed, we can keep you caught up."

I tuned back in momentarily. "Re-mainstreamed?" I
asked, turning my voice toward my mom.

"Going back to Lake Main someday," said my mom. Her
voice had coal in it.

But a small figure eight of hope took shape in my heart.

"I am pleased to see that you've decided to take braille
for beginners in the afternoons with Mrs. Leonard. I com-
mend you on that choice. At Briarly we believe that braille is
an essential tool for full literacy and independence, and Mrs.
Leonard's course will be an excellent complement to technol-
ogy with Mr. Crane."

I didn't know if this meant she didn't think I would ever go back to Lake Main, because if I would, did I really need Braille? And who had decided to sign me up for that? My mom? My dad? Both? They hadn't consulted me.

I didn't want to get into it. So I said, "Spark is going to freeze to death in the car," to my mom, who stood there for another full minute, as if unable to move. "Mom? Are you going to stay?" I asked, and Mrs. Antoine said, in a voice so gentle it would have made me angry if she'd been talking to me instead of my mom, "I'll walk Emma to class, Mrs. Silver. She'll be fine. Why don't you come back and meet me at two forty-five and we'll go and collect her together?"

I thought, *Collect?* But it worked. My mom tore her body and Benj away, stumbling back to the door we'd come in, calling, "You'll do great, Emma, sweetie. See you at three," over her shoulder.

And then Mrs. Antoine walked me to what would be my first class every morning for the next six months, American history. It was a split-level class, she said, with ninth-, tenth-, and eleventh-graders. I could hardly hear her, because my blood was pounding in my ears and I was trying to walk in a straight line, with my white cane along the shoreline where the wall met the floor. Several times I touched the wall with my hand; it was scratchy plaster. I wondered where the lockers were. Mrs. Antoine told me what we were passing: the gym, the library. "Here's the life skills center, where students can hone their abilities, from cooking to laundry to typing," she said. The detergent smell made me think of Leah, who was at Lake Main, in eleventh grade, still in the life I had left. Where was Logan at this moment? It seemed impossible to me that we were all still in the same world, that they were alive in this minute, miles away at Lake Main. I couldn't focus. Or I couldn't choose what to focus on, anyway.

In the doorway to history, I heard and felt the whole room come at me like heat; a puff of chatter and chairs and books and bags unzipping and bodies moving. Mrs. Antoine put her hand on my arm and delivered me to a desk. Almost immediately, a boy's voice said, "Hey, welcome," and I shuddered, because I couldn't be sure if the boy—whoever he was—had said it to me. How did he even know I was there? And even if he had meant me, how was I supposed to respond? I didn't want to be at Briarly, didn't want anyone to know me or know anything about me, didn't want to be welcomed.

But the boy said it again, louder. Was I supposed to turn my body toward the source of the voice? Was he blind? *Of course he's blind,* I thought. *Everyone here is blind.* Although some people are blinder than others, and how much sight you have matters at Briarly. Some people can still see a little, and seeing is a kind of currency. In the normal world, once you're even a little blind, everyone just assumes you're a total, and therefore an absolute lost cause of an invalid. But at Briarly, kids want to know exactly how much vision you have left. If any. I'm a total, meaning I can't see anything, which qualified me for some cred with people like the boy who welcomed me that morning, Sebastian. When he was a kid, he had a tiny slip of vision in his right eye, and a pair of glasses with a giant magnifying glass built into the lens on the right eye. He had learned to read through that magnifying glass, by holding pages up close to his right eye, and taking half an hour a page, but his sight was deteriorating still and his parents finally insisted that he admit he was blind and go to Briarly. But unlike me, Seb was good at passing—he told me once that he looked like he could see. He never used his cane at school or anywhere familiar.

When I still didn't answer in history that first day, he put his hand on my arm, to my surprise. "Hey," he said a third time. "What's your name?"

I felt a fleeting moment of relief. Here was a question clearly directed at me, one I could answer.

"Emma," I said, but as soon as the word was out, my relief was replaced again by panic. I didn't ask what his name was. I felt exhausted, wrung out by jitters, like my bones were giving up on me. I needed all my bravery and energy just to get through the next four hours; I couldn't waste breath on small talk.

But Sebastian wasn't daunted, even if he assumed I was such a savage that I couldn't manage to say "what's yours?" after someone asked my name. Maybe because he's a kind person who assumes the best about other people, even if we don't deserve it.

He waited a beat and said, "Hi, Emma, I'm Sebastian. I'm in tenth grade." I felt my sunglasses start sliding dangerously down my nose and reached up to push them back as our teacher, Ms. Raymond, came clomping in. It sounded like she had stilts strapped to her shoes, which made me think of my sister Sarah. The door closed, her throat cleared, the voices in the room turned off. I pivoted away from Sebastian, tried to face the front of the room, to be polite, correct, unremarkable.

"Greetings, guys," Ms. Raymond said. Her voice was a hot copper color. I thought about the formality of *greetings* against the casualness of *guys*, both words turning 3-D in my mind in a way they never had before. *Greetings* was a penny of a word, jingling and written in metallic ink, and *guys* was like a little light reflecting off it.

"We have a new student joining us today," Ms. Raymond said then. "Everyone, meet Emma Silver. Please make her feel welcome."

When I heard my name, the colors drained away, and whatever she said next went so dull I could barely make it out.

I detached from my body enough to think what an unlucky girl that new blind kid Emma must be, even to wonder who she was. She had, I felt sure, nothing to do with me.

But Sebastian's hand was back on my arm, and then on my hand. His was warm, and I realized how cold I was. He leaned in close to me and whispered, "It gets a lot better, by the way."

I felt shy, afraid to speak lest we get in trouble, but I swallowed and whispered back, "How do you know?"

He kept his hand on mine, and I felt fluttery about it. "Because," he said, like he'd known me forever, "you're sending out total sonic misery, like a radar. But everyone has a story. I mean, not to be mean or anything, but we've all had stuff happen, you know? Briarly will wring the PBK bullshit right out of you."

"What's PBK?"

"Poor blind kid."

He took his hand off me then, and Ms. Raymond started talking about the 1960s, as if any of us could have cared less. How was I ever going to get a job? Or live in the world again? And why could I still feel where Sebastian had touched me, as if his hand was actually still there?

It was in my braille classes those first weeks at Briarly that I started getting a feeling I now have a lot of the time: like I've died and come back too many times to keep a record.

I'm another me, and then another, always versions of myself I never knew before. A switch flipped in me last year at Briarly; my mind and my fingers started working together, making patterns, textures, shades. That's when A became red, B blue, C orange, D brown. Monday went white, Tuesday blue, Wednesday yellow, Thursday brown, Friday red. The weekends were a forest I saw for the first time only once I couldn't see: green Saturday, gray Sunday, the color of the sky right before there's no more light left. At first, braille was confining and confusing—the cells too close together, the figuring out exhausting. Was this an R, with dots 2, 4, 5, and 6 raised, or a W, with 1, 2, 3, and 5? Why was the W in the wrong place in my alphabet sheet? Because Louis Braille was French and so originally there was no W. R and W were mirrors of each other, which made me think of mirrors, which I would never see again.

The first time I realized I'd memorized the braille alphabet, after Briarly one night, I was lying on the gold couch with Naomi, listening to *Alice in Wonderland*. I loved Alice last year, because she fell down a dark hole and was lost. She made me feel like no matter how weird the world got, or even how much you changed, you might still stay yourself. And I loved Naomi, because she was willing to sit with me, even when I was just listening to the same story over and over. I realized that night that my fingers were typing braille along to the story. Dot 6 (capital) and dot 1: A; dots 1, 2, and 3: l; dots 2 and 4: i; dots 1 and 4: c; dots 1 and 5: e. I saw the dots in my mind, the cells, the lovely 1, 2, 3, and 5 of the R for *rabbit*. The W, a mirror image of the braille R: 2, 4, 5 and 6. I had been confusing R and W constantly in my braille class, but when I was listening to the story and thinking of the White Rabbit, I saw the letters as braille dots, rather than letters. I felt both thrilled and miserable. Would I actually manage to get braille? And if I did, did that mean I'd forget what letters had looked like?

On good days like that one, I thought, *I can live like this. I can live in my colorful mind*, and hoped that slowly, the way they do, things would keep coming together, the dots in each cell forming A's, 1's, B's, 2's, C's, 3's; that everything would some-day make sense, the way braille does if you have no choice but to learn it.

Then I started grade-two braille and realized that every-thing I'd learned in grade-one braille barely mattered, be-cause spelling words out letter by letter was absurd, and there were endless symbols I still had to learn: one symbol for *with*, another for *for*, still others for *because, before, behind, below, be-tween, beyond*. Even the word *braille* itself was just b (dots 1 and 2), r (dots 1, 2, 3, and 5), and l (dots 1, 2, and 3). So I cried.

And for months, I couldn't figure out words until I got to their final syllables or letters, like a five-year-old; like Jenna, who was learning to read faster and with more accuracy than I was. Only Benj and Baby Lily were behind me. And on those bad days—and there were a lot of them—nothing made sense at all, braille was impossible, the world was dark and loud and utterly inaccessible and oppressive, and my fingers and ears and I had no choice but to tune the world out. We needed a break.

I can still feel Seb's hand now, even after four months of not talking to him. I can feel his face, too. Because once, somewhere in that early tangle of days repeating themselves mercilessly, while I was trying to make braille take shape in my mind, trying to figure out how I was going to survive, Seb asked me to go outside with him during lunch and I shrugged yes. I often thought last year that I had nothing to lose. Which wasn't true, but I didn't realize it, maybe because Claire hadn't died yet.

I followed Seb outside, clicking my white cane along the way, and hating it. It was an oddly warm day, and I was thinking about the difference between piano, which I loved, and braille, which at that moment I did not love. Of course, right now I prefer braille to piano. Maybe someday I'll be able to tolerate both. Or neither.

I kept thinking during grade-two braille with Mrs. Leonard that if only I could cheat, just use my eyes once or twice to memorize the cell patterns, then my fingers might be able to follow up. But I couldn't remember them, couldn't see them. Why hadn't I learned braille when I could still see? Oh, right. D's and H's mixed in my mind, and under my fingers, which began, after long days at Briarly, to ache. The pads of my index fingers were tired of touching, working, looking, trying to read. Seb kept saying I needed braille; that even if I got mainstreamed, I could never finish all my work without having some way to read it. He said listening wasn't the same as reading, and that braille would be worth it. He said, even though I never told him how hard it was, that it wasn't always going to be this hard. He tried to tutor me, but I resisted. He tried to invite me places, but I said no, said I couldn't go anywhere, do anything. My mom was always waiting to drive me off to Sauberg, where I never invited Seb or Dee, who was often with us.

I thought Seb wanted to be my hero, and he tried: reading me his papers in the hallway, unwrapping my sandwiches, finding things when I lost them, walking me from place to place. But maybe he just wanted to be my friend. I don't know. I don't know how to think of it. That one warm day I was too tired of saying no all the time, and for once it seemed easier to go along. So I let him take me outside to play his favorite cloud game.

We lay on the cold, hard grass on our backs by the track, and pretended to be looking up at the sky while he talked. Like Logan, Seb was always, always talking: "There's an alligator and a huge shoe, maybe a group of all-white balloons."

Making up plush, lovely clouds you can't see, in other words. He said, "I love this game," and I thought how gutting and hopeless it was, but stayed silent, flying furiously around my own mind, stinger poised.

But then out of nowhere Seb quit with the fake clouds and said, "I want to see what you look like." Maybe he'd heard me hating it, hating him, hating Briarly, hating being blind.

I said okay fast, because I was curious. I wanted to see what he would do, felt like testing him. Or myself.

He reached over and took what seemed like hours, tracing my face with his fingers, moving them through my hair and then slowly down my forehead to where my sunglasses were. He had touched my hands countless times by then, but never anything else.

"Please don't move my glasses," I said, and my voice was someone else's, hot and bubbly and strange, as if it came from a fountain underneath us. I put my hands on the damp ground to steady myself while Sebastian kept his on me, skipping the band around my eyes and feeling my mouth instead, my chin, throat, collarbone, the dip in my V-neck T-shirt. I didn't know if he was going to put his fingers inside my shirt, decided not to stop him if he did. But he didn't—just reached down, found my hands where they were on the grass, and lifted them up to his face.

"Here's what I look like, Em," he said, and his voice was gruff, different, too.

And when I felt his face, I was surprised by how smooth it was, how young. He was only in tenth grade, like I am now, but I'd thought of him as way older, maybe because he was so confident. His jaw was sharp, his chin had a groove in the middle. He had a preppier face than I was expecting, and I was surprised by his lips, but it took me a minute to understand why. I kept my fingers on them, trying to feel the shape of his smile. His mouth was softer than I'd imagined a boy's—or anyone's, really—would be. His breathing was fast and raggedy, and I left my fingers there, on his slightly open mouth, for what felt like forever. I could hear my own heart beating, and I thought maybe he was kissing my finger. But maybe not, too. I let my hand slide away from his face and we never talked about it again.

Sometimes I wish I'd done something then. I don't know what—kissed Sebastian, maybe. Or thanked him. Because that was the first time I knew that I could have good, melty secrets again, not just fear and a ruined heart. I even thought maybe that new, 3-D feeling could become my own kind of vision, a way of being extra alive instead of less alive.

But I said nothing. Not that day or the next or the next, and then it would have been weird. Seb never asked me to go outside with him again at school, or to play the cloud game. He invited me to ski, and to watch his beep ball games, and I said no so many times that I saw a page of no's in my mind, raised in their braille cells: all those 1, 3, 4, and 5 N's and 1, 3, and 5 O's. They were round blue and white words: *No, no, no, no.* I wondered whether every time I spoke, Seb saw a girl made of round, impossible braille dots. But I never asked him anything, because asking might have made our friendship real, which would have meant last year was happening, might have made me blind.

The last time I talked to Seb was on the final day of Briarly, five months ago. It was June. He said he was going to take his driving test over the summer, that there was nothing his parents could do to stop him. He was as proud as anyone I've ever met, because in the late spring he'd gotten a job at a cemetery near the school, unloading flower arrangements off of trucks and delivering them to graves. He got hired without telling the guys who ran the place that he wasn't sighted; I know because he had confided in me and Dee the week before that he wanted the job—his friend worked there and said they had an opening—but Seb was worried he wouldn't be able to fill out the application. So he showed up one night right before closing time, wearing sunglasses and not carrying a cane, and asked all casually if he could grab an application and bring it back the next day. They said sure. And he spent the whole night filling it out and then dropped it off the next day. He didn't mention he was blind, or that the application had taken him six hours to finish, with help from his sighted brother. They hired him. And they were right to, because he immediately memorized every shoreline and landmark in the yard, which he said was simple; it was just a grid of paths and graves. And either they never found out he was blind or by the time they did, he was already doing such a good job that no one minded. That's Sebastian. His hands on me—the way he felt, and made me feel—are the best things I've felt since my accident. And they're still pure secrets. I don't know if it's because I want to remember or forget, but I've never told anyone, including him, what he showed me that day.

The first person I invited to our Mayburg meeting was Blythe Keene. I went straight to her voice in English, and I could smell her mint-flower hair. Something clicked in her mouth, against her teeth—strawberry hard candy, maybe. It smelled pink. No wonder boys love her so much; Blythe is a bouquet of delicious things.

"Um, Blythe?" I said, the *um* turning bright like a blush in my mind. "Logan and Zach Haze and I are having a kind of small meeting Saturday night, and we'd like to invite you."

This was just how I'd planned to say it, with Logan's name first, then the big, cool surprise of Zach Haze being involved, and then *small* because it sounded exclusive, and who could resist that? Only the *um* had been wrong and clashing.

Blythe answered in a voice that sounded lower than her usual one, maybe because she was surprised that I had invited her to something. I felt nervous, but she just said, "Thanks, Emma. Um, so, when and where?"

So I said, "The Mayburg place, at ten p.m."

She laughed a little. "Are you serious?"

"Yeah. I know it's kind of weird, so, um . . . If you come, just please bring a flashlight and a notebook. And, well, it's kind of not public, so if you wouldn't mind not telling other people?"

Then she said, in her normal musical voice, "Okay if I bring someone?" And I didn't know what to say, so I said yes. I wondered who the lucky guy might be, felt glad it couldn't be Zach.

At the end of English, Ms. Spencer called on me to ask about Atticus's glasses in *To Kill a Mockingbird*. Even though I hadn't raised my hand and was kind of mad that she'd made me talk, I said they were symbolic of his perspective; that losing them meant he would see the world differently. I didn't actually think that was exactly true, but I knew what she wanted to hear, and that my saying it would make it especially meaningful, since I was even blinder than Atticus. Sometimes I can't help saying what I think people want to hear, instead of what I actually want to say. I wish I could do that less. Ms. Spencer gasped and clasped her hands together the way she does; said, "That's fabulous, Emma. Let's end there," and dismissed us.

I managed to invite Amanda Boughman, Joshua Winterberg, and Deirdre Sharp, in that order. If Amanda was surprised, she didn't really show it; just said in her crackly voice,

"I'm not sure, because I have to go to this Pendleton party, but maybe I'll come." Pendleton is the private high school in our town, and unless you're dating someone who goes there, it's very hard to get into Pendleton parties. I shrugged and walked over to Josh, trying to be like Logan.

Josh said he'd try to make it, and I floated up above my own life for a second. I saw me, Emma, with light blue sunglasses and Spark, asking people to come to a meeting at the Mayburg place on Saturday night—and having them say yes. I felt a little brave again, like I had when I managed to thank Zach for complimenting my slate and stylus.

A whole day of tiptoeing on that thin limb way above my comfort zone, and Deirdre Sharp was the only one who asked an actual question. Deirdre, with what Logan calls her billboard glasses, because apparently they're so big and square that they "advertise nerd," said, "If you don't mind my asking, what's the meeting about?" I said we were hoping to have a kind of no-bullshit conversation about how we could take care of each other and ourselves, since it seemed like the people in charge weren't doing such a fabulous job.

She was quiet for a moment, but then she said, "Wow. I like that idea. I'd really like to come, Emma. Thanks for inviting me." I was impressed, because her parents are the most religious and conservative people in town, so going out late at night to the Mayburg Place might be a big risk for her.

Elizabeth Tallentine said yes fast, like she wasn't even considering not coming, and I felt totally comfortable. Maybe because I'd already asked a bunch of people scarier than her, or maybe because she's like me, also a weirdo. I like her.

Then I skipped gym, because we're swimming for the next two weeks, in the dank, cavernous Lake Main basement pool. And even though I'm brave enough to invite five people to the Mayburg place, and probably will be brave enough to show up there at night myself, I can't get near the school pool. Water sends me into a spasm of fear. Which is too bad, because so does fire. Next I'll have to medicate myself against the breeze. And dirt. Gym was the first class I've ever skipped intentionally, by the way. It's formally the end of the A+ me. And the beginning of someone I don't really know yet, but who's also apparently me.

The Friday before our Mayburg meeting, I was leaning into my locker, feeling around for my sunglasses with the band on them, when Christian Aramond materialized from a blank void and said, loud, "Hey, Emma!"

I jumped out from the locker, almost whacking my head. "Oh, hey," I said, trying to recover.

"Sorry," he said. "I didn't mean to scare you." There was

something in his voice I didn't like, a taste, almost like sulfur in tap water.

"No, no, it's fine," I said, kind of embarrassed, but less embarrassed than I might have been with anyone else, because Christian is so awkward himself that it's hard to be embarrassed in front of him. Leah once pointed out that there are two kinds of people in the world: those who get embarrassed and those who embarrass other people.

Christian's dad is the French teacher at school, and he's always rubbing girls' backs in a creepy way. So I bet Monsieur Aramond being the butt of countless jokes probably hasn't helped Christian feel great about himself. We both waited, and it was like when someone calls you but then doesn't talk. Like you called me, so it's your fault and I'm not going to bail you out. I tried to outlast Christian, but he was quiet for so long that I eventually thought maybe he wasn't even standing there anymore, so I said, "Christian? What's up?"

"Um, so, I just wanted to see if, maybe, you wanted, well . . ." We stood there, aging.

"Wanted what?" I tried to say this gently, before the human race ended, but it came out impatient anyway. Now that I can't read people's faces, I feel like they can't read mine, either. So I work hard to get the intonation right. But sometimes I can't control it.

He spoke very fast then: "To go to the Mayburg thing together tomorrow night?"

My heart popped a bit in my chest at this. Christian had been on Zach's list, so had Zach told him I was going? Was Christian Aramond asking me on a date? Was he afraid to walk over there alone? Or did he think I might be scared? Because I definitely was, but not scared enough to want to go with him. Christian seemed scary in some vague way, too, suddenly. But why? Spark gave a little jerk of his head, like he was looking around to see what had made my blood move faster. I moved my leg over so that it was touching him.

I said, "Uh, I think Logan and I might meet at the, uh, you know, statue and then head over. Do you want to come with?"

"Oh, okay," he said, and his voice had a blurry lining of disappointment around it, fuzzing his words. Which made me think maybe it had been a date he was after. But why?

"I could pick you up at your place and maybe go to Logan's and get her, too?"

"I'll already be at Logan's, so we'll probably just come from there, but—"

"No problem!" he said, embarrassingly loud. "I'll just see you guys at the statue," he shouted. Then he turned and ran away.

"What was that all about?" Logan asked. I hadn't heard her come up. I felt frustrated.

"I have no idea," I told her. "He wants to go with us on Saturday night."

"With *you*, Em."

"Whatever," I said.

"He's only been in love with you since second grade."

"Yeah, but," I said.

"But what?"

"Oh, come on, Logan," I said.

"You're the only one who has no idea how hot you are."

"What are you, my mother?" I said.

"Love is blind!" she said.

"Ha-ha," I said. "I've never heard that one before."

Then we both waited a minute. I wanted to ask her something—about Halloween without me, maybe—but I couldn't think of what it was, and she didn't help.

After school that Friday, while Logan was driving, I told Dr. Sassoman that I was full of dread. I did not tell her about the Mayburg plan.

She said, "Dread? Can you unpack it?"

Dr. Sassoman likes the word unpack way more than I do. It reminds me of a suitcase, of arriving somewhere and staying, and I don't want to stay anywhere near who I am. I said, "No."

She waited.

"It's probably just anxiety about school or whatever," I said, and *whatever* sounded tinny, fake, like a wrong note in a piano song I'm pretending to have learned for Mr. Bender.

But Dr. Sassoman is irritatingly patient, so then we just sat quietly for a long time until she said, "We never expected that going back to Lake Main would be painless, Emma. You're making steady progress, and there were bound to be bumps. How is Logan?"

"Logan's fine," I said. "She went to a Halloween party without me and won't tell me anything about it."

"I see. Did you want to go?"

"No."

"But you'd like to hear about what it was like?"

Hearing Dr. Sassoman describe the way I felt made me sound stupid. I said nothing.

"Is Logan still helpful at school?"

"Yeah."

"What about Ms. Mabel?"

"She's okay."

"And other than piano and gym, have you been skipping classes?"

"Not yet."

"Why 'yet'?"

I shrugged. "There are things I can't do anymore."

"What things?"

"See."

"Indeed. But you managed perfect attendance at Briarly nonetheless."

"Well, that place was designed for me, right?"

"I don't know. I think there were some things about Briarly that were better for you than Lake Main and some that worked less well. Wouldn't you agree?"

I shrugged and then outlasted her through the long, dry pause that followed. I felt thirsty. Finally, she asked, "What about at home? How are things with your parents and your sisters and Benj?"

"The same."

"As what?"

"As they have been since."

"I see. Are you feeling more independent?"

"No."

"Have you gone out alone yet, like we discussed?"

"No."

"Okay. Are you sleeping well?"

"Not really."

"Do you want to talk about it?"

"Not really."

"Let's see each other twice next week, okay, Emma? I want to unpack that 'yet,' and make sure you're feeling less anxious. Or if that doesn't work, will you give me a call on Wednesday, just to check in?"

I knew she was worried, because Dr. Sassoman never asks to see or talk to me extra times unless she's freaked out I'm going to die.

I rode home silently with my mom, pressing my face against the cold passenger-seat window, thinking of Logan, when my phone rang. Logan.

"Where are you?" I asked. "Did you hear me thinking about you?"

"I skipped my class," she said, and I knew her mom hadn't shown up to take her to driver's ed and she had missed it, because Lo's voice was cool blue and even, the way it gets when she turns her heart off. "Can I come over?"

I was thrilled. "Of course," I said. "I'm in the car with my mom—we'll be there in two minutes. Come now." And she was at the door when we pulled up, which meant she had already begun the sprint to my house when she called.

At dinner, Benj recited the story of how they had "bernied" Bigs, and now she was a garden, just like she used to eat gardens. We had all heard it more than a hundred times. "Soon Bigs will be another rabbit," he concluded, as usual.

"She's not going to be another rabbit," Naomi said.

"It's okay, Naomi," Leah said. "You don't have to be so literal all the time—it's just a way of understanding, okay?"

"If Bigs will be another rabbit, why can't we just keep her until she's that rabbit and then that rabbit can be Bigs?" Benj asked.

"I'm with Naomi," Sarah said. "If we let him believe things like that, then he'll want to keep the dead rabbit around until it happens." I agreed, although I stayed quiet.

"It doesn't happen as fast as that, Benj," Leah said.

"Mom!" Benj yelled. "When will Bigs be another rabbit?"

"I don't know when she will, Benj," my mom said. "Maybe she'll be something else, like flowers, or a tree."

"How can a rabbit be a tree?" Jenna asked.

"She's not really a rabbit anymore, guys," my mom said. "She's more like . . . I don't know, rabbit energy." Then she sighed, the universal sigh for people who are in impossible conversations with toddlers, who, it turns out, are totally irrational and also, I've noticed, weirdly rational. That's why they're hard to talk to.

Last year, when she was four, Jenna asked how Baby Lily had "gotten in mama's tummy," and my mom launched into a shudder-worthy description of "falling in love" and "putting this in that" and yadda yadda, and then Jenna asked, "Do sperms have eyes?"

"Um, I don't think so, no," my mom said.

"But they see eggs?"

"I don't know if they really 'see' eggs, honey," she said.

"But they're alive?"

I was parked on the couch, as usual, fingering a page of illegible braille, but I perked up, interested to hear whether Jenna thought you could be alive or not if you couldn't see.

"They're alive, yes," Mom said.

"If they're alive and they find the egg, then they have eyes!" Jenna insisted.

"Maybe they feel their way, Jenna," I told her. "Just like I do."

"When you get eggs?" she asked.

"What?"

"When you get eggs from the 'fridgerator, you feel for them, like a sperm," Jenna said.

At the table, things were melting in my mind in a way I don't like: the eggs in my mom's description, the eggs I had thrown with Dr. Sassoman, the eggs in tonight's challah. I told myself to focus in, and tried to listen to what was happening at the table, but it was difficult and chaotic. My dad was there, because he eats with us on Friday and Sunday nights.

Jenna was screaming, "Aigh! Benj, no! I hate peas!"

"Just leave them on your plate, Jenna. Don't scream," our dad said.

"Benj is throwing them at me!"

"Benj!" my mom shouted. "Stop throwing peas at your sister! Eat your chicken!"

"Chicken meat has arsenic in it," Sarah said. "We read an article about it in bio. It's disgusting." Most of us ignored her, but my dad was like, "Tell me about bio these days, Sarah."

"I'm not throwing peas; I'm rolling them," Benj said. My mom cleared her throat, and she must have thrown my dad a glance, because he laughed. Sarah hadn't bothered to answer his question about bio. She just wanted to pick a fight.

"This is organic chicken, Sarah," my mom said. She's more easily provoked by Sarah than my dad.

"The arsenic is in the chicken feed," Sarah told her. "All chickens eat it, even the lucky organic ones."

"More challah! More challah!" Benj shouted. I was trying not to fret about the candles my mom had lit, thinking, *Dark is cool, light is hot,* even though nothing helps with the smell of heat. For the first six months after the accident, we used fake electronic candles, because the first time my mom lit the candles my face and hands went numb and I thought I was paralyzed. My dad said it was an anxiety attack, so we just stopped lighting fires in the house. This fall, we started lighting actual candles again. Leah or Logan sits with me and whispers candle updates.

Naomi was chattering about the story she's writing at school, something about a warrior princess cheetah, and Jenna was singing "Oh, I Had a Little Chickie," the way my mom taught us: "Oh I had a little chickie and she wouldn't lay an egg, so I poured warm water up and down her leg. And the little chickie danced and the little chickie sang. And she laid a hard-boiled egg. Bang, bang." She had to add the bangs to make it rhyme, because it's supposed to go, "So I poured hot water up and down her leg. And the little chickie cried and the little chickie begged. And the little chickie laid a hard-boiled egg." Yet another pathetic attempt to hide the hideousness of the world from us.

Naomi refused to eat her chicken. Benj started crying because he didn't want to eat anything other than challah. Then Jenna and Naomi had a fight over who was hogging the saltshaker. Sarah's phone rang and she answered it and stood up, and my mom started bossing her furiously because we're not allowed to take phone calls at dinner, and I seized the beautiful moment to say, quietly, "So I think I'm gonna sleep at Logan's tomorrow," into the air.

Both my parents froze like I'd stun-gunned them. My mom immediately forgot Sarah's infraction and turned the scalding beam of her attention toward me.

She smoothed out her voice like a bedsheet. "Did Logan's mom say that was okay?"

"It's fine, Mrs. S.," Logan said, and she cleverly took a big, wet, crispy bite of salad, to win my parents over. Because watching kids eat salad puts grown-ups in an unconsciously good mood. It makes them feel like civilization will continue after they die. Something biological, I mean, which is why watching us eat junk food makes them hysterical; it gives them the feeling that we'll all be obese heart-attack victims and the human race will die out either with them or—if we eat enough "crap," as my mom calls it—before them.

"Well, it's okay with me, then," my mom said. "Robert?"

My dad cleared his throat. "You'll take Spark?"

"Of course," I said.

"And you'll call if you need anything?"

I sighed. "Yes, Dad."

"And Logan's mother will be home?"

"Yes, Dad."

"Fine then," he said, and I heard him put his hands against the table, as if he were bracing himself for the impact of letting me spend a night out of the house.

"Just give us a call to let us know you're all right at some point during the night, okay?" my mom said. "And it's so cold out. Do you want me to drive you?"

"No thanks, Mom. We'll walk."

I haven't slept at Logan's—or anyone else's house—since the accident. I was impressed that my parents didn't insist on convening a meeting about it; that they didn't have to talk it over "privately," while we all secretly listened, first. Or maybe they had their conversation in a series of glances at each other—the kind that used to annoy me. Maybe I don't get as much as I used to. But whatever. I could go to Logan's, and therefore to our meeting at the Mayburg place.

The fact that my accident happened with them one foot away is sometimes lost on my parents. They've had this feeling ever since that if they're just nearby all the time, nothing bad will ever happen to me again, but it's totally irrational. I mean, I was standing right in front of my dad, leaning back into him, when it happened. He still had his hands on my shoulders.

Spark and I were giddy on the walk to Logan's. He galloped along and I kept up, the rubber bulb of my white cane finding sticks and wet November leaves and sidewalk cracks and the shoreline, the edge of the grass. It smelled just right, the hint of winter around a corner.

Maybe because the night was unfolding so deliciously in front of us, I felt as good as I have in forever, kind of extra human. Like a cartoon hero with sidekicks and special powers or something, my bones and my ears and mind and dog and stick doing the work my eyes used to think they were doing. Work they weren't necessarily doing all that well on their own. I wish I felt that way more often. Lots of kids at Briarly hate their canes, and some kids, like Seb, fake that they're not blind. But I can't do that. And I sometimes like the way my white cane feels, the noise it makes, the way it finds things for me. I like it folded neatly in my bag; like to unfold it, feel its parts snap together, the rope inside go taut. It's part of me, like Spark.

Logan jingled her keys as we approached her door, and I bent down to give Spark a kiss. He nuzzled me back with his wet nose. He doesn't like Logan's place, because her mom keeps millions of plants and it smells green and loamy, which makes Spark think we're outside, so he gets disoriented. I also dislike places that smell wrong.

"Mom?" Logan called out.

"I'm downstairs!" her mom shouted, and I heard shoes on the backless wooden stairs that lead up from Logan's basement. We used to do chemistry experiments down there, and when I heard her mom coming up, I remembered vividly, in full-color 3-D, adding borax to boiling water, stirring to dissolve it, and then squeezing out drops of red food coloring. The way that fake blood bloomed came back into my mind so brightly it was almost more beautiful than it had been when I could actually see it. I tried to hold the image.

"Emma!" Logan's mom said, high-pitched, excited. It was only then that I smelled food. I hadn't noticed it when we came in. I don't like it when what I smell or hear feels random or disorderly. Logan's mom said, "I made spaghetti and meatballs!"

"Oh!" I said. "Thank you." Spaghetti and meatballs was my favorite when Logan and I were in first grade, and her mom has remembered it forever, even though I actually stopped eating meat three years ago, after my parents took us to a farm and I saw some chickens snuggling each other and realized that chickens are actually just people, except bumpier and smaller and covered with feathers. They snuggle their family members, is what I'm saying, and that was enough for me—I could never eat anybody's body again, even a chicken's. But I made Logan swear not to tell her mom, because once I didn't mention it the first time and instead made a huge deal about how great her meatballs were (and hid them under my napkin and threw them out later), it was already too late. Now I'd rather toss some meatballs to Spark once every few years than have Logan's mom realize I've been lying to her for years about the giant balls of ground-up flesh she feeds me.

"Thank you, Ms. F.," I said. I kicked my Converse off and felt my way to Logan's room, which is smaller than Naomi's and my room, and which she has described to me so many times I feel like I can still see it. Every time Logan changes a poster, she tells me, so I'll still know what her room looks like. She does it as much for herself as for me, but I don't mind.

"I put up that picture of us. From the first week back? On the field?" she said. I closed the door behind me and sat on her bed, felt Spark relax and curl up next to me.

"What picture?"

"One Trey took on his phone. It's super cute of you—you're leaning your head back and your hair looks especially dark in the sun and your glasses are perfectly balanced on your face and you're laughing. You look amazing, and you have my lipstick on—remember I put X-S on both of us? Anyway, I'm right next to you, looking over at you. I'll give you a copy. And I posted it on Facebook so everyone can see how hot we are."

"Thanks," I said.

"Um, Em, do you mind going up to my mom's room with me, just for a little bit?"

"Of course not," I said.

We sat in Logan's mom's room while she was getting ready to go out, because Logan likes to, even though we're too old and it always ends up making Logan feel bad. She can't resist; there's some magnetic pull between her and her mom. Whenever her mom is in the house, Logan slides and drags and races, almost against her own will, toward her. Probably she just wants to spend as much time as she can with her mom. So they chatted about dresses her mom might wear, and the whole room had a silvery feeling, the glittery clicking of her heels and the smell of her perfume, which was sweet and sharp, nothing like my mom's. My mom smells like shampoo and bread, and she's soft when she hugs you.

Logan's mom is skinny, and if she hugs you, you can feel her breasts like they're attached to her bones, olives-on-a-toothpick style. She came over and told me to touch a dress. It was crunchy and awful, and she laughed when she saw my face.

"You're right, Emma," she said. "It's synthetic and itchy." She changed, and when she came back, in a blaze of perfume, the next dress was so silky it felt cold.

"I like that one," I told her, but Logan didn't like it, said it looked too much like a nightie.

Her mom laughed: a metal sound of money, coins touching each other in a pocket.

"That's the idea," she said to Logan, which made Logan unhappy, and her mom must have noticed, because she added, "I'll wear a little bolero over it, of course," and I heard Logan breathe in a bored way, and then she stood up from the bed and I sank.

"We're gonna eat now, Mom," Logan said, and she paused for a minute, waiting for me, before starting out of the room. I bounced up off the bed, relieved.

"Let me come down and get your dinner on the table before I head out," her mom said, and followed us down the stairs. Then she put pasta on plates for us, heated it up, and left for her date. The night felt deep blue and cool, and Logan and I sat at the table, eating noodles and tossing meatballs down to Spark.

"You okay?" I asked Logan. I could hear her moving food around on her plate, almost rhythmically.

"Yeah," she said. She stood up, cleared our plates, and ran some water over them in the sink, and then we went back to her room to get ready for our meeting at the Mayburg place.

"It would be nice if—" she started, and then cut herself off.

"If," I repeated gently, thinking maybe she just didn't want to finish whatever it was.

"Whatever," she said. "Nice if I had to sneak out, I guess. It's not a big deal. I was just thinking how your parents have two hundred kids, but they're still all like, 'Don't freeze to death, and call and check in,' and if they knew my mom was gone they wouldn't let you stay over in a million years. And my mom only has me, but she didn't even—"

I cut her off, knowing she'd feel bad in a minute and say something kind about her mom. "That's because I was blinded in an accident and my parents can never forgive themselves."

"I know," she said. "My mom is great. It's not that bad. It's not like I'm that unlucky or she's doing a horrible job or whatever."

I felt a stab of pain for Logan. "Your mom *is* great," I said, tasting the faint, purple, fake-grape taste of the lie in my mouth. Maybe learning to lie to Logan was part of growing up. And even though I didn't want to keep doing it, didn't mean to, for some reason I couldn't stop.

"Yeah," she said, and then we were both quiet, agreeing in our silence to pretend this was true.

I hadn't been to the statue since my accident, and maybe Logan sensed my fear, because she held
my hand the whole way there and didn't drop it even when
we arrived and heard Trey Brighton's voice. I could hardly
believe they were there waiting for us, for our meeting, but
they were. Everyone used to hang out on Lake Street at night,
but since Claire there are always adults present: Officers Crag
or Muscan, the town cops, or someone's parents. It's almost
as if there's some weird, unspoken law in the town that we
can't be left alone. Because we might kill ourselves. The only
difference it makes is that if you're going to drink, you have to
do it in someone's basement before you come hang out at the
statue. There's never been much to do in Sauberg; everyone
always just went "downtown" and wandered around looking
for other kids who were also wandering around looking for
other kids who were also . . . you get the point. Like most
towns, I think. And now we still do that. One of the weirdest

things about being alive—being me, especially—is how much stays the same. Even when everything has changed.

"Hey, guys," Logan said, a shimmer in her voice, probably because Trey was there.

"Hi, Lo. Hey, Emma," Zach Haze said. So he was the one Trey had been talking to.

"Hi, Zach," I said. Then, as if we were doing a cheesy dance number in a musical, we all turned and headed together toward the woods.

The walk wasn't as terrible as I thought it was going to be, except for the part along the highway, cars whipping by, the wind they created almost knocking me down. I was terrified that Spark would get hit; I could not live a single day without him. I tried to listen to the traffic and also hear the conversation. I've learned how to pick words out of the stream, and I know everyone's voice from everyone else's in a way that's almost impossible to describe. There's a weird clarity to it—like each voice is a ribbon, stretched out, glittering, unique in its color, depth, variety. I hear them like hearing is seeing. Trey has a purple voice, low and dark and deep, and he was talking over the traffic about how his brother had tickets to this upcoming Cannons concert that was going to be so badass that they were holding it at Sable Arena in the city because no other venue could possibly accommodate such massive throngs of people, and his brother had apparently slept outside the night before tickets went on sale so he could wake up and buy the first ten that were available, because ten was the limit you could buy so they could discourage scalping. But radio stations and super-rich people had vouchers so they could buy fifty, which was total bullshit, but his brother had three extra tickets and blah blah.

"I love the Cannons!" Logan said, a little too loud, right into an unlikely moment of silence in Trey's endless rock 'n' roll monologue. Her pale, naked words hung in the air, shivering. I was getting my brave on to say something bland, anything, to unembarrass Logan, but before I had a chance to choke out, "Yeah, the Cannons are cool," Zach's molten voice flowed out: "Me too. How about two of the tickets for Logan and me? I'll buy them from you."

Something tumbled down from my chest, past my stomach, and into my feet, maybe whatever boring words I'd been about to say. I felt like I might sink to the core of the earth. Logan tried to save me. "Aren't there three? Emma, you like them, too, right? Why don't we all go?" No one said anything.

The night was getting colder, the air so damp I could feel it chill my skin and hair. All the channels of my mind clogged with a thick, slushy feeling about Zach. It's a big deal in our school if someone asks you out alone. It essentially makes you instant boyfriend/girlfriend. Hooking up doesn't, but if you go out on an actual date with someone else, everyone knows and makes fun of you and you might as well get married.

We began to slow down, and I could hear the heaviness of the trees as they thickened at the side of the road. The leaves had fallen and the dense smell of winter seemed to originate in the woods. Fear slowly took over my misery about Zach. Spark nuzzled his way into the trees, because I was directing him that way, but then he lifted his head and turned back to me, whimpering a little, as if to ask, Are you serious? Are we actually going in here, and if so, why?

Josh Winterberg and Zach and Trey got up in front, shone flashlights, and cleared a path for us in the branches, which we powered through. Logan took my hand again and walked in front of me, leading me. I tried not to cry. Spark was panting, and my heart rattled around in my rib cage. We walked for five or six minutes in silence, listening to the branches snap under our feet, pushing leaves and twigs out of our faces. I had another floating moment—imagined suddenly that I was my own mom, watching me, and I felt an opaque, climbing fear; thought, What is she doing in the woods at night? Will she trip? Will she get hurt? But then it went away, and I was me again, stumbling along with Spark, smelling the rotting wood of the Mayburg place, and we were there. Trey and Zach were arguing over who would go in first; they both wanted to, maybe because they were competing for who could impress Logan the most.

But then once we were inside, Trey said, "Oh man, why didn't we just do this at someone's house, with all of our parents there?" and we laughed, relieved. I thought it was cute that he was willing to be a huge public chicken. I would never have admitted how scared I was.

"What time is it?" Logan asked him, in her lavender voice.

"Nine fifty-two," Trey said, which I thought was flirty because it was so specific. But maybe he's the kind of guy who's so detailed and controlling that he can't just be like, "Ten of ten," or, "Nine fifty"; he has to have his fifty-two exact. Maybe I just wanted Trey to like Logan back so there was no chance of her and Zach falling in love.

Whatever Trey was thinking about Logan, I wanted to be her, and hated myself. A yellow envy was tearing at me, and I saw it in my mind, like a mouth full of wolf teeth. If I couldn't be Logan, then why not Blythe Keene? Or anyone other than me? Well, anyone except Claire.

Logan touched my shoulder. "We have a few minutes. Maybe we should set up a little bit."

"Set what up?" I asked, more sharply than I'd meant to. I was feeling around in the dark, unable to make out anything.

"You know," she said. "Find things to sit on, make a kind of circle, get all the flashlights and lanterns on, that kind of thing. Shit. This place is hell on earth. What was I thinking?"

So maybe we were all going to admit how afraid we were. I liked the idea. I hung back with Spark while everyone else banged random, noisy, broken things into a circle.

"Shit!" Logan said again. "What was that?"

"Mice, probably," I said, with my brave metal voice on. Spark was breathing fast, like he was scared, or hunting, or worried for me. I petted his head, but he kept on with the barbed breaths.

"This place is perfect," Josh said. I thought this must be his way of compensating for his tragic nerdiness and, probably, fear.

"Perfect for what?" Trey asked. "A horror movie?" Trey was too confident to have to hide his babyishness.

Just then there was a banging sound and we all jumped ten feet, in sync, as if we had been choreographed by terror. Blythe Keene came into the room, laughing. I listened for information about the guy she'd brought.

"This is Dima, you guys," she said in an exhale-y way. I smelled cigarette smoke, wondered when Blythe had started smoking. It was possible that she had always smoked; it's not like I had hung out with her on the weekends since we were kids.

"Hey," Dima said. She didn't go to Lake Main, and I had never heard her voice.

"Oh my god!" Blythe said then, in her minty, twinkling

way, the inimitable popular-girl inflection I had learned to recognize even more after the accident. It was like, no matter how few syllables were in a word, she could break it up into tons of them, and make the sounds of the word climb hills, duck into valleys, move all over the map. She reminded me of Ariel's voice in The Little Mermaid, every note bursting with want. Blythe has this huge appetite and sometimes it seems like the world exists just to feed her. And to want her back.

"This is horrifying," she said. "What are we doing here?" Her friend Dima laughed again, and in her laugh I heard a puff of smoke.

"We're having a get-together," Logan said in a crunchy voice that was like salt on sidewalk ice. "Please sit."

"You guys may be having a get-together," Blythe said. "I'm having a heart attack. Here, Deem, you sit here." She must have pulled something over for Dima to sit on, because I heard it scrape along the floor. Spark whined uneasily, while Trey Brighton laughed louder than was necessary, maybe to show how charming he found Blythe, and then shuffled toward her voice. I heard Logan inhale like something had given her physical pain, and Blythe said, utterly indifferently, "Thanks, Trey." I didn't know what she was thanking him for. A box to sit on? A backrub? An offer of undying love?

Logan sat me down next to her on a single milk crate. I reached out to feel for it, and she said, "Not a germ on it."

Then Blythe was like, "Hey, Deem, can I bum another one?"

And to my amazement, Logan chimed in, "Me too?"

When Logan flicked the lighter right next to me, the sound and fuel smell made me flinch with fear. Then Lo sucked in noisily, maybe so everyone would know it wasn't her first cigarette ever. It was her third. I knew because she and I had smoked our first one together in her backyard when we were twelve; I stole it from Sarah's purse, after I found out she was smoking. Logan and I put on lipstick and practiced posing like movie stars with the cigarette. We took some pictures, but then we deleted them because we were so dramatic about "oh my god, what if our parents found out we smoked a cigarette?" Now I'm pretty sure they would have laughed, but at the time it felt important to think we were doing something criminally dangerous. Logan had smoked her second cigarette in California the time she got her period. She was feeling wild on her solo maxi-pad run, and apparently as she walked to the drugstore, some guy who lived in her dad's building was outside smoking and he offered her one. When she told me the story, she reverted to the Logan she'd been when he asked her, because she was like, "I just had to have a smoke, you know?"

"Are you ready?" Logan whispered to me as Amanda, Deirdre, Carl Muscan, and David Sarabande came in. Logan smelled like smoke, unfamiliar, scary. Logan and Zach and I were sitting next to each other, with Spark at our feet. The room quieted down and Logan nudged me.

"So, um," I started, "thanks for showing up, you guys. Obviously this is kind of a weird and crazy time to be meeting, and a weird, you know, place." My sunglasses were sliding down my nose, and I pushed them back up. "So, the reason we wanted to get together—well, there are a couple, actually, and, well . . . here." I reached into my pocket, unfolded my notes, and ran my fingers over them. "We wanted to talk, you know, try to figure out what's going on around us, and maybe, I don't know, try to figure out some way to have some control. Over our lives, I mean." The room was scarily quiet.

Then Blythe Keene asked, "Why?" into the stillness. There was no color or music in her voice anymore, no cartoon.

"Why what?" I asked.

"Why are we meeting like this, if it's just to talk?"

"Lots of reasons," I said, just like I had planned to, since I had known this question would come up. I hadn't expected it so soon, or from Blythe Keene. Her being the one to ask made it harder to answer, but also more urgent. I said, "Mainly because of Claire. Since she was, you know, one of us, and we were just feeling like, well, no one's really said why she . . ."

There was a collective surge in the room's pulse. I felt our chests tighten and our breath get short. There was a dead girl among us, and we had done nothing to save her. I didn't have to explain this, it was obvious, but I had chosen to make it explicit by inviting everyone and speaking her name in a dark, abandoned house near the beach where she'd washed up. I broke an unspoken rule: that we weren't going to admit, at least not in a giant group, that Claire's suicide was our fault, that we hadn't done enough, and still weren't doing enough. Were we really just going to lean back into the story of her drug-induced "accident" and relax for the rest of our lives until another one of us died? Didn't we have to know what it was to avoid it? But sometimes making everyone face what you've all already been thinking is just as dangerous as saying something new, unknown. Because admitting the truth locks it into the world in a terrifying way.

"Uh. I'm having trouble following the bouncing ball here," Trey said. "What do you mean, exactly?" He just wanted to be on Blythe's side, but wasn't even sure what side that was.

Zach spoke up quickly, rare for him. "We just mean if what had happened to Claire had happened to one of us, we would want the rest of us to talk about it, figure it out, be honest about it in some way that it doesn't feel like anyone's being."

I was more in love than ever.

"For one thing, shouldn't we all be trying to make sure nothing like this happens again?" Logan added. "I mean, maybe if we have an actual conversation about what's going on, we can figure out how to protect each other." She sounded amazing, like a warrior pumping her fist in the air, eyes flashing. I was really proud of her, even though I'd wanted to say that part myself. I wanted to speak next, too, but I was still out of breath from having talked first. I tried to channel Leah, dug around for some of her words. I'd been storing them up for so long, and if not for this, then for what? But I came up blank.

"What *is* going on?" Amanda Boughman asked. "I mean, if we were going to 'tell the truth' or whatever?"

"And do we not know because no one knows? Or just because no one wants to tell us?" Zach added.

"I agree," David Sarabande said. "It's some real bullshit."

I ran my fingers over the notes again, mainly for comfort.

Josh Winterberg noticed, because he said, "It's cool you can read in the dark."

My face got hot. "Um, thanks," I said.

"So what can we do about Claire?" Deirdre asked. A cell phone went off and someone scrambled to turn it off. "Sorry," she said. Amanda Boughman.

"We were thinking we could start by just kind of saying what we remember about Claire," Logan said. No one said anything and I could feel her start to shuffle, move her feet like she wanted to walk away, but since that wasn't going to work in this instance, she added, in a new, different voice, "Anyway, so we got a group together, to talk, or whatever."

"Is this it?" Josh asked. "Is this going to be the group?"

There was a shuffling and lighting and smoking. I felt a swirl in my chest—the cold night and the smoke and some far-off sound I imagined was Lake Brainch. I used all my courage to say, "Anyone who wants to can come and talk. We just thought we'd start with people we knew and, you know, ask how we could all help each other. I mean, if anyone feels like they need help, or wants to help, or . . ."

I trailed off, nervous, in the real dark and my dark, with a thousand insect eyes on me. Why had I set this up again? If I were someone else, someone not insane, I would have been at home in bed rather than at the Mayburg place, holding a secret, possibly stupid and pointless meeting. I gathered myself, tried to sit tall. Running my fingers along my notes made me feel a little better, safer, stronger.

Josh asked, "Was this your idea, Emma?"

I couldn't gauge his tone. I said, "Um, it was a bunch of ours. I mean, it's not even really—" I stopped, not knowing where to go. Not even an idea? Just something I thought we needed? I didn't want everyone to think I wanted to be in charge or that they were, like, pawns in some plan of mine.

So I said, "Whoever has ideas, we can always add them." I know from my family that it works better if you act like other people have a say, even when you don't want them to. Otherwise, you never get your way.

Deirdre Sharp said, "I think it's a great idea, Emma."

"What do you guys mean by helping each other out? Or being honest? I mean, is there some way to say what we're going for?" Coltrane asked.

Logan answered, "So, uh, back to Claire?"

"What about Claire?" Blythe asked, her voice odd and cold.

"Maybe we should talk about her," Logan said.

"We talk about Claire all the time," Monica Dancat said. I don't know her very well. She's a runner and spends all of her time doing track, and Logan's always saying she's manly, whatever that means.

"Exactly," Blythe said. "Did it ever occur to you that maybe she would have wanted privacy? That her family and close friends might want to deal with it alone, and that's why the news teams don't get to know every intimate detail of her life?"

"Yeah, but we don't mean the news teams," Logan said. "We mean us. Her friends."

"We should talk about what happened," Deirdre said, "if there's going to be hope for Sauberg." *Hope* is a funny word;

it's clear, like a plastic container, and turns the colors of whatever words it holds in the rest of a sentence. "Does anyone want to say what they think happened? Or why?"

"What's there to say?" David Sarabande said. "She was high and she killed herself. What more do you want?"

"Seriously, David? If you died, you'd want us all to be like, whatever, he was high and killed himself? There's a lot to say," Logan argued. "Like, how about why would someone like Claire kill herself?"

"Yeah, but I wouldn't kill myself, Logan," David said.

"What do you mean by 'someone like Claire'?" Blythe asked. She sounded furious.

"It's not our job—it's the cops' job to figure out what happened to Claire," someone said. Carl Muscan, I realized, which made sense. His uncle is a police officer.

"I just mean someone so much like all the rest of us," Logan said to Blythe, backing down, her voice cooling off. "But obviously you were her best friend. I mean, why don't we talk about Claire before? Just, like, say what we thought or knew about her—or whatever."

Blythe said nothing.

"Claire helped me when my parents got divorced," Amanda Boughman said. Amanda was a gum-cracking dancer who talked about herself all the time until sixth grade, when her dad, who traveled a lot on business, admitted to

Amanda's mother that he had another family in Houston, and then moved there to be with them. This was before my accident and before Claire M., so his leaving was the biggest drama our town had ever imagined. Everyone talked endlessly about whether Amanda and her mom would stay in Sauberg, and then they did. And her mom became single, and it seemed like maybe it had always been that way. The only real change, at least from the outside, was that Amanda stopped talking so much and never mentioned her family again. Until now. I was interested that she brought it up at the Mayburg place.

"How'd she help?" Logan asked wistfully.

"One thing she said was I shouldn't think my life was over, because I would be a totally different person in two years. So if I killed myself then, I'd be killing that other person, too, and who knows, she might be super happy. Not to mention the one I was going to be in five years and ten years and fifteen years. She was like, 'Someday, your dad leaving will seem like it happened to someone else. You won't be her anymore.'"

"I told *her* that," Blythe said. "But apparently it slipped her mind."

I hadn't realized until she said that how angry Blythe must be at Claire. If Logan killed herself, I'd be furious. Would Logan kill herself? And if she did, how many of us would blame ourselves? I'd blame myself. And her dad would probably finally feel bad for leaving her and Lo's mom.

"But the thing is, I wasn't thinking about killing myself," Amanda said.

"But anyone could kill themselves if the circumstances were right," Josh pointed out.

I thought about Claire's parents, wondered if they wanted to kill themselves now that she had. Maybe there'd be a domino effect and now everyone in our town would want to die. Mr. M. had cried so wildly at Claire's memorial that he had to be carried out, and Logan said that after Claire's death, Mrs. M. had become like a statue, that her eyes had gone completely blank. I thought of my eyes, and the awful white word *blank*. Sometimes we ran into Mrs. M. at the grocery store, and once she was at the Bridge Café when Leah and I were there, and Leah said she looked like a zombie. Which makes sense. She's probably just drugged out of her mind, like I was after the accident. There are certain things we're not meant to be alive for, never mind being awake, like losing your kid—or your eyes.

I hoped that Josh was wrong, that it wasn't just circumstances that dictate whether we die on purpose or not. Because if it's that random, then how can we go on with our lives? Is there some amount of misery we'd each need to push us off the sand into Lake Brainch at night? I didn't ask. I just sat there, with churning black water in my mind, wishing terribly for Leah.

"I don't know about that, Josh," Monica Dancat said. "I think you have to be mentally ill to kill yourself."

"Yeah," Amanda said. "I mean, I kind of feel like, I don't know, no one I know would make that choice. I mean, I get that that's what it was, but I can't stop thinking something must have happened. I mean, every man I saw all summer, I thought . . ."

"What?" Carl said. "They said right away there was no foul play." Apparently there's so much meat in his head that he isn't able to consider anything but the hard fact of what actually happened. Or maybe he just doesn't want to.

"Why every *man*?" David Sarabande asked. "Women never kill anyone?"

"No, of course. I didn't mean that. I just . . ." Amanda said. I was disappointed that she apologized, even though I probably would have, too.

Josh Winterberg interrupted. "Did you guys know that if you're afraid of heights, it's not about falling, it's about jumping? It's like, you don't know who you're going to be in five seconds, so who knows if that person will be crazy enough to jump?"

Then Elizabeth Tallentine said, "I don't want to be the one to . . . you know . . . but wasn't Claire kind of . . ."

"Kind of what?" Blythe asked.

"I just mean, didn't she have a kind of drug problem?" Elizabeth asked, super politely.

"Define problem," Blythe said, and some people, including Logan, laughed. I didn't think she had meant to be funny, and I didn't laugh.

"Speaking of drug problems, who wants a drink?" David Sarabande asked. I heard something metal, a cap, maybe a bottle being unscrewed, or a flask. David Sarabande is the type to have a flask. He used to play football last year, but then he got kicked off the team because his grades weren't good enough, and as soon as that happened, he was like, "At least now I can be a total slacker and a drunk," because when you're on the team you can't drink.

I could hear people gulping from what turned out not to be a flask but a giant bottle of whiskey, which Logan passed to me after taking a swig. I didn't really want any, but I didn't want to be a blind virgin prohibitionist either, so I took a huge, proving-myself sip, a way bigger one than I meant to, and it burned a hideous path from my mouth to my stomach. I came up coughing like I had dived into the bottle. Someone laughed, but I couldn't tell who.

"Take it easy, Emma! Save some for us!" David shouted.

I tried to laugh, to show I was a good sport.

"So Claire was popping pills," David said then. "She was a wild hot mess; we all knew that."

"Like you knew shit about her," Blythe said.

"What kind of pills are we talking about?" Carl Muscan asked. "I mean, was it like weed? Bath salts? Crack? Or her mom's meds?"

I was interested that Carl could divide drugs up into categories. Most people in Sauberg talked about drugs like they were all identical, and if you smoked a puff of weed you would die instantly, or lose your mind to a crippling pot addiction. My parents always made a point of telling us which drugs were legitimately terrible, because they thought it would help us survive. They came at it from different angles—my mom as a hippie artist who absolutely snorted everything in sight when she was young and thought we'd probably try ourselves and wanted to help us sort so we could do our drug-gobbling "safely," and my dad as himself, a teetotaling, fact-lover extraordinaire.

"Everything they said she was on was all painkillers," Blythe's friend Dima said. I was surprised she had joined in.

Maybe Blythe was, too, because she asked, "Why are we talking about this again?"

"Where was she getting them? Who was her dealer?" Monica Dancat asked.

"Her dealer? Get a grip," Blythe said. "Hey, Emma, can I ask you something?" I tuned in sharply to Blythe's voice.

"Sure, of course."

"Why do you wear sunglasses even at night?"

I hated the question. I didn't want the attention of the meeting to shift toward me, and I felt like Blythe was making a point about me being a hypocrite, because why was I talking about the truth if I didn't want to admit anything about myself? I got that, but I was hardly going to admit that I wear them because I know my left eye is too gross for anyone to see ever again, even though I've never even seen it myself. And I don't want everyone else to be in on the secret of how disgusting I look.

"I have to wear them all the time to protect my eyes," I said.

"Oh, okay," she said, and I could tell she sensed it wasn't true. I had a jolt of longing to tell the truth, to say I was afraid I might look like a monster, and have everyone encourage me to take the glasses off, show my face. They would all rush to tell me I was beautiful anyway, still fall-in-lovable. Maybe. Then they would carry me out on their shoulders while Zach proposed.

I waited out the awkward pause.

"Sorry," she finally said. "Just curious."

"That's okay." I folded my hands on my lap, wanting to end the meeting now, to be anywhere, anyone else.

"Can I ask something, too?" Josh asked. "If it's not rude, I mean? Is this place, like, not as creepy for you because the dark's, like, what you're used to? Or . . . I mean, sorry if that's . . ."

I felt angry and claustrophobic, which was what Blythe had wanted, I thought. We had gathered to discuss Claire, and I wanted to get back to the real conversation. But I got that it would be hypocritical and unfriendly to refuse to answer a small question that wasn't even mean. So I recited my stock answer, the one I made up for Jenna that time in the bath: "It's . . . whatever. For me, the dark is like swimming. Like shades of blue, cool and kind of relaxing."

The truth is, when I first woke up from the accident and realized I couldn't see, it was so soul-wrecking that I wanted to climb straight out of my body and run, shrieking, away from my own life. The feeling of that moment comes back to me sometimes, especially when people ask me about my eyes or my glasses, or the accident itself. But obviously that's not Josh Winterberg's—or anyone else's—business.

What if I had told the truth myself at the Mayburg place that night? *I asked you guys to meet here so I could say that after Claire I can't stop wondering why I didn't and don't kill myself. Is it because I have hope? And if so, of what? What color of hope? The fake plastic pink one, that I'll see again? The milder, blue hope that my situation will change, get better, be something other than what it is? If it stays like this, will I stay alive?* I don't know who I'd have to be to ask my own worst questions out loud, but I'm not her.

The voices began to blend for me, until I couldn't really tell who was talking. I felt like I was melting into sleep. At some point we were all like, yeah, let's meet again here in a few weeks, maybe during the day next time. No one argued with that idea, obviously.

"One more thing about Claire M.?" Elizabeth Tallentine said as we were about to leave. I tuned back in.

"Yeah?" Zach asked.

"I think she was a very secretive person."

Logan said, "Apparently," under her breath. She's never liked Elizabeth.

"Whatever," Blythe said, so quietly I'm pretty sure I'm the only one who heard it.

Walking out into the woods together, we were all quiet. Logan was on my right, holding my hand again. It was midnight. Zach, Trey, Josh, and Coltrane were behind us, and Spark was just ahead. No one spoke. We staggered ourselves, walking back in the trees, rather than along the road, and then ducking whenever a car went by. It was the first time I'd ever been intentionally bad, if you don't count smoking Sarah's cigarette, or skipping piano and gym a few times. It felt pretty good, although maybe that's just because we didn't get caught.

Or maybe it's because we were hanging on to the few small honest things we'd said inside, inspired by the possibility that even though we knew well enough to stay scared, at least we weren't going to have to stay completely powerless, too. And maybe this is a disturbing way to put it, but I took comfort from the fact that Claire had floated up. She was underwater long enough to fill her lungs, and maybe she had hoped to sink out of sight forever, to be vanished and irretrievable. Maybe Elizabeth was right that Claire had been secretive, and maybe she had wanted to keep her whole story secret. But her body rose to the surface like truth.

Just before Thanksgiving break,

someone put a skateboard in front of my locker. Whoever did it apparently thought it would be funny if I stepped onto it and—what? Went flying headfirst into the bank of lockers? Slipped like a cartoon character on a banana peel? Cracked my skull against the floor or a wall?

What happened instead was that Logan (and everyone else) saw it there and Logan threw it in the trash chute that goes from the third floor to the inaccessible garbage dump in the basement. So everyone got to imagine me slipping and falling without it actually happening. And Logan got the unsavory task of telling me that it was there, and the heroic one of throwing it out. In other words, the humiliation happened, but not the actual killing myself in the hallway. Small mercies.

Some people are absolute assholes, but I already knew that, and I worked to remember that it didn't have that much to do with me. But it made me miss Briarly, where no one would have done that. There are lots of stupid things about Lake Main. Including whoever tried to kill me, and the idiotic announcement they made, definitely Claire-related, that for the rest of the year we would be focusing on our own "life histories." Ugh! All the teachers are frothing with delight about a "new curriculum that connects subjects in an organic way," and since the only thing connecting our subjects is that we're the victims of them, now we have to do "memoir work" in our classes: family history, history of our town, literature of childhood.

The art teacher, Mrs. Fincter, has pretty much made it clear that I'm a tragic special-needs invalid. So until now, she's been letting me do an "independent study" and leaving me totally alone, which I love. But now I have to make something that "represents my life." I tried to talk her into letting me use a collage I've been working on, but she said that was just an exercise, and I have to make a piece of "representative art" for this assignment, and it should "work well for me," the idea being that I can make something you feel instead of see. It has to use more than one kind of material. My mom is going to die of excitement when I tell her, and I know this is mean, but it makes me not want to tell her. Of course I'm not a complete monster, so I'm not going to tell her about the skateboard, either. I don't want to make her happy or sad.

In Mr. Hawes's history class, we had to do horribly embarrassing presentations. Basically, we had to pick a piece of history that was meaningful to us in a personal way and tie our own story to the story of someone who lived before us. And then stand up and yammer away about the connection, in front of a roomful of people who can see me but who I can't see. Which I hate, even when I'm the one who makes myself do it, like at the Mayburg place.

Anyway. Coltrane Winslow blew everyone's minds, or at least mine, by doing this presentation on Langston Hughes, even though I didn't think he was the type to read poetry because he's so law school. He ended by reading a poem about America, and saying how this was all of our Americas. Zach did his on a radical antiwar group in the 1970s, because apparently his parents were hippies before they became Republican bankers. Trey Brighton did the Rolling Stones, even though he had no way to tie them to his life, and Logan did Susan B. Anthony and the suffragettes because her mom gets to vote or whatever. I went right after this guy Jason Kane, whose presentation was this totally parallel-universe thing about the history of UFOs, which he tied to his "memoir" portion by saying that there was "no possible explanation" for what he and his dad saw one night over their house, and that they had no choice but to join the thousands of believers who aren't believed by anyone else, and how that's a lonely place, but they know for certain that UFOs exist.

I made a point of not laughing with everyone else, not only because I was in a mounting frenzy about my turn, but also because Jason Kane is batshit crazy, and isn't that bad enough? I mean, should he really also have to endure people making fun of him all the time?

I walked up the narrow aisle between desks, and a hum of oohing and aahing about Spark rose in place of the tittering over Jason Kane. I found Mr. Hawes's lectern, set my white cane down, took out my notes, and turned to face the class. Spark sat at my feet. Ms. Mabel had offered to come and help, and I had turned her down, not wanting to stand in front of the class with a babysitter. But now I regretted it.

"So, um, I'm going to tell you a little bit about the origins of the organization called Lighthouse for the Blind," I said, very fast. "There are Lighthouses for the Blind in more than thirty of the fifty states of America. The first Lighthouse for the Blind came into being because two sisters from New York, Winifred and Edith Holt, traveled to Italy and saw a group of blind kids listening to a concert. And, um, they were amazed by how much the kids were enjoying the music."

I felt extremely embarrassed then, and a flash of rage went through me, at Sebastian and Briarly and everyone who had ever mentioned Lighthouse for the Blind. Why was I drawing unnecessary attention to my predicament, right as everyone was starting to forget I existed, that I read braille or had a dog? I had to follow Seb's model and do a whole show about the Lighthouse?

I remembered the sound of Sebastian's laugh, and how I had never seen him. The rage subsided and I fell dangerously into sorrow over the unfairness of my having to stand in front of a room of people I couldn't see, of having no photos or video, of not being able to look at whatever images my classmates had beamed all over the walls. But I pulled myself up, took a breath, and continued. "According to the *New York Times*, if you lose one sense, your other senses may be heightened, especially your hearing, in order to compensate for that loss."

Long before the Lighthouse presentation, I had heard this stupid "fact" from roughly a billion people who were trying to make me feel better about my accident. But actually, only if you've been blind since birth or since you were really little do you get the bat ears. I bet Dee from Briarly has them, and maybe even Seb. If you go blind after you're ten, then you're stuck with your original, craptastic hearing. I didn't admit this, though, because if everyone wants to think I'm a superhero, why not let them? Anyway, when I said *senses*, I meant my mind. And my mind *was* heightened after the accident. I used to take seeing for granted, like everyone else, and now I don't. Now I can focus my thoughts, find things, taste them, hear, understand. I might have called it magical, but I didn't, because I know how to toe the line and not be Jason Kane talking about UFOs.

If I were brave enough to say the truth, in front of a class or to anyone at all—even Leah, my mom, or myself—it would be something like this: what's so terrible about the accident isn't even the me I've become; it's just the endless fear of not knowing who she'll be. Who I'll be. Leah's always telling me that we all contain dozens of versions of ourselves, and it's only the lucky ones among us who get to try out being more than one. She says change, even when it feels tragic, can actually be okay, lucky, good. And she said this even before my accident. I'm trying to believe it. But sometimes I miss the other me, the one I don't get to be—the innocent, okay one, who can still see like everyone else, who can still be young. And I don't get to know who I would have been if the accident had never happened. Leah says someday I'll love myself enough to be glad it happened, to be glad I get to be the person it made me. But I don't know yet if that's true.

The sisters who founded LFTB discovered that the blind kids were at the concert because someone had given them free tickets. And apparently they loved this idea and set up a free-tickets-for-blind-kids program in New York. Then it grew into this huge organization, with Lighthouses for the Blind everywhere, including one that taught blind people how to make brooms, which was better than nothing, because before that happened blind people couldn't get work at all, and apparently the brooms were really good quality. This made me think of how everything in the world starts as an idea—even human beings, who are just ideas that parents had, not even as literal as "I want a baby," but sometimes just, "I want you," or "I want this," and people come from those ideas, those drives. That's why ideas are wants, desires. And tangible outcomes—I mean literally tangible, like brooms or music—can come from small thoughts. Because of my giddy feeling about the Mayburg meeting, the possibility of making a difference, I said this during my presentation: that the reason the story matters for me "memoir-wise" isn't so much that it's about a blind organization, but just because it shows that thoughts are the beginnings of everything, including tables and airplanes and governments and organizations "like LFTB."

The room went silent when I said this, and that's how I knew it had been too weird to include. Sometimes, I'll make an observation that to me seems mundane and obvious, and some other kid will be like, "You're a freak." It's one of the reasons I prefer to say nothing.

I was already twitching with misery when this girl Riley Grossman was like, "Is that why you, like, love music?"

"Excuse me?" I asked.

"I just thought . . . you're really good at piano, or whatever, so is that, like, connected to your being . . . you know?"

"Um, no, I don't think so," I said. "Any other questions?"

"How come you decided not to stay at the blind school, if you don't mind my asking?" this guy named Casey asked. "How come you came back to Lake Main?"

I tried not to turn toward Mr. Hawes, even though I hoped he would say that the Q&A hadn't started yet or something. He didn't. So I just said, "Well, my friends are here, and I realized I could do whatever I needed to, so, you know . . ."

Then Savannah Clark, who just moved to Sauberg this year, asked, "What exactly happened to your eyes?"

I shivered. Obviously that wasn't related to my LFTB talk, and she had just arrived anyway, so she kind of had no business asking me private questions. And did she really not know? Had no one told her?

I said, "I had an accident, but it's kind of a long story, so maybe some other—"

I wondered then for a brief but terrible moment who had put the skateboard in front of my locker—whether it was someone in the room, someone like Savannah. Or someone I'd known forever. What if it was Zach Haze?

Mr. Hawes said quickly, "We are actually out of time today, guys. Great job, Emma. If you could stick around for one minute, I'd like to chat. Everyone else, have a great weekend and don't forget to read from pages 377 to 397 in *A People's History*."

People started to close their books and grab their bags, and I stayed in the front of the room, feeling cheated because everyone forgot to clap for my presentation but grateful to Mr. Hawes for cutting off the class early to save me from Savannah's rubbernecking, even though we still had seven minutes left before the bell rang. I walked over to his desk, and he said, "That was an excellent and brave presentation. I want to apologize for not chatting with you beforehand about what the parameters of the questions should be."

"It's totally okay," I said. "Please don't worry. That was fine." Was I no longer able to speak in sentences that weren't three words long?

I heard his planner clap shut. Then he opened and closed a drawer.

"Here," he said, and I realized he wanted to give me something, so I put my hand out, palm up. Immediately, I felt embarrassed by this gesture, by the way I thought my hand might look, empty, waiting, so I closed it, just as he tried to hand me something, so the thing dropped. I knew it was a pen from the way it bounced off my knuckles and hit the desk. I started apologizing, but he picked it back up and handed it to me while I tried not to feel so frantic. *Who cares if the pen dropped? Stop apologizing,* I thought. I rolled it in my hand, feeling the weight. It was smooth and heavy.

"This was my pen in high school," he said in an unsentimental way. "I want you to have it." Then he stood up, pushed his chair toward the desk. "I think you're an amazing student, and I wanted you to know that," he said. "I don't know if you still take notes with . . . but I thought—"

"Thank you," I said, hoping to save him from the awkwardness of remembering out loud that I was blind and might not want a regular pen. Because I did want it. And what was he going to give me, his braille stylus from high school?

"It's really nice. Thank you," I said. I thought I might combust with embarrassment. "So yeah, um, thanks again," I managed, willing my blood to calm down, my brain to quiet. I put the pen in the back pocket of my jeans and walked out with my white cane and Spark. Logan was waiting just outside the door. She had definitely been peering into the window the entire time, and was practically panting.

"What did he give you?" she asked.

"Nothing," I said. "So, what are—"

"No fucking way, Emma—you're not going to try to change the subject. What just happened in there? Was he like—" She cut herself off, because the door opened and Mr. Hawes came out and walked by.

"Whatever," I said, and started to walk, but Logan put her hand on my arm. "Oh my god," she said. "Did Mr. Hawes ask you out?"

"Are you insane?" I said. "Of course not! He just wanted

to tell me I did a good job on my presentation, and make sure I wasn't unhappy about Savannah's question."

"What did he give you? I saw him hand you something, Emma."

"You're crazy. He just handed my stylus back. Jesus." I felt the full force of lying to her as a kind of awful power and weight. I wasn't even sure why I didn't want to tell her that Mr. Hawes had given me his high school pen. But I knew I didn't want to, rule book or not. I felt bad instantly, but not bad enough. I was selfish. I wanted the pen for myself, the whole heavy, lovely secret of it. Like Seb's face and hands, my own secrets, the best ones no one else could touch or feel or see. I also didn't want Logan to be jealous, because if people are jealous of you, then they hate you. That's why I try so hard not to be jealous of her, especially about Zach, who's definitely flirting with her. When I was little, whenever anyone was mean to me, my mom always said, "They're just jealous," totally missing the point, which was that they still hated me. Who cared why?

Before Logan could press me further about the pen, or ask what Mr. Hawes had been doing with my stylus, or talk about the Mayburg place meeting we were cooking up for right after Thanksgiving, someone screamed "Boo!" and I was so startled that my teeth chattered.

"You're an asshole, Chad," Logan said, and I heard her

hand fly out and smack somebody. Chad Andrews, I assumed. Logan has a beautiful life. When guys make fun of me, or threaten me, she sees it first and beats the shit out of them. She gets to throw the skateboards down the trash chute and smack Chad Andrews. What would it feel like to be the one protecting her? And how could I have thought Logan would ever be jealous of me? What did I have? A pen?

I had to tell my mom about Mrs. Fincter's project over Thanksgiving, because I haven't started and the class has met roughly two million times since we got the assignment. My mom was wearing Baby Lily and roasting a turkey. The smell of the cooking bird was like noise for me, hot and complicated. As soon as I told my mom about the assignment, she asked Leah to watch the oven and took me to her studio in the backyard.

It was sharp and cold and quiet in there, a giant relief from the house. It smelled good, like glue and turpentine. My mom was so thrilled she could hardly contain herself. She set Baby Lily in this swing she has, with plush seafood rotating over her head. The thing clicks and rocks and plays tinfoil lullabies. Benj once identified the creatures for me, because after squeezing them myself, the only one I guessed correctly was the octopus.

"You knew because of the tenstacles!" Benj said.

"Exactly," I told him.

My mother put two giant lumps of unformed clay in my hands, and then fabric and buttons and wires and all manner of junk I had no idea what to do with. I was going to make a "representative art memoir" out of some clay and wires and recyclables?

"Let your mind guide you," my mom said. "Just listen to your thoughts and your hands will do the work." My mind rolled its eyes. Then I listened to my thoughts, but all I heard was the clicking of Lily's swing.

I snorted. But for the rest of Thanksgiving break, whenever my mom was busy, which was basically every second, I sneaked into her studio by myself, feeling the walls, the concrete floor under my bare, cold feet. I left Spark in the doorway, and found the clay, which she took out of a huge wet bucket. I listened to and smelled it: it was off-red to me, and prehistoric, like my mom had dug it up from the core of the earth. I smushed it around for a bit, thinking about my face, wondering if human beings would be extinct soon anyway, and if so, whether that made my problems any less real. It kind of did, I decided, and I made a mental note to think about the apocalypse anytime I started feeling sorry for myself. Then I thought, as I always do, no matter what train leads me there, of Claire, under the ground. Is it worse to be dead if everyone else is still alive? Yes. Just like it's worse to be blind if everyone else can see. Even though being different is the only way we can define ourselves against each other, it still sucks. If everyone were blind, it wouldn't be a big deal that I can't see. And if everyone were dead, then Claire wouldn't be at a disadvantage anymore.

I made a ball out of the clay, and picked up a twig of wire my mom had also given me. I twisted the wire into a spiral, and then picked up another one, and made a spiral out of that, too. My mind was quiet while I was doing this, a rare relief until it became like a creepy, empty room. Then I gave up and, in an odd move, carried the lump of clay with its spirals out of my mom's studio. For a week I kept it on my nightstand, until it was dry and crumbling, but the wires stayed in.

Then I wrapped it up and brought it to Deirdre Sharp's house the first weekend after Thanksgiving, for the second sleepover of my blind life. I guess it was like a blanky or teddy bear or something, but smaller and grosser, since it was crumbly. I was really nervous about the sleepover. It was me, Logan, Blythe, Amanda, and Nicole, a girl whom none of us had ever met before but who was apparently Deirdre's best friend from summer Bible camp. And I don't think Deirdre would have invited that group if it hadn't been for the Mayburg meeting we'd already had—and the one scheduled for the day after her party.

My mom had insisted on calling Minister Sharp and

Mrs. Sharp to make sure they were okay with having a dog at the house for the sleepover. They said yes, likely because my mom made it clear that it was a deal-breaker for me if Spark couldn't come, because of my "situation." And even if she hadn't called ahead and made a huge thing of it, no parents really want to be the ones who don't let their child befriend the blind kid. Having a blind friend might widen your kid's small, homogeneous life experience, especially if you're raising her in Sauberg. I didn't come up with that by myself, by the way. It's something I heard someone say to my mother after I got out of the hospital and everyone came to our house with lasagnas so we wouldn't first get blinded and then also starve to death that month. That's what we do in this town: we make lasagna. No matter what. When my eyes caught fire? Lasagna. When Claire drowned in the lake? Lasagna. When our second-grade teacher, Mrs. Jacobson, had to stay in the hospital for two weeks after her baby was born? More lasagna. The only death or emergency that ever went uncelebrated by a two-ton brick of pasta was Bigs the rabbit's. So maybe it's a species thing. Maybe you have to be a human being to warrant a snaking lasagna parade arriving at your clan's dwelling in the wake of a maiming or death.

Deirdre's dad is a minister, and her mom is a mom, but for some reason (one that interested Logan intensely), their house was fancier than either of ours. Deirdre also wasn't interested in stuff or popularity or clothes. Logan asked if Deirdre would take us on a tour of the house. The walls felt beige, like Dr. Sassoman's. There was no smell of cooking, or chaos, or art supplies, or animals, or even people, really. Logan held my arm and whispered in my ear, "I had no idea her house would be so posh. And she never shows off, you know?"

Deirdre's parents were hugely conservative, and maybe they preferred a modest, quiet daughter. I wondered why they'd been successful in making one, while Claire's parents would definitely have loved a Deirdre-like daughter but had gotten Claire. Blythe's parents, too. I thought of my own mom, who has so many daughters that she gets to have it every way possible, maybe another reason for wildly overpopulating the earth with your offspring.

Mrs. Sharp ordered pizzas for us and then vanished upstairs. Minister Sharp came down and said that he and Mrs. Sharp would be on the fourth floor.

"Enjoy yourselves, girls," he said. "And if you need anything at all, don't be shy. Just come up to the fourth floor and tell us right away. Or text me, Deirdre."

"Okay, Dad," Deirdre said, clearly impatient for him to leave and not embarrass her any further, although he didn't seem to me to be more or less embarrassing than any of our dads.

"We are at your service," he joked. Okay, so that was embarrassing.

"Thank you, Minister Sharp," Logan said in her pink-flower-and-glitter voice.

"Bye, Dad," Deirdre said.

"I'm going, I'm going!" he said, and then his footsteps bounced up the carpeted stairs. He was wearing socks. I wondered what they looked like—whether they were sporty and white tube socks like Benj wears, or sleek man-tights like Logan's dad's, or argyle socks like my dad wears under his loafers. You can tell a lot about people from what socks they wear. If they're unmatched, or have holes, or are pristine or whatever. But before I could ask Logan about Deirdre's dad's socks, a question only she would have understood and forgiven, she leaned into my ear. "Minister Sharp is hot," she said. "He's super young and looks like Mr. Hawes."

"I gathered," I told her.

"How'd you gather? From his beautiful voice?"

"From yours, actually."

She giggled again. "He was wearing jeans," she said. "And blue socks, in case you were wondering."

"I was, actually."

"I know, you weirdo. Can you believe they have a four-story house?"

We all gathered in the kitchen and ate pizza and drank Coke. I poured my own, dangling my pinky slightly into the Styrofoam cup like Mr. Otis had taught me, so I could feel when the soda reached the top. Nicole, Deirdre's summer camp friend, lived in the city, and you could tell she thought she was a super-cool urbanite among a bunch of hayseed-chewing bumpkins, because she was like, "Oh, your accents are so cute! No one in the city talks like that."

While we burned all the skin off the roofs of our mouths on pizza, Nicole chattered about her private Catholic school in the city. "It's a total celibacy prison," she said. "We're the inmates." Only Deirdre laughed. I wondered if they were like Logan and me.

"Can Nicole come to the Mayburg place tomorrow afternoon?" Deirdre asked, and I said, "Sure, of course." Then Nicole said, "Cool, thanks. I'll check my schedule," and Logan snickered.

"Yes, do that!" she said. "And have your people call my people."

No one laughed; it was too hostile. Nicole said, "Um, did I piss you off in some way? Because if so, I'm sorry."

"I was just kidding," Logan said.

"I don't think you should haul in just to sit in that creepy dungeon and listen to a bunch of whiners from Lake Main," Blythe said. I was surprised, but didn't say anything.

"Whiners?" Logan asked. "We were just trying to have an honest conversation."

"Yeah, well," Blythe said.

Deirdre was like, "Let's have cake."

Nicole had a mind of her own, apparently, because she said, "'Creepy dungeon' sounds cool. Why don't we go over there tonight?" No one answered her.

We ate a chocolate cake that Deirdre's parents had set out on the counter, and then she opened up the presents we'd brought. Nicole got her a locket, Logan and I brought leopard-print pajamas and slippers that matched, which Deirdre claimed to love. Logan had picked them, obviously, and I felt shy and sad giving a present I had never seen. Amanda gave Deirdre a Ouija board, which I thought was an awful and unfunny joke, and Blythe brought three bottles of wine she had stolen from her parents. I wondered how Deirdre felt about that. I mean, we were in her perfect house with her minister parents—were we really going to risk them coming down and catching us drunk? And if so, why? She also got Deirdre a set of lipsticks I would have found insulting, maybe like a hint that Deirdre wasn't working hard enough at being pretty.

We took Blythe's wine to the basement, where there was a dull hum of machinery, which reminded me of a hospital. It would be weird to be an only child like Deirdre, with her super-adult parents and life and immaculate house. I was thinking maybe she did homework all day long, taking breaks only to go to church. Nothing in her house was loud or broken or dirty. I had a rare stab of envy. I was never jealous of Logan's house, because it felt terrible and lonely, but Deirdre's felt luxurious to me. There were many ways to live.

"Let's break these open!" Blythe said, and then there was laughter.

"What if your parents come down?" I asked.

"No chance," Deirdre said. "They promised to leave us alone. They have no reason not to trust me, and they can't hear us; they're, like, a mile away upstairs."

Suddenly they were all laughing again, but I didn't know why. "It's a miracle you got that out," Amanda said, and Logan whispered in my ear, "Blythe had the wine opener in her pocket, and her jeans are so tight she had to pry it out with a crowbar."

I was sitting on the carpet, with Logan's sleepover voice in my left ear and my back against a couch that smelled of new car. I had a hand on Spark; he and I were both twitchy and homesick, and I was petting him, wondering if I was going to have to relearn how to relax and have fun at a slumber party now, too. Although honestly I couldn't remember if I had ever found a slumber party much fun, even before the accident. Are slumber parties fun or just one more thing we all do because we don't want to be the only ones not doing them, the way grown-ups have dinner parties and go to holiday "functions" at the hospitals where they work? If I could have gone home the instant we finished pizza and cake and presents, I would have, just like a four-year-old. I would have snuggled my mom and Benj and Babiest Baby Lily and Naomi and gone to sleep in my own bed, happy.

At least Spark was there, in between me and Blythe, who was on my right. We had opened all three bottles of wine and started drinking them simultaneously when Amanda brought up the Ouija board idea again. I stayed quiet. I was hoping that Amanda would drop it and we could hang out and talk and maybe put on some music. But I didn't want to be the one to admit to being scared, of course. I can always find a reason to say nothing. Logan handed me wine; we were drinking straight from the bottles so that Deirdre wouldn't have to hide wine-stained glasses from her parents in addition to the empty bottles, which Blythe had already said she'd take out in her sleepover bag in the morning.

"This present includes delivery and removal service," she said, swigging from the bottle and passing it to me, and for some reason—maybe the wine taking effect and warming me up—her voice gave me a jittery feeling. I was oddly aware of it every time her arm brushed mine over Spark, or her hand grazed me when she passed me one of the wine bottles.

"You okay, Emma?" she asked.

"Yeah," I said, and took three quick sips from the top of the bottle, before passing it to Logan, her familiar head leaning in close to mine. *The wine,* I thought. *Taste the wine, focus. Relax. Close your eyes and relax, Emma, focus in.*

But as soon as I narrowed in on the taste of the wine, it reminded me of finding my mom drinking in the kitchen last year, and I went hurtling back toward that night, toward my own left eye and the word *livid* and my mom's weird, sad laugh. I tried to hold my nose. Not smell the wine or laughter, not think of mud or rubber ducks or *livid,* even though the braille cells lit up in my mind: the straight, clean, logical line of the L; the 2 and 4 of the I; the V, just like L except that dot 6 is also raised; another I; and then D, which I no longer confuse with H. D is 1, 4, and 5.

Stop, I thought. *Just let the heat pour down your throat. My throat.* But my nose, used to working overtime, couldn't turn off. The wine tasted like burning tires, like raised braille dots for *livid,* for flames, for my mom, for mud, for Claire, for dead, for rubber ducks, for chaos.

"I'm drunk." Amanda was giggling, and there was a murmur of agreement. "Let's do it."

"Do what?" Blythe's voice was close to me. I felt a drumbeat in my stomach.

"The Ouija board!" Amanda said.

"I don't know," Logan said, and I was glad, since I didn't want to be the one to say no.

"Come on, it'll be fun," Amanda said. "It's just a game."

Deirdre said okay, maybe because she didn't want Amanda to think she hated the present. Or maybe she actually wanted to play. So just like that, we all decided we would "try it out." Nobody mentioned summoning Claire—we were all just like, "Well, we'll see what happens if we open the game, and blah blah"—but raise your hand if you're too daft to sense it's a bad idea to play with a Ouija board in the middle of the night at a sleepover that your dead friend would also be at if she weren't dead.

"You guys go ahead," I said. "I have to go to the bathroom." I waited just a beat, until Logan asked, "Want me to come?"

"Sure," I said, and stood up and followed Spark and Logan down the hall. Spark waited outside, but once Logan and I were in the small room, which I knew somehow was peach colored, I told Logan I was freaking out.

"Why?" She hugged me. "Are you okay?"

"I don't know. Something about the wine, or the crowd, something." Spark scratched the outside of the bathroom door.

"Do you want to go home?" she asked. "I'll take you if you want. We can sleep there instead."

Just hearing that calmed me enough that I no longer felt like I needed to leave.

"No," I said, "that's okay. But thank you."

I could tell that she was relieved; that she hadn't really wanted to leave, but had been willing to on my account. This made me both grateful and lonely, because it meant Logan was actually having fun, but I was just pretending to have fun. I secretly wished I could go home and be with my mama. Pathetic. Would the original, not-blind Emma have felt this way? Or was this just the new, damaged me? And how would I ever know who I would have been if I had just kept growing up on my normal track? I decided I'd try to have fun. To be more like Logan, more like everyone else.

"Do you think Deirdre'll wear lipstick now that Blythe got her some?" I asked Logan in a fake bubblegum voice. "I mean, I took Blythe's present as a kind of hint. Did you?"

"Maybe," Logan said, and she popped something plastic back in place, maybe the top of her own lipstick.

"Are you putting on lipstick?" I asked.

"Mmm-hmm," she said, and then, "You want some?"

"No thanks," I said. "And I don't think she should, by the way."

"Who should what?" Logan asked me.

"I don't think Deirdre should wear lipstick just because Blythe got her some. I mean, unless it's something she wanted to do anyway." I pulled my skirt up and my tights down, sat down to pee, thinking this hadn't come out as fun as I had hoped. Why was I such a downer?

"The colors Blythe got her are insane," Logan said cheer-fully, zipping her purse. Then I could feel her leaning over the sink, maybe peering at herself in the mirror. I put my hands to my face, felt my same familiar skin, my hair, longer than it had been in a while, wavy and probably still super dark like all my sisters', but who knew? I smoothed my former bangs down and tucked them behind my ears. They've gotten longer and I've started kind of using them as a curtain over my face. Maybe if my eyes still worked, I wouldn't be able to see any-way. Dr. Walker and my parents like to talk about how lucky I am that the rest of my face was "unaffected" by the accident, but we all know that's utter bullshit. How much better would it have been if that rocket blaze had burned my forehead? I could have worn bangs and seen for the rest of my life. The band of my eyes seems to me to be the worst-case scenario, the word *unaffected* outrageous, insulting.

"She got the absolute slut pack—all dark blood reds and blacks and a hot-pink iridescent one. I think it's kind of funny, actually. Isn't it the rule about a good present—that it has to be something you'd never buy for yourself?"

"I guess," I said. "But not if the reason you'd never buy it is that it makes you feel like shit or is totally out of the realm of anything you'd ever want."

"I dunno," Lo said. "Deirdre *should* have more fun, and she could be really pretty if she tried."

"Maybe she doesn't care as much about being pretty as Blythe does," I said bitterly, and we both knew that I meant Logan, not Blythe. And that she'd meant me.

"You don't have to worry about it, so you don't understand."

I stood up and pulled my tights and miniskirt back up. "What the fuck does that mean?"

Sebastian's friend Dee from Briarly wore makeup. She's a total, too, and she once told me she kept one rubber band around her blue eyeliner and two around her black. She had her own systems and never seemed to forget what was what. I didn't ask her what the point of wearing makeup was, even though when I told Logan about Dee once, that's what she asked. I didn't have to ask, because I got it right away: it's not like because you're blind you don't care what you look, or feel, like. You can still feel fat or ugly or sweaty or whatever, all the ways you can feel when you're not blind. Maybe Dee thought wearing makeup was fun, or that being beautiful was something you should be allowed to do even if you weren't sighted. However she thought of it, I don't agree with Logan that blind girls have to worry less.

But apparently she meant something else anyway, because she said, "It means you're prettier than me, which is why you get to be above worrying about prettiness."

I almost spit. "I'm *disfigured*," I said. "In case no one mentioned that. I can't even take my sunglasses off, because if everyone saw my face they'd run like it was a zombie movie. And I can't see. So how about we all just agree to talk about what's pretty less often?"

"Why are you so mad at me all the time?"

I didn't answer her, not because I wasn't mad at her, I realized, but because I wasn't sure why.

Once, Dee asked me what I looked like, and I said, "I don't know." Because I was mad at her, too, and tired. She asked how I could not know, so I gave in and said, "I have long, dark hair. And I wear sunglasses."

"Why?" She came up to me then and touched the edge of the plastic frame of my cat glasses. Her hands smelled bright pink, like the soap that came out of the dispensers in the Briarly bathrooms.

"Because my best friend gets them for me," I told her, and then, after a beat, I added, "And I don't want anyone to see my eyes."

"No one here can see."

"Not true. The teachers can."

"Only some of them."

"Well, I don't want the air to see my eyes."

I thought about the Briarly soap as I washed my hands in Deirdre's bathroom, where the soaps were little shells in a dish; I could smell the pastel colors. While I was picking each one up, turning it over in my wet hands and then returning it to the dish, Logan said quietly, "I'm sorry if I said something wrong, Em. I just meant you still look like yourself, that's all. And I still think if you just were more yourself around other people—just, like, let go a little bit, talked more the way you do when you're with me—then anyone who didn't already get how awesome you are would know—"

"It's fine," I said. "Don't worry about it."

Even though I didn't think I liked her when I was at Briarly, I suddenly missed Dee. How could I explain to Logan that I hadn't even cared that much about what I looked like before the accident? And what could how I look to other people possibly mean now? Any conversation about it infuriated me. The way we talked about looks at Briarly was way better than this; looks were a feeling. I couldn't see myself, and as far as I was concerned, no one else was allowed to have an opinion about what I looked like. Not even Logan. This was something Dee would have understood, even if she didn't feel the same way.

"What do you mean by 'like myself'?" I asked Logan.

"Like this," she said, and she took both of my hands and put them on my face. I felt the familiar skin, the bones of my cheeks and jaw. She ran my hands, under hers, down to my shoulders, over my breasts, down to my stomach.

"Just like you always did, except even better with your big

boobs," she said, and I could hear her grinning, feel the dimples in her cheeks deepening. I put my hands up to her smile, felt her cheeks. I thought of Seb then, almost the way I think of Dr. Sassoman: like Seb was a part of me. Maybe I'll remember him for the rest of my life whenever I touch anyone's face.

I can feel my body more and more lately, maybe because I'm blind but maybe just because I'm older. It feels good sometimes, and strong. But since I can't see anyone else's body, what do I have to compare it to? I can hardly ask the other girls if I can feel their bodies to get a sense of where mine fits in.

As if she had read my mind, Lo said, "Now, if you want something to compare that to, I'll ask Elizabeth Tallentine if you can feel her up. But trust me, everyone talks about your body all day long at school."

"That's mean," I said.

"I didn't mean instead of your face. I just—"

"I meant about Elizabeth."

"Oh. Right. Sorry. I take it back, okay?" Logan opened the bathroom door and headed out into the hallway back toward the game room as a way to end the conversation, which I found annoying and manipulative. But I followed her out anyway. What choice did I have? I grabbed Spark's leash as we went back toward our friends. It was oddly quiet.

"Hi, guys," Logan said.

"Hey, have a seat here," Deirdre said, standing up and putting her hand on my arm. She led me to an open spot on the carpet and I sat. Spark sat behind me, and when he realized I was going to be awhile, he curled up and rested his head against my back so I'd know he was still there. I petted him gently.

"We did one round while you guys were in the bathroom, just to get started," Deirdre said, and her voice sounded unhappy, far away.

"It was crazy," Amanda said giddily. "We think maybe she's trying to talk to us. Here." She moved something on the board; I heard it click and slide, and tried to turn my fear into focus. Someone had lit candles. I could smell the lingering sulfur of the match, the waxy, burning crayon of the candles. I leaned over to Logan and whispered, "Where are the candles?"

"They're on the table," she whispered back. "They're fine—no dripping or anything."

"What's the clicking noise?" I asked Logan, slightly louder but still whispering.

"That's the planchette," Amanda said, to my annoyance.

"The what?" Logan asked her, in a loud, rude way.

"It's the piece that slides along the board and spells out what Claire is trying to tell us."

Logan sucked in her breath. "This is a horrible idea," she said.

"Lighten up, Logan," Amanda said, and Nicole was like, "Yeah, Jesus Christ!" and I could feel Logan straighten up like she'd been shocked with a cattle prod. I knew Amanda's insult would be echoing in Logan's ears for a while, especially since city-Nicole had put a big exclamation point after it. I should have stuck up for her, but I felt too swirly and blurred.

"Fine," Logan said, giving up, giving in. "Whatever you want, Amanda." And she scooted forward to join in whatever they were doing with the board.

"We need two more people to put their fingers on the planchette," Amanda said. I hated the way she said *planchette*, like she was a big expert on spiritual communication tools, or speaking a foreign language we all had yet to learn. Or wanted to learn, for that matter.

"Why don't you join in, Emma?" she asked. "Don't you have, like, special sensitivity in your hands?"

"Uh, not really," I said.

"Come try anyway," Amanda said. "You guys didn't have a turn last time." Logan put her hand on my back, helped move me in toward the board. I felt backward with my left hand for Spark.

"Come on, Blythe. Put your hands on, too," Amanda said.

"What about Deirdre?" Nicole asked.

"That's okay. I'll watch this time," Deirdre said. She sounded upset.

"Okay, so it's me, Blythe, Emma, and Logan," Amanda said, and if I'd thought she had said it for my benefit, I would have considered it thoughtful, but it was clear she'd made the announcement for the sake of some ghost or other.

"Here we go," Amanda said. We each put our fingers on the board, over a little wooden piece that felt, when I picked it up for a moment, like a guitar pick. Amanda took it and set it back on the board.

"We all just hover above it; no one needs to grab it or hold on to it or anything."

"Okay," I said. No one else responded.

"Ask the board a question," Amanda said.

"Does it have to be someone who's touching it?" Nicole asked.

"No, it can be anyone," Amanda said.

"Okay," Nicole said. "Are there any spirits here?"

We all sat there, and our fingers started pushing at each other's. I don't mean to be a giant killjoy, but I was pretty sure that Amanda was guiding the movement. Our hands moved together, even though I couldn't feel the planchette anymore.

There was a squeal and everyone inhaled sharply. "Okay, so yes," Amanda said. "It went to the 'Yes' on the board, for anyone who can't see from where they're—oh my god! I'm so sorry, Emma. Was that, like . . . was that—"

"Was it what?" I asked, wanting to punish her for being

rude to Logan a minute ago but only succeeding in coming off as an uptight shrew myself.

"I don't know," she said. "Rude? I mean, I didn't mean—I just meant anyone who can't see the board."

"Right. And that includes me. It's fine, Amanda."

"Oh good, okay. So anyway, the yes? That means there are spirits here." She dropped her voice back into its creamy, ghost-ass-kissing register.

"Who are you, spirits?" she crooned. "Will you please tell us your names?"

It wasn't lost on me that Amanda talked to both me and the Ouija board "spirits" in the same patronizing baby voice. I wondered if the ghosts found it as annoying as I did.

Our hands were moving again, and this time I let myself get lost in it, feel the group push of what I figured were our imaginations and desires, which Amanda and maybe everyone else believed were Claire's thoughts. And who knows? Maybe that's what a spirit is, right? The collective memories and thoughts of people who knew a dead girl and want to believe that her energy still exists in the universe.

"H," Amanda said. "H what, spirit? Is that your name?"

"O," they read.

"Ho?" Logan said, laughing. "The spirit is a ho?"

I laughed, too, but Amanda shushed us furiously. "Shut up!" she said. "Do you want to piss her off? Are you crazy?"

"I thought this was a game, Amanda," Logan said. "Remember how you just told me to chill out? Maybe you should chill out."

"God, Logan. You really need to back off. I'm just saying, why not be respectful about what you can't be sure of?"

"What is it I can't be sure of?" Logan asked.

"What exists in other dimensions," said Amanda. "Do you think you know everything there is to know about science and the universe?"

"Obviously not," Logan said. "Do you?"

"Shhh," said Nicole. "Do you feel that?"

Our hands were moving again. "U," everyone but me said. "S. E."

"H-o-u-s-e," Nicole said. "It spells *house*."

"What house, spirit? Can you tell us your name? Or the name of the house?"

This time I worked to keep my hands still, to let them move only if I actually felt like some power beyond me was moving them. But I felt nothing but the pressure of the fingers of the group, making my hand move with theirs. And the whole operation was the opposite of piano, or even braille—anything that has color in it, depth, joy, or meaning. I was all blank.

"B," Amanda said.

"L," said Logan.

"X," said Logan.

"This is bullshit," Blythe said.

"Come on, Blythe!" Amanda said. "What if Claire is trying to tell us something? Don't you want to hear what it is?"

"What if you're trying to pull some of your regular bullshit, Amanda?" Blythe asked. "I don't want to hear what that is."

"Okay," Amanda said. "Everyone, shake your hands out. Let's start again."

We all shook our hands at the wrist, and even as we were doing it, I was thinking, *At least three of us don't want to be doing this, so why are we?*

"I only want to do this once more," I said, "and then can we please do something else?"

"Me too," Logan said. "Let's have this be our last round."

"Fine by me," Blythe said.

"Whatever, you guys," Amanda said. "Fine. Let's start. Who wants to ask the question?"

"Why don't we all ask together?" I said.

"Okay, if we can agree on a question," Amanda said. "How about, 'What are you trying to tell us, spirit friend?'"

If my eyes had worked in their old way, I would have rolled them endlessly. But they didn't and I didn't. I just synced my voice with everyone else's: "What are you trying to tell us, spirit friend?" we all asked, and the room vibrated with our vocal cords. Then our hands moved quickly, and I got nothing—no texture, no truth, nothing. I didn't care what they said; just wanted to have the stupidity over with, to be home in my own bed, a baby, safe in my mom's orbit.

"L," Amanda said.

"P."

"Space."

"L, P, space?"

"W," Nicole read.

"*Lap? Wow?*" I said, as our hands went all over the place into a huge scramble of letters and I felt furious in a way I hadn't since my days on the couch with my braille cube. Nothing meant anything, and we were making it worse, further confusing ourselves and each other. And for what?

"You know what, you guys? Fuck this," I said. "It doesn't mean anything." And I went back to the bathroom alone, called my mom, and asked if she'd come get me.

And she did, and I left, and Logan stayed.

Logan showed up at my house at one o'clock the next afternoon and forced me out of bed, where I was listening to *Alice in Wonderland*, still in my pajamas. I had my clay head on the nightstand next to me and Mr. Hawes's pen and a valentine Zach Haze made for me in third grade under my pillow. Zach made one for everyone, of course, but I spent hours poring over mine, hoping to find a clue in it that mine was extra special in some way. And now it is, because I've kept it a million years and it's definitely the only remaining one in the universe. Normally I kept these treasures in my desk drawer, but lately I've been putting them under my pillow. Maybe because things, including parts of me, can disappear without warning, and I want to keep them close. Maybe I'm going crazy.

"What happened last night?" Logan asked.

I didn't say anything. She went and got me a hoodie and basically pulled me out of bed.

"Come on," she said. "We have our second meeting and you can't miss it. Everyone is counting on you."

"Yeah. I'm such a pillar of strength."

"No one said anything about you leaving, Em. That Ouija board thing sucked, and everyone blamed Amanda. But it got better after. We—"

"Yeah, Lo? I don't really want to talk about last night. Maybe we should just—"

"Okay, fine."

I got dressed in silence and then we breezed by the kitchen to the mudroom to put on boots and a parka. As we left the house, I called back to my mom, who was cleaning up lunch, that we were going on a walk.

"But you haven't eaten, sweetie. And it's freezing!"

"We need fresh air," I said. "And I'm not hungry."

It was so cold that I could feel the steam coming off me. I could almost see our breathing, but neither Logan nor I spoke until we were halfway to the Mayburg place, when she brought up Deirdre's again. "So, Em, I know you don't really want to talk about last night, but I just thought, in case it came up or whatever, that you might want to know that some of us snuck out for fun. It was no big deal, we just wanted to see if we could do it, so—"

"You guys snuck out of Deirdre's? Who's 'some of us'?"

"Me and Blythe and Nicole."

"Wow. Where were Amanda and Deirdre?"

"Asleep."

"Don't you think it's kind of rude to sneak out of Deirdre's house and risk getting her in trouble?"

"I wanted you to come, Em," she said, "but you had already left—"

I said, "I didn't mean me, okay? Forget it." And we walked the rest of the way without talking.

The Mayburg place was so cold it felt like a cave, and I imagined icicles coming both up from the floor and down from the ceiling. But in spite of that, and the fact that our first meeting had been a disaster, there were twenty-one of us by three o'clock, fifteen from Lake Main, four from Pendleton, and two friends of friends, Nicole and some guy visiting Carl Muscan.

"Is Blythe here?" I asked Logan.

"No."

"What about her foxy Pendleton friend?" David Sarabande asked, meaning Dima. He had heard us? How close was he standing?

"Shut up, David," Logan said.

Then Amanda Boughman shouted, because she apparently thinks I'm deaf, "Hey! Emma? I know you're in charge or whatever, but is it okay if I say something?"

Obviously I said, "I'm not in charge. Go ahead."

So Amanda said, "Well, this is really crazy, but last night some of us were at Deirdre's and we think Claire was trying to talk to us," and naturally that made everyone freak out for all sorts of reasons: first of all, it's rude in human society to bring up a party that no one else was invited to, so Deirdre started apologizing all over the place and talking about how her parents only let her have a few people or whatever, and then a bunch of guys were criticizing Blythe for not showing up, saying how if we were going to make any progress figuring out why Claire "offed herself," Blythe's input would be necessary. Of course, that expression freaked out other people, including Monica Dancat, who was like, "Why do you guys have to be so rude and degrading?"

And David Sarabande made this whiny sound like he was imitating her, even though he sounded nothing like her at all. "Yeah, why can't you be a big *feminist* about her overdose?"

The word *feminist* was like a gray, spitting snake, weaving through us like something toxic and awful. No one, not even Carl Muscan, laughed.

"I'm not a feminist," Monica said. "It's just, 'offed herself' is kind of, I don't know, disrespectful."

"What would you call drugging yourself to death and then drowning?"

"I don't know," Monica said. "Passed away? Died?

Drowned? Why does there always have to be such an asshol-ish value judgment in everything you say?"

"Whereas 'assholish value judgment' is respectful?" Da-vid said.

"Fine, you're right, whatever," Monica said.

But then Coltrane Winslow shocked everyone by asking, "Why aren't you a feminist?"

I felt bad for Monica. I would have hated to be on the spot like that. "I don't know," she said. "I just meant I don't, like, hate guys or whatever." At this point I heard clouds in her voice.

"But *feminist* just means you think men and women don't get treated like equals," Coltrane said. "And they don't. Women make seventy cents for every dollar men make."

Someone—one person—was clapping. It sounded like a death cough. Apparently someone wanted to join Coltrane in social suicide, and it was Elizabeth Tallentine, because she stopped clapping to say, "I totally agree with Coltrane. I mean, look at Congress—it's eighty percent men? And Fortune 500 companies run by women? Ten of them. What the fuck?"

I agreed, obviously, and so did my mom and dad and Sarah and Leah, and everyone I'd ever met who had a brain, but there was no way I was going to be like, "Yeah, I totally agree! Hooray for women!" at the Mayburg place. It's shame-ful, but I didn't want everyone to think I was a guy-hater lighting my bra on fire.

"I totally agree," Logan said, and my self-loathing was complete. "And I think it's relevant, because if girls could feel better about ourselves, then maybe—"

"Yeah? It was because men earn more money than women in certain jobs that Claire OD'd? You can't be serious," David said. "Guys kill themselves more often than girls anyway, so it's not society's fault."

"No, they don't," Coltrane said. "Girls attempt suicide more often. Guys succeed more often because they use guns."

"Have you guys ever heard of the rule of three?" Amanda asked. When no one responded, she said, "It's just that suicides happen in threes, so probably at least two more of us—"

Logan cut her off. "I'm just saying we'd be less suicidal if society was better for girls, David; not that we—"

"I think it's pretty fucking good for girls," David said. "How about you work and pay the bills and I get to stay home and play with the kids?"

"*Play?*" Logan shouted. "My mom works like a slave so she can feed us, while my dad . . . whatever."

"Well, not every dude is a complete slacker, Logan," David said. "You can't really hold all males responsible for the bad choices of a few females. The *many* bad choices." Then he laughed. "Like mother, like daughter."

"Shut the fuck up, David," someone said. It took me a minute to accept that it was Zach.

"Why don't you take that shit up with her?" David said.

"What's your problem?" Zach said, and I heard scuffling and then something hitting something else—hands, maybe, on something. I couldn't tell what was happening, and I put my head in my hands, half to rock and half to protect it in case the sky fell. Something was happening on the floor— were they fighting on the floor? I kept trying to move back, but there was something behind me—boxes, or a shelf. I heard Logan shouting, "Stop it! Quit it!" And then the door opened and there was more shouting outside, but I held my hands over my ears for what seemed like a long time.

Logan came back in. "That was horrible," she said. She put her hand on my back. "It's okay. Emma. Emma, stop." I stopped rocking. I heard movement around the room as people came back from whatever they'd all seen and I'd missed.

"Em? You didn't miss anything. A bunch of guys rolled around in the grass punching each other like fucking idiots," Logan said. "And then Josh broke it up and they all ran into the jungle. We should keep talking, instead of everyone just leaving now and proving Sauberg right that we're too stupid to have a conversation at all."

"Josh broke it up?" I asked her, because he's shy and nerdy. She shushed me.

"So where should we start?" Josh asked. So he'd heard me. I vowed never to say anything about anyone ever again. People shuffled chairs and lit cigarettes and settled.

Coltrane said, "I wanted to say that I don't really believe in accidents. I don't mean that in a religious way, but I think Claire's killing herself does matter for the rest of us."

The sound and color of his words made me feel like everything could be understood eventually if we all just worked and talked and tried hard enough. Like meeting up had been worth it, the exact opposite of how I'd felt literally thirty seconds before.

But Carl Muscan asked, "Matter how? What difference does it make? Dead is dead, right? We're not going to bring anyone back by talking about shit here."

"But we never thought we were going to bring her back," Logan pointed out. "We just thought if we could understand why she did it—whatever *it* is—we could prevent—"

"You're not going to prevent anything by sitting around in here smoking and talking about whether Claire slipped or jumped into the lake, Logan," Carl said.

"We might, actually," Coltrane argued. "People don't kill themselves unless they have an opportunity—like a gun or a cliff to jump off of or a lake to drown in."

"So, what?" Carl said. "So the lake is cordoned off at that beach now; you think if it had been cordoned off before, Claire wouldn't have found some other way to OD or die anyway?"

"He has a point." One of the Pendleton kids—or someone I don't know, anyway.

"Where was Claire getting the drugs?" Josh asked.

"Carl, I don't get why you have to shoot down everything everyone says," Logan said. "We're just trying to imagine what Claire felt like, or what happened to her, so we can all do better in some way. What's wrong with that?"

"Nothing," Carl said. "What's wrong with me disagreeing with you? Why are you so insecure and bitter?"

"Um, excuse me," I said quietly. "But what about Josh's question?"

"Thank you, Emma," he said.

"I'm sure she got the drugs from her pill-popping mom," someone said. Again, I wasn't sure who it was.

"Or Dr. Keene's office," Amanda said.

Blythe's dad, Dr. Keene, is the town dentist, so I guess he can probably get drugs. But I thought it was really weird that Amanda would say that. I was glad Blythe wasn't there. Everyone started shouting then, arguing about whether Dr. Keene was giving Blythe and Claire drugs and if there was a point in trying to guess and if it was slander to say Dr. Keene's name and did Amanda know something and how you could get drugs anywhere, on any playground, including at Lake Main, and blah blah.

Finally, we were all wrung out and deflated and everyone was shouting about Zach and David's fight and the stupidity of our having decided to meet here again, and I was just trying to ignore it all when Logan grabbed my hand and pulled me out the door and into the thick trees. I walked quickly, with my face down, holding Logan's hand and Spark's leash, breathing as evenly as I could. I had to lift my legs high to come down safely on the bed of twigs and leaves covering the ground. When we emerged onto the highway, I heard gasping and realized Logan was crying. Unlike the rest of us, Logan never cries. I stopped walking and hugged her.

"That was horrible," I said. "I'm sorry. We'll never do it again. This whole idea was—"

"It's not that," she said. "It's . . ."

"Carl and David are complete assho—"

"No, it's just . . ."

"What? Amanda? Claire?"

I wanted to keep cutting her off. I must have had a sense that whatever was bothering her was going to be trouble for me, too. And I was right, because as soon as I was quiet for three seconds, she said, "Remember how Zach asked Trey about the Cannons show?"

"Yeah."

"Oh, Emma," she said, and started crying again.

"Yeah?"

"I ended up kind of going."

"What do you mean?" My voice sounded sad and far away, and I saw the words appear in a speech bubble about my head. Then they floated off.

"Well, Zach called?" Lo continued.

I decided not to talk anymore.

"He called to see if I still wanted to go to the concert with him and Trey? But he only had one extra ticket?" Why was she telling me this like there were questions in it?

We were in the middle of the sidewalk, frozen, leaves swirling around our feet. The date came at me, the time: December 7, 5:49 p.m. I turned on my GPS and it told me where I was standing, even though I already knew. It smelled like winter, and I knew I had to be home that second; that I couldn't stay, couldn't listen, couldn't speak, couldn't see. I had to be in our kitchen, smell whatever my mom was cooking, touch Benj and Jenna and Naomi, hear Leah's voice, eat my mom's dinner, answer my dad's barrage of doctor questions, and listen to whatever shouting and crying and wild drama was taking place there. I thought suddenly and clearly of Seb, took a breath and got my white cane ready, bent my knees like a sprinter at the starting line.

She had gone to a concert with Zach. Okay. I could feel my mind trying to file this information in the right place— 1. *Let go, try not to suffer over it; 2. Deny this until much, much later, maybe even decades from now, when you won't care anymore; 3. Panic fully and cry uncontrollably, etc.*—when Logan said, "So, um, Em, there's something else."

I still said nothing.

"Last night? When Blythe and Nicole and I sneaked out of Deirdre's, we went over to Trey's for a minute and Zach was there, too, and we were drinking a lot, and, well, Zach and I kind of—we've been kind of, I don't know . . ."

I didn't help her.

"So, okay. So I wanted to tell you, but, okay. I should start with—I lost it."

It took me a minute to recover, but then I said, "Congratulations, Lo. You . . . last night, you mean? With—? I mean, that's great. I'm happy for you." It fell to the ground like a body. I was shuddering.

And she said, "No, no, not last night, not—it's kind of complicated. I mean, it's a disaster, actually."

"What's a disaster?" I asked, trying to keep my voice neutral, trying to imagine what it would be like to be Logan, to be having secret sex with Zach Haze, gobbling up the gorgeous world with my eyes.

"The sex thing," Logan said. We'd been planning this conversation for years, planning to fall in love at the same time, with best friends (Trey and Zach, for example), losing our virginity on the same night, feeling identical, telling each other everything. Did anyone have that friendship? How did other girls work out their secret differences?

"I totally regret it," she added.

"You totally regret what?" I repeated like a feverish parrot, confused, trying to remind myself that this was about Logan and not me. I had walked her up onto an embankment, and she came around the other side of me.

"Losing it," she said. "I fucked it up, because this guy from Pendleton, Brian, I—"

"Who's Brian?"

"He's no one. Just this guy."

"You lost it to him?"

"Kind of."

"But then you and Zach—why 'kind of'?"

"Because I didn't tell, you know. I didn't tell . . ."

"Who, Zach?"

"I don't want any of the guys to know. I was hoping they didn't know, so they wouldn't think I'm—But I am. I'm—" She made a noise that was worse than any real word could have been, a collection of a's, c's, g's, and h's that didn't belong together. I recognized what it was without effort or thought: it meant disgusting and ruined, and I got it so clearly I might as well have made the sound myself. It was how I felt about my left eye, but I would never have felt or thought or used it about Logan—or anyone other than myself.

She was chewing her hair. "I don't know. Last summer, Brian and I were—"

I tried to think. Last summer. When I was finishing at Briarly. When she was begging me to come back to Lake Main. When Claire died. Who was Brian? She had had sex with someone last summer? When? Was that what David Sarabande meant when he'd said "like mother, like daughter," and why Zach flipped out? And if so, did everyone else on the planet know more about Logan than I did? I stopped walking and tucked my head down for a moment, rocked, dug my elbow into my side to stop the weird feeling that was threatening to topple me.

"Emma? Are you okay? Why do you keep doing that?"

"Why didn't you tell me?"

"I didn't want . . . It was an accident; it didn't count."

I couldn't help myself. "So you didn't tell anyone?"

She didn't say anything. Everyone knew. Except me. She hadn't told me because I would have been a babyish, jealous PBK about it. I was inexperienced and pathetic; how could Logan confide her tortured, sexy secrets in someone like that?

A tiny switch in me flipped. "Run," I said to Spark, and I took off, with my white cane bouncing in front of me and Spark by my side, also running. The white cold air hit my lungs like smoke, and froze me from the inside out. But I kept running. I didn't need to hear the rest of whatever Logan was about to tell me. Once, we had never lied to each other, and now? What did any of it, even our whole history, even mean? The pavement rose up and pounded the bottoms of my boots. Spark galloped, pulling the leash in my right hand taut while my graphite finger scratched furiously in front of me, as if it would save me from something in my way. Maybe it wouldn't have. But there wasn't anything.

I made it to my house alive, gasping the freezing air, and feeling, in spite of my tremendous rush of fear and sorrow and the real danger that running put me in, proud. My mom was flying down the front steps as I came up the walkway.

"Emma! Jesus!"

"Hi, Mom."

"Logan just called, she said I had to come and find you, that you were running by yourself, that you, I was just—"

"I'm fine, Mom. I just felt like running." I had only been three blocks away, and the fury started to rise up my body. Did she think I couldn't survive a three-block run alone? Because I could. I just had.

"By yourself? Logan was so worried," my mom said.

"You mean *you* were worried," I said meanly. "But I'm fine. As you can *see*."

The phone started ringing and my mom went back inside, hurt. I headed straight into my bedroom and slammed the door. The Mayburg place? Meetings about Claire? How stupid had I been to think that I could do anything, have any effect on anyone? I pulled back the green curtain and climbed into my tent bed, hid. I would never go out again, I decided. Two seconds later Logan knocked, but I stayed in bed, half hoping she would go away and half hoping she would come into my room and never leave and say something that could undo the whole thing, make it all right. Except, what would that be? She came in, pulled the cold lime curtain open, and sat with me. I thought, for some reason, of the moon. Its broken surface and green curtain color. *Focus in,* I told myself, *and please don't cry.*

"Emma, I'm so sorry I didn't tell you about Brian. I know it broke the rule, and it was totally wrong of me, but please, I'll tell you now. It was just because I was embarrassed, or . . ."

I didn't tell her that I had lied about Mr. Hawes's pen, about actually thinking her mom was a terrible mom, about Seb or the way his face felt. I didn't say I wished for last year again, to be back at Briarly.

Had we both changed so much that we couldn't know each other for real anymore? And either way, why shouldn't she get to be the love of Zach Haze's life, someone I couldn't know, let alone be?

"Are you in love?" I asked, hoping this was a deeper question than the one burning at the surface, which was whether they had had sex last night while I sat in a pool of my own chills at home, too scared to sleep over at Deirdre's, a blind crybaby? When had they started? Just now? Last night? At the concert? Last summer? Right after Brian?

She paused, then asked, "Me and Zach?" in a quiet way that reminded me more of my voice than hers.

"Yeah," I said, too loud. "Are you in love with Zach Haze?"

"What do you mean by *in* love?" she asked.

I did the math fast. "That's fine, that's okay," I said. "I don't like him anymore anyway. My thing was just . . . whatever."

"Really?" Logan asked, and the relief in her voice almost made me take it back.

"Yeah," I said. "I like someone else."

"Seriously?" she asked, fake happy.

"Yeah. I have for a long time."

We both sat there. She didn't ask me who, and not even because we both knew it was a lie; just because she didn't get to ask for my secrets anymore.

And that's how the L&E rules shattered into a web of windshield glass. Because even if we hadn't both been lying to each other unstoppably, our other big rule was we had to tell each other what we were thinking and feeling. Which I could obviously no longer do—ever again.

-10-

For the two middle weeks of December, it snowed all over Sauberg, just like last year. And just like last year, I couldn't see the flakes as they twirled and blew around, as they landed on the frozen surface of the lake, Lake Main, our yard, the Sauberg cemetery, everyone's eyelashes—or, in my case, sunglasses. I've been wearing plastic ones because my metal pairs are too cold now.

I listened to everything everywhere go silent; the listening gave me images of the places I couldn't see. I thought and tasted white. Hanukkah happened, and I performed the motions, which my parents and Dr. Sassoman giddily called progress. Progress was me, at sundown, smelling candles without blacking out, opening presents: audiobooks, a deck of braille playing cards, a new collar for Spark, a beaded necklace Naomi and Jenna made me, fur boots from Leah. Progress was me handing my sisters presents my mom had bought and put my name on.

Days, I went to school in a numb white daze, one that felt like snow. Nights, I lay awake listening to Naomi's sleepy breathing, thinking how a steady diet of tragedy teaches you to rank what matters. I told myself that how I felt about Logan mattered more than how I felt about Zach Haze, and that fifty years from now, unless we're dead, Logan and I will still be friends, and neither of us will be dating Zach Haze. So who cares which one of us gets to date him now? Because even though I'm young and most people think that being young means you have no perspective and are stupid about what things will matter in the long run, I'm aware that Logan and Zach being in love isn't the end of the world. Because I've seen the end of the world twice—when I stopped seeing and when Claire stopped being alive. So I can fake that it's okay even though it's not. And I can try to convince myself that my experiences—even the accident and Claire, and Zach loving Logan—will eventually add up, the way dots in their proper cells do, into a structure I can understand. Maybe even something "worth it."

I was in my room, working on my clay memoir, when my mom confronted me. The sculpture was now a clay dog and a disposable chopstick that I'm turning into a white cane with surgical tape and a small marble. I was sitting at my desk, surrounded by my treasures: a rock I had found once in the lake and spun in our rock polisher until it felt like a jewel; some plastic, hollow rubber grapes that Leah had popped off the string they had hanging over the produce in the supermarket and that she had then given to me. They feel green and purple, give me colors. And Mr. Hawes's pen, my journals, my L&E notebook, some notes Logan had written me over the years, even the Zach valentine. Two pictures: one of me holding Benj when he was first born, and one of me and Leah and Sarah in a play garden that was outside our apartment in the city. I can't see them, can't tell which is which, but I also can't give them up.

"Em?" my mom said, and it sounded like maybe she'd already said my name several times. I turned toward her.

"Yeah, Mom?" I felt a tumbling in my chest. Maybe she knew something. About the Mayburg place? Or Logan? I wondered how she'd feel about my having set up two meetings at the Mayburg place, one of them in the middle of the night. Probably hysterical. The thought gave me a surge of defensive pride, like the running had.

But instead she asked, "Have you been skipping Ms. Spencer's class?"

That was it? "Maybe a couple times," I said. I'd been skipping for a week straight, since we got back and Ms. Spencer assigned us *The Inferno*, which was clearly as terrible an idea as the Ouija board. It's typical that no one thought to revamp our educations toward maybe preventing us from dying of fear. I mean, a terrifying journey through hell? During our "memoir" coursework? And when we were already unable to sleep and living in cold-dread fear of death and ghosts and Claire and our town and ourselves and each other?

"Ms. Mabel called me. She's worried. Do you want to tell me what's going on?" she asked.

"Nothing's going on," I said.

This was so obviously untrue that my mom and I both sat there for a moment, wondering what to do about the lie.

She sighed. "Em?" she said. "If you don't want to tell me, you don't have to, but please go back to class tomorrow. Please. Spare me a meeting with Principal Cates and Ms. Spencer."

"Ack, blah, effff," Baby Lily said, as if she'd been listening the entire time and only now felt that it was appropriate to contribute to the conversation. I reached my arms out gratefully and took her. She felt twice as heavy to me as she had two days ago. My misery lifted a bit.

"Hi, big girl!" I said to Lily. "How'd you get so big? How did you, big girl?"

"Blarp bun doot!" Lily said to me, grabbing at my sunglasses and trying to tear them off so she could shove them in her mouth. I gave her my hand instead, and she put my fingers straight into her slobbery beak and chomped down.

"When will she talk?" I asked my mom.

"She is talking," my mom said.

"Right, I get that, but I mean, when do the words become actual words?"

"Benj didn't talk until he was two," she said, "but you had words at ten months."

"So only three months left for you before *ark* and *ack* and *blurp* become English, you big baby," I told Lily hopefully, and she laughed her fat belly laugh.

"Do you think Baby Lily is like me?" I asked my mom.

"I think she's the most like you of all my girls," my mom said. "But also herself."

"We're reading *The Inferno* in Ms. Spencer's class," I said.

"I know, honey. I got you the audio—oh." She thought for a moment. "Is that why you're not feeling up to going?"

"Ms. Spencer keeps asking what we think of it," I said.

"What do you think of it, Em?"

Baby Lily was making a *pfzzing* noise with her drooly lips and stuffing my hand into her mouth. I leaned in for a big baby kiss and then wiped my mouth on the back of my other hand.

I decided to tell my mom the truth, which was that I had listened to the *Inferno* CD and the words "my heart's lake" on the first page of the first canto had electrocuted me with terror. I didn't know if I'd ever be able to forget the way those words sounded or felt, and I couldn't undo them, like the *livid* of my scar. I didn't want to talk about any of that in class.

After I said I hated "my heart's lake," I added, "I think we're all shadows. And that we're vanishing bit by bit, especially me." I handed Baby Lily back to her. This was the most I'd said to her about my secret inside life since the accident, and the worst and the weirdest. My mom knows I'm weird, and she's weird, too, and there are good and bad weirds, as she's always told me. My parents don't love normalcy, like everyone else in Sauberg, who are all, "My kids are so average, it's fabulous!" Still, I try not to say things that freak my mom out, now that she's a fragile person who slashed her own paintings and needs my dad to take care of her. But she's always asking me everything, and for some reason, lately I feel less like sparing her. Maybe she's getting better and can take it more. I don't know.

"What do you mean you're vanishing, Emma?" Of course she would land on that. She sounded desperately unhappy.

"I just mean when someone dies, they're gone. So Claire vanished, and so did part of everyone who knew her. And I already lost my eyes, so it's like, I don't know, I'm being erased every time some new terrible thing happens, and they keep happening. Like the rabbit. And other things. It's like I'm losing pieces, disappearing, kind of dying, even if it's, whatever, gradual."

I don't even know if I meant to make it better or worse, but my mom stopped breathing, and I kept on, picking up speed. "Now all that's left of Claire is a conversation no one can even agree on—and a huge pile of meaningless junk: trophies and notes and photos. And that's what it will be for all of us. Some pens and plastic grapes and diaries or whatever. It's like we're already ghosts stumbling through our own useless *stuff*. I mean, that's it. That's what gets left from our lives! Who cares how you live or who you are if it adds up to balls of clay and boards you formed into walls and a roof? And it does. That's what I mean by shadows. That we're all going to be utterly gone *forever*, so how real are we even now?"

"But Emma," my mom almost shouted, "we're alive! And my god, what about love? What about family? Joy? And why is stuff meaningless?" She was panicking. "Objects help! They're not meaningless, and we make them *because* they outlast us," she went on, missing my point so wildly that I actually imagined her swinging naked into the conversation from some incredibly weird angle and crashing into what I had said. She was thinking of her sculptures, of course, trying to make everything better, but I didn't want her to make it better. I just wanted her to hear me.

"Stuff helps people when we lose each other. It's not meant to replace human life, but to represent it, to memorialize. We need graves, shrines, art," she said.

I hadn't been to Claire's grave. Maybe it was covered with snow. Frozen lilies, teddy bears, goggles. I thought of Claire underneath all the stuff, alive. She ran into class once, late, flushed, her face all blotchy, almost as multicolored as her hair. I thought of her putting melty pink pills on her tongue, and then her tongue, also pink in my mind, like taffy. I saw her drinking, or doing whatever it was that made people say she had a problem—dizzy Claire; smart Claire; night-swimming, dancing-naked-on-the-roof-with-Blythe Claire; betraying-her-parents, taking-the-ghosty-bowl-that-day-from-the-Mayburg-place-when-we-were-kids, washing-up-dead-in-the-lake Claire. Which Claire had dragged her down to the lake and thrown her in? Which Emma might drag me into the water? Had Claire been terrified of herself?

Baby Lily started crying, and I realized it was because I was crying. My mom reached out for me, but I pushed her hand away, recovered. "I'll go, Mom," I said.

"That's fine," she said. "I'll even write a note excusing you from the discussion if you—"

"Absolutely not," I said. "I already have people throwing special-needs favors at me day and night. Do you think I want to be considered mentally ill, too?"

"Emma," my mom said. "Everyone agrees that you're doing brilliantly, in school and out. I mean, look at what you've accomplished, and it hasn't even been two years! There's no reason to throw barbs like that."

I almost told her about someone leaving the skateboard

in front of my locker, because I knew it would be exponentially more painful for her than it had been for me. I almost told her about Logan and Zach. But I settled on a different and equally successful attack: "Yeah? Everyone agrees? Even Dad?"

My mom swallowed hard, and Baby Lily's crying turned into straight shrieking. I put my hands over my ears, saw flashes of the screaming, like lights in my mind.

"Especially your dad," my mom said over the screaming, loud enough for me to hear. I felt bad for her.

She carried Babiest Baby Lily downstairs, and I pulled the wire glasses out of my new hideous lump of wet clay, rolled it back into a ball, and stuck two big, round plastic grapes in where the glasses had been. Then I taped surgical X's over the grapes. Eyes. Isn't it weird that in art, crossing out your eyes equals death?

My mom must have said something to him, because first thing the next morning, my dad came and found me in her studio, where I was shredding paper. He asked if I would go to the hospital with him. It was Sunday, so I was surprised.

"To work?" I asked.

"I don't have to work, but I want to take you there. Would you mind?"

I said of course I'd go, and felt excited and honored, even though I thought it was probably a trick of my mom's to make me feel excited and honored. Sometimes placebos work even if you suspect they're placebos.

In spite of the thrill of being asked to go somewhere alone with my dad, I felt so tired in the car that my head kept falling down onto my chest and then snapping back up. My dad was telling me a story about a colleague of his who thought a patient had one disease but then it turned out she had some other disease. Then he asked me about school, about Logan, about Mr. Hawes, about my LFTB presentation, about gym, English class, *Antigone*, *The Inferno*.

I felt like I couldn't really respond. "You tired, Em?" my dad finally asked, and I felt him turn away from driving, toward me, and the car swerve a little. I reached up involuntarily and grabbed the bar above the window. "Why don't you rest a little bit and I'll wake you when we get there," my dad suggested.

But I didn't want to. Even though I didn't want to answer his endless questions, I also couldn't remember the last time I'd been alone with my dad, except on occasional doctor visits and once when he took me in for my final surgery. But I could hardly remember that, and I had been too afraid and miserable to think, let alone enjoy his company in the car. Now here I was, in the front seat, going to work with him for some reason other than my own tragic health, and I was too tired and distracted to absorb it.

"I'm fine," I said. "I don't want to sleep. Tell me why you wanted me to come."

"There's someone I want you to meet," my dad said.

"A doctor?" I asked, my hope sinking.

"No," he said. "A child, actually."

"What's his name?"

"Her name. Annabelle," my dad said. "She's nine."

"Why do you want me to meet her?"

"Because I think you might be able to help her," he said, and I was surprised. I was used to my parents taking me to people who they thought might be able to help me.

"Really? How?"

"Wait until you meet her," he said. "I think you'll understand each other."

By the time we pulled into the parking lot at the hospital, I felt both accomplished and also wrung out, like I'd just taken a standardized test. And, as always, unsure of whether I'd passed.

The smell inside the hospital made my pulse quicken, and the birds inside my body started flying in opposite directions, pulling my ribs and lungs apart. I held tightly to Spark's leash with my left hand, and my white cane with my right. My dad put his hand on my shoulder and guided me to the cafeteria, where I said "no thanks" to food or a drink but he bought two muffins and two juices anyway, and a little bag of Swedish fish, so I would have something to take to Annabelle. I began to feel nervous that I would be a disappointment to her, and therefore also to my dad. When he'd first asked me to come with him to the hospital, I thought it was a favor to me, but in the café, when he was buying the Swedish fish and asking me what else I might want or thought a nine-year-old might want, I began to feel like I was actually doing him a favor. And I didn't mind, but I also didn't want to get it wrong.

"I don't know her, Dad," I said. "Maybe after I meet her, I can come back down and get something she'd actually want."

"Good point," he said.

"Have a good day, Dr. Silver," the cashier said, and I had a flash of his being famous at the hospital, everyone knowing him as Dr. Silver. I wondered if I'd ever be known anywhere for anything other than being a tragic disaster girl. I moved along the slick floor and into the elevator, where my dad said, "Em, can you please push sixteen?" This was another test I wanted to pass. So I slid my index fingers across the cold steel braille, felt for the backward V that turns letters into numbers, then found the 1 and the 6 and pushed.

"Thanks," my dad said—proudly, I thought—and his voice bounced off the metal walls of the elevator as we rode up and up. There were other people in the elevator. I wondered who.

On the sixteenth floor, my dad pushed open the door to Annabelle's room, and I smelled lilies and balloons and something else—candy, maybe; a plasticky red cherry smell I couldn't quite identify. Maybe lip gloss. Or Twizzlers. It reminded me of Logan.

"Emma, this is Annabelle. Annabelle, I brought my daughter Emma to meet you today."

There was no voice, just a sound I recognized right away as the movement of a mechanical bed. I couldn't tell whether its occupant had moved it up or down. I can tell if people have moved higher or lower only if they speak; closer or further away I can hear in other ways.

My dad waited a bit for Annabelle to say something, so I tried to be Leah about it, said in a friendly, big voice, "Hey, Annabelle, so nice to meet you."

Still nothing.

"Emma is blind, too, Annabelle," my dad said, and I heard a swallow come from the bed, like maybe some crying was rising up in Annabelle's throat.

"Can I sit on your bed with you for a little while?" I asked.

My dad said quietly, "She's nodding."

I nudged Spark forward, and we made our way to the side of Annabelle's mattress, which I felt with my hands before hoisting myself up and sitting on the edge. I felt small suddenly, my legs dangling off the mechanical bed. Annabelle still didn't speak, but I felt her hand come out from under the thin, bleachy hospital quilt and feel around for where I was. She found me and, once she had, left her hand limp on my lap, like it had died there. I picked it up and held it.

My dad must have been watching this. His voice sounded like a clogged drain when he said, "I'm going to let you two hang out together for a bit. Emma, push the call button on Annabelle's bed when you want me to come back."

"Okay, Dad," I said, and the words sounded strong to me, like soldiers marching out of my mouth in a neat line. Maybe because my dad was sad and scared for us, or because Annabelle was too freaked out even to speak yet, the fact of my being able to talk seemed suddenly like a huge achievement, one my dad would have no choice but to notice. We knew something he didn't know—what it was like to lose our sight. We were older than my dad in this regard, more experienced. His shoes made a shiny sound on the floor, and then he pulled the door closed after him. I heard the swallowing sound in Annabelle's throat again, and I knew she was trying not to cry.

"You can cry in front of me," I told her. "I can't see anyway." I laughed a little bit and squeezed her hand, hoping to cheer her up, but she took a short, gasping breath and started to sob. I was afraid then, because I didn't know her story, or what had happened to her or her vision or her face, but I reached over and felt her face anyway, thinking if it was as terrible as mine, she would be bandaged. I put my fingers lightly on her cheeks, then moved them up to her eyes, which were closed and wet from crying but not wrapped or patched.

"It's really scary, right?" I said. "I cried all the time, too. But not anymore." I didn't mention Claire, or the fact that I had cried the day before.

I felt Annabelle's small face bob up and down on the pillow. She had a cute nose, I noticed, tracing my fingers over it: little, with a slight tilt up at the bottom. I leaned forward and felt around on the tray I knew would be right next to her bed. I found a box, felt its edges, slid it toward myself, and pulled a tissue out. I put it in Annabelle's hand, and she took it, lifted it almost involuntarily to her face to wipe the tears, but I stopped her hand. "Feel it for a second," I said, and she did.

"It feels white, right?" She said nothing, and remained motionless on the bed.

"You can wipe your face if you want to," I said, and she did. I felt her little arms move up to her face and scrub at the tears, and deduced that she hadn't been in an accident, because she wasn't gentle with her face. It must have been a disease that made her eyes stop working.

"Do you want to tell me what happened?" I asked her,

partly because I thought she might, and partly because I thought she might want me to tell her what happened to me; I think it's weird for older kids to talk about themselves before younger kids get a chance to. It's something I learned from Naomi and Jenna and Benj. Mostly, if a little kid wants to know something about you, they'll ask. Adults who talk about themselves in front of kids are creepy. And so are big kids who don't ask little kids questions first. But since Annabelle didn't say anything, I was kind of at a loss.

So I asked, "Do you want me to tell you what happened to me?" I put my hands gently on her chin, so I could feel her nod.

"I was at a Fourth of July party with my family—my mom and dad and my sisters and brother. I have five sisters—I only had four then because my littlest sister, Lily, wasn't born yet—and my brother, Benj," I said, feeling like I was falling headfirst down a mole hole. I steadied myself, remembering. "We were standing in the front—my dad and I were, I mean; my sisters and my mom and Benj were on a blanket. But anyway, we got there early, just so we'd have a good place to see the fireworks, and my dad and I love them most, so we wanted to be right up near where they were lighting them. But then when they started, one of them blew up backward and sprayed fire and pieces of the bottle rocket into the crowd right where we were standing. And some of it hit my eyes, and they were burned." My face felt very cold, and there were colors all over the place in the room.

Annabelle was making the swallowing noise again.

I tried to focus on her instead of myself, even though it was the first time I'd told the story. It hadn't sounded sharp and broken and dangerous, the way it felt in my mind. I added, in a quiet voice, "So that was a really bad thing that happened, right?" I could hear her crying, and feel her nodding.

"I don't know what happened to you," I said, "but I bet it was also bad. And scary. Did you used to be able to see?" She nodded again. "And now you can't, right?" Right.

We both sat there for a while, thinking about each other.

"I learned to read again," I told her. "Braille. I can get all my favorite books, and my computer talks to me." She stirred a bit at this, not enough that anyone watching would have been able to pick it up, I think, but just enough that I could sense it, feel it.

"You like computers?"

More nodding.

"Me too. I like science, too," I said, thinking before I added, "Especially robots."

At that, she sat up a little straighter.

"There are robots to help kids like us," I said. "Computers that read to you, sticks that feel the ground in front of you, music players that put on whatever song you ask for. Sometimes," I said, "I even feel magical."

She was so still I thought she might be holding her breath.

"I pay really super-close attention to stuff, like this." I squeezed my face into its tightest focus position. I had never even considered doing my focus-in thing in front of anyone else, but I knew she needed it, and besides, just like I couldn't see her crying, she couldn't see me struggling, wishing, hoping so hard it made my head explode.

"When I focus as hard as I can now, I can understand— or kind of see—almost anything," I told her. "I couldn't really understand as much before I was blind. Maybe because I didn't have to."

She swallowed. I was thinking how shy I would have been if she hadn't been shyer than me. How scared I would have been if she hadn't been more scared than me. How everything we feel depends on who we're feeling it next to. I felt grateful suddenly for my sisters and Benj.

"Do you have brothers and sisters?" I asked her. She nodded.

"One?" She shook her head.

"Two?" She nodded.

"Brothers?" She nodded.

"Both of them?" She nodded again.

"Are they older?"

At this, she took my hand and put it on hers, so that I could feel she was holding up one finger.

"One is older?" I guessed.

She nodded, vigorously this time, and I had the thought that she might be smiling. I smiled, and put her hand on my mouth so she could tell.

"What about the other?" I asked. "Younger?" She nodded, and put my hand on her mouth. She was smiling, too.

"They'll be able to help you figure out fun ways to set up your house so you can get around. And maybe read you stories. My sisters did that for a long time, before I learned to read braille. But now I read to them, late at night, when we're supposed to have the lights out, because I can read in the dark, under my covers, and nobody knows."

I could hear Annabelle's breathing. It had picked up, and had a smooth rhythm.

"Do you want to know the best thing, though?" I asked. And before she could even respond, I said, "You might get a dog like Spark."

At the sound of his name, Spark perked up. "Stand up, boy," I told him, and he stood up on his hind legs, putting his face up to where Annabelle and I were. "You can pet him," I told her, and she reached over with both her hands and felt the sides of Spark's face. He wagged his tail happily, and she leaned her face in close to his. He was so overcome with delight that his tongue came flying out of his mouth and he slobbered all over her face.

"Spark!" I said, but she kept her face right up in his.

"He really likes you," I said, genuinely impressed. "He's not usually such a kisser."

We stayed like that for a minute, and then I asked if she wanted a Swedish fish. She took my hand, which I took to mean yes, and I pulled the bag from my pocket, tore it open, and gave her a handful. She ate one and fed one to Spark. I don't usually give him candy, but he loved it and I didn't want to do anything to make her sad, so I let her feed him the rest of the fish.

There was a knock at the door, and then the sound of my dad's shoes squeaking across the floor. He said hello, and I said to Annabelle, "Did you hear my dad's shoes?" I still had my right hand resting lightly under her chin. She nodded. "That's the sound of black on a white floor."

"How are you guys doing? Emma, you ready to head out?"

I said I was, and leaned down to give Annabelle a hug. When our faces were right next to each other, I heard a tiny whisper of a word come out of her mouth into my ear. It was so soft and weak, maybe from however long she hadn't spoken, that I wasn't even sure what it was or that I'd heard it, except I was, and I had: *Spark.*

My dad kissed the top of my head as we walked outside, a little, awkward peck, like a dad bird. Then he cleared his throat.

"So, that was an okay exchange between you and Anna-belle?" he asked.

"It was fine," I said.

"Did she confide anything in you about her experience?"

"I told her what happened to me and then she told me she has an older brother and a younger brother and that she loves robots. Oh, and dogs."

"She said all of that?"

"Not with words," I said. "I don't think she's in the mood to talk yet. She mostly used her hands and her face."

"Thank you for meeting her, Emma," my dad said. "And telling her your story."

"What happened to her?"

"She has a disease called RP, or retinitis pigmentosa."

"What is that?"

"We don't know that much about it, except that it runs in families. It's extremely rare to be blind from RP so young, and we're concerned because in some cases it's caused by syn-dromes that create other problems as well."

"What kind of problems?"

"Deafness."

"Oh." I took this in for a minute. "Will she be deaf, too?"

"Well, it's not always . . . well . . ." he stumbled, not want-ing to tell me.

"So she will."

My dad sighed. "In her case, yes, it looks like—"

"When will she lose her hearing?"

"We don't know yet."

"Does she know she's going to be deaf, too?"

"No."

I took this in. "Are her parents blind or deaf?"

"No."

"What about her brothers?"

"What about them?"

"Are they blind or deaf?"

"No."

"But will they be?"

"Her older brother is unaffected, but her younger brother appears to be suffering from RP as well, yes."

"Oh." I imagined Benj, awake in his toddler bed at night, snuggling Champon, knowing that he would go blind, too. Like me.

"Why is she in the hospital?" I asked.

"She had some gene therapy that was meant to improve her vision."

"But it didn't."

"The results were not optimal, no."

"That's horrible," I said.

"Well, not if she ends up being a brave and brilliant warrior like you," said my dad.

-11-

We decided to try again at the Mayburg place in January, after New Year's, which I spent reading and sleeping. Logan went to California to see her dad, and the Sunday she was supposed to get back, Naomi woke me at five in the morning. She said she wanted to give me a card she'd made; she was too excited to wait until I woke up. I was still basically asleep, but I propped myself up, tried not to be annoyed, and opened the envelope.

"Want to read it to me?" I asked her, yawning.

"Nope!" she said.

"Uh, how am—"

I opened the card up and felt the surface on the inside. Up bumped two dot sixes, for "all caps," and I laughed. Then a raised 2 and 4: I; 1, 2, and 3: L; 1, 3, and 5: O; 1, 2, 3, and 6: V; and 1 and 5: E. Then, the crowning triumph: a solo 1, 3, 4, 5, 6: Y for YOU.

I screamed.

"What!? How did you get the YOU like that? Have you been learning grade two already?"

She was laughing gleefully.

"I found a glossary on the computer! To surprise you!" she said, so proudly I could hear the warm color of her cheeks.

"It's the best card ever," I said, kissing her. "I love you, too." Then I pulled the covers off. "Follow me," I said. "I want to show you something."

We went upstairs, where everyone was still asleep, and I told her to pull down the attic ladder.

"Why?" she asked, scared. We all hate the attic.

"You'll see," I said. I lifted her up and she pulled the hatch open and released the ladder, and we made our way up slowly, with her in front. I touched and counted the rungs, five of them; pulled myself through the opening into the attic. Then I felt my way over to the window.

"Open this," I said, and she did. A blast of icy air came toward us, and then we climbed out, Naomi holding my hand. And we sat in our pajamas on the winter roof, feeling the sun come up. Naomi told me where it was—over the lake, over the roofs, directly over us, and I felt and smelled it, bright yellow in a mint-blue sky.

"Emma?" she said, when we'd been sitting for a while. "Can I ask you something?"

"Of course."

"What happens at the May-Bird place?"

I was quiet.

"Emma?" she said again. "Are you going there again?"

"Yes."

"Can I come with?"

"How'd you know about the Mayburg place?"

"I didn't mean to listen, but I just heard you always talking about it to Logan." I couldn't tell what kind of look she had on her face, and I felt sad but didn't want to reach over and look. "You can say no," she said. "I was just . . . I don't want to be home with the babies all the time. It's boring."

"You can come with," I said. "We just meet to talk, but maybe Leah can come, too, because I don't know if I can get you there myself."

"You took me here to the roof!"

"*You* took *me* here," I said, and she laughed. I felt around for her hand and held it.

I was both horribly nervous and thrilled the following Saturday. Knowing Leah would be at the Mayburg place embarrassed me, but I had asked her to come, and to bring Naomi. What if Leah found the whole idea stupid? What if Naomi changed her mind and told on me? On the other hand, what if Leah was impressed? I wanted to impress Leah at least as much as Naomi wanted to impress me.

Logan got back from California in a very sad and weird

mood, but at least she called me to see if I wanted to head to the Mayburg place early that Saturday, because some of us were going to clean the place up a bit. Carl and Josh and David had already driven away a bunch of junk in Carl's dad's truck. Logan and I walked over, and she told me about California, how her dad went out at night, too, like her mom, and she was mostly by herself at his place, watching TV. Spark and I half listened to Lo and half focused on where we were walking, what was in front of us. And as we approached the Mayburg place, my slight hope of the meeting going well was smothered by a thick, sudden smell I got before anyone else: cooking bacon, cigarette smoke, burning wood.

"What is that?" I asked.

"Hello? What's going on here?" Logan asked.

"Nothing," said a slightly laughing voice I didn't recognize. "Why?"

"Are you here for the meeting?" I said, and immediately regretted it.

"Sure," said the voice, and then laughed. "What meeting?"

He was older than we were. And we didn't own the Mayburg place; we were trespassing. We could hardly demand that someone else, someone older, leave because we were "having a meeting."

"We're trying to figure out what happened to our friend Claire," Logan said. "Did you know her?"

He whistled a low whistle. "I know who she was," he said. He sounded pretty sincere, and Logan's voice softened.

"What's your name?" Logan asked him.

"Jason," he said.

"Hey, Jason, I'm Logan," Logan said in an unnatural way that made me think he was good looking. "And this is Emma. So, we've been meeting here, but we don't want to get caught, because this is, you know, trespassing?"

"Right," Jason said.

"So would you mind maybe not lighting fires out back, in case the police or our parents notice?" Logan continued. Now her voice sped up; she was losing confidence, didn't want to sound bossy, and was definitely embarrassed to have mentioned that we had parents. She added, "I mean, it's fine to eat here, but maybe we can all bring things that don't need cooking."

Other people had begun to come in. I heard Deirdre and Amanda, Elizabeth, Carl and Josh, Christian and Coltrane. People were laughing and chatting and gossiping and tearing open bags of chips. Someone had french fries. A few more people came in. Logan introduced Jason like they'd been friends forever, and Amanda asked where he went to school.

"I don't at the moment," he said.

"What do you do?" Amanda asked.

"I work," Jason said.

"Are you from around here?" Christian Aramond asked.

"My pop lives in Sauberg," was all he said, before there was a numbing pause, and into it, he injected, "What happened to you?"

It took me a minute to realize he was talking to me.

My heart lurched and sloshed around, giant and dangerous. How did he know something had happened to me? That I wasn't born this way? I shrugged, hoping to seem casual, thinking about how I had told Annabelle the whole story. "I had an accident," I said. "I got burned." It was the first time I'd ever said it that way, out loud.

"Brutal," he said. "Nice dog, though."

"Yeah, thanks."

"Maybe we should get started," Logan suggested, and there was a shuffling of chairs, milk crates, pillows, sneakers. The door swung open and I heard more kids come in, including Leah, who shouted across the throngs of people and noise, "Hi, Emma, we're here!" She made her way over to me and touched my arm, and I could feel Naomi clinging to her other side. "Hey, Naomi," I said.

"There are so many people here, Emma," Leah told me. "This is amazing." I heard Jason's voice ask, "Who's that?" But I didn't know who he was talking about and maybe no one else did, either, because no one answered.

Logan whispered to me that Emily McIntyre had shown

up. She was this girl who had apparently gotten pregnant the year before, by this older guy, and had an abortion. She was famous for it. I wondered if she knew that, or thought it was her secret. I wondered what it felt like to be her.

Then, to my surprise, Blythe came in with Dima, whispering. Maybe everyone else was surprised, too, because the room hushed, and Blythe said, "I thought if you all were going to talk shit about my dad again, I'd show up for it this time."

No one spoke.

"And this whole . . . whatever it is, is stupid and insulting," Blythe added. "In case you hadn't noticed, Claire's dead, and there's no way everyone sneaking out to talk shit about her behind her back is going to help her, so how about we all just admit that and give her and her family the privacy they deserve."

"But we're not talking shit about anyone, Blythe. Just trying to make sense of what happened to Claire," Logan said.

"Sense?" Blythe said. "Claire killed herself. There's no such thing as being by the lake, by yourself and high, and falling in, unless you meant to, right? And killing yourself means you care more about yourself than the people you abandon when you do it. None of this is anyone here's business, except maybe mine."

"Come on, Blythe, Claire was all of our friend," Amanda

said. "We all hung out; it's not like you guys were the only ones who—"

"She has a point, Blythe," Logan said, and I was really surprised, because what did Logan know about it?

"You guys are all fucking idiots," David Sarabande said. "Blythe gets to decide everything because her and Claire were—" And even though I couldn't see whatever gesture he made, I got it, and it was like most things you've always known but didn't know out loud or in Technicolor or whatever. I was surprised not to be surprised. Of course: Blythe liked girls, which was why she was sparkling and radiating, which was why she brought Dima; because Dima was her—

"Fuck you, David," Blythe said.

"Why? Is it not true?"

"It's none of your business, is what it is. If anyone here wants to talk about my dad, and accuse him of being a drug dealer, do it directly." She started to walk out.

"Wait, Blythe, don't go, please," I said. "We didn't mean to . . ."

Everyone waited.

"To what?" Blythe asked me.

But I couldn't continue.

Monica Dancat asked in a super-quiet voice, "Um, did her parents know?"

"Know what? Did Claire's parents know what?"

"That she was, you know, into girls or whatever?"

"She wasn't *into girls*, Monica. Okay? And I don't know what the hell her parents knew or thought they knew. Or why we're talking about this, since it's all totally moot now anyway."

Amanda said, "I don't mean to be . . . but didn't her parents—"

"Are you serious, Amanda?" Blythe said. "Shut up."

"I just think if it's because they found out, and they're keeping the whole thing secret, that we should actually talk about it. I mean, when we took the—"

Monica said, "I agree with Amanda. I mean, if Claire was gay, and that's why she . . . I mean, it is kind of everyone's business. She made it our business by dying."

"Maybe we should move to a different . . ." Logan said, in a fluttery, fake voice that made me think of a butterfly in the winter, freezing as it tried to flap its overly colorful wings against the absolute white of the cold. I wondered why she would want to change the subject when it seemed to me we had finally arrived at the point of all of our meetings and work and arguments.

I couldn't help myself. "But was *that* why? Claire killed herself because she was, whatever, gay?" I asked. "Or because her parents caught her?" I couldn't help the rage in my voice; how easy would being gay be compared to being blind? I didn't have a chance to ask that directly, though, because Blythe's weapon voice came down like a blade from above where I was sitting.

"Fuck you," Blythe said, and I wondered suddenly where Naomi was sitting, whether she was okay. Blythe's voice was quiet, but it felt like she was yelling: "You fill a stadium with people so you can pry into Claire's private life, like you're doing her or her family some big favor? By what, outing her? By accusing people of shit you know nothing about? If Claire's parents want to keep the details of her death private, that's totally their right."

"But why?" I asked. "I mean, isn't keeping secrets just worse?"

"Keeping secrets? That's rich. Why don't you two catch up on each other's secrets instead of publicly announcing Claire's and mine? Have you told Emma about last summer yet, Logan?"

My voice had that sound it sometimes gets, like it's coming from someone underneath me, underneath the floorboards, the dirt: "Told me what?" I asked, beating like the dead guy's heart in that Edgar Allan Poe story.

"Watch it, Blythe," Logan said. My heart was up in my throat, gagging me.

"Watch what, Logan? Who the hell made you two God?" Then she stormed out. I felt the room start to spin, and put my hand down on the side of the table I'd been sitting on, trying to steady myself, but it didn't work. I felt like I might throw up. I stood, said, "Let's go, boy," to Spark, and stumbled toward the door, reaching out as I went, feeling chairs, people, stuff. I didn't care what I touched.

"Blythe, wait! Please?" I called. I could hear Blythe and Dima moving through the grass, and then I heard them stop. I tried to walk toward them, but stumbled, and heard them move back toward me.

"Be careful, Emma," Blythe said. "It's a mess back here."

"I know," I said, tripping a little again. Someone reached out and held my arm. Dima, I guessed. "Blythe, please forgive me. I didn't realize . . . I mean, I didn't want this to be . . . we won't tell anyone about—"

"About what?" Blythe said. "You have the entire world talking about my private life, which is what you wanted, right?" Her voice was too far away to be connected to the arm that was holding mine, so I said, "Thanks, Dima," and she said, "You okay now?" I nodded and she let go of my arm.

"This is not what I wanted. We can stop, okay? We'll make everyone promise not to mention the—I mean, we can keep your secrets secret. I thought it would help to . . . I don't know. I just wanted to know something about Claire—something I thought would make us all understand—"

"Well, now you know something," Blythe said, and she walked away.

Leah and Naomi were outside then, and when Leah called my name, I jumped. "Let's go home," she said.

But I called after Blythe, "What did you mean about last summer?"

Blythe turned around from where she was, at least fifteen feet away in the trees, so I barely heard her, but I did. Maybe my bat ears were on duty. She said what I knew she would: "Ask Logan."

"Emma, are you okay?" Naomi asked me in a tiny voice.

"I'm fine," I said.

We were starting to make our way out of the woods when Logan came up behind us.

"Emma, wait," she said breathlessly. "Please. Let me walk you home. Leah? Can I walk with Em? Can you guys go ahead?"

"Okay, Emma?" Leah asked.

"I don't know," I said. "I guess so."

"We'll be ten feet ahead, so if you change your mind, just shout," Leah said. I nodded, and fell into step just behind Logan, who took the hand I was using to hold Spark's leash and led him and me out of the woods. I let her. She used her other hand to pull branches out of the way and waited to speak until we were on the grass strip along the side of the highway. During that silent, thorny walk I was thinking how many hours we'd spent together in our lives, and how being quiet had never sucked before.

"I have to tell you something," she said as soon as we were out of the trees.

"For a change," I said. My voice sounded controlled, even though my brain was racing with painful guesses. I wished intensely that Sebastian and I were friends, that I hadn't ruined that, too. Maybe I just wanted to confide in him whatever Logan was about to tell me, shed some suffocating, miserable lizard skin onto someone else.

Lo's voice was low and crunchy, like boots on rocks or bike wheels over gravel. "Blythe got the drugs from her dad's office."

"How do you know that?"

"I was there."

"You were where?"

"It's no big deal, Em. It's just . . . so I went swimming with them a couple of times last summer. A bunch of times, I mean. And we met up with guys sometimes, and whatever, partied, but I guess Blythe and Claire were . . . whatever. I didn't realize they were—we all hung out is all."

"Is that all Blythe meant by, did you tell me about last summer?"

"I guess so."

"That you went swimming naked with them? And what else? Spent the summer doing drugs and losing it and telling them instead of me because you all know what a baby I am?" My voice was rolling into something dangerous and Leah shouted back to me, "Em? You okay?"

"I'm fine," I called. We were past the statue. I felt my legs tense, and Logan felt it, too. "Don't run away from me this time, Emma, please. Just listen, just hear my side for once."

I took the "for once" and filed it away with Sebastian and Dee and last year and the fact that I'm blind, under "unbearable if true."

"That is not what it was," Logan said. "You are my best friend, not Blythe or Claire or anyone else. I just hung out with them sometimes, because—whatever. I felt bad about it. And I told them I was upset about you not being there, and they were nice about it. That was all. They got why it was hard. And with my parents. I needed—" She stopped, but I knew she was going to say "someone to talk to."

She tried instead, "That guy Brian was just . . . I met him because Amanda knew him, so that's— Even if I hadn't told them, he would have. I didn't tell you because I felt like I couldn't tell you part of it, because then I'd have to tell you all of it."

I slid my white cane side to side along the sidewalk with my right hand and felt Spark tugging his leash, which I had wrapped around my left hand. In step, back step. I walked forward, wishing I could disappear.

"Emma, I wanted you to come with, I wanted to invite you. But I couldn't, because . . . because, you know, it's not safe or whatever. I didn't tell you because I didn't want you to feel like we were leaving you out just because—"

"Because I'm blind," I said.

She was chewing her hair feverishly. I didn't tell her to stop. Maybe she would devour herself bald. I thought of a poem Naomi loves, called "Hungry Mungry," where Hungry Mungry eats the entire world and then his teeth have to gnaw on themselves once there's nothing left.

"I'm like your Jenna," I said, my voice numb. "Like the toddler sister you've been hiding everything from. I'm the only one who—" I hated the pathetic sound of my dried-weed-yellow PBK voice even as the words straggled out.

"No, no, Emma. First of all, since when do you hide anything from your little sisters? And anyway, that's not what—"

"Yes, that *is* what," I said, because it was. It was a perfect description, and my voice was full of lava, my heart grinding and spitting into my throat and mouth. "Honestly? The only reason I know anything about you—having sex with Brian and whoever else, Zach; anyone else now, too?—is because Blythe—Blythe Keene!—forced you to tell me. You were never going to tell me any of it."

I repeated, "You were never going to tell me." I wondered how many times I'd have to say those words before I could make them lose their meaning. Logan's lies stacked inside each other like nesting dolls: Brian, Zach, Blythe, Amanda, drugs, what drugs Logan had done, what other things I hadn't done, would never do. A whole summer of nights whispering her life with other people while she acted like she cared if I came back. Why?

"Come on, Emma, please don't be like that. I've told you now. I didn't think the part about Blythe and them was—"

But she stopped, because Leah was calling for us all of a sudden, and then my mom's voice came into our ears, shouting from the porch. Logan pulled me the last stretch toward my house, half running. Spark bounded up the stairs and I followed him, touching each step with the front of my foot, until I was standing right in front of my mom. My mind reeled and tangled. Did my mom know where we'd been? How?

"Naomi, honey," she said, trying to rein her voice in, "head into the kitchen for a snack. Sarah is in there waiting for you. Emma and Leah and Logan, come and talk to me for a minute."

Naomi dutifully marched to the kitchen, but I knew she would ooze her way back into the hallway to hear whatever it was Mom had to say. I tried to brace for the impact, found myself clamping my teeth together until my jaw began to ache.

"I've been frantic," my mom said. "I had no idea where you guys were. Leah, where were you?"

I waited to see if Leah would lie, hoped she would, so it could be her fault and I could follow her lead, but she said, "We were in the woods."

"In the woods? With Emma and Naomi?" my mom asked, incredulous. "You took Emma and Naomi into the woods at night without telling me? Why?"

"*She* didn't take *me*, Mom. I took her and Naomi."

My mom was speechless for ten seconds. "Well, then maybe you can explain to me how you thought that was a good idea," she finally said. "Do you have any idea how dangerous it is for you to be in the woods at night? And how did you get there? Along the highway? Something terrible could have happened, Emma. I thought you had better judgment."

"Something terrible *did* happen," I said. "But not in the woods or along the highway. When I was standing with Dad, you may recall." I could hear my mom swallowing, and imagined the sobs, the pills, the words, the dread—everything she'd been driving down inside herself since my accident. Just like I had.

I didn't stop. "And then *nothing* bad happened tonight. Some of us met at the Mayburg place and argued about real stuff—in a conversation that for once isn't completely and utterly full of shit."

"The Mayburg—the abandoned house on I-92? You thought it was appropriate to take Naomi there at night? Your ten-year-old sister?"

Okay, so taking Naomi hadn't been a good idea, maybe, but she had asked and I hadn't felt like patronizing her, so I'd said yes. And Leah hadn't intervened—she'd agreed to it, too. We had scared Naomi. Was that because I wasn't capable of paying attention to anyone other than myself?

"Where are Jenna and Benj and Lily?" I asked, maybe wanting to show my mom that I had realized my mistake.

"They're asleep, obviously," my mom said.

"I wish I were asleep, too," Naomi said then, from the hallway where she'd been listening to us. "Why did you take me to that terrible place? I wish I didn't know anything about Claire or you and Logan and Blythe or any of it!" She scrambled by, whacking into me and tripping before rushing upstairs and slamming the door to our parents' room. My mom got up instantly and followed Naomi upstairs, as she always does when one of us storms off. Leah went with her, and Sarah got up, too, but headed into the kitchen, probably to get something to eat. She has a mechanical heart. Suddenly the living room was quiet, just Logan and me.

"Naomi's totally right," Logan said. "That was fucked up of us."

"She wanted to come," I said. "And kids have a right to

know what's happening." I spat the last part out.

Logan came closer to me. "Maybe," she said quietly, "but timing matters. I mean, there are times when you can handle knowing things and times you can't." Her voice was amping up, because how was she going to justify all her lying to me? There was no way. She said, "It's like Santa. There's a moment when you're ready to know that's bullshit, but a lot of moments before when you're not, and it's like—if you find out before you're ready, it ruins your whole fucking childhood."

"This isn't my childhood, Logan. I'm your age. We're the same age!"

"I didn't mean you, Em. I meant Naomi coming to the Mayb—"

Sarah had come back into the room. "We're Jewish," she said in a bitchy way, setting a heavy mug on the table and sitting practically on top of me. I moved over, smelled coffee. "We never believed any of that absolute crap about Santa." Logan stiffened next to me. She hates it when Sarah snaps at her.

"Jews can't understand a simile, Sarah?" I said, turning the force of my wrath toward her.

Leah came back in and sighed. "She's okay," she said, about Naomi. No one responded.

"Whatever, Emma," Sarah said. "Make it all literary, as usual." Sarah can never let anyone have the last word about anything. I was so sick of it.

"It's no surprise you never believed in Santa, Sarah; you never believed anything good about anything," I said. My words felt like darts spinning toward a bull's-eye. "Because you're so self-involved you've never given one second of thought to anyone else. Ever. Honestly, it's unbelievable that you're Leah's twin." Once I got started, I couldn't stop. Maybe because of Logan, I don't know. But I kept going, like my brakes didn't work. "I guess Leah just got everything good and God left you as a husk of a fucking person. It must be miserable to be you."

There was a half-second silence and then Sarah stunned us all by bursting into tears. She cries even less often than Logan, and hadn't cried over Claire or any of the legitimately horrible things that had happened in the last two years. I'd always assumed Sarah couldn't possibly care less what I thought or said or did, as long as it didn't bankrupt our family or absorb too much attention. I was angry that she would cry now, as if this were the worst thing that had happened, and make me look as mean and ugly as I felt.

"Jesus Christ, Emma," Leah said. "What's wrong with you?" And she went after Sarah the way my mom had gone after Naomi. My stomach flipped and started sinking.

"Whatever," Logan said, knowing Leah's disapproval was terrible for me. "You were totally right; she needed to hear that."

I said, "I have to go to sleep. Maybe when I wake up, it will be from this whole nightmare."

I didn't invite her to stay. It was the first time since we met—when we were four, both of us on the jungle gym at the playground, and Lo was hanging upside down and saying, "Hold my hand so I can jump!" and then, after I did, "Want to be best friends?"—that I had let her leave. Now I turned, pressed my hand against the hallway wall, and slid my way to my room. Spark hopped off the couch and followed me. I felt the chipped paint, the groove; reached down and turned the cold brass knob. Behind me, I heard the click of the front door shutting behind Logan, and wondered—worried about—where she was going. Home, to her empty house? Or who knew, maybe she was headed straight to Zach's? Or to Brian's, whoever he was? Maybe she'd go to Amanda's, since I had been wrong at Lake Main. They had become close friends; I had thought everyone was just interested in me. Shame licked up at all my edges. Maybe Logan had gone back to the Mayburg place. Maybe everyone was still there, except Blythe and Dima and my sisters and me.

I sat at my desk and shuffled through my treasures again: the new braille love note from Naomi, Mr. Hawes's pen, the grapes, the rock, my photo envelope. I found the stack of Lo notes, our L&E book. My fingers caught the edge of Zach Haze's cardboard valentine, which I could identify because it's shaped like Spider-Man, and because Zach glued glitter to the back, mostly gone but with still enough scratch left to touch. I have probably run my fingers over it seven hundred times since the accident. Because I love it. I held the L&E book for a few minutes, along with the envelope of notes from her, and wondered what would happen to them over the years, how long they'd survive. They were still here, even though I couldn't see them anymore, even though she had gone swimming every night last summer with Blythe and Claire, had known all about Claire and told me nothing, had been drinking, smoking, gobbling drugs, laughing, trading secrets in the lovely, safe-scary dark. Until it wasn't safe. Did they blame themselves for what happened to Claire? What were their secrets?

I forced myself to imagine Logan lying back, Zach kissing her neck, taking her clothes off, having movie sex with her, whispering *I love you, I've always loved you*, the whole time. Had she risen from his bed and gone straight to her real, grown-up, undamaged friends to gossip and celebrate? Or cry? Had they all felt sorry for me out loud, Emma Sasha Spinster Silver, trapped forever in the worst year of my life, my "horrific tragedy," no longer a part of their glorious society, where girls could giggle and swim and see. Where they could have sex. And tell each other about it. Girls like Claire, I guess. Claire's life had been so lovely, no matter what had been wrong with it; it was so much better than my life, with everything she could see—but maybe she couldn't see that.

What if I just decided to kill myself? Is that what happened with Claire? Was she like, "This is too much—too miserable, too impossible. I'm out"? But if I were going to do that, wouldn't I have done it the summer of my accident? Or that terrible fall I spent on the couch—wouldn't I have stopped thinking, *I'm going to die*, and actually died? But I didn't. So does that mean I won't? At what point can you say someone is safe from herself?

The next morning, I took the L&E book, the clay lump with its X'd out button eyes and wire glasses, the dog and stick I'd made, and a bunch of cutout paper I'd been gluing into a book of tiny braille notes and headed to the kitchen, still quiet. I chucked everything into a paper lunch bag. I grabbed a small rectangular box from the middle drawer, where my mom keeps the secret cigarettes we all pretend not to know she smokes. I went out into the bright morning and stood at the edge of our backyard. My fingers prickled and then ached. I felt the heat of my breathing, changing the air around me, and slipped a stick out of the matchbox; felt its scratchy red bulb like the glitter on Zach's valentine. I held the other end between my index finger and thumb. Then I whisked it along the side of the box and heard the thump of the tiny flame, smelled the sulfur, and felt my heart swell and ignite in my chest. It was the first time I'd lit a match. I said, out loud, "Focus in, Emma," then set the paper bag down and held the match to it. Immediately I felt and smelled the fire, heard the crackling as the bag went up, saw the flames, the smoke, the end of my shitty project, the pretense that I could create "memoir art," our rule book, the paper bag, Logan's and my childhoods. I stood, wondering if I might throw up, inhaling the smoke, thinking, *This is what fire looks like to me,* waiting to see if it went out or burned me and the entire town to the ground, thinking, *How afraid am I now?*

"Emma?"

Benj was there, and I heard splashing, popping. He was pouring water on the flames, which sizzled so quickly I knew they had been a joke, not even a dangerous, real fire. How afraid had I been? And of what?

"Benj?"

"What are you doing, Emma?"

"I was making a little fire," I said.

"I ended that fire," he said, scared. "I'm sorry."

"That's okay. It was a good idea to put it out."

"It's cold," he said. He bent to set something on the ground, a watering can, maybe, or pitcher—whatever he had used to pour the water on my embarrassing fire.

I reached down and felt his little face as he stood back up. Then I slid my hands down to his neck and shoulders, realized he had on nothing but cotton pajamas and a cape.

"You're right. We should go inside, Benj. You'll freeze."

"That's why you made a fire, right, Emma? You were cold?"

"Sort of. Actually, I made it because I was feeling kind of blue," I admitted.

"I'm feeling blue, too," he said.

"Why?"

"Do you remember that rabbit, Bigs?" he asked. We began walking toward the house. I held his hand, felt him move Champon the turtle into his other hand and then flop the raggedy thing against his face.

"Of course I remember Bigs. We all remember her."

"She eated that plant and died and we had to bury her and later she was going to be another rabbit but she never was and we never saw that rabbit. And then we also never seed Bigs again, either. That made my heart blue."

"I know," I said. "I can see why you feel blue."

"Why are you blue, Emma?"

"It's something smaller than Bigs," I said, and Benj laughed his noisy, shouting laugh.

"Smaller than Bigs!" he said, having moved from devastated to hilariously cheerful in under one second, still a baby, still able.

"You made a joke, Emma," Benj reminded me.

"I get it. Smalls. Your blues are Bigs and mine are Smalls."
He laughed again, but this time it was a forced *ha-ha-ha*. Even
Benj had to humor me. "But why do you feel blues?" he asked.
We walked up the back porch steps and into the house, kicked
our boots off in the mudroom next to the kitchen.

I settled on, "Logan and I are in a kind of fight."

"Your friend Logan?" Benj asked.

"Right. My friend Logan."

"Logan is your best friend," Benj told me. "Like Taylor
and Sophie and Paolo are my best friend."

"Exactly."

"Maybe you can have a playdate and you'll share better
then," he suggested.

"That's an excellent suggestion," I told him. "Thank you
for helping me with my blues."

"But what about my blues?"

"What about them, Benj?"

"You didn't help me with my blues."

"I guess that's true," I said. "I have an idea, though. Do
you want me to take you to visit Bigs's grave?"

"What's a grave?" he asked. "Is it like a grandma?"

Benj is on his way to being weird, like me and Naomi.
Maybe the kids in our family will eventually be divided almost evenly between outsiders and people who can blend
seamlessly in with the rest of society: Sarah, Leah, and Jenna

will have normal lives, whereas Naomi, Benj, and I will never escape our own freakishness. I guess Baby Lily will shoulder the burden of being the tiebreaker.

"A grave is the place where you and your best friends and your teacher, Nancy, buried Bigs. Remember? Do you want me to take you to Bigs's grave? Maybe we can even bring something that she liked."

"Bigs liked me," Benj said. "I was her favorite boy. Just like I'm Mom and Dad's favorite boy."

We walked into the kitchen, where people were up having breakfast now. I could hear my mom shuffling around in the fridge. It's funny how even when the sky falls around us, people still have to make pancakes.

"Is it in the cabinet?" Sarah asked my mom. Syrup, probably.

Benj tugged on my hand. "Emma?"

"Yeah, Benj?"

"Do you think I would still be Mom and Dad's favorite boy if there were other boys in our family?"

"I can't speak for Mom and Dad, Benj, but you would still be mine," I said.

I went straight to my room and turned on *Antigone*. She was reburying her dead brother and I was taking notes in my brailler when someone came in without knocking. "Naomi?" I asked, taking my headphones off.

"It's me, Emma," Leah said. I was losing track of who was who, even among my sisters.

"I think you should apologize to Sarah," she said, coming to sit on my bed with me. She put her hand on my back, started to make the motions of "X marks the spot," which we used to do when we were little. I couldn't remember the last time she'd done it.

"Whatever. Everything I said was true," I said.

"Maybe so," Leah said, "but why hurt her feelings?"

"She hurts my feelings all the time," I whined, knowing even as I said it that it wasn't exactly true anymore.

"Come on, Em," Leah said. "There's so much horrible shit going on—just be generous. I mean, she's a mess and you're a champion." I thought of Principal Cates. Champions are made in the mornings. Champions are blinded in the summers. I felt my brain clicking and locking in the wrong places.

"Do you hear yourself?" I asked, angry. "I feel like I'm going to die. Look at my life!"

"It's been a brutal stretch, no doubt," Leah said, and she didn't even know about Logan. "But do you really not know what I mean about you and Sarah?"

"I'm not sure I do," I said.

She sighed. "Sarah can hardly survive a hangnail, Em. You know that." She lowered her voice. "Whereas you get blinded and are going to be fine. She can't pass a math test to save her life, and you can't even see anymore and are acing your way through school without even thinking about it. You don't even notice, because school is so easy for you. It's impossible for her. And you're Dad's favorite, his hope, the one he takes to work to save children. You can acknowledge that or not, but you should say you're sorry."

"Can you do 'X marks the spot' for real?" I asked.

She put her fingernails inside my T-shirt, tracing the figures out on my back as she spoke: "X marks the spot, with a circle and a dot. Spiders crawling up your back, stabbed the knife so hard you crack. Blood pouring down your back. Cool breeze, tight squeeze, makes you get the shiver-ies."

I saw the circle and dot like they were 3-D—glowing, moving—and the spiders and the blood. I saw the cool breeze across my back and the lake, and thought of my dad saying I'm a warrior, Leah saying I'm a champion.

But I didn't apologize to Sarah, because my dad and Leah are wrong about me.

I surprised my mom and myself by saying yes when she asked if I wanted to come to a concert with her on Valentine's Day. She was going to the city to hear some chamber music, she said, and did I want to bring a friend? We could pick Logan up on the way, she said, but I told her I wanted to bring someone else. I had no idea what Lo was doing on Valentine's Day, and I didn't want to know.

When we got to Annabelle's house, her mom led her to the door, holding her hand the entire way. She put Annabelle's coat on her, and said, in a very shivery, nervous voice to my mom, "Are you sure you can handle watching her for the night? I could try to—" It was funny; she sounded like my mom, making my mom sound like someone other than herself when she responded, "It will be just fine. I'll hold Annabelle's hand and Emma does okay on her own. We're just going to the Symphony Center and we'll park right in the lot and walk into the hall and listen and then I'll text you when it's over and drive her straight back."

"Thank you again for doing this," Annabelle's mom said, and I had the terrified feeling she might cry. I wanted to leave before that happened, to rescue Annabelle.

"Bye, Mom," she said in a whisper, and reached out. My mom grabbed her hand and helped her down the porch steps. I wondered if they had hired Mr. Otis, or someone like him.

"Do you have a mobility coach?" I asked Annabelle.

"No," she said. "My mom mostly helps me."

"How do you get dressed and get to school and stuff?"

"My mom drives me. And she picks my clothes."

"I could come over and teach you some tricks, if you

want," I said. "I don't have to, I mean, but if you think it would be fun or whatever."

We were climbing into the backseat together when I said this—my mom had moved the car seats out of the way in honor of our hot concert date with Annabelle, and my mom stopped buckling Annabelle's seatbelt to give me a grateful squeeze. I don't think Annabelle noticed or felt it. I nodded at my mom.

"I'll call your mom, Annabelle, and maybe we can make a date for Emma to come over and help you label clothes and locate shorelines."

When my mom said *shorelines*, I cringed down into my bones. She sounded like an old person trying to be cool. But then I realized there's nothing cool about knowing the word *shorelines*, and that made me realize, the way I often do, stumbling into it from a seemingly unrelated thought, that I'm a blind kid.

In the car, we talked about Annabelle's favorite book, which is *Charlotte's Web*. She told me she'd watched the movie and listened to the audio, but it was in an old man's voice and she didn't like it. She said she wanted it in her mom's voice, so her mom had made a recording of herself reading *Charlotte's Web* so Annabelle could listen whenever she wanted to. She said she was dying for a dog, but her mom had told her she had to prove she was responsible enough to take care of a living thing before they could get something as big and complicated as a dog. Apparently she had a cactus now, and if she was able to keep it alive for six months, she would graduate to a fish, and then from there to a turtle, and then a hamster, and maybe by the time she was my age, she'd have her skill set and her dog.

When we arrived at the Symphony Center, we were underground first in a parking garage that smelled like concrete and sounded like danger, engines, and oil, in a black swirl around me. I missed Spark terribly, but the Symphony Center was apparently one of the few places where they distinguish carefully between legitimate guide dogs and K9 buddies, and they didn't want Spark barking along to Tchaikovsky. As we walked from the car to the escalator up to the street, my mom talked about some composer who was still alive and had written the other piece the quartet was going to play, and the whole time I tuned her out I was thinking in a claustrophobic way that I would have to add being underground to my growing list of what terrifies me.

Annabelle seemed okay, though, walking quietly, holding on to my mom's hand, and listening to her talk about music. My mom was the happiest and most excited I had heard her in a long time. She loves live classical music, and I realized she hadn't left the house in the evening even once since my accident. This was the first time she'd left

Baby Lily at night with anyone, and it was my dad.

The concert hall was warm and shiny. It smelled red and gold and black, and I could hear the kind of light that comes off of chandeliers, reflecting into rainbows all over the walls. People were everywhere, in expensive coats that smelled like fur and mothballs, clicking in heels along a marble hallway my mom told Annabelle and me was lined with photographs of the musicians. I'll never see a photograph again. My white cane finger kept track of the floor and the depth of each step on a winding staircase up to a room with ceilings so high it felt as if the roof had blown off. The place bounced with voices and echoes.

"This is just a quartet, girls," my mom said. "It's my favorite." Her voice sounded like a string instrument, running up and down the notes of the words, all vibrato. I felt bad for all the piano lessons I had been skipping and bombing even when I showed up. I vowed to start practicing again. My mom ran her hand through my hair and then fluttered the pages of a program. She read us the biographies of the violinist, cellist, and pianist; told us the places they'd been, awards they'd won. "There's a part in the Moravec that's played by a bass clarinet," she was saying. "Caliban, the villain part. The song is based on *The Tempest*. The violin is Ariel."

The room hushed. "They've dimmed the lights," my mom whispered. "Here come the musicians." And then she finally stopped talking, as a line of people walked out onto the stage, women's heels, men's shoes, men's shoes, men's shoes. I couldn't tell after that because they were drowned out by clapping. I could almost feel the heat of whatever lights must have been shining onstage, and the silence of the audience was dark and oddly safe. I sat back against my seat, listened to the few lonely, hopeful tuning notes shudder out into the giant cave of a room and then vanish.

Then one of the musicians, I couldn't tell which one, breathed in sharply and they all started playing together on an exhale, and hearing the music start that way made me put my hands on either side of my chair. I steadied myself and listened hard; I could hear that the violinist was to my left, the cellist in the middle, and the clarinetist to my right. The piano was coming from behind the other instruments. At first, it was as if my way of separating sounds out got in the way: I could only hear the individual strands of music, but then, as I reminded myself to breathe, I started hearing all of it: the ridges and drops and the notes swelling and falling, and sometimes they were purple, dark like velvet curtains, and then the clarinet would come in and the notes were summer, lemonade, sand, and then the piano behind them became a drum for me, became fear, became Claire, a chorus was pounding and she was drowning, and then the violin was playing a shivery line alone, above everything else like a bird, or something smaller, a bird so small and delicate it was invisible. To everyone except me.

When the piece ended, I was crying.

"Are you okay, sweetie?" my mom asked. She stopped clapping and put her hand over mine.

"Can you take me and Benj to visit the rabbit's grave?" I asked.

My mom leaned right up to my ear. "You want to take Benji to Bigs's grave?"

The clapping around us was still thunderous, and I thought about people who climb into barrels and send themselves over waterfalls. "Yeah. Is that okay?"

"Of course," she said. "It's lovely." She leaned over and kissed me, brushing my hair out of my face with her hands. "We should get you a haircut," she said.

"I don't want a haircut."

"No? Okay.

"Annabelle, honey?" she asked. "It's intermission—would you guys like to get some M&M's or something? Or go to the bathroom?"

We said yes, followed my mom in a row out the door. Annabelle held my mom's hand, and I thought how we should get her a white cane. Everyone was everywhere, talking about how beautiful and Pulitzer and composer and tempest, and the words were boring compared to the music and I wanted to keep the sound of them away from myself so they didn't replace the notes in my mind. We bought M&M's at the bar, peanut ones for Annabelle and plain ones for me, and then we went back to our seats.

They played Tchaikovsky and the notes melted in my mouth, turning the colors of M&M's—red, green, yellow, blue, brown, a rainbow—and I thought of rainbows over the lake when we were little and it rained, and my chest hurt and the chocolate melted on my tongue and I thought how Claire will never taste chocolate again or see a single color, let alone hear a symphony. I held my mom's hand through the scary parts of the piece and remembered to breathe, and smelled colors and fire and lightning and the peanut M&M's Annabelle was eating. I heard Logan night-swimming with Claire and then without Claire, felt in the rawest bow strokes of the cello the bottom of the lake. I saw Claire deciding her life wasn't worth it—right as I saw the rainbow the day Lake Main called and said I could come back, right as I danced around the living room with Logan and banged into Sarah and she shouted at me. The music raced up a scale toward a terrible question mark: what changed? How do you decide you'd rather be dead, and never hear music or eat colors again? I both wanted and didn't want to feel what Claire had felt. And I didn't know whether it was possible to feel what someone else feels. Whether you wanted to or not. Being me at that concert was so shatteringly specific—could anyone else ever have understood what that music sounded like inside my head, my eyes, my ears, my fingers? I couldn't tell anymore, listening to the strings vibrate into colors and textures and mountains, what was imaginary and what was actually happening. Everything blurred, even though the world was sharper and clearer to me sitting in that rush of beauty than it had ever been before. It was like dreaming, and this is really weird, but all those notes, conflicting and moving and working themselves out, the way I could feel the rush of the music underneath, above and inside me, made me want to be even more alive than I am, than anyone is. It made me want to feel everything, to be in love. It made me want to start my piano lessons again immediately, to ride a bike again, to call Sebastian, to swim.

-12-

At the rabbit's grave, I bent down to touch the letters BIGS carved into it, and then, underneath, I felt the braille: B, I, G, and S. So my mom had made it. Under Bigs's name, it read, AUTUMN TO AUTUMN, the dates of his life. That's such a my-mom way of putting it, making the rabbit's dead life endless, ongoing, somehow okay. Benj was crouched down with me, touching the stone, too. Then we stood up together and I held his hand. It smelled green outside even though it was only February.

"Do you want to put down what we brought for Bigs?" I asked him.

He set the carrot down and then stood up and leaned into me, sighing. "Do you think Bigs will like the carrot?"

I felt Spark move closer to the carrot. He sighed longingly. Spark loves carrots and green peppers. "I think it's a very nice way to remember her, and to celebrate her life," I said, and I was suddenly catapulted forward in my mind to when I would have a little kid like Benj. I hoped someone would love me enough to have a kid with me someday. And that if anyone did, my little kid would be just like Benj. I also hoped Benj would let Spark have the carrot, but I didn't want to be the one to suggest it, in case it felt like Benj's dead pet had to sacrifice for my live one. We both stood there, and I could feel Spark tugging on the leash, nosing the carrot.

"Emma?" Benj asked. "Can Spark eat the carrot? Or will that make Bigs be frustrated?"

I laughed. "I think it's okay for Spark to eat the carrot," I said, and fast, since Spark was already crunching it delight-edly. "Spark and Bigs liked each other, and Bigs will be happy for Spark to share her carrot."

"But they can't share, because Spark already eated the whole thing," Benj said. "I want to give something else to Bigs, a toy for her to sleep with."

"Okay," I said. "We can get a toy for her and bring it next time."

"I want to leave a toy for her now."

"But I don't have one here, Benj."

"I have Champon."

"You want to leave Champon here for Bigs?" I asked.

I didn't hear anything from Benj, so I reached over to feel his solemn nod. I wanted very badly to see Benj's face, sud-denly. I knew his eyebrows would be scrunched up, that he was furrowing his small brow, and I couldn't believe I hadn't seen him in almost two years. How was such a horrible thing possible? I felt furious and crushed, like the accident had happened two days ago, like I was only realizing it now. I hate it when that happens. I took a deep breath, the way Dr. Sassoman taught me to, and touched Benj's face.

"Is that how you can see me?" he asked.

"Yeah."

"What do I look like?"

"You look like you," I said, thinking of Logan. I felt his little shiny nose, and his soft baby cheeks. I felt his eyebrows, but if they'd been furrowed a moment before, they were high above his eyes now, cheerful, puppety. His face felt like Baby Lily's. I was glad he was still a baby. He bent down again, to put his milky, beloved turtle on the rabbit's grave.

"Do you know what I'm thinking?" I asked Benj.

"About Swedish fish?" he asked, because those are my favorite. "The lemon ones?"

"Well, that too," I said. "I was also thinking if I ever have a kid, I hope he's like you."

"You don't get to pick that kid," he said.

"I know, I'm just saying I hope."

"Actually, the egg and the sperm decide, is that kid a boy or girl, and then they tell you."

"You're smart," I told him.

"You're smart, too, Emma," he said. "Because you can see me even though you have no eyes."

The door of the rec center slid open automatically as soon as my white cane touched the mat in front of it; I had to remind myself to breathe. *Think of yourself the way Benj thinks of you,* I suggested to myself. *Or Leah, or your mom, instead of the way you do.* It was hot inside, and I began to sweat the moment I walked in.

"You okay?" someone asked. A woman, maybe in her twenties. She had a deep voice, kind but gruff.

"I'm fine, thank you. Um, I'm looking for beep ball practice—do you know where I might find it?" I had been nervous on the way, and now I was here, even more anxious. Leah had agreed to drop me off on her way somewhere—I hadn't even asked where—and she was going to pick me up whenever I called for a ride. I felt agitated to be out on my own, even though Leah had driven me. It wasn't like I'd taken the bus or ridden my bike. Spark could tell I was doing a shabby job of staying calm, though; he kept shaking his body, trying to get imaginary water off his fur.

"Sure," she said. "That's where I'm headed, too. My brother plays. I'm Alexis." She tapped my shoulder and held out her hand to shake.

"Nice to meet you. I'm Emma Sasha Silver," I said, blushing terribly. Why I had decided to use all three names was anyone's guess.

"Cool name," she said. "There's a turnstile three steps ahead at your waist," she said. As soon as we were through, the smell of chlorine rose up into the thick air and stayed suspended there.

"This way," Alexis said. Spark was relaxing a little; he had stopped doing the dry-off fear shake, and was sniffing around. We went down two flights of stairs, and came into a room I could tell was giant and open by the echo of Alexis's voice. "We're here," she said. "Do you want to sit with me?"

"Sure," I said. "Thanks for your help."

"No worries," she said. "Who are you here to see?"

"Sebastian Metropole," I said. "He's a . . . a friend of mine from Briarly."

"That's where Mark, my little brother, goes," Alexis said.

Then we sat quietly, listening to the game, which is exactly like baseball except that the players are blind and the ball beeps, so they can hear it coming and hit or catch it. Whenever anyone makes a play, the sighted people in the crowd tell the blind people what happened, which was how it went with Alexis and me. I wondered if she resented having to be a sports commentator for me, but if she did, it wasn't obvious. Maybe she was lonely and glad to have company, or used to being an interpreter for her little brother. I don't get why people love watching sports, honestly. I can't bring myself to care who wins unless I know something personal about the players. I used to like competitions where I knew everyone's stories and I could see their faces. I tried to hope that Seb's team would win, but mainly I was busy practicing in my mind what I would say when I saw him after. Whenever anyone hit a home run, the crowd cheered and shouted, "Good eye!" Other than that, we stayed quiet, so that players could hear the ball beeping its way through the air toward them, and feel the arc of it, smash into that sound with the bat, or grab the sound from the air like an electronic butterfly into a net.

"These guys are good!" Alexis said, after what she told me was an "elegant catch." The crowd was screaming, and I asked into the already loud noise, "How old is Mark?"

"Eleven," Alexis said, and I heard sorrow in her voice.

"Was he sighted before? Or has he always been—"

"He was born blind," she said. "What about you?"

"I was sighted," I said. "This"—I gestured up to the band of sunglasses where my eyes used to be—"was an accident."

"That's lucky," she said, and I knew what she meant: that I had gotten to see everything. That I would have those visual, colorful, fluttering memories of what the world looks like forever. And Mark never would.

"I guess it is," I said.

After the game, she took me down the risers to find her

little brother and Sebastian, but when I called out Seb's name, no one answered. "Are you Sebastian?" Alexis asked someone.

"Yeah," he said, so he must have heard me and turned but not responded. At the sound of his voice, still so familiar, I felt sorrow rise up in my throat, and shoved it back down.

"Hey," I said, no tears in my voice. "Hey, Sebastian." This huge name felt oddly formal—I had called him Seb at Briarly, but I knew I'd forfeited any right to nicknames.

"Hi, Emma," he said. "What can I do for you?"

I realized I'd been hoping he would be thrilled to see me. And how unfair that was. "I, um, I wanted to see you," I said.

"No hope of that, obviously," he said. I smiled, but I could hear that he wasn't smiling.

"Good game," I said.

"It was just a scrimmage."

"Um. I was wondering if we could talk? I know I've been kind of—"

"Yeah," he said, meaning no. "I have to get dressed and do a postgame now. I'll give you a call sometime."

"Seb!" It was Dee, who had come from behind him somehow. Then she turned suddenly and her voice came toward me. "Who's this?" she asked, super friendly and casual, sticking her hand out and down to shake and brushing mine.

"It's me, Emma. Hi, Dee," I said. I took her hand.

"Emma Silver?!" She let go of my hand, but whether

out of surprise or because she hated me, I wasn't sure.

"Yeah."

"Wow. We thought you died," she said.

"I know. I'm . . . things have been kind of a disaster, and I was hoping I could talk to you guys about—" I couldn't finish and no one came to my rescue. The beat of silence finished me. "Well, um, great to see you both."

Then, like with Logan, I turned and began to flee, the sobs that had formed in my stomach the instant I heard Seb's voice forcing their way out of my throat.

But before I got to the top of the stairs, I heard Dee calling my name. I turned and groped for the banister on the rising stairs. "Our final ski trip's next Sunday, Emma," Seb called up to me. In his voice was a mean, sharp dare. It came out in a color I'd never heard him use, something dark and metallic gray. "How about you come and try it out this year?"

Their invitation to ski was obviously my last chance to know them. I knew right away that if I said no, as always, as I had nine billion times last year, as I wanted to, well, then I was not only a wretched chicken but also a lost cause of a friend. So I had no choice. I had to say yes. I heard the yes come out of my throat like something yellow and small, fluttering before it died of regret.

And then I had to tell, rather than ask, my parents.

"I'm going to tag along on a Briarly ski trip, because it'll be 'empowering,'" I said at dinner, the word growing on me now that I needed it to convince them. My dad didn't even have a chance to say anything before my mom said, "But there's no snow. It's already almost spring. How can you—"

"It's Mount Crandon, Mom. The snow is fake."

"But will you have to miss school?"

"It's a Saturday."

"But who will take you?"

"I'll go with Seb and Dee."

"But can you sign up even if you're not at Briarly anymore?"

"It's a great idea, Em. We'll absolutely make it work," my dad said.

It turned out, predictably, that my dad was so thrilled that my mom had to give in. I heard them argue it out at night. And we all heard her console herself with hundreds of daily phone calls with Principal Antoine, Mrs. Leonard, and Mr. Crane, the teachers who were chaperoning. Were former students welcome? (She hoped no, but got yes.) Could it possibly, actually be safe? (She thought no, but got yes.) Who would be there? (*Everyone*, including lots of teachers.) How many possible ways were there that I might die? (This sort of speculation they refused to indulge in directly.) It was endless, even after it ended, because once she couldn't call and torture everyone, she decided to come with me.

So my dad took a day off from saving people's lives so my mom could drive to Silverton and take the school bus from Briarly three hours to a fake-snow-covered bunny hill with me and Seb and Dee and a bunch of kids from last year whose names I had hardly bothered to learn. A few of them politely asked how I was and how school was, and I said fine. No one was that excited to have me back, and who could blame them? Sebastian and Dee sat together on the bus, and I sat behind them with my mom. Everyone was so excited that the driver stopped twice to turn around and tell us to calm down or he was going to turn around and drive right back to Silverton. I sat silently, listening to Sebastian and Dee shout about all the near-death experiences they'd had on the slopes the year before. When I had smartly refused to come. We had not acknowledged yet what a psychotically terrible person and friend I'd been all fall. And all last year, too, really. Not when I said yes, I would come skiing; not when I called to get the trip details; and not when I showed up and boarded the bus. We all just acted like nothing had happened. Which was really weird.

"Do you remember how I almost totally wiped out on that huge hunk of ice?" Sebastian was saying. I could hear him bouncing on the plastic bus seat, the tired springs creaking and breaking further every time he slammed his body back down. I had a flash of wonder about his body then, what it might look/feel like.

"Yeah," said Dee, her voice full of awe. When I was at Briarly, I thought no one there could have crushes, that blind kids couldn't fall in love with each other. Obviously that's insane, but I hadn't realized yet that it was possible to be both blind and capable of thinking about anything other than the fact that you're blind. Somehow, now that I'm not at Briarly anymore, I have a better view of life there. It's like life anywhere, at any school, really. Even Lake Main. Except for the life skills classes, I guess, but the truth is, the kids at Lake Main could probably use those.

"Scott was like, 'Look out, man!'" Sebastian was saying. "And I was like, 'Left? Right? What the fuck, man?' And—oh, excuse my language, Mrs. Silver—and he was like, 'Right in front of you, man!' And I swerved at a ninety-degree angle to the left and flew up four feet in the air."

I could feel that my mom hadn't breathed since the story began, and knew that Sebastian apologizing for swearing in front of my mom was fully missing the point.

"Who's Scott?" I asked, trying to distract my mom from the idea that whatever had happened to Sebastian might happen to me, too.

"Our ski instructor," Dee said. "He's amazing. He can

snowboard, too." Her voice pitched up toward her crush register. "He used to be a professional skier. He's cute."

When we got to the slopes, we climbed out of the bus and my mom held my arm on the way to the lodge. I missed Spark, who had stayed home with my dad and the little kids.

"This way! This way!" Mr. Crane shouted. We followed him into a ski lodge and locker room, where those of us with no boots or skis rented them and we all put on our ski equipment. I could hear kids asking their parents why all those blind people were there and how we could ski if we couldn't see what was in front of us. The parents didn't answer, just shushed the kids, which was wrong and stupid. Why not just answer kids' questions? The way the parents acted made us seem like unspeakable freaks. "Doesn't it make more sense to talk?" I said, loud, in the direction of a kid I heard asking about us. "We have a guide who goes behind us and tells us if we're about to hit anything."

"Oh," the kid said, coming a little closer to me—I could hear the volume of his voice increase a bit. "See, Mom? That's how." I smiled. His voice reminded me a little bit of Benj's, and I wondered how old he was, thought about how kids like facts and answers, just like anyone. Everyone acts like reality is unmanageable, which it is, maybe, but putting sugar all over it is also terrifying. Because people, no matter how young, sense both what's there *and* that they're being deceived about it.

I sat on a wooden bench with my mom at my feet, snapping on the giant boots that would then apparently be attached to skis, on which I would blindly fly down a cliff. Why?

Sebastian was sitting on the bench next to me, with his boots already on. He reached over suddenly, grabbed my hand, and squeezed it. I had a blaze of nerves that felt like a light display. I wanted to apologize, to thank him, to ask him to forgive me and let me be his friend again. But I was scared to say anything, lest he drop my hand. So I just swallowed and held on.

"Ready?" he asked me.

"I guess so," I said, and it came out accidentally flat and unfriendly.

"Well, I guess that's the best I can hope for from you," he said. Dee came clomping over then. He dropped my hand.

"You ready, Seb?" she asked him. He stood up.

"Wait," I said, blushing. "Um, Dee? How scary is it?"

"What, skiing? It's nothing compared to what you've been through," she said kindly.

I had a flash then that I should ask Logan the same question about sex. Or drugs. Or last summer. Any of the things she had done and I hadn't. "Will you guys come visit me on the bunny hill?"

"Sure," Dee said, and then maybe she elbowed Seb, because he said, "Yeah, okay."

When my mom finished snapping and bolting and soldering my boots on, I stood up and stumbled forward and she grabbed me. It felt like my feet were encased in blocks of lead.

"I have your skis right here," she said, and clacked them together for my benefit, before leading me out into light so bright I could sense it from inside of my skin. I like light like that; I can't see it, but I can really feel it—it reminds me of what I have left.

"Beginners, over here!" Mrs. Leonard called out. I felt exhilarated suddenly, like I might be able to keep Seb and Dee, and part of myself I'd almost lost, somehow. Like I was actually going to do this thing other-Emma had never even done. Maybe she wasn't always superior to me in every way.

It was weird to crunch through snow when it didn't smell cold. We were all led up to the top of a small hill, and when we got there, out of breath, we put our skis on. My mom set the first ski up next to my foot and told me to step sideways onto it, slide my boot in, and then step back with my heel. I tried six times before we heard the click and my heavy boot locked into an even heavier ski. I did the other side in one try. Then I heard my mom sliding her own feet into skis.

"You're skiing, too?" I asked her.

"Sure," she said. "Why not?"

Because it was ludicrous, and I didn't want her to, and having her along at all was bizarre and embarrassing, to name several of the thousands of reasons why not. But we both knew she couldn't be talked out of it and we both knew why— because she wanted to be holding me up every second, right behind me, on top of me, whipping down the hill in front of me, or wherever she could be, in order to control what was going to happen. I had the unkind thought that if only she'd lavished that much neurotic attention on me before the accident, maybe it never would have happened. But I pushed that away, because it was unfair and untrue, and because if my mom could scoop her own eyes out like ice cream and give them to me, she would.

But she can't. So she followed me like a crazy shadow, shouting, panting, trying to keep her screams to words of encouragement. I was barely even on a hill, just learning to point my skis down toward the bottom of the hill, and to pigeon-toe them in to brake. It was pitiful, but watching me move down a slope of white must have felt to my mom like a metaphor. She was letting me fall into nothingness, because she knew it was good for me. She had agreed to let me do it because I wanted to, because it was empowering, because she had always liked the idea of my "friendships" with Seb and Dee, because my dad would have demanded that I be allowed to go, and because my former teachers had urged her to let me build my confidence and my "ability to trust people." She had no choice but to let me go—over and over.

The first time the beginning ski instructor, Kevin, showed me how to ski down the hill, he was tied to me by a rope and harness and, from right behind me, had the ability to pull the rope and save me, literally yank me back away from any danger.

Yet my mom was next to him, shouting, "Go, Em! Good, Em!" and nothing else—no warnings, for example—because Kevin told her that if she shouted orders he'd have to ask her to wait at the top or bottom for us. I could only have one person telling me to avoid the trees.

My mom's breathing was more frenzied than it should have been from the small exertion of skiing the bunny hill. And her words, although cheerful, happy ones, were like tissue paper over the shrieking fear, which I could hear and feel under even her most convincing cheers: "You're a skier, Em! Brilliant! Keep it up!"

When my mom had to go to the bathroom after an hour, she urged me to come back to the ski lodge with her. And I wanted to. In fact, I had separation anxiety like Benj used to when he was one; whenever my mom left the room, he would hold his breath until he turned blue, in what my parents called "Benji's blue fits." He stopped having them around the time of my accident, when he was two and a half, I guess when he realized he could count on her to come back. I felt on the slope like I could not, must not, follow my mom to the bathroom, but also like if I stayed alone on that fake white hill I might transform backward into a sobbing baby, turn blue, pass out.

And then, furious that I could not do that, would never be able to do it again, I barked at my mom, "I don't have to go to the bathroom, and I'm not coming. Kevin?" I wanted her to know that I was calling him over, that I was about to plunge straight down the cliff without her. On purpose. She wouldn't even be watching this time.

"Are you sure?" my mom asked, her voice a mixture of the buzzing insect sound of panic that was always there and a lavender, fluttering sound—maybe pride that I had made a brave choice.

"I'm sure, Mom. You go ahead."

And she did, because what else was she going to do? Pee our family name into the snow? Refuse to leave her almost sixteen-year-old alone for three minutes on a school trip? I wished I were Logan, smoking, swimming at night, in bed with a beautiful boy like Zach, or that I were Blythe, actually capable of rebelling.

Kevin was making his way over to me. "Hey, Emma," he said. "Did you call me?"

"Can I go again?" I asked him. "Fast this time?"

"Absolutely," he said, and he tied us together, and I took a deep breath in and let go. And I flew down that bunny hill so fast that I almost forgot Kevin was there, almost forgot that I had never been skiing, almost forgot who I was and wasn't, what was and wasn't possible, that Claire was dead and I was blind.

I forgot for one split of a perfect second everything except the feeling of tremendous power in my legs—and my own wild speed. Almost.

Sebastian was calling my name from somewhere at the bottom when I slowed down.

"That was amazing, Emma. Good work trusting me," Kevin was saying.

"How was it?" Sebastian asked. He had come up right next to me, and now he put his hand on the sleeve of my hoodie. All the words in my mind were a flurry, so I didn't speak; just tripped over my own skis to put my arms around Sebastian's neck. He smelled just like himself, leather and tangerines, and his shoulders were wide and thin, almost like wings, his face warm. I hugged him for long enough that it started to feel strange, and he pulled away, embarrassed.

"I'm so sorry," I said, and then, "Thank you. I mean, not just for today, but for last spring, too, for being so . . . I missed you."

"S'okay," he said. It took me a minute to see that Dee was standing there, too, sniffling. Was she crying? And if so, why? There was some other energy blinking in the air. Were they dating? They *were* dating. Why was I hugging Dee's boyfriend? I backed up, trying not to fall over in my huge boots.

"Dee! How was your skiing?" I asked.

"Good, thanks," she said.

I hugged Dee, too. "Thank you for inviting me," I said. "For making me do this."

She laughed, a short bark of relief, and then sniffled again, so maybe she just had a cold.

"You're welcome," she said. "Anytime. In fact, how about we all come back next week? They're open until April." Then she put her arms around Sebastian and me, and we began to tow each other along on our skis toward the lodge. I pushed some words out of my throat. Because I knew I'd be a new me by tonight, and she would hate the me I was right now if I didn't say them. Out loud.

"Um, so, you guys, I came to the game the other day because I wanted to apologize for being kind of, you know, MIA this year," I said. "I guess I was—" I thought about saying how busy I'd been, how tough it had been to start back at Lake Main, how something. And then, instead, I tried for the truth. "I was trying to pretend that last year never happened."

"Why?" Seb asked. I felt sort of sick, my throat hurting, my head hot. But I kept on, as we pushed the doors open and the heat of a giant fireplace met my nose first, then my neck, my ears. I heard the logs popping.

"Because I didn't want to be blind," I said.

"We didn't blind you, Emma," Seb said fairly. "It's not like it's because of me or Dee or Briarly."

"I know. I know that. It just took me some time to sort it out."

"And now you have?"

"I don't know," I said truthfully. "But I'm trying." I paused, then said, "I mean, I've trained myself not to be a PBK anymore. No sulking. No rocking. And I'm working on doing some brave shit on my own. I need to tell you about some of it. I think you guys will be impressed."

"Yeah?" Seb asked, interested. "What kind of brave shit?"

I shrugged. "It's nothing great," I said. "Nothing like you've done with your championships and driver's ed test and beep ball and saving blind kids like me. But I'll tell you about it soon. Maybe you can even come visit me in Sauberg and meet some of my friends there."

"That'd be nice," Dee said.

"How about the driver's test?" I asked Seb. "Did you end up telling your parents you were taking it?"

"Yeah," Seb said, in a kind of flat way.

"Oh. Were they mad?"

"No."

"Did they let you?"

"Yeah."

"So, um . . ." I didn't know what to ask.

"He aced the written part," Dee said proudly, rescuing everyone.

"I'm not surprised," I said.

I didn't make him tell me the rest—about whatever part he'd failed. Why would I?

The first weekend in March, my dad took me over to Annabelle's house. In the car, I asked him how many times Mr. Otis had come to our house last year, when I was first blind. I said it like that, "first blind," and the words had a green, lime taste in my mouth, one I didn't like.

"He came every day for about two months," my dad said, "and then once a week for a third month." I was quiet, surprised. That seemed both like more and less than I had remembered. "How did we start our lessons?"

Now it was my dad's turn to be surprised. "Do you really not remember?" he asked.

"Yeah," I said. "I guess I was kind of in a daze. Did we start with finding stuff? Or labeling my clothes? Or—"

"You listed your goals, Em. You and Mr. Otis talked a lot about what you hoped you could accomplish, and how you would work toward those goals, one at a time."

I felt sudden, nauseating fear. I didn't know who I had

been last year, and I had a harder and harder time remembering who I'd been before last year. If I lost track of every past me, who would I be now? Anyone?

"What were my goals?" I asked, and my voice had a layer of frost over it.

My dad took his hand off the steering wheel then and put it on my hand. "Your main one was to get back to school, to be at Lake Main with Logan and your sisters. Do you not remember that?"

"Not really."

"Well, now that you've achieved it, you have new goals, of course, like more independence. Taking the bus, or getting to and from school by yourself," my dad said. "You and Mr. Otis worked on dressing yourself, pouring things, eating, using the white cane, on listening to sounds that could help you figure out where you were and who was around you, on memorizing routes around the house. Once you acquired those skills, you didn't need to remember the lessons themselves as much."

"Yeah, maybe."

At Annabelle's, my dad sat and drank coffee with her parents while I walked with her from room to room, feeling the walls, talking about what colors I thought the carpets and fixtures were. She giggled every time I got one wrong, and shrieked when I was right (once, about the bathroom being yellow). "How could you tell?" she asked. "It's a lemon room,"

I said. "Everything about it." In her room, she showed me her toys, which were in a jumble, and I said I thought we should organize them. We made a line of plastic robots and glass and stuffed animals along the top of her dresser, and I felt inside some of her drawers. She and her mom hadn't labeled her clothes yet.

"My mom helps me get dressed," she said.

"That's fine, of course," I told her. "But in case you ever want to do it yourself, you can." I reached into my bag and took out a small packet of premade braille labels for her clothes, with colors and identifiers like "TS" for T-shirt or "SJ" for skinny jeans on them.

I had blank ones, too, and my slate and stylus ready, so we could make our own if she preferred that. "You can do what I do," I said, "and pick your favorite thing to wear, and just have a bunch of the same ones. Oh, and I always wear a tan bra, so no matter what T-shirt I pick, my bra won't show through."

She giggled. "I don't have a bra," she said.

"Well, not yet," I said. I thought how she was Naomi's age, and how in three years they'd both be completely different people from who they were now. Sometimes I forget that that's true of everyone and not just me.

I thought for a moment, and then I said, "So, I wanted to tell you that I went skiing. I think you should try it sometime—when you're ready. Maybe we can go together."

She was as quiet as she had been the first time I met her, in the hospital. I thought about how quiet I used to be. I talk more lately. I said that on the mountain, I'd been really scared, but also the bravest since my accident.

Annabelle listened, barely breathing, and I told her every detail of what it was like to ski down a cliff, how my mom's and my words had melted the air in front of our faces. I said the boots had been heavy and I'd thought I might fall, but I hadn't fallen, had flown instead. The more I told her, the more amazing my own stories seemed, and the less I thought they could actually be my stories, that they could actually be true. But they were.

I even told Annabelle how I'd spent most of this year trying to forget being at Briarly last year.

"It didn't work, though," I said. "It kind of made things worse, I guess." I paused, but when she still didn't speak, I added, "It made me a terrible friend, for one thing. To a few people, but mainly to this boy I knew at Briarly. One time, last year, I touched his face? And this might sound weird or funny or whatever, but touching his face made me hopeful, like I might be okay, even though I was blind, and for me, it was the first time I felt that. So instead of ignoring and forgetting him, I probably should have thanked him." I felt a sudden electrical surge of embarrassment and laughed nervously, even though it was just Annabelle. She didn't respond, so I sped up and finished: "Anyway, so yesterday I thanked him and it was too late, but I'm still glad, because it felt kind of like the skiing."

Annabelle asked in a clear voice, full of the kind of Disney want I associated with Blythe Keene, "What was his name?"

And I knew, maybe without her even knowing it, that she was worried she'd never have a boyfriend. And even if she wasn't yet, she would be worried about a job, too, a life, like I was, like we all were.

"Sebastian," I said. "His name is Seb. I hope you can meet him, because he's amazing."

"Is he your boyfriend?"

I laughed, but it came out forced, like a small bark. "No," I said. "He has a girlfriend named Dee, who's also my friend from Briarly. Seb and I are just friends. I'm hoping to be more like him about—I don't know—about being blind. Or being a friend, or whatever." As I said this, I realized it was the stark, warm truth; that truth isn't always blinding, agonizingly sharp, cold, or bright. Each word was a little lit bulb inside a night-light, leading me down a soft hallway in my mind. I wanted to be like Seb, to try to make someone else okay with being a blind girl. Because I had been wrong that forgetting last year would make this year—or anything—easier. In fact, the opposite was true.

If I'm going to live with any of what's happened to me,

unlike Claire, I have to remember everything as clearly as I can. I used to know that, back when I was a spy, but somewhere along the way, I forgot. I'm going to start saving my details again, because that's what being alive is, I think. Not banishing or forgetting or drowning any part of it. Some of my best stories I've already saved, just by telling them to Annabelle.

-13-

It got hot all of a sudden, frying the winter out of our systems and apparently skipping spring. The flowers in our yard and along the sidewalks bloomed straight up through the dirt only to stand thirstily in the sun and then fry into withered stalks. My shorelines have changed; there's nothing slick or icy, nothing wet. I knew before anyone else that the world had decided to skip spring, because of the overly bright and dry way the air smelled.

Leah's acceptance letters started pouring in; she's already gotten into her top two places and now it's just a matter of her choosing. Sarah never finished her applications, so we're all calling the absolute train wreck of her future "taking a year off." What this means practically is that my parents are like trapped animals, caught between trying to celebrate Leah and make life livable for Sarah. I know this is awful, but I can't be happy for Leah. For the first time in my life, I wish Sarah were the smart one, the one who was leaving.

I wish Leah were staying here, because the thought of her being gone sends a vacuum of blood straight out of my heart. But it's happening. It's coming. Just like I'm groping down the barrel of summer and next year myself. Eleventh grade. Ms. Mabel has started talking about next fall, SATs and APs and college visits and whether and how much I'll need her. My parents are talking about my birthday in June, and how once I'm sixteen I can go to guide dog school over the summer and get a guide dog.

Instead of the future, I've been thinking about peekaboo, about the strange and stupid idea you have when you're little that if you can't see people, then they can't see you. Obviously I know now that this isn't true, but what I wonder, late at night, is whether people who can see me know more about me than I do. Or whether what they know is just different. Last night I was lying in bed, listening to Naomi sleep, imagining forever without Leah, forever in the dark, the specific forever of Claire's flesh blowing off her bones underground. I was thinking about spending forever without my eyes when I had a thought that sat me straight up, made me rabbity-awake, like a predator was hovering above me, ready to strike. Except I was also the hawk, about to attack myself. I threw the covers off my legs and swung around so that I was halfway out of the green tent.

My heart started jackhammering my rib cage into cat litter, and I decided I would do it. Just because I had thought of doing it. I stumbled silently out of bed, feeling less like an animal once I was standing and more like two people who hate each other: this Emma, that Emma. But neither could talk the other out of it; I couldn't stop myself. I was determined not to wake Naomi in her bed above me, and tried to be as quiet as I could while I grabbed around for some sweatpants and a jacket, my hands working less well than I needed them to. *Calm down,* I told myself. You can tell yourself to calm down, like Dr. Sassoman once said. I tugged the sweatpants over my pajamas, tripping and trying not to bang into my desk chair. Once I had them on, I pulled on my Converse, threw a hoodie haphazardly over my shoulders, and shook Spark awake. Poor Spark.

"Come on boy, shhh," I whispered, and guided him toward the window, helped him stand and lift his front legs over and out. He didn't bark. I climbed out after him, slipping down onto the bushes and brushing my pants off as soon as I was standing outside. I unfolded the cane and set it down in front of me, felt it describe the grass, a medium-size stick, some rocks.

"Let's go, Spark," I said, and we started walking.

It was a warm night, and smelled peaceful. There was no noise except for the occasional car swishing by as we walked along.

"Dark is safe," I said out loud to Spark, although he seemed delighted to be treated to an extra walk, and not to be too concerned that it was happening in the middle of the night or that we had left by window. It's like he actually thinks of dark the way I pretend to. At least I haven't pushed my fear off onto him.

"Dark is cool; light is hot," I told myself as we made our way down to Lake Street. I listened to my phone tell me where we were until we had made it to the statue. Then we started along the highway, where there were no cars.

"Look at us, Spark! We're doing fine. And who cares if it's night, right? Day is dark, too."

He didn't say anything.

"Right, Spark?"

He padded along cheerfully.

"I wish you could talk," I told him.

When we got into the woods, the crunch of my sneakers on the twigs was so threatening that my teeth started to chatter. "Not cold," I told myself. "You're not cold. Don't worry, teeth."

Ever since my eyes got ruined, it's like all the other parts of my body have stopped trusting me. Maybe my arms, legs, teeth, and hands are afraid they'll be next. The last time Dr. Walker checked the reflexes in my legs with one of those little hammers, I almost fainted. He had to keep reminding me to breathe, because I was certain my legs wouldn't respond, and he'd tell me that I was going to be paralyzed.

The woods were too still and too alive at the same time. I could feel them pulsing and breathing in this wet, dark-green, nighttime spring way. This was my fault, I reminded myself. I had to figure this out for myself: how to sleep, how to live, how not to be so scared that it killed me. I had tried the Mayburg place idea, tried to have a real conversation, but maybe that had failed. It had obviously failed Logan and me. Not to mention Blythe. And honestly, Claire too. I felt like the sound Logan had made about herself. I heard a bird, wondered what birds were awake at night—just owls? This didn't sound like an owl.

Once, Claire came to school early, carrying a shoe box with a bird inside of it. She had found it the night before, on the ground in a patch of ice, hurt. And she had wrapped it in her winter hat, run home, and hidden it from her parents all night. She took it straight to the science teacher the next day, who said it was an emaciated, disoriented woodpecker, and that the reason it was on the ice like that was because of climate change; it had stayed too warm and then gotten too cold too fast. He said Claire was a hero for saving its life, and that he would help her get it to a wildlife rescue facility. But for some reason, this didn't make her feel okay; she stood there with her eyes turning red and then cried until she looked like a puddle. I never knew if it was relief or sorrow that made her cry that day. Was she freaked out about climate change and all the other birds that were lost on ice without her to rescue them? Or just glad her lost woodpecker would live? Or was it something else altogether? And why didn't I ask her? I remember walking out of the science room with a few other girls, Logan and Deirdre and maybe Elizabeth Tallentine, but I can't remember who comforted Claire. Was Blythe there that day?

"This is not fear," I told myself, and the woods rustled and closed in around me. "This is bravery. You walking here? Brave."

I focused on my breathing, kept small-talking to Spark, as if his being there could mitigate the danger and terror. It could. *It can,* I told myself. *You're safe. Spark is with you.*

"Hey! Here we are! The Mayburg place," I said to Spark. Lately the Mayburg place had taken on a smoother, more familiar texture, but walking alone through the night there stripped it back to jagged, splintery, abjectly scary. Spark recoiled at something I hadn't heard or felt. An animal? A movement in the forest? A branch? Keep on, I thought. *Focus in.*

"It's okay, boy," I said. "It's right up here." I counted the steps in, and within eleven minutes of leaving the highway, we were at the door. I pushed it open. It was silent inside, except for the night noises. Wind, maybe the lake a half mile back. Was that the lake I heard?

"Why don't you sit?" I said out loud, and I bent at the knees and felt around for a crate, found one, and sat on it. Spark settled at my feet. My legs felt like overcooked noodles. Spark's must have, too, because he curled up immediately and his breathing slowed. I was too hot-wired to feel sleepy; my fear had every nerve in my body standing at such rapt attention I was prickly, wondering if fear could give you hives, or spikes. Maybe I would mutate into a blind porcupine.

"So, we are gathered here today to talk about fear," I said out loud, to myself, and started laughing. A gust of wind blew loud through the corners of the Mayburg place.

I said, over it, "Terror is a choice. I can decide whether to be afraid."

I thought of Jason, the guy we'd found staying in the Mayburg place, making bacon. Had he slept here? How scary had that been, even for him? Did having sight mean you were never scared anymore? Of course not. He had asked what had happened to me, and I'd said, "I got burned," just like that. Like it was some small fact I could speak out loud and then go on with my day. I said it again, into the blank, crazy night: "I got burned." Then I sat for a minute more, utterly still and quiet, until I was sure I could hear the lake at Point Park Beach. I stood up, wrapped Spark's leash tighter around my left wrist, and held my white cane in my right hand. I felt my way back to the door.

"Fuck you, nighttime," I said, and I walked out of the Mayburg place. Away from Point Park Beach and all the way home. I went slowly, not rocking, not chattering with fear, not talking anymore, just walking. Me and Spark and my white cane and night vision, in the middle of another dark, alone.

The grief counselors reappeared at school. It was as if they had been hiding underground and bloomed alive again suddenly when everything melted. Maybe they wanted to get a word in before vacation comes again. Otherwise summer might inspire more recreational drug and swimming suicides: *We're back! You've never met us before (except for that one time, when your friend gobbled tons of drugs and died in the lake, probably on purpose, and then her corpse floated up right where you learned to swim, and we showed up for a week at your school to ask how you were feeling), but here we are, in our capes and masks, to check in one more time. How are you feeling?* Much better now, thanks!

Logan must have gotten her driver's license last week, but she didn't mention it to me. I know because it was her birthday, and everyone has been going to get their licenses on their birthdays. I have a present for her, but I haven't had a chance to give it to her yet. She hasn't said anything about a party, and I'm too afraid to ask. What if she's having a sleepover and doesn't want me there, wetting the bed and leaving in the middle of the night? I don't think I'll ever be able to tell her about sneaking out to the Mayburg place alone. Not because I'm mad, maybe, but because some secrets only mean something if you keep them for myself.

I was standing at my locker, getting ready to go to English myself, when Logan came up.

"Hey," she said.

"Hi."

"Um, Em? So Zach and I were thinking, maybe we should meet up at the Mayburg place again? This weekend? I mean, now that it's so weirdly warm, it might be . . ."

I waited.

She said, "Fun?"

"You think?" It came out meaner than I meant it to.

"Come on, Emma," she said in a pleading voice. "Don't you want to keep talking? Do you actually not think it's worth it anymore? Or are you just mad at me? Blythe is willing to come, if—"

"Of course it's worth it. I just . . ." I felt sorrow wash over me and threaten to drag me under. "Let's do it Saturday," I finally said. "Why don't you ask people from here? I want to invite some friends from Briarly."

"Oh, okay. Sure," she said, and turned and walked away midsentence.

"Logan?"

"Yeah?"

"Happy birthday."

"Thanks," she said, and kept walking.

In Ms. Spencer's class, when she asked us whether Antigone had done the right thing by "refusing to follow the law," I raised my hand.

"Yes, Emma?" Ms. Spencer said, unable to hide her surprise.

"I think she did follow the law, just not the state's law. Her own, private one."

No one cared that I'd spoken, except for Ms. Spencer, who said, "Good point," and Ms. Mabel, who squeezed my arm. The planet kept spinning, and people kept yawning, talking, passing notes, opening drinks, bags of chips, pop, crunch. I should speak in class more often.

When I got home, I called Dee.

"So, um, hey, do you maybe want to come over this Saturday? I mean, if you don't have other plans or whatever? Or if your mom can bring you to Sauberg? I—"

"Sure! I'd love to," she said. "Should Seb tag along?"

"That would be great," I said, glad it had been her idea. "I, well, I got this kind of group of my friends from Lake

Main together a few times, to talk, you know, about this girl
from our school who died, and just about the world or whatever, and we might be meeting on Saturday in the late afternoon, so I was thinking you guys might want to come and
check it out."

"Uh, okay," she said.

"I mean, I think I need some moral support. So I'm hoping you'll come with me to our meeting."

"Sure," she said.

"Oh, and this is kind of weird, but we meet at this old,
abandoned house near where I live, so one of my sighted
friends or my sisters will come with us, if that's okay."

"Okay," Dee said. "I'll call Seb and see if he's up for it,
too."

That Saturday, Seb's mom drove them in and we all had
lunch in my kitchen, which seemed like the most normal
thing ever. Then I told my mom we were going on a walk, and
that Leah would come with us. My mom didn't object, didn't
even demand to know where we were going, even though she
must have been suspicious. She was working hard to let me
go; I could feel it. We headed straight to the Mayburg place.
Leah had been very eager to come, which I assumed was because she's generous and wanted to help me and my blind
friends find our way into the woods without perishing, but it
turned out she had other reasons as well.

When we got there, a few people had already gathered. Someone walked up to me, and when no one spoke, I did it. I reached my hand out and said, clearly, "Who's this?" I couldn't tell if Dee noticed.

"It's Christian, hey," Christian Aramond said.

"Hi, Christian. These are my friends, Sebastian and Dee," I said, and felt them reach their hands out and shake.

"Nice to meet you," Christian said, and I thought I could hear a lacy edge of envy in his voice. Maybe he thought Seb was my boyfriend. I didn't mind if he did, although maybe Dee minded.

"These are my friends, Sebastian and Dee," I said over and over then, interested in how easy it was, how everyone said "hey," how no one, not even David Sarabande, who amazed everyone by showing up, made a blind-leading-the-blind joke. No one seemed to think I was made doubly or triply blind by having blind friends. When Logan arrived, she came straight over and introduced herself. Her voice made my stomach pitch and flip, as it always did these days.

"You must be Sebastian and Dee," she said maturely. "I've heard so much about you guys. It's great to finally meet you." I thought of her jealousy when I was at Briarly. Now she either didn't feel it anymore or knew she wasn't entitled. I felt sad, in spite of myself. And unhappy that Logan knew more about what Seb and Dee looked like than I did. She could probably see that Dee was half Korean and half black. But I consoled myself with the chilly comfort that she didn't know what their hands or faces felt like.

"You're like the prom queen of your school," Seb said.

"Yeah, right," I said.

"She totally could be," Logan said. "But she's always been super shy because she has no idea how great she is."

Lo meant that as a compliment, obviously, but Dee punched Seb's arm. "She's a union leader, Seb, not a shallow prom queen, you sexist pig." Logan recoiled, probably horrified that Dee felt like she knew me well enough to correct anyone about me in front of her. But Logan said nothing. What could she say?

A few people in the back of the room started laughing, and I didn't know why, because whatever happened, I didn't see or hear it. But the laughter and the not knowing made me start to laugh, too. Maybe I was just really nervous, because I couldn't stop, even though nothing seemed particularly funny to me. After a minute, we were all laughing, and it was surreal because I had no idea why I was laughing, let alone why everyone else was. Except Dima, who shouted, "What is everyone laughing about?"

I stopped laughing fast, realizing if Dima was there, then Blythe must be, too.

"We're sorry," I heard Deirdre Sharp say.

I heard my own voice before I realized I had decided to speak. "My older sister Sarah laughed at our grandma's funeral," I said loudly, shocked to hear the bright, hot words come out of my mouth.

"Weak," David Sarabande said. I wondered why he kept coming, why Blythe did, too. Maybe it's better to be in the conversation than out of it, no matter what the conversation is.

I shrugged it off. "Yeah," I agreed. "I thought our mom would be mad, but she said sometimes people's bodies overwhelm their minds."

"Whatever that means," Carl Muscan said.

"It means that your body is trying to fix you, to heal you when your heart is broken," Leah said, from way in the back of the room.

"I remember that," said a voice I recognized before the word *remember* was finished. The I was Sarah's, the *remember* a kind of onyx word, glinting into *that*. It took me a minute to get it: Sarah was there, with Leah; had come to my meeting, a meeting I had organized. Leah must have invited her. Sarah, peppery, mean-spirited Sarah, was in the room. She had let me tell that story, her story, and not a very nice one, without interrupting. I was amazed.

"Hey," I said. I waved. "Hi, Sarah. I didn't see you come in."

A couple of people, including Sarah, Leah, Logan, and Jason the runaway, laughed at this. Jason was sitting with Leah and Sarah. I listened hard.

"I laughed when I first saw the news about Claire, actually. I know it's horrible, but I lost my mind for a minute and it made me laugh," Deirdre Sharp admitted. "Until I cried."

Blythe, her voice an octave lower than it usually was, said, "Well, I didn't. When my mom told me they found Claire, I wet my pants. And then I blacked out. When I woke up, I was in the bathtub, with my parents trying to wash me."

No one laughed.

An image of Claire came into my mind. She was running, without shoes on. I tried to focus on it, and saw her on a road, barefoot. She looked like both a dream and an actual image. And as she ran, Claire transformed into Logan and then into me. I kept watching her on the screen in my mind. Maybe seeing Claire like that is as close as I can get to seeing at all, or to knowing what it would feel like to be somebody else, even a sighted version of myself. It was like my mind was rebelling about all the focusing in, and doing the opposite; it was projecting itself out onto other girls—and then reflecting their minds, lives, and eyes back onto me. If I had been Claire, would I have died? If Claire were me, would she kill herself? Maybe I've been wrong thinking that after my accident I have no choices anymore. Maybe every minute is a choice I make to be alive for that minute. And the next and the next.

"Emma, are you okay?" I turned toward the orange voice, which belonged to Josh.

"Yeah, I'm fine, thanks," I said quietly.

"Oh, okay," he said, embarrassed. "You just . . . I thought you might be—"

"I'm fine," I said again, quickly, because I didn't want to let him say *crying*. I didn't want to hear him imagine what that might mean for someone with eyes like mine. Josh is nice; he sounds like morning, like juice pouring into a clear glass.

Then I realized someone else was crying, maybe Blythe. I didn't ask. Monica Dancat was talking, and her words sounded familiar, like I'd said or heard or thought them before. ". . . or because people would have been totally cruel about it if they'd known," she was saying. I thought of Logan making fun of Monica for dressing like a lesbian soldier. I thought of her making fun of Elizabeth Tallentine. Would Logan have been cruel to Claire if she'd had ammunition? Would I have? I wondered who talked about Logan, about me; who might joke about Seb and Dee after today. It suddenly seemed like none of it mattered much.

"Whatever," Carl said. "There are plenty of gay people in this town who don't kill themselves. You have to be mentally ill to . . ."

Then Blythe spoke. "Obviously," she said. "And plenty of people who kill themselves aren't gay or young, or whatever, aren't Claire." Her voice was different, deflated, edgeless.

"I'm just saying, I think she felt like she had a lot to hide, right?" Monica asked, and I thought how she probably did, too. How we all did.

"Everyone feels that way, don't you think?" Dee said. She knew no one except Seb and me, and yet she felt like she could say what she wanted, which happened to be what I had been thinking but been way too chicken to say. And interestingly, no one was like, "What is that blind stranger doing, talking at our meeting?"

Logan responded to Dee. "Yeah, I think so. No matter where they live. We're all hiding shit. Maybe Claire was just more of a pressure cooker than the rest of us."

I expected Blythe to contradict this, or at least to be annoyed that Logan had said anything about Claire. But she didn't. She let it go. I wanted to be like Dee. Why was it so difficult for me to be brave and so easy for everyone else?

So I said to Blythe, "Do you think Claire meant to die?"

There was a long silence. But finally she just said, "I don't think everyone's hiding some kind of amazing truth, Emma. I know that's how you see it, but maybe it wasn't simple. And we don't get to know what she was thinking. She didn't leave a note. So who knows what the hell she wanted? Maybe she was waiting for me. I was supposed to meet her that night, so maybe you'll think that's like another huge secret the world's keeping from you."

I ignored the rude part. "Why didn't you meet her?"

"Because my parents caught me sneaking out. So what?"

"Doesn't that make it seem more like an accident? I mean, if she was planning to hang out that night, maybe she just—"

"What I'm saying is, stop it," Blythe said. "It doesn't matter and the guessing and keeping on about it just make it worse."

"So what *should* we do?" Logan asked.

"I don't know," Blythe said. "Why don't we do something she would have liked? Like shut up and go swimming. At night."

Coltrane Winslow said, "I love that idea," which surprised me.

My heart flipped a bit. "What if we each brought her something?" I said quietly. "And left it somewhere? Maybe where she's . . ." I couldn't bring myself to say either *buried*, that horrible blue-gray word, or *grave*, which was so bleak and airless it made my dark seem like sunlight and glitter. "I mean, what if we each left some object or photo or thing that's meaningful to us, so we can all . . . would that be okay?" I was thinking of Benj, of Champon sitting on the rabbit's grave, keeping her company.

A few people said sure, and Blythe was like, "Yeah, okay, why not?" And then we kind of drifted off and talked about school and when the outdoor movie screenings were going to start and how stupid it is that they only show musicals from the dark ages, and then someone from Pendelton took out a box of wine. Zach Haze suggested a drinking game and Logan was laughing and I didn't really want to stay or play or drink. So Sarah and Leah and Seb and Dee and I decided we'd take off, and started walking back through the woods.

Seb hadn't said anything the whole time at the Mayburg place, but as soon as we left with Leah and Sarah, he was showing off. "Let's go swimming in the lake right now," he suggested. "Come on. Seriously. It's warm enough. Let's do it."

Fortunately, Dee said, "No thank you," so I wouldn't have to. But as soon as I felt all relieved about not having to say no, I decided to be a decent friend for the first time in my life, so I admitted that swimming, especially at night, especially in the lake, sounded horrible to me, too. "I second the no-thank-you. Lake Brainch sounds like a horror movie," I said.

"Don't be so chicken, Emma," Seb said. "I thought you were all into doing brave shit lately, holding big town hall meetings and whatnot. And you got over your skiing phobia on the bunny hill."

"And your thing about fire," Dee said.

"What do you mean?" I asked.

They were quiet.

"Uh, your sister said you made a bonfire out of your homework in the backyard, so we figured . . ." Seb started.

"Really? Which sister?"

"Come on, Emma, lighten up," Sarah said. "I didn't think it was a big deal."

"How'd you even know about that?"

"You think there's anything that happens in our house that everyone doesn't know about?"

To my annoyance, Leah laughed at this.

"Yeah. I know. I just thought . . . I don't know," I said.

"What? You thought what?" Sarah asked.

"Whatever, Sarah. Since when have you been interested enough to know what I'm doing?"

"Maybe since longer ago than you know."

"Yeah, maybe."

"You know, it's possible that even you can be wrong occasionally, Emma," Sarah said.

"Apparently I can be wrong pretty often," I said. "But at least I'm willing to admit it."

"That's true," Dee said. "You're good like that. Now that you talk."

We were turning onto Oak when a fat drop of rain fell on my head. Two seconds later, it started to pour.

"Let's run!" Seb yelled, and took off.

"Show-off," Dee said.

"Can you run?" Leah asked me and Dee, and we said, "Yeah, okay," and she grabbed the hand I wasn't using to hold Spark's leash and started off at a slow trot. Then I heard Sarah ask Dee if it was okay to take her hand, and Dee said yes, too. Then we picked up speed until we were bolting through the rain, getting totally soaked and laughing. Dee shouted ahead to Seb, "You got your swim!" and for some reason this seemed really funny to me. I tried to imagine what we looked like, three blind mice and a dog, running with my sisters on either side of us like parentheses. I started singing, "She cut off their tails with a carving knife," and by the time we got home, I was bent over laughing at my own joke, even though no one else seemed to find it that funny.

Then suddenly we heard the roar of an engine so loud I wanted to cover my ears, but I couldn't because I was using my hands to feel the front gate of my yard and to hold Spark's leash and Leah's hand. But Leah dropped my hand as the engine slowed. "That's Jason," she said. "I'll see you guys later. Will you tell Mom I went out for a bit?"

Sarah said, "Sure," before I had time to say anything, and Leah sprinted off. Sarah took my hand then.

"Jason?" I asked. "The runaway from the Mayburg place?"

"He's not a runaway," Sarah said.

"What was that noise?"

"His motorcycle."

"Really? Is Leah going out with him?"

"I guess so."

"On his motorcycle?"

"Apparently."

"In the rain?"

"Jesus, Emma. What are you, Mom? Jason's a nice guy. And they're just friends. So far."

I tried to press down the envy rising in my throat. Did Leah confide in Sarah instead of me? Was it like Logan not telling me about her life last summer, because she thought I'd be jealous or feel left out? Or was it something worse: had I never asked Leah a single question about herself?

In my room, Seb and Dee and I listened to weird music by this band Logan had introduced me to, called Pearl and the Beard, and I took total credit and didn't mention Logan. I think they were impressed. Seb said he'd been practicing biking, because his new plan was to teach himself how to bike to and from school, and Dee told me she was going to Korea in the summer to visit her grandma. Hanging out with them was easy: we didn't have to talk about anything intense or crazy, no one we knew in common had died, and we'd all been blind since we'd met and it was just normal. They didn't seem to think the Mayburg meeting had been that weird, and being in my room with them felt like exhaling after all the drama at Lake Main.

After they left, I was in a good mood, and I went to Sarah's room. Leah wasn't back yet. "Um, so, I'm sorry," I said, hanging in the doorway.

"For what?" Sarah asked, fake confused.

"For saying that you never believed in anything good about anyone. And that you were self-involved or whatever." Hearing it again didn't make it better, and I could feel her bristle.

"I accept your apology," she said.

Then I waited for her to apologize, too, for being such a bad sister that I'd felt compelled to say that to her in the first place. For calling Spark "that dog," and never letting him into her and Leah's room, which was hardly a spotless place of worship. I walked in, pushing past her, and sat on Leah's bed.

Instead of apologizing, Sarah asked, "Why didn't you invite me to your big parties?"

"What? They weren't parties," I said. "I mean, you saw—it was, like, a bunch of us trying to . . . and anyway it didn't work. But it wasn't like we were—"

"Whatever, Emma," she said. She went over to her desk.

"I made these," she said, handing me a fat envelope. "You can have them."

I felt the cream color before opening the thing up and sliding out a bunch of smooth, loose pages.

"They're printed on regular printer paper," she said, "but they're pictures of your thing from before you burned it. And two of the fire."

"You took pictures of . . . Did Benji tell you?"

"Come on, Emma. You think Benji went out in his pajamas with a bucket of water alone?"

I thought about this. "You were there?"

"Yes."

"Why didn't you say something?"

Her voice was quiet, maybe unfriendly, or maybe just hesitant. "I knew you would take it the wrong way if I—" I didn't say anything. Sarah's voice rose to a slightly more cheerful register. "Whatever. I just thought you'd prefer Benji. I didn't want you to think I was trying to, like, criticize you or control what you wanted to do. So I sent him."

"But you took pictures of my . . . ?" I was too embarrassed to call it "memoir sculpture," or anything else at all, and my words seized up. But the truth is, I missed that stupid lump of clay with the chopstick white cane and the half-dog. Not to mention my L&E rule book. Now I'd never see any of it again. I shouldn't have burned it.

Sarah said, "Show these pictures to Fincter to prove you did the work," she said. "You don't want to fail art. Take it from me."

"Did you fail—" This seemed like the wrong question, so

I started again. "But you took these before. I mean, why did you take pictures of that stupid, hideous lump of clay in the first place?"

Now her words were pinched flat and ashy. "It wasn't stupid. It was good, especially the white cane and the wire eyes and everything. Mom loved it, of course."

I didn't know my mom had ever seen it. I hadn't shown it to her.

"Did she ask you to take pictures of it?"

"No," Sarah said in gray, annoyed way. "I was going to use them because I was writing about what happened, but I didn't. Because like you said, I'm no Leah or you."

"What were you writing?"

"Nothing," she said, and I heard her stand up. "I didn't do it and it doesn't matter."

Her college essay. She had been writing her college essay about my accident and she hadn't been able to finish.

"Why didn't you ask me to help?"

She didn't answer, but I knew why. Because she'd been afraid I would be possessive about my story, or think less of her for being too stupid to write her essay herself. Both were possible.

"Maybe I could help now?"

Her teeth scraped against each other, and two opposing parts of my mind clamped shut on a thought like teeth on teeth: How much had my older sisters suffered? How scared or traumatized were they? I know this sounds crazy, but it wasn't until I heard Sarah's teeth make the sound that I really thought of it. My accident had seemed like mine alone, or mine and my mom and dad's or something. But how terrible for me has Claire's death been? And I'm as far away from her as anyone else who knew her from childhood or school or whatever small intersections there were between our lives. So isn't it possible that my accident might have been life-wrecking for Sarah in more ways than just costing her our parents' attention?

"Yeah, no thanks, Emma," she said. "I have to write my college essay myself, you know." In her voice was the same hiss of self-hatred I'd heard in Logan's. I thought of the snake tattoo I would never see, moving up Sarah's leg, hidden by socks.

"I don't know about having to do it yourself," I said truthfully. "I think most people have to ask for help in whatever areas they need it in. I obviously have a lot of those areas. And I get a lot of help."

I slid the pictures back into the envelope. "I wish I could see these," I said. "Thank you for taking them. Sometimes I wish so much I could open my eyes. I just . . . even just once, so I could, you know, take one last look at . . . well, at everything. Or stay friends with my friends. Or do any of the things that I should be doing. Like grow up, for instance. But I can't. I can't do anything right anymore."

She didn't argue with me, or offer stupid advice. She just said, "I'm really sorry." And, "I can't imagine."

I shrugged. "Maybe you can."

-14-

It stayed the hottest spring in the history of the world, and the funny thing is, I felt relieved: not that we're destroying the earth, but that summer was almost back. I wasn't surprised or enraged, like last year. I guess that's progress, because I'm glad that almost a whole year has passed since Claire, almost two since my accident. It makes me feel further away from both of those things, closer to something else, something better. Maybe just summer break, cheesy musical screenings on Lake Street, lazy mornings in the house. Maybe I'll even make it to the lake with Logan. Or Seb and Dee.

Ms. Spencer told us this week in class about the pathetic fallacy, and how easy it is to think what's happening outside of us is related to or representative of what's happening inside of us. Then she read us a poem in English about how stupid spring is anyway, maybe to make us feel better about the fact that we'll never experience it again. The poem was by Edna

St. Vincent Millay, and I loved it, and I said in class that I liked it because it wasn't cheerful or fake. Coltrane came up to me after and said he'd liked it, too. I was like, "Yeah. It's almost good enough to forgive Spencer for making us read *The Inferno*," and then I laughed a little too loud. He was quiet for a second, but then said, "I kind of liked that one, too, though." And then I wandered off, feeling awkward—even though, why? I mean, shouldn't it be okay to disagree with people some of the time? Why do I always feel like everyone has to see things the way I do?

I had a snack after school with Sarah and my mom. Leah was out with Jason again, and I've noticed that the more she's out with him, the more Sarah's around. And the more Sarah's around without Leah, the more of an actual human being Sarah can be. She even walked home from school one day last week with me and the little kids, because Jason picked Leah up on his motorcycle, which our mom still doesn't know about. Maybe it hasn't been that easy for Sarah to be Leah's terrible twin. I'd never really thought about it before.

On the first really hot Saturday, some of us met up at the cemetery. It was dusk, and the air was thick with sudden humidity, pollen, the steady hum of a cloud of gnats above us.

Zach and Josh and Logan and Blythe and Christian and Deirdre arrived, followed by a trickle of kids, including Amanda, David, Carl, and Coltrane.

"Mr. Hawes is here," Logan said, grabbing my arm. "Weird."

"And Mr. Aramond, Christian's dad," I heard Deirdre say. "Did someone tell the teachers?"

More adults were apparently gathering. Mostly teachers, from the whispering, and some parents. I didn't know who, exactly, but my parents weren't there. We just did what we had planned to anyway: took turns walking up to Claire's grave and leaving whatever objects we'd brought. Logan whispered in my ear: now Blythe was unscrewing her nose ring and setting it down; Carl Muscan left a police badge his uncle had given him. Zach put a book down, and when Logan told me that, I didn't ask what book it was, or even whether she knew.

"I'm going now, Em," she said. "Do you want to come?"

"No thanks," I said.

She let go of my hand and walked away from me, toward the grave. A little time passed, during which no one told me anything about what was happening. Then Logan came back and she picked up my hand. I felt bad for not walking up with her.

"What did you leave?" I whispered.

"My chemistry set," she said, the one her dad had given her when we were little, when he and her mom were married; the one we'd made borax snowflakes with.

When it was my turn to go up, I asked Logan to come with me, and she said sure. She told me when we arrived at Claire's grave, and I bent to touch the stone, letting go of Lo's hand and passing Spark's leash to her. Then I gently set down Mr. Hawes's pen. I whispered my quiet thank-you—to Benj, because who but Benj would have thought to leave his most beloved possession for a dead friend? And then I said, silently, "I'm sorry," to Claire.

Then Logan held on to me on the way back to the crowd of quiet kids. She touched my arm with the hand she wasn't using to hold mine. "Why a pen?" she whispered. And I could hear that she was hurt even before she found out why it was that she wouldn't know about an object I loved enough to have considered using it for this.

"Because Mr. Hawes gave it to me," I said. "It was his in high school." I heard her take this in. "I'm sorry I lied about it."

She was quiet. Obviously her giant lies trumped my tiny ones, but she still minded. In a way, I was glad. Not to have lied to her, but that she still cared about our sad, lost pact, too. Eventually, while other kids filed up with their treasures, she said, "It's okay. About Mr. Hawes giving you a present. I get why you didn't want to tell me that."

When everyone was done, Blythe went back up to the front and stood at Claire's grave. "Hey, everyone," she said. There was a buzz of hellos.

"So we're all here," she said shyly. Then she paused for a long moment, as if deciding something, and added awkwardly, "This is a vigil for Claire, who, um, as you know, committed suicide last June. We were all her friends, and so we've been talking about how to remember her life? So, she was my . . ." I could hear people crying, but I couldn't tell who. I didn't feel like I was going to cry, just felt really quiet and calm in a way I don't think I've ever felt before. "She was my best friend, since we were kids, and my girlfriend, so . . . Anyway, we've left some things here today for her, and, um, if anyone else wants to leave something or say something, anyone who wants to can."

Dima said, from behind us, "I do," and she moved toward the grave while we waited. "So no one's really said this out loud in the news or whatever, but we all know Claire was, you know, a wild one," she said, and there was laughter, soft, in-joke laughter, like we all knew her and it's okay, now that Blythe talked, to say she was wild. Dima's voice blended with the air coming off the lake, slowly moving through the leaves and branches around the cemetery. Dima sounded nervous, unlike herself, and I wondered for a moment what her throat looked like, her jaw, her cheekbones. I had never seen her, and I wanted to. Dima was saying, ". . . pure fun, too. I guess we all know she was kind of crazy. In a good way, I mean. And I think she would want us to keep telling her story."

Some people clapped awkwardly, but that seemed wrong, and then Dima walked back into the crowd.

Josh was standing behind us, and Logan whispered to him, "Hey, Josh, what'd you leave for Claire?"

"Nothing," he said. "I mean, something, of course, but . . . well, forget it."

I perked up, interested that he could be embarrassed. Spark barked for some reason. I reached down and petted him.

"No, come on, what was it?" Logan asked.

"Just an old note," he said.

I smiled. "I save those, too," I said, but he didn't say anything else, and I turned my attention back to the ceremony. Logan let go of my hand, walked back up to the grave, and said that Claire and Blythe had taught her to be braver.

When she came back, she told me Amanda Boughman was walking up.

She started with, "I was always jealous of Claire," but I didn't hear whatever she said next, because I felt a hand on my shoulder and I turned. It was a boy's hand. "Emma," someone said, and I flinched. Christian Aramond.

"Um," he said. "So, I, uh . . ."

"Yeah?"

"I'm sorry."

"Why are you sorry, Christian?" I asked, trying to sound more patient than I felt, as always with him.

"I wanted to apologize for something I did."

"Okay."

"But I only did the thing because I wanted to fix it, not because I wanted to, you know, hurt anyone or . . . I know that sounds . . ."

In honor of the occasion, I tried especially hard to mask my annoyance. "What, Christian?" I asked, failing.

"So, um, my skateboard? I just . . ."

My voice dropped with my stomach, as if they'd been holding hands. "That was you?"

"You're a fucking asshole, Christian," Logan hissed.

He sounded like he was crying. "I didn't want to—I just wanted to move it out of the way after, so you would know, you know, that it was there, and that I took it away, but then Logan—" Had he been trying to wound me? Or save me? Maybe this is weird, but I felt distinctly like I didn't care.

"Fuck you, Christian," Logan said. "How dare—"

"No, it's okay," I said. "Forget it, Lo—let's drop it. Just . . . why did you even bother telling me?" I don't know what I expected. That he'd been moved by our Mayburg meetings, or by Claire's vigil?

"Mr. Hawes told me I had to . . . but Emma, it's—"

"Forget it. Please." I didn't want to talk to him, or hear anything else about it. Ever again.

I turned to Logan. "Did you do something for your birthday?" I asked, as afraid of her answer as I had been about anything.

"No, I . . . I didn't, because I—" she said, and her voice was broken into a lot of just-stepped-on pieces.

"Because you . . . ?" I asked, and even though I tried to sound worried and sad for her, the words were shimmering with relief and joy.

"I was waiting until we're friends again," she said.

"Shhh," someone said from behind us. We shut up and I tried to listen. UFO-spotter Jason Kane was up at Claire's grave, speaking now, and I felt bad that we'd talked over him, which probably seemed intentional and mean, especially given that he was saying, ". . . and Claire didn't laugh. So, uh, I just wanted to say that. And neither did Blythe Keene. Okay. That's all." There was a silent pause and then some slow rustling, so I assume he walked back to wherever he'd come from. Logan put her hand in mine again.

Right as I started wondering why the quiet was lasting too long, a man said, "Hello, kids," and I knew. The quiet changed then, became thousands of feet deep, went blue and almost solid. It was so silent that I wanted to put my hands over my ears. I felt the air moving behind the man, through the trees that lined the side of the cemetery facing the street. I thought I could hear, almost see, the grass against his shoes, parting and flattening where he stood. I imagined his shoes were black and polished, and thought of Sebastian, unloading flowers at his graveyard job last summer. I thought of Claire, underneath where we were standing, dead; how the word *underneath* doesn't come close to the literal thing.

"I just wanted to stop by and say hello," the man said. "Mrs. Montgomery couldn't make it, but, well, we both wanted to say we hope you kids have a good summer, okay? Be safe."

"Thank you, Mr. M.," Amanda Boughman said. I wondered what Blythe was doing, whether she was looking at Claire's dad, or holding hands with Dima, or looking down at the ground. Then Amanda asked, "Um, Mr. M.? Is it okay if we keep on with our vigil?"

I didn't hear anything; maybe he nodded, or maybe he shook his head. Either way, people were too shy to keep talking about Claire in front of her father, so then Josh said a little too loud, "Well, maybe now is a good time—for our quick dip in Claire's honor."

Then I heard Josh grin, I swear. And I remembered suddenly that I'd seen his dimples when we were kids, and that they were uneven—the right one up by his cheek, the left lower. "Ready?" he asked us. We headed toward the woods. I checked the band on my sunglasses and held on to Logan as we walked, a group of us, back into the woods until we were at Point Park Beach. We shed our clothes and I decided not to think about the fact that I couldn't see anyone; figured Logan would tell me later who swam in what. She and I had bathing suits on under our shorts and T-shirts. We stood for a short beat, facing the darkening lake: Logan, Amanda, Blythe, Zach, Josh, Carl, Coltrane, Deirdre, and a bunch of other kids, although I didn't know exactly who. It smelled like water moving, grass and flowers in a riot of sunshine and spring, the world ramping up for another round of living and dying. I could hear people shouting, but not their words. I thought of Claire's dad's voice, his *hello*, his *kids*, his *be safe*, the sound of wishing so desperate and blindingly bright in each word that my eyes hurt.

I thought about *be safe* as we all felt for each other's hands—if I'm being totally honest, I was hoping to be next to Coltrane, so I could hold his hand, but I was disoriented and ended up between Josh and Logan. I held tight. Then we ran, our feet crunching twigs and leaves until the ground turned to sand. I held my breath, trusting Josh and Logan to keep hold of my hands. When our feet hit the water we let go. We were laughing, splashing, running shallow until the lake deepened and slowed us down, swept us up. The water came to meet me, and I braced for a moment before I dove under, to the quiet, dark blue. I held my breath, pushed my arms forward and my legs back, stretched and moved and sliced through the water so smoothly and powerfully that it gave me a surge of courage. When I came up for a breath, breaking through the cool surface into the air, I said Claire's name out loud. And then I listened to the other voices nearby, like lightning bugs in the dark, little flashes of remembering. And I turned and swam, supported by the water and my own breath, back toward my friends.

It's staying light later, and last week we went to the Mayburg place even though there was no reason except that as usual, we have nowhere else to hang out. At least nowhere that our parents aren't hovering above us. A bunch of us stayed at the Mayburg place through dinner; we decided to order pizza and have it delivered to the closest highway exit. Then we were eating pizza and it was dark out and our being there morphed from whatever we'd been calling it—a meeting, I guess—into a straight party. It was like a shift in the color of the night, and as soon as it happened, I wanted to go home.

I was standing in the doorway, wondering how I'd get home alone—I knew Logan wouldn't want to leave and I didn't even want to ask her. I was also worrying about whether I'll always hate parties, when an orange voice asked, "Can I get you a drink?"

Josh Winterberg. I said, "Sure, of course, yeah, thanks," embarrassed that I had been standing there like a terrified animal about to get plowed down in the road. Not to mention, why had I felt the need to use so many words when I could have just said "yes, please" like a normal human being? But he didn't seem to notice, just handed me a cool, plastic cup of something, which he must have already been holding. It smelled pink, like lemonade, icy, sparkling. It smelled like summer. I took a cold sip—it was some kind of Kool-Aid or juice, and I thanked him again and then he said, "So, uh, do you want to go outside for a minute?"

I said, "Sure, okay," and he kind of took my elbow, which made energy shoot through my arm like I'd plugged it into a socket. We walked outside, until he was like, "So, um, should we sit here?" And I had no idea if we should sit there or not, so I said yeah, okay, and he took my elbow again and helped me sit down on what turned out to be a log. I could hear him breathing. I was nervous enough that it took me a second to realize how nervous he was. But once I did, it made me want to slide my hand into his, so I did. Mine was cold from being scared and his felt big and warm, like an oven mitt or a glove. He wrapped it around my hand right away, like he was happy about it. I suddenly couldn't wait to tell Logan, even though she was obviously way beyond thinking that holding hands with Josh was a big deal. I had the mood-wrecking thought that if I told my mom, she might be the only one as thrilled as I was. We sat there on the log, listening to the noise of the warm night, crickets, dry grass, and the lake, close enough to where we were sitting that we could hear it.

"So, um, I mean, that note I left at the vigil? The one that was—whatever? It was from fifth grade."

I waited.

He laughed a nervous, unfamiliar laugh. "So, I guess it's pretty obvious it was from you," he said. "I don't know if you remember that you wrote it to me—about the floor hockey thing in gym? I'd saved it since grade school. But now I don't have it anymore because I . . . um, I—" Maybe he realized that nothing he said was coming out right, because instead of finishing, he took my other hand and pulled me toward him and put his mouth on my mouth. Our noses bumped, and then his touched my sunglasses, which I reached up and steadied. My senses rushed at me, and I could feel his jaw and hands and mouth and shoulders, taste a mint he'd maybe just eaten, and a kind of boy-soap and boy-sweat-and-sneakers navy-blue feeling about him. His shirt and something spicy, maybe cologne or deodorant. I thought how the only boy in our family was Benj, and he was still so little that I didn't really know much about what teenage guys wore or smelled or sounded like up close.

Josh held pretty still, with his mouth on my mouth, and I was trying to turn my brain off, so I could feel instead of think. *Feel it,* I thought. *Feel his heart racing, and your own heart beating*. I felt both, moving so fast I wasn't sure whose was whose. I was giddy and breathless, trying to turn my mind down to a quiet hum, trying to *focus out*, to concentrate on kissing him back, on what he—and I—felt like. I had just opened my mouth a little, and put my hands on the back of his warm neck and then up a little bit into his hair. It was soft and wavy. Then I heard footsteps and Christian Aramond's voice: "Oh, sorry, man, my bad." Josh and I sprang away from each other, and Christian crunched away through the woods. We were alone again, but it was too embarrassing to leap back into each other's arms.

"Well, um, I guess we better, you know, get back or whatever," Josh said, in a voice that was still orange, but lit from the inside with embarrassment and also excitement, one that gave me the feeling of a giddy kind of falling, like a roller coaster right at the magenta moment when the rise becomes the fall. Like skiing, too, I guess, except not cold or solo.

We stood and walked back to the Mayburg place, holding hands. When we arrived at the door, he offered to walk me home, and I said, "Oh my god!"

Josh stopped walking so fast he almost tripped.

"What's up, Em?" he asked, and I liked the way my one-syllable name sounded in his voice. It was sexy, a kind of gruff *Em*, the way he said it. Like he wanted something. My stomach felt fizzy again.

"I forgot about Spark," I said. He was still in the Mayburg place, had been inside this entire time.

It wasn't until I said the words—to Josh Winterberg—that I realized that there were moments when I was forgetting to need Spark. I wondered if I would admit this to my parents, who were pushing me to go to guide dog school and get a registered mobility-assistance dog as soon as I turned sixteen in June. I decided I wouldn't tell them anything. When you're little, you feel like your parents know every private thought you have. I remember vividly the moment I realized I could actually keep secrets from my parents. I was sitting with my mom on the porch and she had her knees up and her arms wrapped around them and she was looking off into the distance, thinking. And I said, "Mom?" and she didn't hear me. And this weird wave came over me, because I knew she was far away in her own mind, and that it was a place where there were thoughts I didn't and couldn't know about. At first, I was sad and scared. But then, almost in the same second, I realized it was true of my mind, too; that I had thoughts my mom couldn't know. It seems truer to me the older I get. I can even see my parents feeling and reacting to it, especially now that Leah's off to college in the fall and Sarah's finally working on her applications. It's in the questions they ask us, the ways they think about our days, even how they touch or look at us; it's like the more we know, the more they're in a state of constant wonder.

Kissing Josh added another layer to my secret inside life, the one that belongs only to me, and that other people can't really touch or see, even if I choose to tell them. I think I love that layer, the lava at my center.

"I'm sure he's fine, but let's go get Spark," Josh said, and I liked the way Spark's name sounded in his voice almost as much as I liked my own.

At first I thought everyone must be noticing us as we came back in, still holding hands, and I was glad. And then I realized they were probably all occupied with their own dramas. And I was still glad. I had just let go of Josh's hand to squeeze by people and find Spark when Logan came rushing over and jumped on me. "Em! I've been looking all over for you!"

"I'm just grabbing Spark and heading out," I said.

She went silent.

"What's going on?" I asked.

"It's about Zach, he just—" she said. "Can we talk for a minute?"

"Em, you ready?" Josh said from somewhere in a crowd of people behind me.

I stood still for a minute, waiting for Spark, who I could now hear padding and panting his way toward me, and Josh, who was standing behind me in the mass of people.

"Of course, Lo," I said. "Tell me what happened. Josh, can you give us a sec?"

"Sure, yeah, um, I'll wait out front," Josh said. I blushed.

"Okay," I said, turning back toward Logan. "Is everything all right?"

Her voice dropped to a whisper. "Wait. Is Josh waiting out front for you?"

"I can tell him to go ahead, just—"

"Is he walking you home? Did you just make out with him? Is that where you were?"

When I said yes, quietly, she screamed with delight, grabbed both my hands, and started literally jumping up and down. She was like Baby Lily or Benj, going from crying to celebrating inside of an instant.

"*What?!* What are you waiting for? Go!" she said. "Do not send him ahead. I'll walk my dumped self home. I deserve it. Walk with Josh and take his pants off and—not a germ on it!—call me the minute he leaves!" She gave me a gentle push. "But don't do anything I wouldn't do! Get it? Ha!"

I didn't let go of her hand. "Don't be ridiculous," I said. "I'm not leaving you here. Come with us."

"No," she said. "You don't be ridiculous. I'm staying; let Josh walk you home."

"Come with us, Lo, and sleep over. Then we'll have time to talk."

If Spark felt betrayed that I had left him inside while I kissed Josh in the woods, he didn't seem to hold a grudge; he just came up beside me and nuzzled my hand. I pulled a Milk Bone out of my jean skirt pocket and gave it to him. And if anyone else at the Mayburg place even noticed that Josh and I were holding hands, they didn't mention it. Maybe no one else is as surprised as I am that someone would want to kiss me in the woods.

As we walked, I wrapped Spark's leash around my wrist so I could hold my white cane in my right hand and Josh's hand with my left. I had to work to walk steadily, because I didn't want to drive Josh up onto the embankment. I wondered if Logan missed holding my hand. She talked the entire way home. Zach had broken up with her. He had apparently known about the Brian thing, and thought it would be okay with him, but now it bothered him too much that she had lied about it or not told him the whole story or whatever, and apparently she didn't mind Josh—or me—knowing all the details.

When we got to my yard, Josh and I stopped. Spark barked. I laughed, reached my left hand down to pat him. "It's okay, Spark, he's our friend," I said. Josh kind of leaned in toward me and Logan was like, "Jesus, you two, get a room!" But then she bounded up the porch steps, leaving us on the lawn. We stood there, awkwardly, and when Logan opened my front door I could hear the light and chatter coming from inside the house: Sarah's voice, Leah's, my mom's, and then a boy's, maybe Jason's.

"Is there a motorcycle in the driveway?" I asked Josh. Maybe my asking this kind of stupid question would remind him that I couldn't see, freak him out.

But he just said, "Yeah," and then leaned forward and kissed me again. Our noses and my glasses were in the way of each other, but I kept my hands still and tried not to think. I also had a little bit of a tickle in my throat, and tried not to obsess about, what if I coughed? What if you do cough while someone you never imagined would kiss you is kissing you? Does the person faint with horror? Do you both pretend it didn't happen? Do you say excuse me, or say nothing? How does Blythe Keene think about these things? I landed safely on the fact that Logan was staying over; we could stay awake all night analyzing the nose and glasses and possible coughing problems. And I could tell her about the feeling of Josh's pulse through my chest and back and hips, my lips and legs. And maybe this is crazy, but kissing Josh made me realize that I was also going to kiss other people, including, I hoped, Coltrane Winslow. And maybe Seb, too, if that ever became okay with Dee. I planned to amaze Logan by telling her this.

In fact, maybe I'd shock the whole town by being "the guy about it," and telling Coltrane I want to kiss him. I won't botch it like I did with Seb. I'll just call him up and ask him to meet me at Bridge for coffee, to talk about justice. Ha! He'll like that, I bet. I like Josh, and I also like Coltrane, and I'm going to like other people, and hopefully be like Blythe—at least a little bit, I mean—picking whom I like, not just getting picked by whoever likes me.

I kissed Josh one more time then, exactly the way I wanted to, fully, turning my mind off and my body on. It was kind of mind-clearing—I stopped thinking of Logan, Coltrane, Seb, Dee, Sarah, Blythe, Claire, the past, the future, anything at all; just let the world go blank and quiet, like water, how it used to be. Warm and beautiful, before I was scared all the time. Everywhere I could hear and feel and see the rainbow-sparkle liquid heat of that kiss.

-15-

Sometimes, I know for a fact that I can't imagine how Claire felt. But other times it seems to me like saying "I can't imagine" is the worst thing you can do to anyone else. So I try as hard as I can to imagine, while also trying not to die of fear, either my own or someone else's. Because maybe the whole point of being a good human being is trying to imagine—for real—what it feels like to be someone else. Maybe Claire was in an irrational amount of pain over Blythe, or her parents, or something complicated and private enough that there can be no record of it except the one her death created. Maybe she had what Monica Dancat calls "mental illness" but I think might just be regular human suffering.

When I can imagine, it's bottomlessly terrible. So maybe she felt that way all the time, without the bolts of joy to balance it out—maybe she never got the feeling of the braille dots rising up to mean something, or the piano sounding good again, or sisters laughing at a stupid joke only the five of you can get. Maybe Blythe never skipped her own birthday and then suggested going to the city at the end of the summer for a day to celebrate both birthdays. Or maybe she did, and the feeling of it made Claire desperate instead of happy. Maybe she took drugs to feel the way she thought she should feel more often—fun, or happy, or numb, or safe—and then she went swimming. Either to feel brave or to see blue or to feel dangerously alive.

And maybe in that moment, after the drugs, during the water, it's possible to think that you don't care whether you die. If it is, that's only because you don't know what it means to be dead, inside forever in the dark. You can't know about death until you're dead, not even if you're me. No one can see that forever, but we all know it's coming. Death is both the only thing we can be certain of and the thing we know least about, so I guess it makes sense to find it terrifying.

Here's what I think: Claire forgot for a second that she would be a million other Claires over the course of the rest of her life, and some of them would have been happy. Even though she once told Amanda Boughman that, so we all know she once got it. Or maybe, like so many of us, she got it about other girls, but couldn't hold it in her mind about herself. So I can totally imagine how she felt. And maybe the truth about Claire is like most truths: hard for everyone to agree on, kind of liquid, changeable—a weird, inconsistent lake.

The last week of school, Elizabeth Tallentine invited me to her house for a sleepover, and I said yes right away, the way she did when I asked her to come to the Mayburg place for our first meeting in the fall. Even though that was a crazy, terrible invitation. I didn't want to say anything that might make her think I didn't want to come. Because I did. And I didn't tell Logan. Maybe I was worried she'd make fun of it, or feel bad, or not care. Or maybe telling someone everything all the time isn't necessarily the definition of a good friendship. I mean, I don't know what Logan was up to that Saturday night, and it's okay, I guess, if sometimes we do our own things. Elizabeth's house smelled like my house, warm and busy. She has two brothers and the little one wanted to hang out with us and she said yes and I liked her for it. We stayed up really late talking about sex, even though neither of us has had it yet, and we're not 100 percent sure we'll ever find anyone who wants to and who we also want to do it with. We also talked about the world, because she wants to travel, which I think is brave and awesome. She wants to go to India someday, and Greece, and Latin America. I knew she had a big map in her mind, and it was fun to hear about it. She said she thinks I'd have an amazing time traveling the world, and maybe I could write a book on the way each country feels or smells or something, a totally original perspective with all my "colors" built in. I didn't even really know that I had mentioned the way I see things to her, but I guess I had. And she pays close attention. She was nice about it, too; I mean, I didn't feel like she was patronizing me or trying to make me feel better or anything—just like she thought it was a good idea.

Elizabeth and I came up with a self-dare for me: to call Coltrane Winslow. She had this great idea, which is that if I want to dare myself to do stuff, it should at least be stuff I want to do anyway, not stupid, random things like jumping out of tree houses or sneaking out to the Mayburg place, which I told her about and she seemed to think was both amazing and also not that surprising. But once we thought of the Coltrane call, I couldn't get out of it, and I was kind of glad. So maybe I'll dare myself to kiss him, too, the way Josh kissed me.

Coltrane didn't seem surprised to hear my voice on the phone; was just like, "Hey, Emma, what's going on?" And I said, just like I'd practiced with Elizabeth at our sleepover and even recorded myself at home saying, "I was wondering if you wanted to meet up at Bridge sometime?" I had deleted all the extra words from my early versions—where I was like, "to talk about our meetings," or "to talk about next year," or anything that would sound like an excuse.

Coltrane said, "Sure. When were you thinking?"

I hadn't planned this part. "Um, I don't know, maybe this week?"

And he said, "Are you free after school tomorrow?"

I wasn't; I had a piano lesson with Mr. Bender. "Yeah, totally," I said, thinking I would call Mr. Bender and just tell the truth for once. Not skip without calling, not have Leah call and pretend to be my mom; just call and explain that this week, Tchaikovsky had to wait for my date with Coltrane Winslow. A date I had initiated!

But Coltrane paused for a minute, and I could feel my heart clench. Should I have been harder to get, even though I had called him and asked him to meet me? Should I have put it off? I hadn't wanted to.

"So, um, I'll come by your locker after sixth period and we can walk over together?"

It was the first time I'd ever heard Coltrane say "um." Maybe he was nervous. I felt ecstatic. "Sounds good," I said, and my voice was lavender and fluttery like Logan's.

At Bridge, we each ordered a sparkling lemonade and we shared a blueberry muffin, which was his idea. We took turns taking little bits of the muffin, and our hands touched a few times while we talked about the year, Fincter, Spencer, Hawes's class, swimming at Point Park Beach, and Mr. M. showing up at the vigil. Coltrane asked how I came up with the idea of all of us meeting at the Mayburg place, and I totally took credit, didn't even mention Logan or Zach. We talked about Sauberg and America's justice system and the Edna St. Vincent Millay poem about spring. I told him about Briarly, and how braille felt like piano, and then he asked if I have extra sensitivity in my hearing or touching.

"Depends what I'm touching," I said. It's hard to say which one of us this surprised more, but maybe him, because I think he was too shocked to respond. We were both quiet until I started laughing, and then he laughed, too.

When we stopped, he asked, "Um, so, can I walk you home?"

"Sure, thanks," I said. We had finished our drinks and it was cooling off outside and there was no way to sit at Bridge anymore without it just being really weird. So I roused Spark, who was under the table, probably desperately bored. I felt bad for Spark as Coltrane and I walked out onto Lake Street. The walk was quiet, but it wasn't awkward, for some reason.

"So, Emma, can I ask you something?" Coltrane asked when we were halfway home.

"Of course," I said.

But then he waited kind of a long time, like whatever he was going to ask, he decided not to. He finally just said, "So, uh, are you coming to the Mayburg place Saturday?"

I said yeah, even though I was curious what he had actually wanted to ask.

"I was thinking maybe we could walk over together," he said, and my stomach fluttered.

"Sure, okay, yeah."

We were at my house. I was thinking about what it would be like to kiss him, what he might taste like—lemonade, or vocabulary, or summer? I don't know how to explain this, but he felt familiar to me: like love, or hard candy, or home—something I'd been waiting for. I could tell he wanted to kiss me but didn't know how to go about it. I wondered if he'd get home later and wish he had, or think of clever things he might have said on our walk. I really liked him; I think I liked him even more because I could tell he was unsure, too. I wished I were brave enough to make it easy for both of us and just kiss him myself.

But I said, "So, um, I guess I'll see you Saturday," and I bounced up the porch steps with Spark—one, two, three, four, five—confident and fast, without teetering or anything. At the top, I turned and waved, smiling, because I could tell Coltrane was still there, watching me.

As soon as I was inside the door, I dialed Logan. "You are not going to believe what I said to Coltrane Winslow," I said, and then I told her that I had asked him out and met him for coffee and said "depends what I'm touching," and that he was walking me to the Mayburg place on Saturday. And even though I had chickened out and not kissed him, she screamed so loud throughout the entire description that my mom heard her through the phone and came into the living room to check on me.

"I'm fine, Mom," I said, holding my hand over the mouthpiece.

"You're totally going to lose it to Coltrane Winslow," Logan was shrieking into the phone, loud enough for my mom to hear.

When we hung up, I went into the garage and felt around until I found my bike, still propped up against the wall where it had sat, untouched, for the last two years. I pulled it away from the wall and wiped the dusty seat with my hand, which I brushed off on my shorts. Then I climbed up and sat on my bike for what felt like hours but was probably ten minutes. Would it occur to me to ride it, and then would I force myself to open the garage door and careen forward into the driveway, across the sidewalk, into the street? How would I listen for cars if the breeze was fast or loud in my ears? Holding the handlebars, I thought of the eggs I'd thrown into the crosswalk with Dr. Sassoman. I put my right foot on the right pedal, and balanced my body by leaving my left foot on the ground. Then I focused as hard as I could on imagining what it would feel like to ride forward into the dark. Scary, and fast, and probably good, too.

Then I climbed off my bike slowly and carefully, and

leaned it back against the wall. Maybe I'll ask Sebastian to bring his bike over here someday and give me a courage transfusion. I wonder if Dee rides her bike, too; I've never asked her. I bet she does. Maybe even if they came over, it wouldn't help, but I think I want to see them ride their bikes either way.

Baby Lily took her first steps the same week I turned sixteen. She was already one, and my dad had started worrying about the walking, even though Leah and Sarah and I agreed with Mom that she'd walk when she was ready. Why pressure even the tiniest person in our family to hurry up and achieve everything? It turns out we were right, because one afternoon we were sitting on the living room floor—my mom and Leah and me in a kind of triangle across from each other, encouraging Lily to toddle on her own—and then she did it. She stood up and walked from my mom to Leah and then from Leah to me. We were only two feet apart from each other, but still. Sarah took a bunch of pictures while we all clapped like Lily had just won an Olympic gold medal. Benj came down to see what the noise was about, and Lily was laughing and shouting like, *Yeah, I told you so*, and then she let go of my hands, probably so she could clap with us or race over to Benj, but in any case it made her fall over. And then she crawled across the room.

I wished so hard I thought I might black out: that she would be safe, that nothing like what happened to me or Claire would ever happen to her. And I knew, as the joy over her walking rose like a balloon, that there was still, in me and in all of us, the sinking, scary truth: we couldn't be sure.

Logan was on her way to pick me up in her mom's car. I climbed up onto the gold couch to wait for her by the window, listening to Benj singing "Oh, I Had a Little Chickie," the warm-water, dancing, bang-bang version. Babiest Baby Lily was pulling herself up and standing at the edge of the couch, listening to Benj sing, then falling down, then pulling herself up again and falling again and screaming and pulling herself up again.

The doorbell rang and I got up to let Logan in.

"You ready?" she asked.

"I don't know," I joked. "How good a driver are you?"

"Logan, be careful, please," my mom said, coming to the door. "Emma, wear your seat belt and call me when you get there."

Naomi's voice was so small it sounded to me like it came from between the floorboards somewhere. "Emma? Can I come with you?"

I said yes fast, without asking Logan.

"She has to have a seat belt on in the backseat. Emma, make sure," my mom said.

"Fine."

Once we were all belted in like we were taking a trip to the moon, Logan backed out of the driveway so insanely slowly that I thought she might be kidding.

"Are you terrified or just protecting Naomi and me so my mom doesn't kill you?" I asked her.

But she answered in her serious voice, "I'm just trying to be more careful, I guess. About everything."

I laughed. I couldn't help it. "I'm trying to be less careful."

"Well," she said, "we should be good influences on each other, then."

Then Naomi said from the backseat, "Do you guys know what puberty is?"

I could hear Logan stifling a laugh. "Um, yes, I think so."

"Well," Naomi said, "it's disgusting."

At that, Logan laughed out loud. Naomi was silent and we both wondered if she was offended. Logan said, "You should talk it over with Annabelle. Aren't you guys the same age?"

"They are," I said, and I thought about how much easier it would be for Naomi to be in middle school than it would be for Annabelle. It seemed really unfair.

As soon as we got to Annabelle's and she came out, Spark went wild.

"Hi, Spark!" Annabelle said, dropping to her knees to smother him with kisses. "Hi, Emma." Then she went back to Spark. "I missed you! I missed you," she said, muffling the words into his neck.

"My friend Logan and my sister Naomi are with me, Annabelle," I told her.

"Oh," she said, not moving her face from Spark's. "Okay. Hey, Naomi." She didn't say anything about Logan.

Her mom invited us in, and Logan and Naomi and I followed Annabelle toward her room, where she showed us all her stuff. Logan hung back a little bit.

"These are my robots," she said, and I ran my hand along the surface of her desk, feeling a row of toys, lined up neatly. I picked one up, a square plastic robot whose head turned and who felt heavy, maybe battery-operated. "That one's remote-control," she said. "I can almost do it again, but not as good as before."

"These are cool," Naomi said shyly. And I thought again how different their lives were. And how unfair it was; Naomi could see all of Annabelle's stuff, and Annabelle would never see her own toys or friends or her mom again, and she might lose her hearing, too. And why? I wanted so much to make it better for her.

"You have a great room," Logan said.

"How'd you know which robot I was holding?" I asked Annabelle, impressed.

"I can hear which is which," she said proudly. "And I

memorized what order they're in. Just like you told me! And look!" She pulled open a drawer in the dresser, and I reached my hand in and felt dozens of neatly labeled shirts.

"Damn!" I said, and she giggled, scandalized. "My mom and I labeled them," she said.

I sat on her bed, and Annabelle must have heard the springs because she immediately said, "Spark can get on the bed if he wants."

"Up, boy!" I told him, and he leapt gleefully onto the little bed, where Annabelle and I both sat for a minute quietly, petting him.

"I came because I wanted to talk with you about Spark," I said.

"Is something wrong with him?" she asked, and her voice was so desperate I could hear every fiber of her fearful self in it.

"No, no! Not at all," I said, putting my hand on her arm, feeling the soft, skinny shoulder, thinking how hard a time she had already had, and how hard it would still be for her. When she couldn't hear anymore, what would colors be for her—music? touch? taste? I squeezed her shoulder a little. "My parents want me to go to guide dog school and get a trained guide dog at the end of the summer. And, well, Spark needs to be best friends with someone young and bouncy and playful. Someone who understands him as well as I do, and who can play with him more full-time than I can. Someone who really, really needs him."

"Do you mean me?" Her voice had all the air squeezed out of it.

"I do mean you," I said, and then the rest of the speech I had planned never happened, because Annabelle's joyous screaming drowned me out and brought her mother running.

Obviously her mom had already told my mom it was okay, so it wasn't like she was surprised, but she was weeping anyway. Naomi held my hand, shyly, or maybe proudly. She loved Spark, too, but she never showed a minute of jealously or unhappiness that I had decided to let Annabelle have him. Naomi is a good person.

"Emma," Annabelle's mom was saying, "it's not possible for me to express how much it means for her—and us—to have a friend like you. It's more than—"

My face felt hot, and I didn't want her to go on, especially in front of Logan, so I jumped in fast: "I have friends—and sisters—there's no way I could survive without," I said. "So I'm just, you know, trying to be like them, I guess." I don't know what Logan thought of this; she was quieter at their house than I've ever heard her anywhere. I squeezed Naomi's hand and she squeezed mine back and I thought I could feel her smile. As for Annabelle, she didn't hear any of it, because she was with Spark, sprinting for the yard.

• • •

The last day of school was a half day, and I told my sisters I would walk home from Lake Main alone. I wanted a minute to think, before Logan and Annabelle and Spark came over and we headed together to the Mayburg place for the afternoon.

On my way home, I listened to my neighborhood, wind coming through the green summer leaves. The concrete sidewalk was a chalky scratch under the heels of some short cowgirl boots Leah had just handed down to me, all like, "You can remember me by these when I'm away in the fall." They were very different from my Converse, and made me feel weird, almost like Leah instead of me.

I thought of Sarah, working on her essay, hoping she can get in somewhere for next year. Leah will already be a sophomore then. Maybe it wasn't that much fun always being in the same grade as Leah; maybe Sarah waited on purpose so she could have her own year, between Leah and me. I can't even take credit for that idea, actually; it's something I heard my mom say to my dad late at night. But unlike anyone else in my family, I managed to keep it to myself.

My white cane clicked out its efficient rhythm. I thought of what it showed me: cracks, leaves, a wrapper, small rocks—lots. When I got to our house, instead of going inside, I pushed open the gate to the backyard. It smelled like my entire life up until that moment: rustling red and gold leaves, wood smoke, Halloweens, new pencils, binders, notebooks, library books, cold nights when icicles hung from the roof of our house, summer dinners, listening to the hiss and pop of my parents' grill. I thought of the bristly night I sneaked out alone, held it close like a proud secret, like flying blind down the hill on skis and finding Seb and Dee at the bottom, waiting.

Music was pouring from my mom's studio, and the faint smell of cigarette smoke, and even though I felt it coming and tried to avoid it, I remembered the accident suddenly: the wet cut grass, paint on the buildings, hot bricks and barbecue and dogs and water; then the icy metal machines and plastic tubes of the hospital, even the moments, days, and months just after, full of terror. The burning dark of it, the way I felt, screaming, when I woke again and again and couldn't open my eyes. I took a breath, let the memory play out, tried not to put it into my blood or bones, not to store the fear of it for later.

I thought, walking into the yard, how little there now was to trip over, how the riding toys and soccer balls and wading pools were put away each day. How it had taken my mom and me forever to organize our drawers, closets, house. How we were still at it, and how *ongoing* is a shiny word and *done*, *over*, and *gone* are grimy, sad ones. I remembered how my mom walked my fingers over spoons and forks, scissors, tape and paper, the night she retaught me to wrap a present, poured shampoo in a huge, round bottle and conditioner into a tube. How every time I had gotten a haircut the year I was at Briarly I cried because what difference did it make? So I stopped cutting my hair at all. I haven't had it cut once this year. Because I couldn't see, so what difference did it make what my hair looked like to everybody else? I thought how everyone in my family had stopped using the word *see*, as if it was synonymous with *get* or *realize* or *understand*. Can't you see?

But now I'm going to start using that word again. Because why not? Because I can still see Seb's mouth, even though he and Dee are in love and I'll never touch him again. And I can see Baby Lily's little sharp teeth, and her walking. I can see a lot about what's true and what truth does—which, as Coltrane says, is to free us. If we're careful with it. Logan's mom is going to be out this Saturday night, though, so we're thinking maybe a few of us can hang out there. Logan has already picked out my outfit, which consists entirely of her clothes.

I made my way to my mom's studio, my white cane like a magic wand, sparkling and lighting up the way there, and knocked gently on the door, which I could feel was slightly open anyway.

"Come in, sweetie," my mom said. I walked over to her voice and she put an arm around me. Pasta, talcum powder, and the metal tang of paint, lavender, smoke. Her skin was warm and damp, and I snuggled in close for a long minute. My mom kissed the top of my head and we stood there, listening. Baby Lily was in her swing; here was her milky, sleepy breathing, here was the mechanized rocking. I imagined the octopus, seal, clown fish, starfish turning a slow circle overhead.

"How was your last day?" my mom asked when I pulled away. I thought how if I hadn't moved, she might have kept her arms around me for the rest of the day and night, even though—or maybe because—time doesn't stop even if you stay still. I didn't blame her. It must be weird to have the tiny people who were once your babies in swings grow up into huge strangers who don't sit on your lap anymore. I hope Benj and Baby Lily never stop sitting on my lap or burying their faces in my neck.

"It was okay," I said. "I missed Spark kind of terribly."

"Of course. He's coming with Annabelle, right?"

"Right."

"You're the best person I know, Emma Sasha." She thought for a minute. "Did you and Ms. Mabel say good-bye?"

"Yeah. She cried," I said. "But I reminded her I'd still need her next fall."

"Not as much as she needs you, I bet," my mom said. "How were your other teachers?"

"Ms. Spencer and Mr. Hawes didn't seem that sad," I said. "But Mrs. Fincter actually hugged me; it was like falling into a well of turpentine and mothballs."

My mom laughed.

"She said if I burn another project, can I please tell her in advance so she can watch the installation. She totally knew I was bullshitting." I sat down on the old corduroy couch against the wall. "But she loved Sarah's pictures. And she gave me an A, so."

I suddenly asked what my mom was making. She only smokes cigarettes when she's actually working. As soon as I asked, I thought how it might be the first question I've asked her about herself since I lost my sight.

Her voice cracked a little bit over the surface of the words. "It's a painting, actually."

"Oh. Are you going back to painting?"

"Maybe," she said. "At least for the moment." Her words were sorrowful gray and black pebbles you'd see in a bowl of water, wavy and blurred maybe, but still hard stones.

"Would you like to see it, Emma, sweetie?" she asked. She was apologizing to me.

"Is it dry?"

"Dry enough."

I stood again. My mom took my hands in hers and guided them to the surface of the canvas, where I felt around and started to make out the edges of a raised circle with other circles in its middle—buttons, maybe, something smooth and round. I felt the places where the paint stood up into stiff little mounds, marking a figure: arms, legs, and, at the bottom, a soft scrap of fabric, maybe velvet. I let my fingers pause over each edge, felt another small circle with smaller buttons on it. Eyes, maybe. And two long, soft pieces of something else.

"What do you think?" my mom asked.

"Is it me and Spark?"

"You're a genius," she said.

"If you glue cotton balls and buttons and a long, velvet tail to a canvas, then doesn't that make it a sculpture?" I asked.

"No," she said. "It's really a painting."

I ran my hands up and down the shape of what I could feel was a body—legs bent, in motion—and, at the bottom, a fabric dog whose legs also felt like they were sticking out almost horizontal. My mom had outlined all the edges, maybe so I could get each shape.

"Are we running?"

"Yes. It's the day you ran home."

I thought maybe if I ignored the fact that she was crying, she might stop. "What am I wearing?"

"What do you want to be wearing?"

"Am I not filled in yet?"

"I'm willing to take requests, if they're reasonable." The weepy sound in her voice was gone.

"How about a red hoodie? A velvety one? Maybe like whatever you made Spark's ears out of?"

"Velvet it is," my mom said. Now she sounded almost cheerful, almost red again herself.

"And Converse," I said. "Or maybe the cowgirl boots Leah gave me. Up to you." I felt the face quietly for a minute, first the forehead and then the buttons where my eyes were. I lingered on the left one, felt a line, maybe made of wire, across it.

"Are these sunglasses?" I asked.

"No," my mom said. "Would you like me to add them?"

"What's there now?"

"Just your eyes," she said.

"Like they are for real?" I asked.

"Pretty much."

"With the scar? Is that what this is?" I ran my fingers over the extra diagonal line again.

"I can add sunglasses if you'd like me to."

I kept my hands on the painting, imagining peach and pink, the way I thought of the skin on Jenna's and Naomi's cheeks, or my mom's or Babiest Baby Lily's, even my own. I ran my fingers again and again over the ridge and wire of the closed left eye button. My mom had used something soft for the eyelashes, maybe embroidery thread. The paint on the sky and grass and background felt dry and flaky, and I was gentle so I wouldn't ruin any surfaces.

My mom named the colors as my fingers moved over their surfaces: purple, black, red, gray, white. When she was done, I moved my hands from the painting to my mom, touched the cotton of her T-shirt, her upper arm, her face. She wasn't crying. Baby Lily was starting to stir in her swing; I could hear her smacking her lips and babbling.

I said, "It's lunchtime, big girl!" toward her, and she said, "Mema," which is definitely Emma, because she only uses one syllable for "Ma." "Right. Emma!" I told her. Then I touched my own face; slid my sunglasses off my nose and pushed them up into my hair. I was thinking as I did it that maybe the gesture would become a habit. Sunglasses make cute headbands. And it felt good to get the hair out of my eyes—I hadn't realized how hot it had gotten until I moved it.

I felt the scar on my eye, as familiar as my mom's skin or the sound of her voice, speaking colors to me. When the doorbell rang, I stayed still for a minute, facing my mom before I went to let in Logan and Annabelle and Spark.

"Don't bother with sunglasses," I told her. "I like it how it is."

Acknowledgments

Thank you to my daughters, Dalin Alexi and Light Ayli, for inspiring me to write *Blind*, for introducing me to the inimitably beautiful children's book *The Black Book of Colors*, and for believing that Emma Sasha Silver is a real person. Thank you for blind millipedes, military Braille, hours of practice on the Perkins Brailler, and for drawing the most stylish and beautiful Emmas ever. Thank you for understanding—in your profound way—the inextricable link between fiction and nonfiction, between what's dreamy and what's real. Thank you to your sweet friends, Pilot and Ever, Solange and Deji, Jessie and Zachary, Penny Lou, Lola, and Lillie, who keep our house and life lit up with childhood friendships. I love you two "more than the world," as you've taught me to imagine and say.

Thank you, Chicago Lighthouse for the Blind, for being such a generous and gracious organization and resource. James Kesteloot, your driver's education test and first job anecdotes shaped Sebastian's life, bravery, and heart. Thank you for your wisdom and warmth, for letting me try on your glasses, for showing me so much about sight and insight, and for being a dream reader. Thank you Dominic Calabrese for the tour, for encouragement, and for so many introductions. Katie Howe, thank you for the months of wildly inspiring braille lessons. I loved them. Mary Zabelski, thank you for the beautiful writing by and about your daughter, Cara Dunn-Yates. Wilma McCallister, thank you for welcoming me into your home and sharing your talking computer, slate and stylus, guide dog, and math tools; for jump-starting my braille; and for Rick's and your fabulous gallon milk-carton clothing label idea. Thank you, Salmaan See, for Beep Ball, for meeting me for ice cream, for the tutorial in white canes, for explaining what the world feels and looks like to you. Charli Saltzman and Johanna Brooke, thank you for being so forthcoming and generally awesome, and for your thoughts about blind adolescence, prettiness, nude bras and rubber-banded eyeliners.

Thank you, Jill Grinberg, my friend, agent, and ally in all, for reading this book and all my books at every stage, for being honest, compassionate, ferocious and everywhere all the time for me.

Regina Hayes, I will keep your elegant editorial letters forever with Emma's polished rocks, plastic grapes, and valentines. You are a treasure and I am enormously grateful for your wise, gentle, and essential input. Ken Wright, your constant support and engagement made this book a pleasure to work on and publish. Thank you Joy Peskin and Jen Hunt for your belief in and help with early drafts of *Blind*.

Robert Pinsky, Rosanna Warren, and Derek Walcott, thank you for being my teachers first when I was really young and then forever. You are still and always the first row of readers in my mind.

Anne Carson, thank you for the idea, expressed magnificently in your writing, that loneliness has an opposite. And thank you to the writers, readers, and friends who make my work and life that opposite: Emily Rapp, Cheryl Strayed, Nicholas Montemarano, Gina Frangello, Dika Lam, Thea Goodman, Molly Smith-Metzler, Emily Tedrowe, Zoe Zolbrod, Beth Hopson, Kristen Garrison, Bess Miller, Raisa Tolchinksy, Daming Chen, Anke Schrader, Cui Jian, Alex Jie, Yan Ping, Dallas Roberts, Olivier Sylvain, Alex Federman, Teri Boyd, Sasha Hemon, Gabe Lyon, Vojislav and Ivanka Pejovic, Yvette Charbaneau, and Brendan O'Connell (Lara Manalli, thank you for the best-ever line about puberty!), Bear Korngold, Logan and Stephanie Hart-LaVail, Malik Dohrn, Lisa Frecerro, Jacai Dohrn, Chesa Boudin, Harriet Beinfield, Efrem Korngold, Kathy Boudin, BJ and Dandara Richards, the Ayers-Minters, and David Gilbert. Jamie Klassel and Danielle Slavick, thank you for giving me eggs to throw at the walls. Yuan Qing, thank you for the imagination-shaping music—in my life and this book. Ann Thomas, Dan and Hannah Rubenstein, you are amazing models of graciousness and courage, and the inspiration for Emma's name, after your brave, beloved Emma Rubenstein.

Thank you to the community of generous, smart, compassionate, and hard-working teachers, staff, and parents at Nettelhorst Elementary School in Chicago, and Huron and Community High Schools in Ann Arbor Michigan.

Christine Jones, Donna Eis, Erika Helms, Julia Hollinger, Lara Phillips, Olati Johnson, Heidi Schumacher, Shanying Chen, Tamar Kotz, and Willow Schrager, thank you not only for reading my endless drafts, but also for understanding and loving me all my life.

Bill Ayers and Bernardine Dohrn, thank you for an endless supply of support and energy—for so many who need you. You defy every stereotype I've heard about in-laws (and outlaws). You are the village it takes to raise us and our girls, and the activists we need to help countless people work toward a more just world, particularly for children and teenagers.

Thank you to my utterly unique family, Kenneth, Judith, Jake, Aaron, Melissa, Adam, McKenna, Gail and Isaac, and the Mazurs, Silvermintzs and Kaufmanns, particularly my beloved great aunt Naomi and uncle Saul, who have shown us all how to live big, thoughtful lives, and how to be fabulously married.

Mom and Dad, thank you for being so loving that I'm unable to write a bad family, for our surreal, fantastic (ongoing) childhoods all over the world, for buying me a new book for every book I read, for all the teaching and reading and talking, for summers in China, for editing and thinking and grand-parenting with such adventurousness and thoughtfulness, and for celebrating us and all the small people, projects, buildings, books, (and even mistakes) we make with your fierce, loyal, absolute love.

My final thank you's will forever be for Zayd: you are my co-pilot, closest writer, reader, thinker, editor, world and word explorer, imaginer, analyzer, understander, father of my dream-real girls, day and night light, unequivocal love of my lives.

Q&A with the author

1. What inspired you to write *Blind*? Why did you decide to narrate it from the perspective of a character who isn't sighted?

I began to imagine and write *Blind* when my two little girls and I read *The Black Book of Colors* every night for a year. I was both frightened and inspired by that shiny, embossed wonder, a children's book full of images you can feel rather than see. The more we touched those pages, the more I wondered what it would be like to be able to see and then lose that ability. Would my memories stay visual? Would my senses cross so that I could taste, smell, and hear colors? What if one of my daughters lost her vision? The stakes would be astronomical.

I wrote Emma Sasha Silver's story so I could try to feel my way through someone else's experience, my favorite part of both reading and writing. I always imagined the story as one about what it feels like to see the world differently from how you're used to, and from how those around you see it, so it was essential that Emma narrate the story herself. And I wanted to make her powerful, because she's the heroine I wanted for my daughters, a complicated girl who manages to be a warrior when faced with staggeringly painful circumstances. Like so many teenagers I know, she is tenacious, scrappy, funny, and difficult. She is resilient not only because she musters up her own courage, but also because the girls around her are kind. Emma's friends, sisters, and parents are like mine: flawed but loving, trying to be their best selves even in the worst possible moments.

2. What were the challenges of writing a blind character?
Any time I write about a community of which I'm not a member, I try to ask as many questions as I can, as widely as possible. I knew I wanted Emma to be brave, but not perfect, to find herself in a painful context, but not to become that context. It was important to me that she not be either a victim or a symbol. For me, *Blind* isn't ultimately a book about blindness, or even a "blind girl"; it's a book about being a girl in the world in general, about figuring out how to make meaning in (and of) your life, no matter how difficult the hand you're dealt.

3. What sort of research was required? And what were the most surprising things you discovered while doing your research?
I spent a year studying Braille, going to "beep ball" games and eating ice cream with blind teenagers, trying on glasses, tripping over white canes, and learning basic geometry with a teacher who taught me to feel shapes on a magnetic board.

I talked to blind girls who told me they always wear nude bras, so the colors won't show through, no matter what shirt they might accidentally choose. I felt clothing labels Braille-d onto little squares cut from milk jugs, learned to tell a blue eye-liner (one rainbow loom band around the top) from a red lip-liner (two bands).

I learned a lesson that I kept finding fascinating even as I learn it again and again in my grown-up life, which is that kids are unbelievably resilient. And, at their centers, so similar to one another, no matter what differences appear to define or set them apart. I think part of what gives them amazing bravery and grit is the ability to juxtapose life's most profound difficulties and joys with its most daily matters. To go from the zero of a social interaction at school to the infinity of our socially unjust world, or of a life-changing accident, of a death, even— in mere seconds. And, importantly, to come back. In the visually impaired kids I met, this quality is particularly inspiring, because they've had to recalibrate how to live in a world designed for people who are sighted. Many of them have done so with incredible creativity, grace, and humor.

4. How does Emma figure out what tools will help her survive? What makes her fate different from Claire's?
I think when we make progress in our lives, it usually happens

in a backward and forward motion, becomes a liquid process, even. When *Blind* opens, Emma has moved past the worst moments of her accident and its aftermath, partly because I didn't want the novel to capitalize on the shocking value built into a scene like that. I didn't put that first, and I didn't want to make her disaster the climax of the book. But as she's not in the first moment of it, she has to remember it and figure out how to live with it. And sometimes remembering—which I believe is work we all have to do if we're going to create palatable narratives from the substance of our lives, can drag you back under the water of your own most difficult moments. Emma lives on a wide spectrum, and she's trying to figure out how to think about and understand what happened to her, how to be truthful about it with herself. And both versions—the one that features her heightened ability to feel a world she used to be able to see and the one that features her gutting loss—are true stories for her. She figures out a way to live between (and with) them.

5. Why did you choose to write about disability?

All my books are about sameness and difference. About girls and women on the peripheries of their societies or social groups or worlds. I'm interested in how we communicate with (and betray and forgive) each other, across whatever chasms divide us. Sometimes those are cultural and linguistic;

sometimes they're political and generational. Lately, I've been writing some about physical difference; my novel *Big Girl Small* is about a teenage little person who wants to be Judy Garland but feels forced to identify with the "munchkins" of our cultural media world. *Blind* is the furthest reach of that question for me, an exploration of ways we see the world, no matter who we are. I wrote it in a fit of wonder about what it would feel like to have to change, to have your perspective and identity made irrevocably different both from what it was and from those around you. And how a tough heroine (I always write with my daughters and mama and mama-in-law and an army of my best girl friends in mind, thinking: how would we keep each other afloat, no matter what the circumstances?) can get through almost anything.

6. What is your writing process and why are you a writer?
I write many pages in fits of inspiration; I have endless ideas. But I don't make the work good until I revise, and I often have to revise for years in order to shape my ideas and pages into books that have momentum and meaning. I do it because I love books, and because I've always needed to write. There are certain ideas and stories I want in the world. When I wrote my novel *Big Girl Small*, I did it because I wanted to think and write and talk about how resilient I think girls are (and how rarely I think young girls get credit for being the warriors

they can be, no matter how difficult their contexts or circumstances). One of my daughters, who was four years old at the time, loved *The Wizard of Oz*, we watched it 93,000 times, and she spent her days dressed as Dorothy while I watched with horror the actors playing the "munchkins." Why did the professionally trained actors have to wear rompers, lick giant lollipops, and then get no billing in the final credit sequence? What would it feel like for my daughter if she were her exact same self, but in a small body? So I wrote that book about a kid who has an external manifestation of an internal situation I think we all have: she feels small. And I gave myself (and all kids) a way to imagine her being amazingly brave and okay anyway.

7. What is your inspiration for your writing?
Books. Love. My girls. My parents. My husband. Cities I love (Beijing, New York, Chicago, Shanghai), the way the light looks, losing a friend I needed and adored when we were both only twenty-five, and so much more. I want to write down almost everything I see, think, feel, and wonder. So I can be in a conversation with the world about it, and so I can understand what questions to ask, what narratives to build.